Dancers

of the

Third Age

Judith Granahan

Acknowledgments

Writing a novel is similar to giving birth. In both endeavors, one needs a lot of help. This novel is dedicated to all my helpers. My partner, Robyn who's always supported and believed in me. To the memory of my mentor Maureen LaJoy who encouraged even my bad stuff and showed me the value of criticism.

To my critique group, Night Writers of Maple Grove, Minnesota. They appear alphabetically because one is never above the other. Genny, Jack, Janet, Judd, Laura, Lyn, Ross, Stephanie and Sue.

Special thanks to:
Robyn Anderson for her editing help, Fran Forsman, and Jack Stanton and Laura Vosika for preparing my novel for printing.

Chapter 1

Anna Mae read again the letter she'd gotten from the Tucson police yesterday. It clearly stated that her husband's death was an accident. It even had an official seal. Of course the police had to investigate his death; he'd fallen off his very highest ladder. It could have been an accident or it could have been murder. She neatly folded the letter and tucked it away in her underwear drawer. To have it declared an accident on official paper was very comforting. That meant she was now free of him.

She closed the drawer. No, she wasn't quite free. She still had all those blank spots in her head about his death.

She'd been there, watched him fall, but she still couldn't remember any more of the details. No matter how hard she tried, nothing came into her head except the strong feeling that she'd killed him. She prayed it was her fault that he'd died. She'd been very lucky that day because someone had dropped something just as she was about to smile and tell the paramedics the sun had risen in her soul when they told her Benny was actually dead.

With it officially an accident, she could now go back to their house, walk out to their workshop to try and remember exactly what had happened just before Benny died. She had no more excuses to stay away. Today with their official notice the police were done with the workshop. Completely done. They'd said so when they'd taken down their yellow tapes two months ago but she couldn't believe it until yesterday.

Today would have been their wedding anniversary; the perfect day to go there and investigate for herself. She'd gotten a good night's sleep, a rarity lately. Her body wasn't stiff, or sore. Her mind was as sharp as it could be these days. She limped around, picked up things she'd left on the floor.

Then, as it often did, her mind wandered off to think about other things. Might she stay here if the other tenants stopped pestering her to be social? If they did, would she like living in an apartment building instead of her house? It was fun listening to all the stories the other tenants made up about what it must have been like to live here back before the Wild West days when the huge stone building was a very popular brothel miles away

1

from Tucson. Today, the city of Tucson had grown up and swallowed the building, making it part of the city.

When the laws changed, the ladies moved along. The building became a series of businesses. A hat factory, clothes manufacturing company, law offices, a medical office building until it finally became too outdated and just sat there looking tired and dilapidated.

Four years ago the beautiful stone building with its rotting interior, was put up for bids to the wrecking ball companies. Her friend Cece stepped in and out bid them all, took two years to renovate it into a modern apartment building. Cece, liked the humor of renting only to single women who were collecting their Social Security checks, then named her new place the Bordello.

Benny's death was why she was living here now. A month after he died, Cece had stopped by their house to see how she was doing and was shocked at how much weight she'd lost. Of course she'd lost weight, what with Benny's ghost flitting around the house taking her appetite away, but she didn't tell Cece that.

Cece had even said her house smelled like old rotting food. So when Cece, her only friend, insisted she move into the Bordello, she'd felt obligated to do it. Cece said it could be a temporary move until she got her life figured out and that she'd adjust better to being a widow if she were with people, not sitting around in a dark house.

She'd brought only a few things with her. Her best clothes, her kitchen stuff, her bedroom furniture, the coffee table Benny hated and the sofa he never sat on because it was green, their old television set. Seeing how bare her living room was, Cece had her maintenance man Carlos bring up a few chairs from the basement storage area. Moving really hadn't fix anything. Benny had come with her, plus she just didn't know how to be around people.

For most of her life, she'd had only Benny and her cats. Now she could sit in any of the three lounges, listening to the stories that Birdie, and all the others made up about the 'ladies of the night.' How they'd dressed up in fine clothes, teased the men, entertained them, then took their money and sent them on their way.

It was her freedom that scared her. For all their years together, Benny told her what to do, when to do it and how badly she'd done it. With him now dead, even trying to make the little decisions sent her to bed. Eating alone, she couldn't eat. Eating with people, she didn't know what to say.

Anna Mae limped over to where she kept her purse. She needed to go over to the house now, today, and try to remember if it was her who had killed him. Plus, she should search in the workshop for more of their money. Before Cece had spirited her away, she'd searched only in the house and found almost one hundred thousand dollars in cash and stock certificates hidden in Benny's room.

She still had to fix the problem with their names. The funeral people had been very nice. They'd told her how to notify the government of Benny's death so she could get his Social Security benefits. To do that, she needed to find the papers that said she was Anna Mae Brown and he was Benjamin Brown. Trouble was, she'd never seen the papers that proved it. Benny had kept track of all those things.

The only place she had left to search for money was in their workshop and it was the one place she was still afraid to go. After the police had removed his body and studied where he died for another week, they said she was free to go out there. She'd stood in front of the door into their workshop but could never make herself even touch the doorknob. For most of her married life she'd wished Benny dead. She'd been there when he died, but there were holes in her head about it.

She pounded her grey head with her fists to knock the details back into it. As usual, nothing happened. All she remembered was Benny being up on his high ladder, then falling. She didn't see him land or know why he fell. The next thing she remembered of him was seeing him in his casket at the funeral home.

Pushing her watch up her arm to get it to stay in place, she realized it was almost nine o'clock. Nine was a good time to leave. The tenants who volunteered in Cece's free daycare center out in the carriage house were there by seven-thirty. Those who went golfing, or running, usually left by eight to beat the golf leagues. Nine was her best chance of avoiding most of the women who lived here. It wasn't that they weren't nice women; it was that she wasn't.

Suddenly she felt an eagerness to go. Starting out the door, she looked down. "God damn it! I've got my fool slippers on."

She rushed into the bedroom. "People will take notice of me if I go out looking like an idiot."

She enjoyed talking out loud now. Saying whatever popped into her head. Even swearing. Benny swore but he'd forbid her to do it. Trouble was, now she'd been speaking out loud in public when she shouldn't.

She put on a pair of slacks, cinched her belt so they wouldn't fall down. Shivering in the air-conditioned room, she grabbed a long sleeve blouse then threw it on the floor.

"Damn it! Think Anna Mae. Think! Use your friggen head; you damn old fool! The house is all closed up. It'll be hotter than hell over there!"

She slapped her face and muttered, "Shut up, Benny". She had to stop Benny's foul words from spewing out of her very own mouth.

Giving a swift kick to the blouse, she sent it flying into a corner. It felt so good now, being messy, doing whatever she wanted. She finished dressing, checked herself in the mirror. Her face was a sag bag of wrinkles.

That was what some of the women here called their faces. She checked her hair. It was sticking out in short gray sprigs. A few strokes with a wet comb and she was ready to go.

Digging in her purse for her car and house keys, she peeked out her door into the large, open lounge. The Shady Lady Lounge was for watching TV on the big screen, and visiting with each other. Anna Mae chuckled. The prostitute manikin was sitting on the red velvet settee, touching the male manikin on the knee. Someone kept moving them around. Yesterday when she'd seen them, they'd looked like they were glaring at each other from across a table. Just like her and Benny. She rushed past then and down the back stairs, went through the first floor Scarlet Letter Lounge where they had their weekly pot-luck dinners. Then she was out the back door into the warm morning sun. So far her luck was good; she hadn't run into Liberty Price.

She let out a long sigh. It was hard to understand people. Libby seemed to be a nice person, but there had to be something wrong with Libby. Just two days ago, she and Libby were sitting in the Shady Lady lounge having a pleasant conversation, when Cece suddenly came by, grabbed her arm, hissed 'stay away from Liberty Price' then led her up the back stairs to her office. It was still all very puzzling. Getting into her car, she couldn't dwell on that. No. It was time to figure out if she'd killed her husband.

Concentrating on the traffic, she drove up to the house she'd lived in with Benny for thirty-six very miserable years. Cece's handyman must have been there. The grass had been cut and no papers blew around her yard. Busy checking it out, she drove up and over the curb.

"Pay attention, you dumb old fool! You could've wrecked my car." Anna Mae slapped her mouth.

"Shut up, Benny!"

Backing up, she drove into their wide driveway, stared at the house, their repair shop, blinking back tears she shut off the car. Her life might not be perfect yet, but it was better than before. She could plan a future for herself, she could. She'd keep telling herself that until it came true.

She started to get out of the car, but couldn't. She was doing it again, trying to do something and her body was refusing to do it. Humming a tune to make herself feel less nervous she suddenly got out of the car. Limping as little as possible, she went to their front door, had no trouble of unlocking it and slipped inside. Turning on a few lights in the darkened house, she went into their small kitchen, put her purse on the table and stopped in front of the door that led into her and Benny's workshop.

Just like all the other times, it seemed like a pulsing, living thing, with Benny standing on the other side waiting for her. How many times since his death had she gotten this far and never touched the doorknob? Fifty? A hundred? She thought back.

She'd been fixing their lunch when Benny started yelling, "Get your sorry ass out here."

She'd ignored him at first. Wanted him to sound really angry before she went out there. Suddenly, now her courage let her open the door and walk into that day.

"You sure took your damn sweet time coming out here!"

Her body shook. Benny was perched at the very top of his tallest ladder next to the huge fan set into the peak of their workshop ceiling. He liked to brag that it was twenty-five feet up there. The fan sucked the chemical fumes from their furniture and antique car restoration business to the outside. Broken for several days, the air reeked of caustic fumes as he shook his fist at her.

"Your fucking cat's hair is plugging the vent fan!"

"That's not true. Ms. Dasher Cat is never, ever, out here in the workshop and you know it!" She'd actually said it out loud! She never dared yell at him before.

Shutting the door behind her, she moved forward, tripped, looked down. Ms. Dasher Cat was lying in a heap on the floor. Her head was turned wrong. All wrong. Anna Mae screamed and screamed, until her throat was sore. A rushing noise filled her ears. About to fall, she grabbed at the workbench. Benny had wrung her precious cat's neck.

"You killed Ms. Dasher!"

When a leather glove landed next to her good foot, she jerked up, screaming, "You wrung her neck! Just like you did all the others."

"Damn right I did! Fucking cat was out here getting hairs all over my stuff."

"Ms. Dasher is never in the shop! Never!"

"Hell of a lot you know. That damn thing snuck out here whenever you weren't watching her."

Moving blindly forward, she edged along Benny's workbench, hit something with her foot, looked down again. It was Ms. Dasher's cat carrier she'd bumped into. The door was open and a small mound of cat food sat inside staring up at her. She gulped air, picked up a wrench and pounded Benny's workbench over and over.

"Damn you. Damn you" Yelling as loud as she could, she added, "You tricked Ms. Dasher into her carrier!!"

"Why would I do that?"

"To kill her. Like you did all my other pets. You know you did! I hate you!" She should have known he'd not keep his promise that this cat would live.

"Do your bellyaching after you throw me the wrench to fix my stuck fan." He waved his hand at her. "Or, I could come down there and do the

5

same thing to you."

A rasping, *come down, kill me, things will be better then*, came out of her mouth but didn't carry far.

Vowing that this time Benny would pay for all the animals he'd killed, Anna Mae picked up a wrench, not the one she knew he wanted. Swinging her arm out, she threw it high and right into his hand, just like he'd taught her.

Benny looked at it, dropped it so it would fall into a basket on the floor. "Bigger. You know I need the bigger one."

"Bigger. Yes." She picked up a much heavier wrench. Flung it hard, felt pain shoot to her shoulder. It was worth it when she saw it clip his leg then fall with a huge clatter to the floor.

"Damn you, woman! You'll pay for that one."

He held out his hand. "Park the right one, right here, right now, you old fool or I'm coming down! You know I will."

"Try this one." She threw him the adjustable wrench that didn't adjust anymore.

Benny flung it back so fast she barely got her head out of the way before it stuck deep into the plasterboard inches from her head. His hard laugh rang out through the huge workshop.

Infuriated she walked slowly to his row of brand spanking new wrenches. Smiling she picked up one, pulled her arm back, then snapped her wrist just so and let go.

That was what she'd forgotten! That wrench. How she'd thrown it. Made it flip end over end until it was just a few inches from his out-stretched hand. If he didn't catch it, it would smash into the center of his precious ceiling fan.

As she'd yelled, "You'd better grab it. It's a new one." Benny leaned far out, laughed at her, grabbed at the wrench. There'd been a snapping sound and his ladder tossed him off. He fell. Hit his head on the edge of the workbench. She remembered the loud whack followed by a dull thump as he landed on the cement floor. Then there was a long silence.

Suddenly heels clicked and Cece was running to her, saying it was all an accident. Why had Cece been there? Anna Mae shook her head. Oh yes, she'd brought them a picture frame, or something, to be repaired.

Cece kept saying the ladder broke, it was an accident. She'd helped her pick up the tools so the police wouldn't think she and Benny were arguing. Cece covered up the hole in the wall with a calendar. Then they went outside to bury Ms. Dasher. Neither of them had looked at Benny not even once.

Cece was the one that called the police and told them to come because Benny Brown had fallen off a ladder that had broken. As they waited for them to arrive, Cece kept telling her how she saw the ladder break and that's why Benny fell. Cece had said it so many times that must be why she hadn't been able to remember her part in his death until now. Not remember she'd thrown the wrench wide so Benny would reach for it and fall.

She rubbed the sides of her head; smiled. Yelling at him, so hard for the first time in her life, must have knocked the common sense right out of him. Made him reach out when he knew better. His weight probably twisted the ladder off its moorings and that's what killed him.

No. She'd thrown the tool just out of his reach so the ladder would twist and kill him. Yes, she'd killed him. That's was all there was to it.

She patted the bench that had broken his neck. "You and I killed Benny Brown."

Chapter 2

Relieved to finally remember, Anna Mae burst out of the workshop and into the Arizona sunshine so bright it brought more tears to her pale blue eyes. Shielding the top of her glasses against the sun, she ran to where she and Cece had buried Ms. Dasher and collapsed onto the warm grass next to the dirt she remembered tenderly digging for Ms. Dasher's grave.

She patted the ground. "I'm so sorry we buried you without any kind words, dear. I wanted to have you nearer to my other cats, but Cece said it would be bad if the police saw fresh grass all dug up. They'd find out Benny killed you and then they might think I killed him. Which I did, Ms. Dasher."

She clapped her hands in joy. "Did you hear me? I killed him! I know you're glad I did."

She rubbed her hand over the dirt, took in some easy breaths. "I should have come to visit you sooner than this, but it just broke my heart to know you were out here."

The dirt seemed to warm beneath her hand. "You have nothing to fear where you are now. You're safe, and I'll bring you flowers very often. You rest well, my dear and loving friend."

She looked around her yard, smiled. "Actually, Ms. Dasher, this is the perfect spot for you. You're higher up than all my other darlings. I promise you, if I sell the house, I'll sell it to people with small children. You'll be able to see them playing in the yard."

She patted the ground again, rubbed the dirt, nodded. "Yes, I like my new place."

Anna Mae listened. "What? You say that's not true, Ms. Dasher?"

She tried to hold back her tears and failed. "It's so amazing how you've always been able to read my mind."

She listened. "Yes. You're right again. The important thing is that I move on."

She knew it probably wasn't Ms. Dasher talking to her. Cats couldn't talk. Maybe they could when they were dead. Or, maybe sitting next to Ms. Dasher, her most favorite cat of all time, shut out Benny's voice in her head. The voice that so often disturbed her thinking, even now after his passing.

She leaned over the mound and whispered. "Is he around here?" She sat back up, waited.

"He's not? That's wonderful. He often came in the deep night shadows to my bedroom but not at the Bordello. He didn't follow me there, because he never liked Cece. Although sometimes I think he pokes me in my sleep. I left his favorite chair here at the house. I use to see him sitting in it staring at me."

She let out a satisfied sigh, patted Ms. Dasher's grave again. "All that will change now that I know I killed him. I'm not afraid of him anymore."

Taking a small locket from around her neck intending to tuck it into Ms. Dasher's grave, something brushed against her leg. Smothering a scream, she pulled away as a small orange tabby dashed behind a bush.

"Shoo. You must go away until this is all settled."

The cat meowed a few times then inched its way out of hiding. Anna Mae clapped her hands. It dashed back only to come out of hiding a few seconds later.

"You're hungry, but if I feed you, you'll keep coming back and no one lives here right now."

Grabbing the cat by the back of its neck she carried it over to her fence gate and dropped it outside her yard.

"Please go away. You can find a better place to live. One that's not a pet cemetery."

She went back, knelt beside Ms. Dasher. "As always, you've helped me by listening. I'm closer to knowing what I should do. I'll come to see you soon and plant many beautiful flowers near you."

Going back into the workshop, she waited for her eyes to adjust to the dimness and listened for Benny. The silence said he wasn't there. She looked at his desk, his chair, and it finally hit her, that she'd killed a person. A real live bad person was dead because of what she did. That dropped her to the cold cement floor.

Pulling her knees to her, she hugged them tight. She'd ended a life. Rocking back and forth, she wailed. She'd put an end to him. The pain shooting down her bad leg reminded her that Benny had brought her to this. Benny's meanness had made her a killer.

She supposed some of their trouble had been her fault. He'd been cruel, and she'd been a coward. She rocked harder, faster, then stopped when her hips couldn't take the pain of the cement floor.

She was not going to feel guilty about this. "I didn't set out to kill him. He was being cruel again. Laughing about killing Ms. Dasher. And he nearly split my head open with that wrench!"

Her guilt lifted and she got up from the cold floor. Benny's precious cabinet starred back at her. She just knew he kept all of his secrets locked in there. Taking a crowbar off a shelf, she calmly walked over to it, jammed the crowbar between the steel door and its heavy padlock.

"Are you watching me, Benny Brown, aka, David Thurgood?" She knew calling him by his real name would irritate him.

"I hope you are, Aka, David Thurgood. I tried to please you all these years and you drove me to kill you." She tapped the cabinet hard with her good foot.

"You just wouldn't quit, would you? So, now you are buried dead and I'm alive."

She cranked the crowbar a little. "I searched the house for our papers. Didn't find any proof of who I am but I found our money. I'll never quit looking for the papers."

She cranked harder. "Are they in here? If not I'll wreck this place until I find them."

She gave a large grunt then yanked at the padlock. The handle flew off and the door opened, spilling a box and it's contents onto the floor. Several seemed to be photos. They were probably Benny's before and after shots of furniture they'd refurbished. More trash for her to throw away before selling the house. Or burning it down.

One photo caught her attention. She picked it up, looked at it, then raced to the window for better light. Turning around until the sun brought out the images, she let out a soft moan. It was a young man and a girl. The cut of their hair said it had been taken many years ago. A closer look and she recognized her son and her daughter at her daughter's high school graduation. She let out the cry of an animal caught in a trap, spun around and collapsed onto the cement floor again.

How had Benny gotten the picture? She and her sister Ruth had been so careful when she'd sent her children away. They'd been so small, just four and nine years. She ruffled through the papers and found five more pictures.

Clutching them to her chest, Anna Mae got up, ignored the shooting pains in her ankle, to pace around and around Benny's desk until she was faint with pain. Both in her leg and in her heart. How had he gotten the pictures? She'd been so careful. Even now, thirty-seven years later, she didn't know where her children were. She stared at the pictures. Touched her son's face; her daughter's long hair. Her children were grown up and they looked happy.

Tears for them, forbidden all these years, poured down her face. She again saw the blue and grey highway bus pull away from the station carrying her brave nine-year old son and his tiny four year-old sister off to their aunt and uncle and away from the cruelty of their father.

She'd stuffed their two small suitcases with clothes, some favorite toys and a note to her sister. No one even questioned her when she'd put the children on a bus with tickets to Flagstaff pinned to their jackets. Today, they'd arrest her for doing that and what a blessing that would be. Someone would have paid attention to her. Back then a woman was all on her own.

She'd run away with them once, after his beating caused her to miscarry. Her father, not seeing her side of it, called Benny to come get his wife. Years of failed escape plans, ended when her sister phoned to say she and her husband were moving. They weren't telling their parents where they were going so she could bring her children and run away with them. Instead, she'd sent her children alone on a bus.

Her sister called hours later, to say the children had arrived. She'd ordered Ruth not to tell her where they were going, in case Benny would try and beat it out of her. That had been her mistake. Three days later Benny moved them from Charlotte to Tucson. She'd believed she'd saved their children from their father's anger but somehow he'd found them. Had he talked to them? Hurt them?

Anna Mae stiffened. Were there more pictures? She threw everything out of the cabinet and found no more. Looking again at her daughter's graduation she realized her son wore an Army uniform. Anna Mae gave out a small cry. Timothy had joined the Army! They'd talked about how the Army could be his escape. And her little girl looked so beautiful and proud and happy. She hurt all over and felt good too.

There was no hint in the pictures of where they'd been taken. She carefully laid the photos on the bottom of a small cardboard box at her feet. Covering them with some business files from the cabinet, she pulled out Benny's stained chair, took deep breaths to slow her heart and still the pounding in her head.

It was intolerable that Benny had found their children and never told her. Anger filled her. He'd never said a word. Not one word! He knew she mourned for them every day. He could have showed her one of the pictures and eased her pain. Maybe they were dead now.

She stood and swiped everything off his desk. Getting his pistol from the cabinet, she carefully laid it on the desk. Dug through another shelf stacked high and found the bullets. Loading them into the gun, she put the pistol into the box under papers she needed, took it all and left.

Fifteen minutes later she was staring down at Benny's grave marker. Reading it for the first time. The small plaque said he was down there in the ground. To keep up appearances she'd spent almost a respectable amount of money on the plaque, and as little as possible on his casket. A plastic bag would have suited him better. Not even the heavy kind, the thin kind that maggots could cut through and get to him sooner.

She looked around the grounds of the small cemetery once again. Fate was with her. No one was visiting a grave, no one was being buried. No Caretaker roamed about. It was just she, the dead, and a few birds, alone in the cemetery.

11

She stomped onto her husband's grave, planted her feet like they showed on TV, then pointed the pistol to where his head should be and pulled the trigger. The gun jerked her arthritic hand straight up and sent her reeling backwards.

Imagining dirt spraying up where the bullet entered the ground, she pictured it racing down, clipping her husband's brain just enough to wake him up.

Birds cawed in the distance as she gripped the gun this time with both hands. Planting her feet even firmer, she aimed at where his heart should be, if he had one, and fired. She thought she heard him bounce in his casket. It was so cheap she was sure the bullets had gone all the way through to his body.

The smell of gun smoke swirled around her. The shots echoed in her ears and she pictured him quivering below her feet. Aiming lower, she shot again, then once more. Fearing someone would come to arrest her, she kicked his grave for good measure then fled to her car. Driving away from the cemetery, she headed back to the Bordello. She had to lie down and figure things out.

Wild thoughts tore through her. What if her children lived near here? What if they were dead at their father's hands? She had to lie down. Think what to do. Benny had grown up pictures of her children. She hated him more that ever.

Driving around a corner someone honked, honked again shaking some sense into her. Benny had found their children; she could too. She was as smart as him, smarter even. She'd hire somebody. She'd found all that money. Tomorrow she'd go back to the house and find more.

Chapter 3

That same morning Liberty Price left her apartment moments after Anna Mae. As if her life wasn't messed up already, two days ago she'd upset Cece by talking to sad sack, Anna Mae. It made no sense. But last night she'd gotten Cece's message saying she could get kicked out of the Bordello just because she'd talked to Anna Mae. Cece was stepping on her freedom of speech.

Driving a few miles over the speed limit, ticket territory in her mind, she made good time getting to the neighborhood she called the Garden of Eden. Botanical Zealots lived in the Garden of Eden. That included her ex sister-in-law and, longtime friend, Ginger.

Every yard in the neighborhood was filled with amazing floral, cacti and plant displays. Their owners had spent years striving to be on the front page of amateur garden magazines. After Ginger retired from her multi million dollar real estate business, her front yard had become the envy of all

Ginger had been avoiding her lately. It was probably the MADD protest she'd dragged Ginger to a few weeks back. That protest had been a doozie of a mistake. She should have read the fine print on the flyer. Should have seen it wasn't Mothers Against Drunk Drivers, but Men Advocating Dirty Dancing. It was just a good laugh being photographed in front of a saloon and a group of men holding up a MADD sign, until it became a featured picture in the Sunday paper. But the, 'Save the Trees' sit-in? Her fault? Libby shook her gray head. No way was that one her fault.

All on her own, Ginger had decided to stand next to the huge pine three not noticing the broken lower branch that was pointing right at her lower region. That too, had made the papers.

Libby got out of the car relieved that today was Wednesday. Only rain or heavy wind, kept Ginger from tending her gardens on Wednesday mornings. Today there was very little wind, it was sunny and not too hot for mid-May in Asheville. It was nine thirty, Ginger would be out there by now. Her plan was to trap Ginger in her garden, then convince her to go over to the Bordello so she could talk to Cece on her behalf. Cece was usually in her office at the Bordello on Wednesdays from eleven to one. The planets were aligned in her favor today.

It was imperative that she catch Ginger outside so Ginger wouldn't see her and run into the house like she had the other day. Then refuse to answer her door no matter how long she'd rung the bell.

Parking her small car behind Ginger's neighbor's thick stand of tall hibiscus kept it well out of Ginger's sight. Getting out, she quietly closed her door, crept up to the hibiscus, took her birding binoculars and zeroed in on Ginger and George's huge sloping front yard.

Right now there was no human in sight. Ginger had perfected the art of timing flowers. From early spring to late fall her yard was a slow moving kaleidoscope of beautiful colors. Libby thought of it as a symphony of sorts. A smattering of yellows, reds, purples burst forth in March, slowly built through the summer to a brilliant crescendo that didn't fade away until late fall.

She could see that today Ginger still had work to do. No weeds, heaven forbid there would be weeds in Ginger's gardens, but many of the flower heads had seen better days.

Inching her way to the edge of the thick hibiscus stand Libby peered up Ginger's half moon driveway. There were no parked cars. She hadn't expected any. Since the Arizona sun and cars were deadly enemies the Logan's rarely parked their, much too, expensive cars outside. Her own car she'd so proudly named Rosa Rita, was now more like Cream of Tomato Soup.

A wheelbarrow and a trashcan sat alone at the top of the drive that meant Ginger had to be somewhere in her front garden. Only the dense, red bougainvillea bushes, filling up the far corner of the yard could hide Ginger from her prying eyes. She zeroed in on them and her heart quickened. Something yellow was moving behind red bougainvillea thick branches.

Steadying her 'binocs', she caught Ginger in bright, canary yellow, busily clipping away. A floppy tan garden hat covered some of her bush of platinum hair. Perfecto! Oh happy day.

Libby rushed back to her car, drove it to the bottom of Ginger's driveway, smiled as the yellow outfit in the bougainvillea disappeared behind the thick bushes.

Ginger peered out in horror out from behind the thickest branches. Libby's junk heap of a car was at the bottom of her drive! Not again? Libby did protest marches, sit-ins and fund-raisers as often as other people brushed their teeth. She was here to beg her to go on another of her hair-brained crusades. It didn't matter how often she said no to these outings. Libby always showed up a few days later with another, even more, exciting crusade. Libby's desperate attempts to avoid fixing her own life was beginning to destroy Ginger's.

She bent low. Remembered she was wearing yellow. Crouched. Went lower until her knees screamed stop. A few minutes in this position and she'd snap them in half. To go lower dirt would make a mess of her Gucci slacks. Slacks she'd paid an arm and two legs for. She looked longingly at her front door. It was too far away to dash there and get inside unseen. She was fast for someone who collected a Social Security check, but not that fast.

Last week Libby's high-pitched engine noise had given her the time she needed to slip inside then dive into her front closet. Thinking back, she could still smell the perfume that had nearly asphyxiated her while waiting for Libby to give up and leave. She should have known better that to wear yellow today.

Ginger stared at the pink monster at the foot of her driveway. This would be a good time to pray for Libby to go away. No, she only prayed for life and death things, a good score in golf, and a plastic surgeon with steady hands. She stared at the small green lizard blinking at her from a branch.

"My saying no to Libby works about as well as telling you guys not to change colors."

Hearing the familiar engine whine of Libby's car made Ginger risk peeking through the thicker branches. Libby was slowly backing up her driveway!

Libby couldn't back her way out of a paper bag.

Libby gripped the back of the passenger seat, cranked her neck around as far as it would go, aimed the back of her car at the top of the drive where Ginger's prize winning, triple blossom azaleas sat, then she started slowly backing up.

Ginger bolted up and out of her bougainvillea. Running fast, she leapt over and dodged her Stargazer lilies, sucked in their sweet smell, raced around her tall blue delphinium, avoided a cluster of zinnias, heard something crunch under her feet and almost swore, zig-zagged across three more flowerbeds while flapping her arms at Libby like a mad woman. Finally, totally out of breath, she stumbled on to the driveway just a few feet back of Libby's car.

Libby squelched a grin. Ginger had looked like Big Bird coming down her front garden. She'd won the first round.

"God Bless America, Liberty Price. Stop before you give me a heart attack!"

Out of breath, Ginger promised herself she'd get back to her aerobic classes right after she broke Libby's neck. She put her hands on her hips, stomped on the driveway, then realized throwing a temper tantrum in rubber clogs had to look like a welcoming jig. She whacked Libby's back door.

Libby stepped out, pushed her glasses up her nose and faced her former sister-in-law.

Ginger ran a nervous tongue over her teeth, pulled herself up to her full five-foot-nine inches, crossed her arms planted her feet then stared down at Libby.

"Why are you backing up my driveway?"

Libby smiled. "And here, I'd hoped your bright yellow outfit meant you were being more sociable these days."

Ginger's glare killed that idea. Wearing expensive clothes in the garden was just, Ginger being Ginger.

"I was in a very good mood until you aimed your car at my prize winning flowers."

"You've been avoiding me."

"Because you won't take no from me about all these crusades you go on so you can avoid figuring out your life. This is my gardening day. Go home. Even George dare not interrupt my gardening day. Scoot. I've work to do."

Scoot? Ginger had said scoot! Libby reached into her shirt pocket, pulled out a yellowed piece of paper, unfolded it, slapped it onto the trunk of her car. "Read it."

Ginger crossed her arms. "No."

"But, you promised."

Chapter 4

Ignoring the paper, Ginger looked deep into Libby's eyes. Her years of sales had taught her that a sincere look usually simmered things down. It didn't work with Libby. Libby knew all her tricks.

"That paper is for emergencies only. Your crusades, your sit-ins, your political protests, are not emergencies." Ginger, about to stomp her foot for emphasis, crossed her arms instead.

"George has barely recovered from his recent brush with death."

"First off Ginger, they caught George's cancer right away. All his doctors say he's made a remarkable, and complete recovery."

"Damn it, Libby. He scared me to death. Still scares me." She'd just broken her rule, never to swear anywhere near her garden, even if Lib was here persecuting her. Ginger uncrossed her arms.

"Let me repeat what you said to me the last time you wanted me to do something."

"You needn't do that." Libby tried to see Ginger's eyes hidden behind her designer sunglasses and floppy straw hat.

"Yes, I do. Two weeks ago, after you promised me I was done with all your crusades, you came here agonizing that the recent ice damage to the pine trees has added to the fact that the Red Cockaded Woodpecker and the Bobwhite Quail were running short of habitat. In fact, you said it so often I can't get their names out of my head."

Libby started to speak, but Ginger's hand in her face cut her off. "So what did I do? I went with you and got in the newspapers again. I don't care if you have to carry three picket signs, I'm not going to another thing with you."

Ginger's anger set Libby back a little. She had to take another tact if she was to get Ginger to Cece in time. "You're right, absolutely right. I'm rotten."

"Don't try that one on me, either. I'm not listening." Ginger turned toward her house.

"Wait, Ginger!" Libby waved her paper at Ginger. "I know I promised never to use this unless I was in dire straits. Now I am. I'm about to get kicked out of the Bordello!"

"Hah! That's a good one."

Libby tapped the paper. "This thing says that even though you divorced my bed hopping brother, I stood up for you at your last wedding. We've been best friends for fifteen years. *Please* listen to me."

"No, Libby. You've hopped on the insanity train. I'm done with your protest marches and picket lines. I am truly done."

Ginger's intensity shook Libby. Ginger almost never shouted. She should leave, come back another day, but Ginger was the only person she knew who could deal with Cece's outbursts.

"I know I've over-played the desperation bit on a few occasions, but your picture with the Saguaro Cacti got our cause so much attention we've got more people on board."

"And, if I'd still owned my business I would've gotten several real estate cancellations."

This wasn't working. Libby put the list in her pocket and turned to her car.

"I'm here with an apology gift for pestering you to death ever since my Phil died. It's a peace offering you can't refuse."

Ginger silently groaned. Now it was a bribe. That was a terrible thought. Phil's heart attack happened over a year and a half ago and her best friend was still floundering from being a widow.

The screech of Libby's trunk lid as she opened it had them both shivering in the warm morning sun.

Libby patted a worn cloth covering her surprise and thought it was cruel to tease a woman who adored presents as much as Ginger did, but anticipation was such a powerful tool she just couldn't afford to overlook it.

Ginger, looking in, told herself, she could refuse whatever it was. *I can refuse it,* ran through her head, followed by *No, I should take it, smile, say thank you, then bring it up every time Lib tries to bully me into saving the world from itself.*

Ginger adjusted the brim of her hat, pushed her sunglasses tight, jammed her hands in her pants pockets, and bumped her thermos. Surprised it had stayed clipped to her garden belt after all her running and dodging, she snapped the cap off then took a long, but disappointing drink of cool water. She'd stopped taking her gin and lemonade mix with her to work in her gardens when 'those in the know' said gin, Arizona heat, her high-blood pressure, and her age were a deadly brew.

The trunk was empty except for a cloth covering something that had lumps and bumps. Was that her peace offering? If so, it certainly had her attention. Leaning in, Ginger's back muscles seized up. In all her years of gardening they'd never complained like they were doing this year. And, she'd really been out of breath chasing down Libby's car. She'd given up her running every day, and exercising, because of the time spent with her husband's cancer problems.

"I should get back to Pilates."

"What?" Libby bending into the trunk, looked up, and banged her head.

Ginger stepped back, "What, what?"

"You said something."

"No, I didn't." Ginger arched her back to slow its spasms.

"You said Lattes, Ginger. Do you want some coffee?"

"No, I said Pilates. It's a strengthening class. I didn't know I said it out loud."

"You did." Libby pulled back the cloth, then lifted out a long metal handle. Turning with it, she bumped Ginger's elbow.

Ginger hopped around muttering 'God Bless America' over and over.

"I'm sorry. I didn't know you were that close to me. How bad is it?"

"Not too much." Actually, her elbow hardly hurt, but she rubbed it for show and mileage. The 'God Bless America' had shot out of her mouth when Libby's cloth moved enough that she recognized an antique water pump lying beneath it. If this were Libby's apology, it was a doozy.

"Good." Libby laid the handle on the ground, turned back to her trunk. "Help me get this thing out. It weighs a ton."

"It says D. Peters. 1857." Ginger stiffened. "It's an honest to god, authentic, signed, antique water pump in mint condition."

Her voice had kept getting louder and louder. "That thing's fantastic."

"It's for the irrigation pond you and George are putting in. I knew you've been looking all over for one." Libby smiled. She'd about split her face grinning when she'd found the pump.

"It's far too valuable to be a gift. We'll pay you for it."

Ginger was embarrassed that her second thought was she'd be forever in Libby's debt if she took the pump. A third thought stopped her. Was this really an apology? Or did Libby need something so bad she went out and tracked this beauty down?

"Where did you find this?"

Libby smiled. "Last week when I was bored with the world I went over to the Kitt Observatory to look into a volunteer position I'd heard about."

"Great!"

"No. The drive is too long to do three times a week."

Ginger held her tongue. That drive wasn't all that long. It was just another of Libby's excuses not to get on with her life.

"On my way back, I swung into to see a friend and saw this thing just sitting in a pile of stuff to be hauled away as junk. I offered to buy it. She said it was junk. I said it wasn't. She refused my money because Phil and his guys had fixed up their house for free and she was thrilled I wanted it. She even helped me load it into Rosa Rita's trunk."

Ginger ran her hand over the engraved name. "It's perfect Lib. And it was in a junk pile? George will be thrilled. I'm thrilled. And you found it just lying around? I'm repeating myself aren't I?"

She could see her gift was working. Ginger couldn't take her eyes off the pump. Ginger would agree to go with her to talk to Cece. She would. She just knew she would.

Chapter 5

Together they carried the heavy pump up the driveway, into the back yard, over two slippery piles of dirt and put it down next to where George wanted a pump to go. The whole way, Libby had nervously rambled on with Phil stories that Ginger heard so often she could tell them herself. Usually she laughed, or got sad, along with Libby. Today, picturing the pump up and running interfered with the stories.

Ginger sighed. Sometimes life was kind. Three months before Phil's death the couple had celebrated forty-five years of marriage. Friends had been expected to show up, but no one had imagined that fifteen of Lib and Phil's sixteen foster kids from all over the country would be there. All had said they'd either be dead or in jail, if it weren't for Phil and Libby.

Libby had shot back that loving them had kept their marriage out of trouble.

There were times now when Lib would go quiet, make her hands into fists. It was so sad that Libby and Phil's Crafty Carpenters could fix everything but Phil. They rarely talked about the day Phil died of a heart attack up on a hot roof.

Ginger blurted out, "It's okay to leave it outside? Right?"

Libby raised an eyebrow. "Yes, it's a water pump."

"Don't look at me as if my mind's gone. I thought the joints might need oiling or something."

"Outside is fine." Libby grunted as she slipped a little.

"How many houses did you, Phil and the Crafty Carpenters restore?"

"Thirty-two. Why?"

"It just popped into my head when you said this came from one of them."

Libby turned. "I've something else for you in my car, and it weighs nothing."

She took off at record speed for a woman with short legs and sandals going over a rough terrain. Ginger followed, getting to the car in time to see Libby lift out a huge bundle of sage from her back seat.

"Finding the pump had me so high I just had to go sage hunting. Libby

21

swished the sage in a wide arc in front of Ginger, the heat expanded and magnified their wonderful smell.

"Isn't that the grandest fragrance?"

"Tis." Ginger nodded. A rare, and valuable water pump. Sage harvested from rattlesnake infested hills. By accepting the gifts, she'd lost the contest of wills without ever speaking of it. Well, one more crusade with Libby wouldn't kill her. Maim her, but not kill her.

"You outdid yourself, Lib." Ginger looked at Libby's faded and tattered baseball cap.

"I surely did." Libby grinned.

Ginger smiled back. "Time to get us out of this skin wrinkling sun."

Ginger's burst of speed had Libby going at a trot, and admiring how Ginger's 'mucho bucks' suit showed off her slim body. Libby brushed her own faded slacks, felt a little flab on her thighs, looked down at her dusty Birkenstocks. They always made her feel right.

In the entryway to the house, Ginger pointed to the ceiling. "How do you like the new fan George had installed?"

Libby looked around. "Where? All I see is your Italian cut glass, chandelier."

"It's behind the sconce." Ginger snapped her fingers. "Give it a minute and you'll hear glass hitting glass."

Libby tilted her head. "I hear gently rippling water. If you put the sage out here the smell will spread all through your living room." Libby kicked off her dusty sandals, slipped on the extra pair of slippers Ginger kept by her front door for guests. It wouldn't do to scratch custom made tiles with dust and gravel from the world outside.

Ginger's tiles weren't tough like the bricks she and Phil had laid in their entryway. Salvaged them from a school being torn down, they'd made it a family project that took months. Cleaning and laying bricks that still looked great when she'd sold their house. Thinking of Phil pushed her a little sideways. She'd only moved into an apartment at Cece's until she could buy a smaller house. Problem now was that she loved it there. She couldn't stand to trouble with Cece. She hadn't done something like burn a hole in the carpet; she'd only sat down to talk with a sad Anna Mae.

Libby shook herself. Time to come straight out and ask Ginger to handle Cece's red headed temper and make things turn out okay.

Realizing she was squeezing the bundle of sage as if they it Cece's throat, Libby let go and looked around. How had she gotten to Ginger's kitchen? She didn't remember going through the living room. Her inattention to things had been happening since Phil's death. She turned to Ginger.

"That tall, oval vase in your front entrance is perfect for some of this sage."

Ginger frowned as much as her surgical 'improvements' allowed. "It's full of dried red berries."

"Yes!" Libby nodded. "Red berries, sage in dark green vase. Perfecto!"

Picturing the authentic antique pump out in her yard, Ginger left to get the vase.

The second Ginger was gone, Libby tiptoed to the refrigerator, opened the door, pulled out the yellow pitcher of lemonade, sniffed. "No gin smell."

She stole a small swig. "Yup, gin."

She put it back, fled to the sink and fiddled with her bribe. The long stems were for the vase. The short, crumbled sage was perfect for smudge pots for she and Ginger and friends. She loved that the smell would stay on her hands for hours. She'd been right to snoop. The liquor taste wasn't as strong as in the past. Maybe Ginger was backing off from the booze now that things looked good for George. Or. Gin could simply have run out of gin.

George hadn't mentioned Ginger's drinking so, she should butt out. She wasn't good at minding her own business.

Out in the front hall, Ginger shook the really dried red berries into a huge wicker basket and hated the ropey blue veins crisscrossing her hands like a road map. Her face 'improvements' had cost as much as her two kids college educations and now her hands gave her away.

There was nothing she could do about them, other than hold them up, let the blood drain away or wear gloves. Gloves in Arizona didn't work. She stared at the closet where she'd almost collapsed hiding from Libby. Libby! Ginger spun around. Good God! Libby was alone in her kitchen! What had she been thinking? She hadn't been.

Libby was probably in her fridge right now checking out her 'gin-aide'. She should have sent Libby to get the vase. Gotten herself a drink, then hidden her pitcher of liquid gold.

Shoving the sprigs of red berries back into the vase, she rushed to the kitchen muttering, "At fifty-five I'm not accountable to Libby."

Glancing in the mirror she mumbled, "Okay, I'm sixty-five."

In the kitchen everything seemed calm. Together they arranged the sage and red berries in the vase.

"Okay. You're here to ask me to do something, so give me your bottom line. I've my gardening to do."

Libby sat down "I'm not exaggerating this one bit. Cece's threatening to kick me out of the Bordello because she caught me talking to Anna Mae and. She was very clear about that on her telephone message."

"Ignore her. Cece changes her mind as often as she changes the color of her hair."

"No, something's rotten in Ceceville. She saw Anna Mae and me

23

talking the other day, and snatched Anna Mae away as if I was about to hit her."

"Cece loves to showcase, Lib. Exaggerating things is how she got all her real estate dealings."

"Well I'm not a building she can fiddle with. Phil and I, you and George played bridge with her and Benny for years. Cece should trust me. Anna Mae mostly stays in her apartment at the Bordello. When she's out her head always hangs down. I thought a friendly chat might help her."

Cece? That's all it was? Trouble with Cece. Ginger fanned herself in relief. "You talking to another tenant isn't a reason to throw you out. You're safe."

"No, Ginger. I think there's something crazy going on. First, Cece moves Anna Mae into the Bordello saying it's because she isn't coping well with being a widow. Then she tells a group of women not to bother her? Does that make sense? No it doesn't."

Libby pushed her glasses up the bridge of her nose, waited for Ginger to pour them glasses of iced tea.

"So I figured Anna Mae had to be sick of talking to herself and I just sat down and asked her how she was doing. Anna Mae said fine, but she didn't look fine to me. Those pale blue eyes of hers looked really sad. Naturally, I started chatting with her.

One word led to another, until we were sitting cozy on the red settee blabbing about how hard it is to do things on our own after so many years of marriage. That's when Cece came roaring up, gave me a dirty look then took off with Anna Mae in tow."

Libby nibbled on a cookie to give Ginger time to think.

"She can't kick you out. You have a lease."

"I don't. I didn't think I'd like living in an apartment. Now that I love the Bordello, I couldn't stand to be kicked out."

She itched to grab Ginger's long hands and beg her friend for help. "Talk to her, Ginger. Please. You know Cece a whole lot better than any of us do."

"Me talk to Cece?" Ginger tried to raise an eyebrow but neither one moved, not her forehead either. "I'm barely speaking to Cece myself."

"I thought you were friends from your real estate dealings."

"No. Not then and it's worse since George's cancer. Cece came to our door telling me, no, almost ordering me, to take George to this doctor and that clinic because her husband's sister had used them when she had breast cancer. She didn't say she was sorry to hear about George's cancer. Or ask, like you did, if I was scared to death. She just started bossing me around as if I had the brain of a day old tea bag. I sent her on her way and she didn't like that."

The sudden tears in Ginger's eyes startled Libby. As she reached to squeeze her hands, Ginger pulled away.

"Did you see what you just did?"

"What did I just do?"

"You pulled away the second you thought I was going to touch you."

Ginger picked up her glass of tea, wished for a more potent drink, put it down, stared at it.

"My dear friend Ginger, you don't let even me touch you. I've heard you tell people that you and George are holding up fine. That you are working with the best doctors here in Tucson."

"It's the truth."

"Ginger, when your life isn't good, you give off stay-away vibes. Your face goes cold. You dress even better when things are bad. You want everyone to see how very capable you are."

"Okay, smarty. What would you have said?"

"The only truth that counts. That George is the love of your life. That his cancer has you petrified and exhausted. Makes you afraid you'll overlook something. You were, and still are, scared to death he'll die on you."

"Cece should have known that. Seen it on my face."

"Come on, Ginger. All your plastic surgery, Botox and whatever else you've had done, has frozen your assets, so to speak. You look fifty instead of sixty-five and you are happy about that. But, it does limit you."

Libby frowned, made her face go sad, raised up her eyebrows.

"You can't do any of what I just did. You can't express your feelings the way the rest of us can. So you'll have to say your feelings in words."

"I refuse to wear my feelings on my sleeve!"

"Then don't complain when people think you're holding up fine."

"Ah, you want me to whine and be pitiful like Anna Mae."

"Not that far. Remember when you divorced my brother and you were reduced to rubble? You let everyone know how you felt then."

Ginger got up from the table so fast, Libby grabbed her glass to stop it from tipping over.

"Your brother was cheating on me with a woman ten years older than me. Older than me."

"And how you howled. How you cried. You cornered everyone too slow to get away and told them how rotten he was. You tripled your drinking and your family jumped in to help. You gave up drinking and found George. Was getting help so bad then?"

"No." Ginger sat down.

"Let me show you what you do when you meet someone new." Libby took her cap off, undid her ponytail, fluffed her hair, leaned forward, waved her hand about as if she had on Ginger's huge diamond ring.

"You laugh, you tell people your first marriage was for raucous sex, two beautiful children and the experience of a divorce. Your second marriage was for love and the building of a huge real estate business. Sadly, you remind people, your love died when a stretch ice that threw his car off the road. Your third marriage, to my brother, was for travel, but unfortunately he preferred to travel other women's bodies. Then you tell them it was all training for your fourth marriage, which is perfect. Am I right?"

Ginger shrugged. "I'm nobody's business."

"Come on, Ginger, be honest. Your first husband didn't grow up. He liked his beer and hated work. Your second husband was a kind, loving, workaholic who fell asleep and didn't see the ice on the road. Your third husband, my brother, was a lemon from the start. And you secretly worry about George being younger than you and that he'll want to stray."

Libby took her last jab. "Plus, you haven't gained a pound in years, probably not since high school. There, that's the worst I can say of you."

Libby sat back, finished off three bite size cookies while Ginger drummed her bright pink nails on the table and glared at her.

"I weigh ten pounds more than I did in high school."

She would never admit she hadn't graduated from high school, not even to Libby.

Libby, relieved there'd been no return fire, tucked away the ten pounds heavier. Ginger must have been a toothpick in high school.

Chapter 6

Ginger glared at her sweating glass of iced tea. She needed the gin-aide in the refrigerator, now. It was time for Libby to go home.

"I'll not make a fool of myself by bleeding all over people."

"A drip or two wouldn't hurt."

"Okay. How's this?" Ginger leaned close to Libby, as if George might come home and hear her.

"I'm falling apart now that George is back to work. I'm mad at the people who get upset because their grass is brown, or their pool needs more chemicals. I'm especially mad at you for bothering me with this Anna Mae and Cece thing."

Libby looked at the clock. Ten to ten. She had to hurry this along. "You need a big diversion, kiddo. You know, when the going gets tough the...."

"None of your Pollyanna stuff!"

"Okay. Then tell me how old Anna Mae is."

"Why?"

"Just do it."

"I don't know. Seventy five?"

"Same as us. Sixty five."

"She can't be!" Ginger thumped the table so hard her glass wobbled.

"She is." Libby nodded. "Birdie, found it on some papers in Cece's office. Anna Mae is the perfect example of how not dealing with life, not facing up to things, wears on a person. I think that's why her face is so wrinkled."

Ginger ran her hands over her face, felt no wrinkles, only smooth skin. "Anna Mae also hunches over, as if she's wearing a fifty pound back pack and she mumbles like a very old lady. I assume your point is that if I don't quit my belly-aching all the money I've spent on my face will be wasted."

"It's a thought." Libby gave her a half smile. "I'm trying to get back to my pressing problem of not getting evicted. I tell you, Cece's jumpy when it comes to Anna Mae."

Ginger dismissed it with a wave of her hand. "If she wants you to stay away from Anna Mae, just stay away."

"Come on, Ginger. Stay away? We are women, we like to talk."

"Look, Cece has always worried about how mean Benny was to Anna Mae and how he ran their lives. Now she's taken custody and obviously she doesn't want help from you. Just sit tight, she'll get bored and quit."

"So, I'm supposed to turn away when I see Anna Mae. Duck behind something. Don't you think she will notice and feel hurt, or insulted?"

"Okay, I'll call Cece."

"No. A call won't do it. Cece is always in her Bordello office on Wednesdays from ten until twelve. Go with me. Help me reason with her."

A whiff of lilac reminded Ginger of the antique pump in their back yard. "Okay, I'll go, but I have to change my clothes and fix my face."

"Wonderful." Libby pointed at the clock. "Hurry."

"You go ahead, Lib. I'll catch up."

"Not on your life. I'll wait right here for you. Cece needs to see the two of us walk in together."

Ginger pointed to the back door. "Then go out and enjoy my early Mexican poppies growing along the back fence."

Knowing 'go see' was code for 'calm down', Libby left. Outside, she welcomed the heat that seemed to be building toward a nice day in May. Next month air conditioning would kick in. It was a fine invention, she couldn't do without it, but sometimes it chilled her to the bone.

A soft breeze swayed the thick row of golden flowers and spun the sweet smell of jasmine from a nearby bush. It was a peaceful garden, not like the mess at the Bordello. She could probably make points with Cece if she promised to help the Bordello's garden. She knew how to make things prosper almost as well as Ginger.

When twenty minutes passed and there was no sign of Ginger, Libby marched back into the house and thumped on her bathroom door.

"Your poppies are gorgeous, as you must be by now."

"Damn it, Libby you made me drop my eye shadow case." Ginger checked herself in the mirror one last time then opened the door. "I'm ready."

Libby smiled. "Khaki slacks, expensive white shirt, a touch of Indian jewelry. Them's serious talk clothes."

She headed down the hall. "Do you follow me or I you?"

"I never follow you. You drive like an old lady. At the first flash of a yellow light you slow down. I see yellow as it's intended to be a warning to get going."

She opened the door to their pristine garage.

Libby looked around, let out a whistle. "Why all the new equipment?"

"It's for George's research on solar waterfalls."

Libby pressed the garage door button, whistled again as the light hit

Ginger's new car. Walking closer to it, she said. "Someone stole your door handles."

"Oh, that's right, you haven't seen this car." Ginger faced her car, said, "Twenty nineteen." and suddenly the driver's door swung open.

"It's voice recognition. I can open one door or all of them. George got it on his last car and insisted I have it on mine because my arms are usually full of plants and things."

"Amazing." Libby started to leave, then stopped. "What happens, let's say when you're driving along and you see an address twenty-nineteen and say it?"

"Well, I wouldn't."

"You're getting old, you could forget."

"Older. We're getting older. The doors won't open if the car is in reverse or drive."

Libby went to the car. "Twenty nineteen." Nothing happened.

"It doesn't recognize your voice. Only George or I can open it."

"And I thought a clicker was amazing. I suppose you don't need a key to start it either."

"Nope. Just my thumb print."

"Wait! What if you lose your voice and I have to open the doors?"

"There's my thumb again." Ginger smiled at the confusion on Libby's face. "I'll wait in my car at the Bordello until you get there."

"Ah." Libby headed to her car then stopped. "You're going to speed ahead so your fancy car won't be seen with my charming older model."

"Who wouldn't?"

Driving out her driveway, Ginger stared straight at Sally Long Nose peeking out her front window across the street. Sally, part of last year's Garden Snoop Group, as she liked to call them had been replaced for being too observant. She gave Sally a friendly wave, then sped up when Libby's raspy Japanese horn blared behind her.

Chapter 7

A half hour earlier, Cece Fontaine had parked her baby blue Beamer convertible behind the Bordello, about the time Anna Mae had broken into Benny's cabinet and Ginger and Libby were carrying the pump to Ginger's back yard.

Getting out, she waved at three kids from her Daycare center, locked her car then hurried in the back door of the Bordello. Blue Beamers were her signature all through her years of buying and selling business properties. Blue because it matched the blue of her eyes and set off her auburn and crimson streaked hair.

The Bordello was her pride and joy. The high point of years of hard work and no one would take it away from her. Especially someone as unimportant as Anna Mae.

Inside, slipping off her stiletto heels, she bare footed it past the empty first floor lounge, up the back stairs. She checked the second floor lounge for Anna Mae and saw only the manikins. Relieved there was no one on the exercise equipment in the third floor lounge, she slipped into her office, locked the door. Then she went to her desk, sitting down, she put her head in her hands and shut her eyes. When that didn't ease her torment, she started pounding the top of her desk with her fists and didn't stop until her hands pulsed in pain.

"Damn, damn, damn you, Anna Mae! I'm in a whole heap of trouble because I've been kind to you."

She took in a deep breath, blew out as her Yoga coach had taught her. Then, fanning herself with a magazine, her eyes caught the most recent picture of her grandchildren; she picked it up and shook it a little.

"Grandma's advice, kids. They say we're to help our fellow man. I say stay out of other people's business. Just send money. I could go to jail for helping."

She took in a deep breath, shook the picture again. "I was just trying to help an irritating acquaintance."

Dancers of the Third Age

Her six grandchildren were her biggest pleasure.

"What will you dear people do if your grandmother is jailed as an accessory to murder? Or manslaughter. What do they call it when a person's killed someone accidentally out of the goodness of their heart?"

She turned the picture away so she didn't have to look into their trusting eyes. They had no idea, nor did their parents that she'd spent a year in jail for battery. It was a long time ago and it shouldn't be counted against her now. Still, she couldn't take the chance that it would.

Her trouble started during her renovation of the Bordello.

She loved the huge, stone monstrosity, built in the mid eighteen hundreds and used as a Bordello. She'd bought it for a ridiculously low price and a promise to restore it to its original charm, or tear it down.

She'd been full of herself. Puffed up. Thought she was Queen of the Reclamation World. She kept her hand in it all. Ran rough shod over contractors because she knew best. And, as usual, it turned out that she did.

She'd even been the headline in the Sunday housing section. *Local Business Woman Restores Former Bordello*. It was during the refurbishing that she met Benny and Anna Mae Brown. They were the beginning of her undoing.

On her way home from checking her Bordello restoration, a road repair project had sent her down an unfamiliar street. Passing a sign, Furniture and Automobile Restoration, she'd slammed on her brakes, backed up and pulled into the parking area in front of a large, barn-like, structure attached to a small white house. She still had several pieces of furniture authentic to the bordello's time period that needed work. She usually took them to The Antique Artiste, a long time friend, but lately he'd been raising his prices on her.

She could try these people. Even if their work was shoddy, she might force the Artiste to lower his prices; competition being the American way.

Walking in, huge fans had whirled overhead sending whiffs of chemicals and wood Cece's way. Pulleys and ropes, for moving things about, hung from the two story high ceiling. A man and woman turned toward her from the back of the shop but didn't move.

Walking past furniture in various stages of re-finishing what she saw met her approval. Nearing the couple, she stuck her hand out in greeting.

"We don't shake hands with people. Your oil. Our oil. It gets on things."

The man's brusque tone left her feeling a bit chastised. That was something new for her. "I'm Cece Fontaine."

"I'm Benny Brown. That's my wife, Anna Mae."

Cece had heard the name Benny Brown before. He was a top-notch furniture restorer with a crabby reputation. Friends told her they would clash and to stay away from him. Seeing his work, made her forget their advice.

Benny Brown was tall, muscled with a thick chest that strained the buttons on his denim shirt but not in a sexy way and his hard stare unnerved her. She gave his wife about three minutes to look her in the eyes, when she wouldn't look at her, she nicknamed her 'The Mouse'.

As a test, a few days later she brought in two pieces, then several more pieces. By the time she was writing a large check, 'The Mouse' had snuck into some of their conversations. She came alive the day Benny brought up duplicate bridge.

"We've enjoyed playing bridge." Anna Mae's smile was brief. "Unfortunately, the people we used to play with have either moved away or are too old."

Cece invited them to be substitute players at her bimonthly bridge club. Benny was the better player. Anna Mae was a subservient player when she was his partner. Alone, she was excellent. By the time they became Bridge Club regulars, Cece was noticing signs of what could be spousal abuse; bruises on Anna Mae's ankles that her slacks didn't hide. Stiffness when she leaned in to gather cards. The way Benny clamped his hand on Anna Mae's when he didn't like something.

Her husband Jack said she was over reacting because of her first marriage, plus she had a tendency to do so. Her first husband had been a brute but she'd taken a bat to him. Defending herself had cost her a year in jail. Those were the days when some judges believed wives should grin and bear it. She'd asked the judge if he meant bear or bare it. He'd said if taking off her clothes fixed things, then he meant bare.

After getting out of jail, she'd moved to Tucson and developed a whole new way of thinking about herself. She was no longer sweet Cynthia. She was Cece, whom no one bossed around. Which meant she ignored Jack and started dropping in unannounced at Benny and Anna Mae's workshop. Always with a piece of furniture that needed to be restored as an excuse.

The day after Anna Mae had made a wrong bid at bridge she made a point of dropping in. The workshop was dark. Thinking they'd taken the day off, she turned to leave. A groan, then a whimper, sent chills up her back. Feeling for the light switch, she turned them on. Anna Mae was near the back of the shop clinging to a workbench, her face a ghostly mix of green and white. There was no sign of Benny.

Anna Mae's slacks were down around her ankles. Her blouse had been ripped open. When she'd run ran to help Anna Mae, comfort her, she didn't know where to touch her. Anna Mae had been beaten nearly everywhere. Pulling up Anna Mae slacks, seeing her mottled skin, she'd almost fainted, but still managed to close her blouse, help her into a chair.

"He's pulverized you. Even I can see that your ankle's broken. And there's blood on your thighs. My God he's raped you!"

Anna Mae had always denied abuse. But now there was evidence right there in front them. Now, Anna Mae would agree to report him, leave him. She was sure of it.

Anna Mae grimaced as she shook her head. "Men don't rape their wives. It's their right."

"Oh for God's sake, no Anna Mae. Not here in America. I'm calling 911."

Surprised that her purse was still over her shoulder, Cece took out her cell-phone.

"No!" A shaking Anna Mae grabbed at Cece.

"No."

"Yes. The bastard beat you everywhere. Raped you. You could have internal injuries. You could bleed to death. You have to go to the hospital."

"Hospital's call police."

Cece was so unnerved, that she had a hysterical vision of a hospital building calling the police.

"Please leave, Cece. He'll be back soon to take me to his doctor."

Cece fought off an impulse to slap Anna Mae. "Wake up, Anna Mae! His doctor?"

Anger boiled inside her. "His doctor'll patch you up and not call the police. I can get you real help."

As started to dial Anna Mae swatted the phone out of her hand.

"Stop, Cece. Benny hasn't hit me in a long time. His doctor is a good doctor. We've used him before."

"Used him before? Damn it, Anna Mae. Fight back! I know how to find you a Safe House."

Anna Mae pulled herself up, inched the chair toward the door to the house. "Go Cece, before he comes back. I shouldn't have called out to you. I'm okay now that I've got my breath."

Cece picked up a heavy long handled wrench. "If he comes I'll clobber him."

"You can't win." Anna Mae had edged herself to the door to her house. "I know."

"I'll take you to a Phoenix hospital. Benny won't look for you that far away. After they fix you up you can stay with my daughter or, I'll find you a Safe House away from here."

Cece, afraid Anna Mae would disappear into the house, spoke fast, swiped at the tears running down her face.

"I'm giving you a chance to get away from that bastard."

"How would I live? I've no money. I'm too old to get a job." Anna Mae reached for the doorknob.

Money? Cece felt hope. "I'll loan you money."

"I can't pay you back, Cece. Ever. I'd be running from town to town, looking over my shoulder. Eating out of garbage cans, freezing at night. It's better I stay here with him."

Anna Mae had the door open.

"He could kill you here."

"I'd welcome that." Grunting, Anna Mae limped into her house and shut the door.

The cold click of the lock, echoed in the garage.

Ever since then she'd felt Anna Mae deserved the limp she got from an ankle that had never healed properly. She'd even stayed away from their shop for over a year, until one of her most cherished picture frames broke in half.

The day Benny died, walking into their shop, she'd heard Benny and Anna Mae shouting back and forth. Anger echoed all around the workshop and she'd almost yelled out, *Hurrah!* Anna Mae was cussing Benny. It was a beginning.

She'd decided to take pictures of what she could. Pulling out her cell phone, she focused on Benny at the top of a very high ladder and clicked. Then clicked on Anna Mae standing near the door into their house. When that wasn't really catching the action, she touched video and filmed them throwing tools back and forth at each other. If she could catch him hurting Anna Mae, she'd file the complaint herself.

Then a huge blur slashed across her lens. Lowering her cell phone, she saw it was a tool that had stuck in the wall inches from Anna Mae's head. The bastard was trying to kill her! Cece dropped her phone, ran and yanked on Benny's ladder.

"Stop it, Benny! Stop." Neither one of them looked her way.

Anna Mae picked up another tool, hauled back and threw it.

Looking like it would go just out of Benny's reach, Cece was shocked to see him reach out for the tool. The ladder moved. Jerking back, Cece felt it twist in her hands, then wrench away.

There was a loud snap, then Benny was falling. His head hit a workbench, sending a sharp thud through the workshop followed by thump when he landed on the cement the floor. They were sounds that still lingered in her head.

No matter how she played it, that ladder always spun out of her hands just before he fell. It didn't matter that the police said it was an accident, she was sure she'd killed Benny Brown.

Stunned, she'd run over to Anna Mae. Tools were lying all over, plus a dead cat. Somehow she and Anna Mae got the mess cleaned up, buried the cat, covered the hole in the wall with a calendar. By the time the police arrived she had Anna Mae believing her lie.

Had her telling the police she'd been at the door to the house when the ladder popped off its moorings and Benny fell. That Cece had just come into the workshop and that neither she, nor Cece, were anywhere near the ladder.

Dancers of the Third Age

Her life had gone quiet then. They'd buried Benny. The police seemed content with the information she'd given them, because no one called her back to ask more questions. Then, sometime around six weeks after Benny died, one of the Bridge Club women saw Anna Mae at the grocery store. She said Anna Mae was as thin as spaghetti and was muttering to herself. That was when she moved her to the Bordello to keep an eye on her.

Now, two days ago, her worse nightmare had come true. Libby and Anna Mae, their two heads together, sat talking in the Shady Lady Lounge. Libby could get anyone to talk. She'd almost screamed at Libby to get away from Anna Mae. Instead, she'd rushed over and took Anna Mae up here to her office. Libby, being a cop's widow, would chew over that one for days.

Cece put her head in her hands again, rubbed her forehead. Sending Anna Mae back home wouldn't help, Libby would trot right over there.

"I guess I have to spend some money. Send Anna Mae to a Spa for a week or two!"

Give her some time to figure out a permanent solution. Someone as insignificant as Anna Mae would not ruin her life.

She looked at her watch; it was eleven. With her office hours about to start, she decided to make her calls when they were over.

Chapter 8

Exhausted, Anna Mae slumped over her steering wheel in the parking lot behind the Bordello. She'd driven so carefully all the way from the cemetery trying not to do anything to make the police stop her and find Benny's gun on the front seat. Fighting back tears, she lifted her head. She was safe now.

Taking her box from the front seat, she checked to make sure the pictures of her children, Benny's gun and several papers from his cabinet were still inside. Several of the day care children were in their fenced yard waving at her. To talk to them, like she usually did, would make her burst into tears. Waving back, she went to a side door and stepped inside.

The large open lounge, half filled with chairs, was empty. Breathing a sigh of relief, she tip-toed up the back stairs, into the second floor landing and stopped. Yes, this was the Shady Lady Lounge, her floor. The red velvet settee with two manikins on it was there, slightly to her left. And that was her apartment across the way with the door wide open. It shouldn't be open! She'd locked it when she left just a few hours ago.

She blinked to be sure she was seeing things right. A man was coming out of her apartment and he was taking her television set! He was pushing it on a cart out her door! She dropped her box and Benny's gun bounced out. She picked it up.

Dare she go over there and question him? No. It was obvious she was being robbed!

Outraged, she shouted. "Stop! Put my TV back!"

Strangely, the man just nodded at her, he even smiled as if she were nothing he had to worry about.

Anna Mae figured she'd confused him by first telling him to stop, then telling him to put the TV back. Straining her voice to its peak, she shouted again, "Stop right there!"

He turned the cart toward her. Was he going to run her over with it? Knock her down? Her hands shook hard as she pointed Benny's gun right at him.

"Get your hands up. Now!"

Somewhere in bending over she'd lost her glasses and she couldn't quite make out his face. All she could tell was that he was shaking his head at her. At least with her gun pointing at him he'd stopped moving.

"Get away from my TV and don't you move."

She'd said it wrong again. He couldn't get away from her property and not move. What a fool she was. She gave him the steely look she sometimes gave Benny when he wasn't paying attention. She wiggled her gun at him indicating he should take the TV back into her apartment. Why was he just standing there like a fool?

A whimpering noise, not from the man, but from her right, got her attention. A quick glance over there said that three women were standing it front of the red, upright piano. Now her whole body shook.

Were they new manikins? No. Manikins never moved on their own. They were real people waving at her. Even their mouths were moving. A roaring noise in her head shut out what they were saying.

Straining to see them, their gray hair made her think they could be women who lived here. She couldn't be sure. No, if they were other renters, they would make the man put her TV back.

The man! The heavy pistol made her hand shake as she turned to him. Who to watch? Him? The women? The man had her T V. She waved her gun at him.

"You piece of shit! Put my fucking TV down!" Benny would have been shocked that she'd snapped out an order like him.

*****

Arriving at the Bordello from Ginger's house, Ginger studied Libby's car. Once a firecracker red it had faded to cream of tomato soup red.

"You really need a new car. Yours is being held together by rope and crossed fingers."

"Hush your mouth, Ginger. If Rosa Rita hears you she'll quit on me."

Ginger pointed to the front windows. "This place just sings of the old days when there were no rules. When these windows were wide open and filled with ladies of the night leaning out to show off their assets and men eager to part with their money."

"Not to me." Libby walked up wide granite stairs that dipped in the center due to a hundred twenty years of foot traffic then pushed open the Bordello's huge, oak, front door.

"I see wives marching down the street with their rolling pins held high."

"Them too." Ginger laughed as she followed Libby, carrying her small bundle of sage into what everyone called the Scarlet Letter Lounge.

"Don't mention eviction to Cece, Lib. If she brings it up, say you talked to Anna Mae because she looked like she was about to collapse any minute."

Libby nodded. "She does and it was obvious she doesn't know how to live without Benny to boss her around."

To prevent her self from saying, *just like someone else I know,* Ginger counted five rows of chairs in the lounge that were turned to face a large square table.

"This looks like a school room."

Libby nodded. "Fran's, English as a Second Language, class is tonight. It keeps getting bigger. Her way of easing people's anxieties brings them in."

Ginger stopped. "You should help out with the classes, Lib. You'd be great. For some reason you speak Mexican as well as any Mexicans I know and you are from New Hampshire."

"That's another long story but me teach English? No. I don't know how to explain words like read, I know how to *read*. I've already *read* the book. And you know what? My dress is *red*."

Ginger glared at her. "Wow. That excuse sure was at the ready. Just like all the other ones you toss out to avoid volunteering or taking a job that won't make you the big cheese. I've met Fran, she'd make you a. . ."

Libby, not wanting to hear it again, sped toward the back stairs. Muttering to herself that Ginger had been her own boss for over thirty years and didn't know what it was like to be in charge of nothing was half way up the stairs to the Shady Lady Lounge when a sharp command cut through her irritation.

She tilted her head. Listened. Felt Ginger's hot breath on the back of her neck and hissed. "I swear someone just told Anna Mae to drop a gun."

"I heard it too." Ginger hissed back.

"Can't be. Anna Mae would never touch a gun."

"Exactly."

Silently creeping up to the second floor landing, Libby peeked out. Anna Mae did have a gun.

The thought was so horrific that Libby's mind erased it. Relief rolled over her until she blinked it all came back. Anna Mae did have a gun, and she was pointing it at someone. Libby dropped her bundle of lilacs.

Anna Mae turned and sucked in her breath. Libby was on the landing. A man was stealing her TV. Women were over by the piano and now Libby. She couldn't keep her eye on all of them.

"You! Stop right there!"

As the gun swung her way, Libby shut her eyes and ducked. Maybe she'd crashed her car on her way here and was having hallucinations. That had to be it! A hand grabbed her ankle and she thought it was Ginger trying to pull her from a car wreck. She opened one eye.

No, Anna Mae really was standing in the center of the Shady Lady lounge with an old Colt 45 in her hand. She grabbed the door frame. She knew guns from Phil's years on the force. If Anna Mae dropped it, it could easily go off and shoot someone.

From somewhere, she heard Phil's voice telling her to *stay calm, study the scene, study the people, but don't argue with them.*

Gathering her wits, she looked at Anna Mae and saw a wild look on her face. Saw a tipped over wooden box, small notebook and several papers at her feet. It was obvious that something had startled her.

Twenty feet or so past Anna Mae, a man was at her open apartment door with a TV on a cart. It was Cece's handyman, Carlos. That was strange.

A whimpering sound turned everyone to the upright piano in the far corner where Lissa, Birdie and Trish were huddled together.

"Carlos is not stealing your TV Anna Mae." Birdie's voice shook.

Libby felt a little relief. Carlos would never steal her TV. Never.

"My door was locked. He broke in and got it. "

Anna Mae's gun shook so violently that Trish let out a high falsetto whine, and collapsed onto the piano bench. Lissa plopped down next to her, white as mashed potatoes.

Birdie seemed about to move forward.

"Don't you dare take a step."

Anna Mae's sharp order stopped Birdie mid-stride.

Libby felt behind her for Ginger and got only air. A quick look back and she saw Ginger crouched down on the stairs in the fetal position. Nothing added up. Ginger was not a coward.

Ginger, glancing past Libby's slacks, to Anna Mae and her gun, quickly covered her head with her arms. This all brought back images of her mother's body dead on the floor. Blood was splattered on the wall. Her mother's suicide happened over fifty years ago and it still plagued her.

Libby hissed, "We have to stop Anna Mae."

"Not me."

Everything in Ginger said run down the steps, get out, but Libby was her friend and in danger. Uncovering her head, she stood up.

Anna Mae narrowed her eyes. Something had moved behind Libby. Yes. It was that dreadful show-off Ginger Logan. With her pouf of yellow hair. As she swung her gun back to Libby, the arthritis in her fingers jerked her gun down, then, up.

What was Ginger doing here? She had no business being here.

Ginger got to her feet, hissed. "Is Anna Mae crazy? Waving a gun around like that? I need a second to think. Say something to her, Lib."

Libby mumbled, 'Okay', cleared her throat so she could actually speak.

"What's going on, Anna Mae? This isn't like you. You're usually so quiet and pleasant."

Ginger was now standing slightly behind Libby. She had to do something this time. She'd been too wrapped up in her own teenage life to stop her mother's suicide. Everyone had excused her, but she should have done something. Today she would. She and Lib were both bigger than Anna Mae, and they were fast talkers. That should give them an edge, even if Anna Mae had the gun.

The pros said talking was the way to go. Anna Mae's crazed face, her spinning around, pointing her gun at everyone, made that idea seem ludicrous.

Feeling stronger with Ginger at her side, Libby stepped a few inches into the lounge. "Anna Mae, we're all friends here. Let's put the gun down."

As Anna Mae turned her gun on them, Libby and Ginger ducked.

"Let's? As in let us? There is no us here. It's me alone and me with the gun. That makes me in charge."

Benny's sarcasm dripped from Anna Mae. "That damn guy is stealing my TV."

"Okay. Tell him to put it back in your apartment." Libby, thinking it a logical suggestion, was surprised when Anna Mae's face went purple with rage.

"I don't want it back now! He stays there so the police will know he stole it. That can't happen if it's back in my apartment."

Anna Mae's tone had gone a bit tentative. Libby now had hope that it would turn out well.

As Anna Mae wiped her gun across her chin, Trish went into another series of squeals.

Anna Mae shook her gun at Trish. "God damn you! Shut up!"

"It's okay, Anna Mae. We're all," The pistol came back so fast, Libby and Ginger leaned back.

"We're all what? Friends? Were you going to say friends, Libby? I don't have friends. Benny saw to that."

"I wanted to say we are all scared. Your gun is scaring us. It's so old it could go off."

"Oh, it goes off all right." Anna Mae locked her knees to stop them from shaking.

Ginger, her heart pounding in her throat, jabbed Libby in the ribs. "Pull a Benny on her."

"A Benny? Benny! Of course, she's use to him." Libby took in a deep breath.

"You're being an idiot, Anna Mae. Put that damn gun in the box right now or you'll shoot your fool foot off!"

Anna Mae looked like she might do it, until she shook her gun at them, let out a long, "Noooo."

Ginger hissed at Libby "That was a Benny?" She took a few brave steps into the lounge, turned toward to the piano.

"Hey! You stupid old women by the piano. Get the hell behind it! Sit your asses down and shut up. You, the tall one, strangle that idiot if she makes another sound."

As the women disappeared, Anna Mae's face turned a blotchy purple. "You don't give the orders here. I do."

"Really?" Ginger thrust her head forward, the way Benny did when he scolded Anna Mae at cards.

"You didn't make them go away. I did. Now put the fucking gun in the box on the floor."

Anna Mae shook her head no.

"If you don't." Libby's loud shout nearly spilt Ginger's eardrum. "I'll tell the guy to knock your TV off the cart!"

Anna Mae collapsed into a heap on the red carpet, moaning.

Ginger mumbled, "I'll sit on Anna Mae while you ease the gun out of her hand, Lib because I never touch guns."

Chapter 9

Quivering on the floor, Anna Mae looked up at Ginger. "Give me my gun so I can kill myself."

This time she really would.

Anna Mae's simper drained the last of Ginger's patience and she growled. "You can't pull that, 'I'm going to kill myself', crap on me. I know better."

Anna Mae turned her body sideways on the floor. "It's the truth."

Ginger couldn't let that go. Getting down on one knee, she hissed in her ear. "No, it's not. Women rarely shoot themselves and it's even rarer they do it in public."

"Lot you know." Anna Mae's voice shook.

"You've no idea what I know."

"I know enough about you, Ginger to know you don't know anything about suicides. They're too messy for you."

Ginger's caution ran screaming from the room. "The hell I don't! I read up after my mother put a gun in her mouth and pulled the trigger."

The instant the words were out of her mouth she saw Libby kneeling on the other side of them.

Ginger's mother had killed herself? No, Ginger's parents were killed in a car accident. She'd told her that, years ago.

To cover the moment, she nodded to Ginger. "You take Anna Mae's arm, I'll take the other and we'll sit her up."

Trish, flushed and excited, arrived with Cece right behind her.

"I've got Cece."

"Why'd you pull a gun on my people?" Cece knelt beside Anna Mae.

"Because that man was stealing my TV." Anna Mae pointed over to Carlos still at her apartment door.

"That's Carlos. I asked him to take your small TV down to the basement storage and bring you my larger, spare one." Cece looked at Carlos.

"I already set it up in her apartment, Ms. Cece."

Dumfounded, Anna Mae looked at all of them. She'd been so foolish. She had to apologize, but now there was a commotion at the top of the stairs. Then two policemen appeared, then several others in uniform.

"I also called 911," Trish said, stepping behind Cece. "I thought Libby and Ginger might need some help."

Ginger leaned over to Libby. "Okay. That's it. I'm not explaining this to the police. You probably know these guys; you tell them, you live here. I'm calling George. I need him to take me to an early dinner."

Dinner? She was going home to drink until she couldn't remember her mother's body.

Two policemen, with their hands on their holsters, did a quick survey of the room. Libby thought that was a bit ridiculous, given all the gray hair floating around. Then they waved the paramedics in, along with their equipment.

"Young cop, old cop, two paramedics, a gurney, more equipment. A bit of an over-kill don't you think?" Libby hissed to Ginger, then instantly regretted the words over-kill.

Cece whispered back. "Trish told me you two took her gun away."

The young cop held his hand out to the women in general. "We understand there's a gun involved. We need the gun."

Ginger pointed her toe at a settee opposite them. "It's under there."

The officer, using a gloved hand, carefully removed the gun, smelt it, checked it. "No bullets."

A collective, "What?" Rang out.

Ginger glared at Anna Mae. "The gun was empty?"

Anna Mae stared at the floor. "I thought there might be some bullets left."

"We need the permit, too."

The young cop now had the gun in a plastic bag and was waiting on Fran who pointed to Anna Mae. "It's her gun."

The older paramedic looked at the older cop. "You know the drill. First, we make sure she's okay. Then, you ask your questions."

He and the other paramedic lifted Anna Mae onto the gurney. "Arm, please."

As one slipped a blood pressure cuff on Anna Mae's arm, the other paramedic attached white patches on Anna Mae's chest.

Ginger, knowing it was too much to ask that they electrocute her, looked for a clear path out of the lounge.

Libby, trying for a little levity, leaned into Ginger. "We must look healthy since he went straight for Anna Mae."

Trish shook her head. "I described Anna Mae when I called 911. But neither of you look very well either."

It seemed just a few minutes later that the paramedics had Anna Mae wrapped up in blankets on the gurney.

One spoke into his shoulder. "Her blood pressure's come down some. Heart rate's still erratic. We're bringing her in for further work up."

"I've never been in a hospital." Anna Mae, speaking to Cece, looked as anxious as when she'd been waving her gun around.

"It's for the best, Anna Mae. I'm sorry. I was in my office and didn't hear a thing until Trish flew through the door yelling she'd called 911 about you."

When Cece patted Anna Mae's hand, Ginger tried, and failed, to raise an eyebrow at Libby. Patting wasn't in Cece's nature. She wasn't the touchy-feely type. Not in all the years they'd known each other.

The good-looking young cop waved his plastic bag holding Anna Mae's gun at Anna Mae. "This gun's been fired recently."

"Yes. I shot my husband to pieces earlier this morning." Anna Mae focused her gaze on the center of the young man's shirt.

Both policemen reached for their phones. "Where's your husband now?"

Anna Mae cleared her throat. "Why he's in the cemetery."

"In the cemetery. Which cemetery?"

"The little one not far from here. He made me so upset this morning I went there and shot him to shreds."

Anna Mae gave a hysterical laugh. "I really enjoyed that."

"That's not funny." The young cop sounded so agitated, Anna Mae just had to peek up at his face.

"Oh! Did you think he was alive and I shot him? I so wish that was true. No, he's been six feet under, in the cheapest casket I could get, for the last two and a half months."

As the young cop reached for his handcuffs, the older cop cleared his throat, shook his head no.

"I peppered his grave with his own bullets. I'll pay to fix the plot. Shooting him was worth whatever it costs."

She started to sit up, but the paramedic pressed his hands on both her shoulders, forcing her to lie back down.

"Please lay still."

"Okay." She looked at the nice policeman again. "I had to make sure he was dead because he's been coming back to pester me. I'm just so mad at him."

Anna Mae turned to the paramedic. "Is there something you can give me to make my dead husband go away in my head?"

"Not right now, Ma'am."

She looked at Libby, then at Cece. "At least I felt good for a few minutes."

Cece nodded. "I'll bet you did."

This story would keep Anna Mae's doctors busy for weeks, if not months.

"I'm sorry I scared everyone." Anna Mae stared again at the officer's buttons. "It's my eyes. They're plain not working right these days. I just couldn't see who all those people were."

"No excuse, Ma'am."

The older cop finally spoke. "Empty gun or not, we don't allow people to wave guns at anything. We'll have to file a report on this one."

Anna Mae lifted her head just enough to glare at Cece. "Hear that? If you'd let me stay in my house none of this would have happened."

Ginger's brief wish to applaud Anna Mae for shooting Benny's grave to shreds vanished.

"Anna Mae! Don't you dare blame, Cece. You did this to yourself! You are responsible for this mess. You! Not Cece!"

Trish edged closer to the gurney. "Cece brought you here because she was worried about you. She thought we all could help keep watch over you."

"Let's not worry about that Trish." Cece motioned to the paramedics to get moving. She needed Anna Mae gone before she had a chance to blurt out things better left unsaid about Benny's death

"You'll get help from experts at the hospital. Talk to them." Libby patted Anna Mae's knees.

Ginger moved away from them all. It had taken her years to get her mother's suicide stuffed down and out of sight. Now she had to go home and try to stuff it back down again.

"My box! Where's my box?" Anna Mae pulled at Libby's arm.

Libby picked it up off the red velvet settee, held it out to Anna Mae.

"Do you see a small blue notebook in there?"

"Yes."

"It's my diary." Anna Mae looked around. Everyone, but Libby, seemed to be involved in talking to someone else.

"Read it. Your eyes only. Don't let that snob, Ginger see it. Read it, then hide it until I come back."

Tears had welled up in Anna Mae's eyes.

"I'm so sorry about the gun. I didn't mean to scare everyone. Please, Libby, when you read about Benny and me you'll understand. Keep my papers safe too. I'll need them."

"I've made sure you have a woman doctor." Cece was back from wherever she'd gone.

"You can get me a woman doctor?"

"I've seen to it. And, as soon as we're allowed, we'll all come visit you."

Libby glanced at Ginger who shook her head no.

"Allowed? You can't just come to see me?" Anna Mae stared at Cece.

"Visiting rules and all that whoop-tee-do."

Now Birdie stretched her neck to peek over the shoulder of one of the paramedics. "Let us know if we can do anything to help out."

"Not me," Trish whispered in Ginger's ear. "I might bake a cake or something, but that's all I'll do."

Fearing the low voices behind her would reach Anna Mae, Libby leaned down to cover them with her own voice.

"Hear everyone talking Anna Mae? Everyone's worried about you."

Anna Mae, looking like a small child abandoned on a dark road, whispered back, "I'll need your help in finding the children, Libby. I have to know if he's hurt them."

Anna Mae's confusion squeezed Libby's heart.

"You'll be fine, Anna Mae. They're very kind in hospitals."

It seemed inadequate, but it was all she could think to say.

Chapter 10

Lining up like a parade, the paramedics took Anna Mae away on the gurney. Then the police left, followed by the gawkers from the Bordello. Suddenly it was just Libby and Ginger in the lounge.

"Wait!" Libby grabbed Ginger's arm before she could leave. "I heard you tell Anna Mae your mother killed herself. I thought your parents died in a car crash."

For a split second Ginger considered lying. Say she'd made it up to get Anna Mae's attention, but she was too tired for more lies and cover-ups, especially to her best friend.

She turned, looked Libby in the eyes then at the male manikin knocked to the floor by someone in the rush to get to Anna Mae. Her mother's death was such a long time ago, how could it hurt her to talk about it now?

"My parents didn't get along. I was sixteen, and didn't know how bad it was until I found her bloody body when I came home from school."

Libby pulled a shaking Ginger to her. "Dear God, your father killed your mother?"

"Not directly. She put the gun in her mouth, she pulled the trigger, but he killed her."

Libby and Ginger sat down on a settee. "Tell me."

"When the police were done going through our house they showed me a court order served on my mother the day before. It said she was an unfit mother so the judge gave my father complete custody of me. I remember yelling at the police saying my mother was a good mother. My father was why she killed herself. Mother killed herself because of my father suddenly being gone traveling for his work as a salesman."

Ginger sat back, wiped her tears. "Mother wasn't unfit. She had untreated depression.

The cops asked me where my father was. I said he was supposed to be back around noon."

"Noon?" Libby asked. "When you were in school. Do you think she planned it so he'd find her, not you?"

Ginger nodded.

Libby hugged Ginger tight, rubbed her back, patted her, generally tried to make things better, unfortunately she was years too late.

"He didn't show up for two days."

"What? Why not?"

"He'd been arrested a hundred miles away for getting mouthy with a policeman after being stopped for speeding. If she'd just waited one more day she could have proven to the court about his temper, then gotten him declared incompetent. My loving father vanished right after her funeral."

"I hate your father for what he did to you, and her."

Ginger held on tight to the strength of Libby's arms and felt her love.

"Where did you go after that? Your grandparents? Aunts?"

The distress in Libby's voice, made Ginger sorry she hadn't said it was all a lie to fool Anna Mae. She pulled away.

"My father's parents." That wasn't quite a lie; she'd run away six months later.

"George doesn't know any of this and you can't tell him, Libby. I poured out my heart to my first husband and he needled me about her suicide every time I got upset. George wouldn't do that, but there's no point in bringing it up now. It happened over fifty years ago."

"It's still a part of you, Ginger. You should share it with your husband."

"No. I was done with it all until Anna Mae waved her gun around. I'll be fine in a couple of days. Therapists have said I should share my story with others but I refuse. I worry that if my children knew their grandmother killed herself, they'd worry about me every time I got excited over a hangnail. Or about them when they got a bit depressed. I can't have that."

Libby looked deep into Ginger's hazel eyes. "You've been all alone in this?"

"I'm fine. I've learned that if you look you can find the good in bad things. Mother's suicide taught me take care of myself. She's why I usually land on my feet. Why, when I'm pushed, I push back. Promise me you'll never utter a word of this to George or my kids."

Libby nodded. "It's your story to tell."

Ginger put her arm on Libby's solid shoulder. "You're the good that came from my disastrous marriage to your brother."

Libby nodded. "For both of us."

She wanted to say you're not strong Ginger. You drink way too much. But, being from New Hampshire, even after all these years, she still hesitated to stick her nose into someone's business when they said not to.

Ginger squeezed Libby's hand, got up, headed for the front stairs. "Don't get all bent out of shape over this, Lib. We got the gun away. I'm okay now."

I don't think so ran through Libby's head.

"Let's go into my apartment so you can call George. Get him to take you to lunch. You don't have to tell him about your mother, but you do have to tell him about Anna Mae."

Ginger checked her watch. "Lunchtime is done and gone, Lib. Besides, George is going golfing."

Libby thought there it is again; proof that the rest of the world twirls on no matter what disaster happens. Maybe it made a person go on too. She was recovering from Phil's death. Wasn't she?

"I'll call George later, get him to meet me at the club for dinner."

Truth was, dinner was too far away and it was only a short drive to her refrigerator and a tall glass of the gin-aide or maybe no aide. Two of those, and she'd be in a better mood for dinner out.

Since is was too early for dinner and not wanting Ginger to go off alone, Libby retrieved Anna Mae's notebook from the box and waved it in the air.

"Anna Mae asked us to read this. It could be very interesting." She and Ginger were a tandem bike when it came to taking on things so she couldn't honor Anna Mae's request to keep her out.

Ginger kept going. "You're lying. Anna Mae wouldn't let me near it. And I've had enough of Anna Mae for the rest of my life. I'll bet my dog it's full of woeful tales designed to get sympathy. I ain't about to touch it, Lib."

"You don't have a dog."

"My neighbor's dog then." Ginger got to the top of the stairs and turned. "I suggest you don't read it either, Lib. I know you'll feel obligated to help her whatever it is."

"We're already obligated. We saved her life. If you save a life, you are responsible for it."

"What? Who says that?"

"The Buddhists."

"We aren't Buddhists."

"Maybe it was Oprah or Bill Gates. Or 'The Donald'."

"Don't get suckered down that path, Lib. Anna Mae owes us for stopping this mess, but I never plan to collect on it."

Libby tired to stall Ginger with another wave of the journal. "We should know what's in here, 'cause they'll eventually let her out of the hospital."

"I truly don't give a damn about the woman." Ginger came back a few steps. "I know you'll read it. So if you think I should read it, burn it."

"Aren't you even a little curious?"

"Not about her."

"But you're a female.'

"And I have to lie down because I'm carrying around a head heavier than George's golf bag."

*****

An hour later, fortified by two tall gin-aides and a whirlpool bath, Ginger faced herself in the mirror. She smiled. Grimaced. Pursed her lips. Tried hard to wrinkle her nose but couldn't. Libby was right. No matter what she did, most of her skin stayed as tight as the skin on an apple. It was doing exactly what she'd wanted. She'd spent tons of money to get rid of the sags, bags, wrinkles and warts of old age. Feeling around she found a soft spot under her chin and pressed it. Maybe that needed looking into.

She'd gotten herself fixed up so well, anyone new to her thought she was in her late fifties. She even looked younger than George and he'd just turned fifty-five. She sighed. Did any of it matter? George loved her dearly. She'd taken what she called 'early' retirement, so now there was no one she had to impress.

She tested grimacing again but nothing much happened. What did it matter if people saw her as aloof just because the skin on her face didn't move very much? What had happened to the art of listening? Well, according to the world as Libby saw it, she didn't communicate with her mouth any better than she did with her face.

She perked up the collar of her blouse and liked how the new shade of green intensified the green hue in her eyes and nicely set off her platinum hair.

George's face came to mind. He'd aged since his cancer scare, but it didn't seem to bother him.

Maybe a few rounds of golf would bring out his natural robust color again, evaporate his tired look. If it didn't, she could give him a facelift for his birthday. Men were getting them these days. She shook her head no. George thought plastic surgeons were today's witch doctors.

She forced a grimace that produced two small frown lines. She stepped back, looked again.

"Maybe I have gone too far. My face does look a little bit like a porcelain mask. I've turned me into a walking, talking, Barbie doll."

She shook her head, pulled her hair back tight. Studied her head. "Shorter? Yes, I think so."

She drained the last of her third gin-aide, dug through her make-up case, giggled, picked out an old eyeliner pencil, anything to keep from thinking about her mother, or Anna Mae. Then, feeling like a naughty child, she scribbled Botox, plastic surgery on her side of the bathroom mirror.

Next, she took out a bright red lipstick and marked a red X through Botox and plastic surgery.

"Enough of you two evils. I'm aging well. I can do my fitness classes better than most of the fifty year olds. Well no, not true now. I nearly died running down my front garden at Libby, this morning."

Was that just this morning? It didn't feel like it. She looked around the bathroom. "Where's my watch?"

When she did find it, she was shocked that time had somehow gotten to four-thirty. She had to hurry if she were to meet George at five. Racing into the garage, she gave orders for her car door to open, jumped in, touched a button so her top lifted up, then folded into its hiding spot as she backed down her driveway. Fresh air would keep her mind alert and evaporate any smell of booze.

Ignoring the yellow lights, she made it to the Country Club in record time. The parking lot was nearly empty. No sign of George's car. Had she been wrong about the time? No, five, he'd said five. Idiot! His car would be around the other side of the club so he could unload and load his clubs.

She knew she looked good striding into the clubhouse restaurant, in her new Hermes outfit and her Minolla shoes. The place was empty. Whoops. No. One elderly gentleman sat at a corner table waving his empty highball glass at the bartender. No dishes. Drinking alone. She remembered that feeling.

Still, no George.

"Do not panic, Ginger Logan. Golf is unpredictable. Your husband can be late. He's been late before. He has not fallen down in a new fit of cancer."

Running it through her head again, did little to comfort her.

Picking a table where she could keep an eye on the door, she mouthed 'gimlet' to Jeremy, the Barkeep, who was looking at her while he polished the bar.

Before George's cancer she never worried about him being late. Now she did. Now her life was before his cancer/after his cancer.

She'd thought that way too, for a long time after her mother's suicide and after her second husband's death. Where was Jeremy with her drink? She looked around, didn't see him. Drumming her long fingernails on the table he suddenly turned up and made her jump.

"Tough day?" Jeremy put the glass of life on her table.

"No, just an acquaintance waving her gun at people."

"A real gun?"

"As real as a gun gets."

"Wow! Anyone hurt?"

"Yes, since I count being scared to death as hurt. They took her to the hospital. I hope to God they know how to deal with her."

"Dementia?"

"No. More like pissed off." She'd forgotten that Jeremy was a third year medical student. She reached into her purse, pulled out three twenties.

"For this drink and the next." She handed him the bills. "The rest is to make sure you change the subject if I mention a gun again."

He pushed the last twenty back. "No need, Ms. Logan."

"Yes." She tucked the money in his hand.

"You medical students always need money. Besides, I think of it as my insurance policy so someday you'll be glad to take care of me." She laughed and took a huge swallow of her golden liquid.

"As always, excellent drink, Dr. J."

He looked worried. "Does Mr. Logan know about your friend?"

"I told him a little when I made our dinner date. That's why we're here tonight."

She looked around the room. Still, just the lone man. "Why so empty?"

"Our Spring Scramble and our Seventy-five years celebration start tomorrow, Ms. Logan."

"Oh dear, I forgot all about them. Can we still get a nice dinner tonight? George should be here any minute." She drained half her glass.

"Better get fixin' me another."

"Sure."

"Sure to the drink or dinner?"

"Both."

"Remember you're supposed to call me Ginger, not Ms. Logan."

Jeremy grinned, nodded as usual, and headed off to fix her second gimlet.

She spun her near empty glass around on the table, trying to remember if she'd seen George's car in the parking lot. No. But, he wouldn't park by the restaurant. He'd park by the Pro Shop. Hadn't she discussed this with herself before? Despite trying not to, she glanced at the clock over the bar. George was now twenty minutes late. Dr. J returned with her much-needed second gimlet.

"Golf isn't precise, is it Dr. J?"

"How you hit the ball or the time it takes?"

"Time."

"He'll be here soon." With that he left.

Hurry up, George. Tell me golf stories so my mother will get the hell out of my head. A few minutes later a tap, tap on her shoulder and a, "Hi babe," made her jump up and spill a little of her second drink. A drink that seemed a little weak.

"Gimlet?"

"I needed it, after what that dimwit, Anna Mae Brown did to us today." Pain welled up in her throat, cutting off a longer explanation.

George sat down. "Dimwit?"

"Anna Mae only rows her boat with one oar. Wait till I tell you what she did today." She giggled. Life seemed so much better after almost two gimlets, and three gin-aides. Plus, her husband was here.

Then Jeremy was there with a tray filled with chips and salsa, a gimlet, scotch. He wiped the table, then gave George an odd nod and then left.

Ginger leaned on her elbows, looked at her husband, thinking he had some color and looked better today.

"How was golf?"

"Good. We heard a guy ahead of us let out a string of cuss words then watched him sail his club into the water hazard. He stormed off, leaving his wife holding the bag, literally."

He took a swallow of his scotch. "Sorry I'm late, but it was so hot out there I had to take a shower or the smell would've ruined our dinner. Now, what's this about Anna Mae?"

She pushed her drink away. She didn't need it as badly now that George was here and he looked so worried she just wanted to hug him and hug him and hug him.

"Evidently she went back to her house this morning, got Benny's gun, went to the cemetery and, for some unknown reason, shot the hell out of the so and so's grave."

"You're kidding."

"That's not the half of it. She'd just come back from the cemetery when Libby and I ran into her in the second floor lounge at the Bordello where she was waving said gun at a bunch of people. Scared the you know what out of us."

She took a sip of her gimlet, then another.

"It's over now. They put her in the hospital under a suicide watch. Which I don't think she needs, 'cause she's usually a wimp. That's my day. Oh yes, it all started when Libby trapped me in my garden and talked me into going to the Bordello in the first place."

She'd wanted to slow the words coming out of her mouth so she wouldn't slur them so much but George needed to know what had happened.

George leaned in close, took her waving hands. "Eat some chips. We need some water."

He waved at Jeremy.

She pulled her gimlet close, looked at it. How had it gotten half gone so fast?

"Who took the gun away? Or did she just put it down?"

"Libby and I talked her out of it. I don't want to think about it anymore." She scooped up some salsa with a chip.

"Talk about golf, or work, or something. Please talk about golf, George. Please."

"Okay, but let's enjoy us for awhile. Later you can tell me all that happened today. Blow by blow."

"Maybe."

"Maybe?" He smiled at her. "Okay. First I have to tell you about my four and a half hours of golf. Hot as hell out there. Glad we didn't carry our clubs. Fell into my swing on the second hole and I shot a ninety-six."

She gripped his arm. "That's your best eighteen holes since your surgery."

There it was, the before and after cancer again. She drained her glass, took another chip.

George slapped his shirt pocket.

"Damn. I forgot to turn in my scorecard. I want that one recorded." He stood up. "Be right back, Babe."

He was gone before she swallowed her chip and could shout out, "Come back here! Turn it in after we eat!"

She watched him walk away. He was tall and thin like she was. What was it someone had said? We marry ourselves? No, George was much better than she. He was kind, patient. Less driven than she'd been at his age. And her favorite thing was that he never brought up old lovers. His or hers.

She waved her empty glass at Dr. J. who now seemed to be ignoring her.

She'd wanted George for her own from the moment they'd met. It was the kindness, yet strength, she saw in his deep brown eyes that had gotten to her. And she wanted to kiss the squiggly half-moon scar on his chin every night for the rest of her life. She'd been doing it for over ten years now.

That was it. No facelift for George. She couldn't stand it if they took his scar away. The wrinkles the Arizona sun sketched in at the corners of his eyes and mouth were such a part of him. She'd be crazy to mess with that.

"On the phone, did you say Libby brought us an antique water pump?" She jumped again. Thank God her glass was empty so she couldn't spill any of the precious liquid.

"Damn it, George! Stop doing that! Twice in the last half hour you could've stopped my heart."

Where was Jeremy with her gimlet? She tipped her glass, nearly licked it clean, and handed it to George.

"Would you get me another one?"

"A third? Shouldn't you wait until we eat?" But he stood up anyway, took her glass.

"I'll start with these." She took a chip, put the whole thing in her mouth. She couldn't bare to look at the salsa. Why did they have to make it blood red?

George had said it would be her third drink. It could be her fourth. Either way she owed Jeremy money.

With her mother's bloodied body floating in and out of her head she tucked several chips in her purse to fool George that she was eating, then heard a laugh. Female. High, like her mother's. The restaurant door opened and relief spread through Ginger. The woman didn't look anything like her mother. Then George, bless him, was back, but with only water. She took several long swigs.

"To continue our conversation, Libby came over to our house this morning with a gorgeous antique water pump. The kind we've searched for, for ages. She told me it was her apology for talking me to all her silly crusades. The darn thing softened me up enough that I let her talk me into going over to Cece's to smooth things out for her and that's when we bumped into all that trouble."

She was amazed she'd remembered the pump but she was still talking too fast and her slurring was getting worse. She picked up a chip, waved it around.

"Now that I think about it, I bet Cece's not mad at Lib anymore since Lib and I got the gun away from Anna Mae. Aren't we women silly? Lib gets in trouble because she talked to someone? Whatever happened to free speech?"

George reached over, took Ginger's hand. "Stay on the topic, Babe. You took the gun away from Anna Mae?"

"No. I yelled at Anna Mae. Lib took it away. I never touch guns. Now Anna Mae's in the loony bin."

Ginger unbuttoned the third button of her blouse. "Whew! It's hot in here."

"You are awfully flushed."

George let go of her hand, felt her forehead. She pushed his hand away.

"I'm just fine. Pay attention, here George."

She tightened her jaw to try and stop slurring her words. "Anna Mae thought Carlos was stealing her TV. That's ridiculous isn't it? It was crazy over there. I yelled at all of them to shut up and hide behind the piano."

"Who hid behind the piano?" George tried to grab his wife's flying hands.

"The women at the Bordello!" Ginger pulled away. "I told you that. Libby tried to reason with her. Now wasn't that just silly?"

"Reason with who?"

"George, really dear, pay attention. Anna Mae, of course. I scared her into giving up the gun."

Ginger slapped the table.

"You scared a person with a gun?" He slid Ginger's empty glass out of her reach. "You could have been killed."

"The gun wasn't loaded." She stared at him as if he'd lost his mind. "Okay, so I didn't say that part. I'm a little muddled up."

She took a breath. "I'll start all over again. I came up the back stairs with Libby. That's when we saw Anna Mae with the gun. That's when my mother's bloody body flashed in front of my eyes, and now I can't make her go away. Oh, she goes away for a little while, that's how I was able to drive over here. But then I remember about Anna Mae and the a gun and, whoooossssh, my mother's suicide comes back."

"My God, Ginger! Your mother committed suicide?"

She reached for George's drink but he wrestled it out of her hand.

"That was rude, George!"

She stood up, steadied herself, then started weaving between the tables toward the exit. She was almost there when George and Dr. J. grabbed her from behind to stop her from falling.

"I'm okay. Libby gave the gun to the police." She gave them a sickly smile. "But yours truly made Anna Mae drop it. Why couldn't I have stopped my mother, George?"

Tears dropped from her chin, she collapsed into a chair. When had she started crying? She must look like that famous clown painting. The one with rivers of black mascara running down its cheeks. No, she wasn't Barbie anymore.

Why was George kneeling in front of her, like he did when he'd asked her to marry him?

"I need to get you home."

"I'll go get your car, Mr. Logan."

She smiled at Jeremy. "You're a third year medical student and you know everything."

"Shhh." George pulled Ginger to him, rubbed her back, held her close.

She gave him a trembling smile. "It isn't my fault that my mother killed herself, is it? My mother should have been stronger."

"That's right, Babe. It wasn't your fault."

"Liar." She smiled at George. He was always kind.

Chapter 11

George drove them home, undressed his wife then laid her gently on their bed.

"My mother killed herself, George "

He wiped the tears running down her face with a cool cloth, laid it on her forehead, then sat down beside her.

"You've had a tough day, Babe. You should go to sleep remembering something good about your mother. Tell me a story of a happy time with her."

Ginger pressed her hands to the side of her head to stop the room from spinning so fast.

"I can't remember any."

"Try. Maybe you've buried them."

Then one came to her so smoothly.

"Yes, mother and I were standing in the middle of racks and racks of clothes in the biggest department store in all of Tucson. It was the first store to have a department just for teens. I was twelve and tall, even then. My mother thought kids clothes looked silly on me, so she gave me three twenty-dollar bills. "

She smiled up at him. "That was over fifty years ago George. It was a fortune for her. And to me. Mother helped me pick out the most stylish things we could find. She said I looked beautiful in them."

She waited for George to turn the cloth over and put the cool side to her head.

"The clothes made me the best dressed in my class. The girls drooled over all my pretty things. Even a star player on the seventh grade basketball team took me to a movie. He tried to kiss me, but I knocked him on the head." She giggled like a schoolgirl.

"My Babe. Tough, even then."

"I knew they liked me just because of my new clothes, but I didn't care. My new clothes made me a part of the In crowd, until I quit school."

She shouldn't have told him she didn't finish high school. She tried to sit up, but he somehow had another cool cloth on her head.

"Then there was the swimming pool incident. Did I ever tell you about that?"

"No." He tucked a light blanket around her.

"I was ten. Mother said we were going to go to the new municipal swimming pool because she knew how to get us in without paying. We waited until the boy who took the money was busy eyeing the girls in the skimpy suits. When his eyes got so far out of his head, we slipped right past him.

I'd never been in a swimming pool before. I was nervous at first, until I got to splashing around with all the other kids. It was a blast until I ended up near the diving board and a big kid jumped off and swamped me. I was sure I was going to drown, until my mother pulled me out."

"She yelled at the kids who'd laughed at me, she really did. Mother made such a ruckus the ticket taker came running. When he saw we didn't have armbands he kicked us out. On our way home on the my mother told me to never swim under diving boards, and never wear white shorts to a picnic."

She looked up at him, tried to smile, said. "Thanks George."

"For what?"

"For making me remember that I did have fun with my mother."

Feeling like she had to asleep, Ginger reached up and turned the cloth over on her head.

*****

After Ginger had fled the Bordello yesterday, Libby returned to her apartment and showered away the smell of fear seeping from every pore of her body.

Dressed to stay home she looked at Anna Mae's small, ragged, bent and stained, notebook lying on her coffee table. She was dying to know what was in it.

Curling up in her most comfortable chair, she turned to the first entry. It announced that on January twelfth, nineteen fifty-six Marian Wilcox married David Thurgood.

"Who were they?"

She looked at the cover of the journal. Yes, it was the same notebook Anna Mae had given her.

The second entry said Marian's parents thought David Thurgood was a good catch for their sixteen-year old pregnant daughter.

"Sixteen and married." She looked over to Phil's chair. "That's not good."

She looked at the journal again, then Phil's chair.

"Someone in here must be related to Anna Mae because it's her tiny,

58

perfect, handwriting. Just like we saw on her and Benny's bridge score cards."

Talking to Phil's empty chair helped keep him close to her. She so believed that when someone died, death only claimed the body and left the spirit behind.

Libby shook her head. "That's strange because neither Anna Mae or Benny ever mentioned their family."

Zipping through several entries, looking for where it might include Anna Mae, she found out that David Thurgood was twenty-one when he married Marian and had a good job with a local trucking company in Phoenix.

She looked over at Phil's chair, which she'd bought because the blue fabric matched his uniform.

"I'm getting grumpy in my old age, because I don't care to read about these strangers. I also feel like a peeping 'Thomasina'. Should I keep going?"

She glared at Phil's silent chair and got up. "You're no help."

Needing no more surprises for the day, Libby shoved the journal into a drawer then cleaned her kitchen as if she was moving out. Bored, she went shopping for groceries she didn't need. At the last second adding a box of frozen apple turnovers because she could pop them in the oven one at a time.

Cleaning up after dinner she became so irritated with all the evening news disasters that she cooked two turnovers then ate both.

Dozing off through most of her favorite program she woke in time to see the previews for the next exciting episode then went to bed.

The notebook popped up in her dreams several times during the night, waking her again around five. Giving up on sleep, Libby went in the kitchen, fixed a pot of tea and took Anna Mae's notebook to the table for another quick peek.

She adjusted her glasses, flipped to where she'd left off and found out that several months after the Wilcox and Thurgood marriage took place he changed jobs and was now employed by an auto-body repair shop.

That caught her attention. Benny had restored antique cars. The next entry gave the birth date and weight of a baby boy they named Timothy Mathew Thurgood. Well, it surely wasn't Anna Mae who gave birth. She and Benny had made it very clear that they never had kids.

Quickly bored with the glowing remarks about the Thurgood son sleeping through the night, sitting up, walking, talking, she slapped the book shut. Why read this thing about people she didn't know?

She jumped to the end, something she rarely did. Read it. Read it again. Then, her voice trembling, she read it again, this time out loud to Phil.

"I now know that I killed Benny." She looked at his chair. "And it's dated yesterday and signed Anna Mae Brown."

She put down the notebook. "Anna Mae killed Benny? And she only now knows that she did it? None of this makes sense. And I know it's Anna Mae's handwriting. Somehow, Marian is Anna Mae. But was the Thurgood guy Benny?"

She stood up, went to Phil's chair. "Why aren't you alive to tell me if I need to show this to the police?"

She paced around her small kitchen back and forth until dizzy. Anna Mae a killer? That was crazy. No mousey, almost invisible, Anna Mae. The wife who always stood in Benny's shadow as if she didn't exist. But mice rise up once in awhile.

She flipped from the front of the notebook, to the last page. Compared the handwriting. Her untrained eye said Anna Mae had positively written it all. That meant Anna Mae was Marian Wilcox Thurgood. But who was David Dale Thurgood? She had to know how and why that happened.

Shivering in her nightgown and robe, she threw on a set of sweats, pulled a blanket off the bed, grabbed some slippers and went back to the journal.

"Okay, tell me what happened."

She'd always run her thoughts past Phil, or talked to her canary. But Harry the Canary had died too. She had to do this alone. One day she'd get a replacement for Harry, because she couldn't replace Phil. Talking to a fridge that rarely let out a rumble left a lot to be desired and it was too early to call Ginger.

Draping the blanket over her legs, she slapped the notebook on her kitchen table and turned to where the boy's progress was recorded. All the praise stopped when the boy was old enough to talk and run around.

"David is always upset with Timothy. He even calls him Timidthy. He spanks him too hard, or scares him to tears by yelling so loud. I now skip Timothy's afternoon nap so he'll go right to sleep after supper. That's made things better for the child."

"Better?" She looked at the refrigerator. "Better? Why does she let this keep happening?"

When the fridge didn't respond, she added. "I keep forgetting that this could be, is most likely, our Anna Mae."

She went back to the notebook, read entry after entry about how the boy irritated his father. The punishments metered out brought her to tears. This was the abuse their foster kids had suffered.

Then a daughter was born. Libby slammed the journal shut and couldn't believe Anna Mae had allowed herself to get pregnant again. She looked at it. Somewhere inside there had to be a redemption, or Anna Mae would have burned this thing a long time ago.

Reading that David beat their son less now and idolized their daughter, fear made her speed through the entries until she came to the one she dreaded would be there.

"This morning, after her father went to work, my dear, four year old, Sarah was in her room crying. Under her pillow I found her poor little blood stained panties."

"Ahhhhhhhhhhh!" Libby pounded it with her fists.

"You Bastard. I can't read more without someone here. And I can't stand it that I ever played cards with you and Benny."

She shoved the notebook in a drawer, pressed her hip against it as if she expected the journal to escape.

It was so far back in time there was nothing she could do now. The kids could be dead for all she knew. At least she knew that Anna Mae had written the whole thing and that she'd killed Benny.

Oh, God. Was Benny her first or second husband? Had Anna Mae killed David, changed her name and married Benny? Where were the kids dead?

Enough! She could not read more of it alone. Taking pail from the closet, she filled it with hot sudsy water and scrubbed the kitchen floor she'd cleaned just yesterday.

61

Chapter 12

Ginger sat in her kitchen inhaling a third cup of steaming coffee. She'd already swallowed two extra strength pills, had a glass of tomato juice, some water, a half slice of toast and still felt like she'd been thrown off a speeding truck. The gnarled hedgerow of red azaleas outside her window was a good example of how her brain must look.

Last night at the Club had done her in, and it was George's fault. He'd ordered her last gimlet, the one that put her over the edge.

His fault? George would probably say she'd drunk everything without quarrel. Well, George didn't have his dead mother living in his head, now did he? Throwing blame around so none of it stuck to her, dimmed her guilt for only a few seconds.

She remembered George propping her up in bed this morning and telling her, her car was still at the club. Why was it still at the club?

He'd also said that maybe their talking last night was a good thing. Talking? They'd talked? What had she told him? Not her mother. No not her mother. That made her head pound again.

Then he'd said he'd take care of fixing dinner tonight. She'd whispered back, don't bother she couldn't eat for a week. He'd told her to call him if things got worse and left.

The peck he'd given her on the cheek had felt like a sledgehammer. She'd had blackouts years ago when she was drinking heavy but now? She remembered being at the club and Jeremy was the bartender. Not much more than that and that her car was still at the club. Damn!

She stared at the kitchen clock. It was almost eleven. George had left over three hours ago and she still was not even feeling somewhat close to human.

Dare she take a shower? Not a hot one. Her head would pound. A cold one would surely kill her. Careful not to make any sudden moves, she went into the bathroom, slipped off her nightgown put on a shower cap then stepped into tepid shower water.

Fifteen minutes later she was feeling better. Dressed in loose fitting clothes she stared at herself in the bathroom mirror. The same mirror where, sometime yesterday, she'd written Botox and plastic surgery, then crossed them out with red lipstick. She'd done it because they had taken away her character.

This morning her face had enough character for Walt Disney and a dozen other cartoonists.

Puffy eyes. Puffy lips. Her color, despite the shower, was still a little green. Ginger ran her shaking hand along the slack edges of her jaw. The ravages of time, salt, liquor, had her so bloated she'd become the Pillsbury Doughboy's twin sister.

What would she look like if she hadn't gotten the Botox treatments or, her plastic surgery? It was all too obvious. When the salt and liquor all washed out of her body she'd look like crepe paper. She'd been out of her mind to think she didn't need plastic repair.

She grabbed the window cleaner and wiped out her wisdom of yesterday.

Yesterday. Anna Mae and the gun. The vision of her mother lying on her bed with blood all over her pillow came rushing back. Her mother had looked tired the day she'd killed herself. Telling her it was a head cold and one she shouldn't worry about. She'd gone over and over that moment. There were no signs that the day was different from any other day. None. Her mother had said, like always when she headed out the door for school, "Goodbye. I love you."

Thank God she'd turned back and said the same to her mother.

All her psychiatrists told her there was nothing she could have done to save her mother. Ginger sighed. Could she ever believe them?

Muttering. "Let it go. Yesterday everything inside me said to get the hell out of there, but I stepped in and got Anna Mae to put her gun down."

Ginger puffed out her enhanced chest. "I risked getting shot to stop Anna Mae from hurting others!"

She shoved the cleaner under the sink. Was yesterday enough to get herself off the hook for letting her mother die? No, it wasn't. Nothing ever would be.

Carefully walking back to her beautiful, cool, kitchen she stood at the window breathing in her magnificent back garden. She didn't know what to do about always being just a little sad around the edges, no matter what.

A persistent buzzing cut into her thoughts. The oven timer? No. That wouldn't be on. The bzzzz bzzzz was the doorbell. Damn!

Like a tiger stalking its prey, she moved to her living room window, peeked through the curtains and saw news of the worse kind. Parked right there at the top of her driveway was the dented, faded, hardly red, car Libby called Rosa Rita, as if the ugly thing were human.

Her first impulse was to hide, but George might have asked Libby to come check on her. To lie, say she hadn't come by, would break her promise to herself never to lie to him. Unless it was for his own good. Like never telling him about her mother.

She'd better head for the front door, cut Libby off at the pass. Opening it, there was no 'Hello Ginger' just, "I've got big, big news."

Without waiting for a response, Libby carried a white bakery bag and a two-cup rack of coffee past Ginger, through the large foyer, and into the living room.

The idea of more news twisted Ginger's irritated stomach. "Has Anna Mae?"

Shutting the door against the heat, she turned, followed Libby as fast as her poor head would allow. Halfway through her living room, there was no Libby anywhere. Was Libby really there? She could be so bad off she was delusional.

The sound of a cabinet door being shut, said Libby was in her kitchen. If Anna Mae were dead, or in more trouble, Libby would have blurted it out in the foyer and now she'd be racing around like a sand storm saying they needed to do something. The kitchen meant no actual crisis.

Ginger took in a large breath, blew into her cupped hands, sniffed. Good. Her breath wouldn't give away last night. "I'm going to kick her out."

She walked over to her beloved watercolor painting of mountains shrouded in the haze of dusk. It always relaxed her. She's built her whole living room around it. Soothing colors, soft lines, comfortable furniture, quiet lighting all invited her to come, sit down.

But today the far end of the living room drew her to where it opened to an alcove with a large bay window. Beyond the window, her Mexican poppies were in full bloom. She'd told Libby to go see them yesterday. Was that just yesterday? Yes. That much she remembered.

"Are you coming?" Libby was behind in the kitchen doorway.

"Let's go out here." Ginger sat down in her favorite chair, a sage green recliner. Pulling a blanket over her legs, she popped up the footrest, heard the storm arrive in the quick steps behind her. Only then did she remember she was going to kick Libby out.

"I've muffins and coffee in the kitchen."

With Ginger looking like something even a wild animal wouldn't drag home Libby added. "Sit still. I'll bring it all out here."

"Wonderful." Ginger stared out the window. Whatever Libby wanted, the answer was no.

Libby was back in what seemed like seconds.

"Trish has called the police to say she thinks Anna Mae should be arrested. She's even hired a lawyer to sue for undo stress. Or something like that."

Libby put the tray down on a low table between two recliner chairs.

"Next thing we know, she'll show up with a note from her doctor saying she's got post traumatic stress disorder because of yesterday."

"If standing by a piano and watching us, is the worse stress Trish has ever gone through, I want her life."

"Good point."

Libby sat down. By this time of day, Ginger should be looking super-duper but she wasn't.

"Here's the worst part, Ginger. Trish has had a free consult with a lawyer who said that if she sues, all of us will have to testify as to what happened."

Ginger groaned, not because of Trish. It was the warm, sweet smell of muffins on the table making her mouth water. They were not on her diet.

"Tell Trish," Ginger moved slowly forward to pick up the cup of coffee with both hands. "Anna Mae could counter-sue her."

"Counter-sue Trish? For what"

"Her screams. I'd be happy to testify that Trish nearly ruptured my eardrums and they made matters worse."

She really wished Libby would go home.

Cup in hand, Libby turned, stared at Ginger. "You look horrible."

"Thanks. You ain't so cute either."

"No, I mean it." Libby put her cup down on the table without taking her eyes off Ginger.

"Stop staring at me!"

Libby shook her head. "Eyes swollen and red-rimmed. Lips out of whack. And you're green around the gills."

"So I'm a little puffy. I forgot to take my diuretics in all of yesterday's hubbub."

"No. It's more than that, Ginger. You look really sick, and your hands shook just now when you took the cup. Do you have any tingling? Numbness? At our age, we have to worry about strokes."

"Oh for Christ sake, Libby. I'm not having a stroke, so just back off!"

She knew Ginger wasn't having a stroke. It was worse. She was sure Ginger had gotten really drunk after their mess with Anna Mae.

"Crabby, too. What did George say about yesterday?"

Ginger couldn't really remember what he'd said, so she just stared ahead and made it up. "He said we did the right thing and should be given a medal."

Libby sat forward. She wasn't going to let Ginger out of this one. "So, why do you look so bad?"

"Because yesterday was a horrible day." Ginger kept staring out the window.

"It was for all of us, but none of us are pasty white or green around the edges."

"No, you're all perfect!"

"And you've got a hangover." Libby got up and stood in front of the window

"The hell I do!" Her reply had deserved a shout but Ginger couldn't bring herself to do it.

Libby clapped her hands next to Ginger's ear and Ginger cringed. Ginger had a bad hangover.

"You're in trouble again, aren't you?"

"It's none of your business, Libby and you can get the hell out."

"No. Ever since George's cancer I've seen the pitcher of gin-aide in your fridge."

"You snooped in my refrigerator?" Ginger, half out of her chair, had to grip its arms to steady herself.

"You told me I should."

"I never did." Ginger stood up.

"Yes. Twelve years ago, your three kids, their spouses, Phil and I did an intervention on you. When you stopped drinking, you told all of us to always be your policeman."

"The statute of limitations ran out on that years ago. You have no right."

"No right? I've an obligation, Ginger. You're my dearest and best friend. You held me up when I collapsed. I won't stand by and watch you do this to yourself."

She paused. "George doesn't know that when you really start drinking, you dive off the cliff. Does he?"

"I've always been able to be a social drinker. You know that, Lib. I just had one bad night. I earned it."

"One night is not why your old trick is sitting in the refrigerator. I tasted that pitcher of lemonade yesterday and it's laced with gin. Just like old times. Gin-aide at the ready. Now that I think about it, you've been wearing a lot of perfume lately. And you smell of spicy foods. You chew a lot of gum too. Have I missed any of the tricks you use to cover up your drinking?"

"No, but you've just missed another opportunity to keep your mouth shut! Go home. First you were my sister-in-law, then my friend, then my ex-sister-in-law " Ginger stopped to catch her breath.

"More of this and you'll be my ex-friend. Get your own act together, kiddo. Since Phil's death, you've signed up for every damn cause or crusade within a hundred miles of Tucson."

"Don't change the subject." Surprised by a sudden rush of tears, Libby looked away.

"I'm not." Ginger shook her head and regretted it as the room swirled around her. "You started this, Liberty Price. Someone picks on me; I strike back. I may drink occasionally to fix things, but you flit around, plunge into things then take off faster than a darting hummingbird."

Now her head was beyond pounding. She had to get Libby out of her house.

"Since Phil died you've avoided your life. You run so fast no one knows you were there. You've made yourself invisible and of no importance to anyone. Me included, now go home."

The next thing Libby knew, she was outside in her car, driving away. Anna Mae all but forgotten, until she sp ed the notebook on the seat beside her.

Chapter 13

Libby screeched to a stop in her parking space at the Bordello and put her head on her steering wheel. Go home. Ginger had yelled at her to go home! Well, where was her home? She didn't have one. She lived in this place, but it wasn't her home, it was Cece's prize apartment building. She'd lost her home and her life the day Phil died of a heart attack up on hot roof because he was too weak, or too stubborn, to call for help.

They wrote cowboy songs about that. The husband dies, the house and barn burn down, killing all the animals except Scruffy, who saves the poor woman from drowning so she can meet another lost soul and all will be well. Trouble was, she and Phil never owned a Scruffy.

She did have an open invitation to move in with any of the three foster children they'd adopted. Come at any time, for any reason, they said. But, being with young people twenty-four seven was just not possible anymore. Now that she knew what it meant, she liked to say twenty-four seven. She was not invisible like Ginger said. She was not.

If she moved in with them, she'd be 'the old one.' The one they shouted to, repeated things for, made lists for, called out, 'make sure you shut off the stove', even though she did all that and so much more everyday.

She did keep in close touch with all of them. Sometime in the next thirty or, maybe even more years, she would have to move in with someone. She yanked her car keys from the ignition, got out and slammed the door.

What was wrong with her? Thinking about her foster kids when her big mouth had just crushed her best friend. Maybe she'd even sent Ginger over the edge, because Ginger had never spoken to her like that.

Should she call George at work and tell him about Ginger's drinking? She should and she shouldn't. Ginger had ordered all of them not to tell him about her former drinking habits when she'd married him. She'd said her drinking was all in the past, but now it has raised its ugly head again. George must have seen it coming. He wasn't dumb. Going inside her apartment, without even dropping her purse, she went to the phone and called Ginger. When she got her recording she told Ginger's machine she was sorry, so sorry, then she hung up.

Dancers of the Third Age

She'd wait until she talked to Ginger again before calling her kids. An hour later she was running away, driving east on Highway 10, headed for the Empire Mountain range.

These mountains were the first mountains to capture her heart in Arizona. Mountains in Arizona were so different from her snow covered mountains of New Hampshire. The bareness of the Empires had drawn her in, were her refuge, whenever she was in trouble or, in joy.

They were her favorite place to gather lizards and other small four-legged creatures. Rocks, cacti, sagebrush abounded. Where she stopped today would depend on how the sun was playing against the mountains. She knew them without a map. If she ended up spending too much time taking in their healing spirits she'd head on down to Sonoita or Patagonia and stay over. Something she hadn't done since Phil died.

Turning south onto 83 she loosened her grip on the steering wheel, exercised her fingers to keep the circulation going. This was a good decision. She could think and no one would interrupt her. She might be confused by Anna Mae's journal and she certainly was still depressed about Phil's death, but what hurt right now was Ginger calling her invisible.

Passing a restaurant, the smells made her wish she'd taken her muffins with her when she'd left Ginger's. A few miles later, craving fried food, or something very sweet, she pulled into the small corner restaurant she and Phil had often frequented.

Opening its door, she was amazed at how everything looked much the same as it had on the hot August day she and Phil had staggered in nearly forty years ago and then over and over again as the years passed. Fake potted plants, glass cases full of trinkets, still greeted her just inside the door. And there was the very same wooden wishing well to her left. Crayons and coloring books filled a Hopi basket sitting next to it.

When her eyes finally adjusted to the dim light she saw that some things had worn out. New tables inlaid with the same style of local tiles filled the small room. She looked for a familiar face and found none. Asking, she was told the original owner had relocated to a town with more people. Unable to deal with another loss, she ordered chicken and chips to go and left.

Muttering, "I suppose there aren't any cacti in bloom right now either, especially the flowers on palm cacti. How about the mountains? Are they gone too?"

A young man heading into the restaurant gave her a puzzled look, and a wide birth.

Fifteen minutes later, she was parked at one of her favorite stopping spots. It wasn't where most people left their cars while they hiked in the mountains, so the lot was usually peaceful. It was a good place to pick her chicken bare, scoop up the crumbs from the basket and leave the bones for the wildlife.

"That was my first good nibble since sunrise." Speaking to her empty car, she licked her fingers clean, picked up the last chip then, getting out, she looked hard at her Rosa Rita. Her color had faded so much over the years there was very little red left to Rosa Rita. Maybe she was like her car. Very little fire left in her.

Sitting on Rosa Rita's bumper, Libby put on her knee-high hiking boots. Standing up, she flipped her backpack over her shoulders then tightened it around her waist. It was mid-afternoon and the snakes would be out for a last ray of warmth. She'd learned to co-exist with the slithering critters still, she was careful.

Reaching into her back seat she got her walking stick and headed out.

Muttering, "Slap the brush. Whack a rock. Let 'em know you're here. Never put your hand into anything without first giving it a good pop."

It's what she'd always told the kids who'd come to live with them, her hoodlums as she fondly called them. And whistle. Whistle, she'd said. She herself favored Yankee Doodle Dandy. Her hoodlums would whistle, then ask her to guess their tune, but she never could.

Making her way down a small slope, she went around a familiar bend in the path. *'Went round the bend.'* How the kids had laughed over that one. Maybe she'd gone 'round the bend' the way she jumped in and told Ginger to lay off the booze the way she had.

She should have known better. Ginger still had a bouncing off the wall hangover. And now she was making excuses for Ginger. She gave a rock a hard whack with her stick.

"That's enough of Ginger. I'm here to soothe my own tattered soul."

It wasn't far to her favorite ledge of rock, well hidden from anyone walking along the larger path. She did as she always did; kept her gaze low, never looked more than twenty or thirty yards ahead. Her hoodlums had called her Scout because they thought she was watching out for danger. She smiled. She'd forgotten that one.

Sure, she'd kept her eye out for danger, but more to the point, she never allowed herself to check her mountain, see how it was doing, until she got to 'her spot' and could really study it. Now, coming to it, she looked east and sucked in a breath. The late afternoon sun was working its magic making the line 'the hills are alive with the sound of music' dance in her head.

This was the best time of day. Which must be why her dear Rosa Rita naturally headed here from Tucson. She'd never cared much for mornings with the mountains. The sun sat behind them making them dark and brooding. She liked midday the least. That's when the bright sun washed everything, showing all the details.

It was the low, late afternoon light that seemed perfect to her.

Watching it creep in, slowly expose the mountain's beauty and peculiarities, light up the ridges in shades of gold, green and so many hues of blue just pulled anything that was bothering her away. Far away.

Sometimes in early morning or late afternoon the foothills leading to the low mountain filled in with a smoky blue haze. That gave her hours of wondering what lurked there. These mountains were her friends.

Holding her pack high over her head, she dropped it hard onto the rock. Several small lizards scurried away, making her pretty sure there were no snakes close by.

Her backpack in place on the large flat rock, Libby settled down next it to wait. Doing her usual soothing trick, she focused on sections of the ridges on the mountains. One resembled a woman lying on her back, her face to the sky. Over the years she'd given it many names. Repose. Wait. Tired. Hopeful. Dreamer. A new journey.

She was on a new journey that had no destination in sight. Libby turned her head slightly to the next ridge. It reminded her of a series of rooftops. A group of homes. Homes meant lots of responsibility. All her adult years. All the kids. All the time Phil was off chasing bad guys she'd always taken care of things. She sighed. Tried to quiet her brain. Mountains called for silence.

Two hawks circled overhead. Were they telling her she was going in circles too? Or were they saying she needed to keep on trying even when she wasn't getting anywhere? She took off her sweater, waved at them, but they were too busy to bother with her. Well, why not them, too?

"Oh, poor me. I'm having me a pity party."

Yesterday, Ginger had accused her of flitting around so much she'd become invisible and useless. It wasn't her fault she couldn't find anything to do that excited her like taking in abused kids, or raising money to help the poor fix-up their homes. Another shot at self-pity.

An hour passed, the rocks cooled under her and she turned to face the sun. It wasn't a blazing red sunset like when a sand storm tore through the desert. It was a pale one, with thin streaks of pink and red, hanging low on the horizon. Her day was running out.

She didn't want to leave. Nothing had inspired her. No animals had passed by to tell her she should look into this or that and maybe her life would count again. The hawks hadn't come back and it was getting dark. Soon there'd be night animals prowling, both the four-and two-legged kind.

Shivering, she jumped up, grabbed her pack and began whacking her way back to her car. Her trip had been pleasant, but a total flop. Maybe the failure was in her. Maybe she couldn't receive messages right now.

There was one more thing that might inspire her. She threw her things into Rosa Rita's back seat and headed for the town called Mountain View and some of the homes Phil and his Crafty Carpenters had restored. She'd raised most of the money they'd needed, had arm-wrestled local businesses for free supplies. There had to be something there that would open up a new world for her.

It was the middle of the night by the time she parked her car back at the Bordello. Her trip to see the houses had also failed, just like the mountains. All they'd done was remind her of the past and all she'd lost. She'd not gotten one hint of what she was to do with the rest of her life.

As she unlocked her door, she remembered Phil saying it was better to wear out than rust out. She sighed. That was her message?

Ignoring the blinking red light on her answering machine, she showered off the dust of the day, but not her disappointments, and fell into bed.

Chapter 14

The soft light coming in the windows stirred Libby and, for a split second, she thought all was well with her world. But then, in a blink, Phil was dead all over again and her very best friend had every reason to want to avoid her for the rest of her life.

Crawling out of bed, she stretched the kinks out of her back then went over to her real desk. The one she and Phil had bought years ago, not the drawer in the kitchen where she threw everything. This desk had character. The scratches, ink stains, food stains, the smells that had taken years to accumulate eased her. Sitting down, she put pen to paper and scribbled without thinking.

My life now and why I hate it.

1. My darling Phil is dead, but I smell him every time I open my dresser drawers.

Well, was that so bad? No, it brought back good memories.

2. I live in an apartment, not our home.

But she had made new friends here. She lightly scratched out one and two.

3. Ginger says I'm invisible and useless.

Ginger had been ruthless! Libby tapped the pen against her teeth. She shouldn't have attacked Ginger's drinking yesterday. People never hear you when they're reeling. That's when they strike back.

She wrote down the number four, sat and waited. What was number four? Oh yes, the mountain had kept its wisdom to itself.

Well, whoop-tee-do. Crumpling up the paper, she tossed it in the wastebasket, got dressed, went into the kitchen to figure out something for breakfast. Yesterday she'd perfectly lined everything up on her counters as if they were on display. An ancient teapot, kept because it was her mother's. Next to it, her cup rack had all the cups designs facing out. That had taken some doing. Four dark green canisters, all with their yellow daisies facing exactly forward and perfectly spaced apart.

"Why'd I do that? I like things messy."

Didn't her life prove it? Wiggling her fingers as if she were warming up to play the piano, she redid her whole counter into its usual chaos and felt a whole lot better. Opening a cabinet door, she stopped, looked, frowned.

"What did I want in here?"

She spun around, glared at the refrigerator. What's wrong with me? I talk to you and yell at my best friend. I refuse to commit to anything lasting longer than a day and then complain no one needs me. I can pay my bills and I know what my car keys are for. But I do everything in my power to keep me miserable. I need to call Ginger and apologize for what I said yesterday.

No, I'm so nuts I'd better practice before I call her. She picked up a spoon and held it as if she were on the phone. She cleared her throat.

"Hi, Ginger. I'm calling to apologize for bringing up your drinking."

She put the spoon down. That was exactly not what to say. She should just acknowledge that her timing stunk. She cleared her throat to try again.

"We've been through a lot lately, you and I. My Phil dying and your George getting cancer and all the struggles that caused. Then Anna Mae and the gun."

She threw the spoon in the sink the clatter sharp in her head. "No, no. I'll just say I love you and I'm here no matter what?"

Deciding to put it off until she pulled herself together, she poured herself a bowl of cold cereal. Cereal! That's why she was in the cabinet!

She thumbed through the Senior Center's summer calendar. There were pages and pages of things to do, places to go. All were designed to keep a person amused, but not very useful. Since useful was her middle name, they all irritated her. She flipped to the education section. Read.

University of Arizona, Phoenix: Reduced tuition classes for all senior citizens.

She adjusted her glasses. Maybe there was something here that would take her out of herself.

Greek mythology. "Nope. Never been interested in that."

The History of China. "Nope."

Memoir Writing. Computer classes. "No. Nada."

How to avoid the pitfalls of aging. "Too late for that one."

Nothing excited her. Pulling open her kitchen desk drawer, she took out her list of local charities and causes she'd visited since Phil's death. Maybe today she was in a better mood for one of them. She'd already crossed off a third as 'not her cup of tea'. The rest she'd given either one, two, three or four stars.

One star meant they had all the volunteers they needed but she should try them again in a year or so. Two stars meant they only needed help during campaigns for money. She was very good at raising money but she preferred to be the organizer not the one doing the calling. Ginger could be right that she liked to be in charge. Three stars meant they wanted her for scut work; make coffee, stack and un-stack things. Four stars said she'd made it to their wait list. Wait until they had some time to teach her how to work all the newest electronic gadgets.

None of them attracted her. She did want to be in charge of something and the volunteers she knew never were in charge. Frustrated she raised her hand high and dramatically dropped the list on top of all the rest of the things that promised her a good life.

"Nothing here, nothing there, nothing anywhere." She walked over to her fridge. "And you! All you do is make ice! You've never made one grunt to help me out."

At least she could fix that. "I'm going to go out and get myself a Harry Canary Jr."

She looked at the clock. The pet store would be open by the time she got there. Ignoring the blinking lights on her message machine, she grabbed her car keys and was half way through the Shady Lady Lounge when Birdie, wearing her running suit and moving fast, closed in on her.

"Oh good, I got here just in time!"

No, no, no, spilled from Libby's brain to the tip of her tongue. No, she wasn't ever going to go running with Birdie again. The last time Birdie's long legs left her short ones in the dust.

"You missed the big uproar here last evening, kiddo."

"Wonderful." Libby gave Birdie a thin smile.

"No. We needed you. Cece came over to see how we were doing after the recent Anna Mae disaster and she sure set off a volcano. There were questions, accusations. Three of us ended up at each other's throats. Cece has set a meeting here for this afternoon at six-thirty."

Libby let her breath out. An offer to go running would have been so much better than a meeting about Anna Mae.

"All of us tenants have been ordered to attend."

"Ordered?" Libby shook her head. "Anyway, I was over at the Empire Mountains yesterday and didn't get back here until very late."

Birdie started walking toward the stairs. "Getting away after Anna Mae's craziness was smart, very smart. I went jogging for so long I thought my uterus would fall out. You do know about Trish's plan to sue Anna Mae. Right?"

Libby nodded.

"I leaned in close to Trish and told her I thought it was her screams that drove Anna Mae to wave the gun around. She stormed out and now Cece's mad at me for ending the discussion on a bad note."

Birdie slapped her leg. "Well, the meeting was so wild I think we should call this place The Cat House, instead of the Bordello."

Trying to look like she needed to leave, Libby shifted her purse to her other shoulder. "A meeting at six-thirty today. I'll be there."

She moved ahead of Birdie going down the stairs.

"Great. One more thing; I'm the rounder upper. I volunteered to make sure everyone shows up. Cece's calling Ginger, maybe you should too."

"Ginger? She doesn't live here." Surprised, Libby reached the first floor landing and turned around.

"She was right there in the thick of things, Libby. Just like you and me." Birdie pointed to herself and Libby then added,

"Since Ginger isn't the sentimental type, Cece thinks Ginger will put the squash on any sob stories some of us might dream up."

"By sob stories, you mean Trish?" Libby headed for the side door.

"Wait, Lib! The meeting is to help Cece decide if she should, or should not, let Anna Mae back in here."

"What? Cece's thinking of kicking her out?"

Libby sighed. "Don't you think, even after being there, that kicking her out is a bit drastic?"

Birdie shrugged. "At least we're being asked."

"Okay. Where's the meeting? I have to think about Anna Mae coming back here."

"In the day care center. No one can walk in on us there. Explain it all to Ginger, if you run into her. Cece's left her several messages, but she hasn't called back yet."

"Will do." Libby waved her purse at Birdie. "I hate to cut it short, but I've places to go, people to see. I'll be there six-thirty sharp."

Moving as fast as her short legs would carry her, Libby sped out the back door and to her car. Cece would have to call Ginger and explain all that. She tossed her purse onto the passenger seat and watched the dust fly up.

Inside, her favorite pet shop, Libby went straight to the bird section and was relieved to see things hadn't changed much. Birds in cages were still displayed against the back wall. Canaries, lovebirds, all colors of finches, were on the left side. The larger birds squawked at her from the right. Cages of various sizes, bird food, supplies sat in the aisle.

Walking over to the two cages of yellow canaries, she looked at the price, pushed her glasses up her nose, leveled them, peered in closer and couldn't believe a male canary cost three times what she'd paid years ago.

"Hello. I haven't seen you here in a long time."

Libby jumped. The birds fluttered. The owner smiled at her. "Sorry, I didn't mean to startle you."

"It's fine." Libby gave an embarrassed laugh.

"You're Liberty Price aren't you?"

Libby nodded. "And you're Betsy. It's good to see you still own the place."

"I'll bet you are shocked by the price of birds these days. All my former customers are."

"They 'bout knocked my glasses off. I was thinking of getting another Harry The Canary. My life's too quiet without Phil."

She looked at the two males in the cage. "At that price, I want to be sure I get one who sings like Pavarotti."

"I've a better choice for you. Come with me."

Betsy hooked Libby's arm in hers and steered them to the back room. A cage with a single yellow canary brightened the large storage room.

"Meet three year old Sing-Sing. His owner died a few weeks ago. The man's son brought Sing-Sing in shortly after that. Evidently, no one in the family has time for a bird. Sing-Sing's has a beautiful voice."

"You're sure he's not been stolen?"

"Oh, no. Father and son came in here together a lot and I've groomed the son's dog for years. The son was teary eyed when he left Sing-Sing, cage, toys and all. I don't think his tears were for the bird. He and his dad were very close."

"Why's the bird out here all alone?"

"I keep all new birds in quarantine to make sure they haven't picked up some disease."

"Has he?"

"No, he's pure as the day I sold him to the man." Betsy walked around the cage.

"Tell you what, I made my money on him the first time. If you will take Sing-Sing, his cage and all supplies, and promise me you'll change his name to something that doesn't remind one of a prison, I'll give him to you."

"Give him? As in free?"

"As in free."

A bit later, stopping at a light, Libby glanced at the small cardboard box littered with air holes.

"You've got very big feathers to fill, my little friend. 'Harry The Canary' was such a singer and oh, could he ever listen. I expect nothing less from you."

The box jiggled making Libby smile. "Good boy."

Getting a free adult male canary, a bright yellow one to boot, had made her feel guilty. So guilty, that she'd picked up a pamphlet listing animal advocate groups needing volunteers. For a split second it seemed like a way out of her misery. Then reality hit. She'd end up wanting to take the shaggiest animals home. Cece didn't allow cats or dogs at the Bordello. She'd shrugged, another volunteering opportunity down the drain. They'd just have to settle for getting some of her money.

After three trips in and out of the Bordello she finally had Sing-Sing, in his cage, hooked to a stand and settled by the sunniest window in the living room. Watching him hop from perch to perch, brought tears to her eyes. She hadn't realized just how much she missed having a living thing around.

"Checking me out and your new lodgings, are you?" He stopped at the sound of her voice.

"Your name's got to go, kid. What do you think of Hop-a-Long?"

Sing-Sing gave her a withering glance. "No? Okay I'll wait till I hear your voice."

Back in the kitchen, Libby poured herself a tall ice tea from the fridge, pawed a few of the brochures of things she could do to keep herself occupied until she died, then opened the drawer and stared at Anna Mae's journal.

"I better finish you off before the Anna Mae meeting tonight." She picked up the small, blue journal, fingered some of the creases and bends in the cover.

"Someone didn't like you very much. You're pretty beat-up. Maybe that's written in here."

She checked the clock. Twelve-thirty. Plenty of time to read the journal or, take it in small doses, if need be. When had she become such a coward? Running away from a notebook. When Phil was alive she took on big companies, twisting their arms until they gave money or supplies for house repairs for the poor.

Determined to read through to the end, Libby flipped forward to the page where Marian told of blood in her little daughter's underpants. Sucking in a breath, she read Marian Wilcox Thurgood's small, precise, penmanship and thought of Anna Mae. Were they sisters? That could be. And Anna Mae wanted to help her sister.

Libby nodded and felt a little better. Although it didn't make any sense that Anna Mae had signed the book at the back.

Frustrated with her what if, and if that, thinking Libby read on.

Marian feared her daughter had been, or would be, molested and if a page could wail, this one did. Angry words, foul words, circled, crossed out, slashed with red ink, underlined, gouge marks rippled the page from corner to corner. Tear stained words.

On the next page, Marian worried her gentle son would turn into a bully like his father.

The next entry made Libby shriek.

"This morning I sent Sarah and Timothy all alone on a bus to Flagstaff where my sister will meet them."

Meet *them*? Not *us*? Libby read faster.

"My darlings will be safe from their father only when sister and her whole family are settled in their new place away from Flagstaff. I must stay

78

here and keep watch on David so he doesn't go after them."

She didn't go. Libby crushed as if it were her own sister, imagined the children on the bus without their mother. Finally she turned back to the notebook.

"Sister didn't know I couldn't go with my children. I left my neighbor's address in Timothy's suitcase and told her to write me where they are. I hope that some night I can sneak out of here and go to them. If I never go, at least they escaped their father."

Stunned, Libby checked the year. It all happened thirty-seven years ago. A girl aged four and her nine-year old brother, were put on a bus alone and essentially evaporated.

Libby's insides crawled. This was the lives of the lives some of the foster kids she and Phil dearly loved. She busied herself making tea and toast, then saw she already had a full glass of iced tea and toast on the table.

"I'm getting too old for this." When the refrigerator had nothing to say she sat down again with the journal.

Marian had written that David, the children's father, was relieved to have them gone. He'd even said she'd done the right thing, because if the children were still with them, he might hurt them in the future.

"In the future!" Libby slapped the diary as if slapping him. "Who are you people?"

Worrying about how this connected with Anna Mae she read on. Marian and David Thurgood had then put their children's belongings in the hallway for the other tenants to fight over. Moved to Tucson where they changed their names to Anna Mae and Benny Brown.

Libby shot up off her chair. Marian was Anna Mae? Not her sister. Anna Mae and Benny had kids? That wasn't possible. Of course it was possible. She sat down again.

This was a terrible thing. To know Anna Mae had children and gave them away. That Benny was an abuser. Yes. She'd seen his flashes of anger, heard the way he spoke to Anna Mae

At least Anna Mae had sent the kids to safety. Or had she? This was so bad there could be more.

She grabbed the journal. Looked, found nothing after they changed their names all those years ago. Anna Mae had kept the diary all this time and wrote nothing?

Quickly flipping through blank pages all the way to the end of the notebook she found Anna Mae's confession that she may have killed Benny.

Why in heaven's name did Anna Mae ask her to read it? Anna Mae must be crazy to have given it to her. Anna Mae's past life was none of her business and now she felt compelled to tell the police about the confession.

She had to do something to drive this ache and anger from her. Leaving her apartment, Libby paused at Anna Mae's apartment door, shook her fist, then rushed up the back stairs to the Wild Women Lounge.

Getting on a stationary bike, Libby pedaled faster than she ever imagined possible and still it couldn't shut out the sounds of their Foster kids crying in the night. Their pain made it impossible for her to let Anna Mae off the hook.

Her legs were going so fast around that one of her shoes sailed across the floor. Out of breath, shaking, she stopped pedaling, slid off the seat and sat on the floor. At least Anna Mae's kids hadn't been raped or murdered. At least she'd sent them to the safety of relatives. Relatives who cared enough to take them in then move away so Benny couldn't find them.

It was the best she could say about Anna Mae. Libby pushed on the bike frame and hauled herself up off the floor went and retrieved her shoe.

Was she any better than Anna Mae? She's played cards with Benny and Anna Mae for over a year, saw Benny's meanness to Anna Mae and did nothing. Nothing. She who'd always thought she'd recognize an abuser and do something about them. All she'd done was put Benny on her unlikable list. It was the same with their card playing friends. Except Cece. She'd seen Benny's meanness tried to stop him.

Ashamed of herself, Libby put her shoe on, looked at the treadmill. No more today. She was already worked up enough over this. And there was the meeting about Anna Mae tonight.

"Damn!"

Her spaghetti legs took her no further than a bench where she sat down and wiped the sweat off her face. What was she supposed to do about Anna Mae's confession?

Chapter 15

Sweaty and shaking, Libby made her way back from the exercise room and fumbled her way into her apartment. The light on her answering machine was blinking three messages. She hoped one was from Ginger. Returning her call would be easier than calling Ginger cold turkey.

About to push the message button she stopped. How to apologize to Ginger, and get her to come early for the meeting to read the notebook?

Libby groaned. It was typical caretaker thinking. None of this was her problem. Cece wanted her here for the meeting. Ginger needed the information in the journal All she had to do was to say so. Tomorrow she'd talk to Ginger about going into treatment. It would be tough. It had taken an army of friends and family the first time.

She walked over to the birdcage. "What's wrong with me? I flip back and forth on everything."

The small yellow canary jumped back and forth as if saying, "I don't have a clue. I just got here."

"Sit still and listen to me."

She smiled when he quieted. "When I decided you should come home with me, I made that decision fast. Not so with other things like is Anna Mae good or bad? I have to decide that before tonight."

When he didn't move she decided not to upset him with the gory details. "Here's another one. What do I do about stopping my best friend's drinking problem?"

Sing Sing flitted around his cage, settled on a perch far away from her. "Okay. So you don't want to talk to her either. That means I have to do more thinking. Ginger has George. I only have you, Sing Sing."

The bird turned his back on her. "Oh I'm sorry. I didn't mean *only* you. I love having you here. I really, really do."

She went over to her answering machine, pressed the red light. Her first caller was Cece, all puffed up with authority, telling her to be in the Daycare center at four thirty sharp today to discuss Anna Mae's return or, no return, to the Bordello.

Libby looked at Sing Sing. "Cece's rattled too, calling me after telling

Birdie to contact us all."

Next was Ginger's saying she'd be over at three-thirty to read the journal before they went to the meeting, then a rushed apology for being so nasty the other day.

"Wow!" Stunned and relieved, Libby deleted a message from an advertiser, went and showered.

Dressed and back in the kitchen, she was running water for a pot of coffee when a series of warbles came from the living room. Sing Sing was singing! Harry The Canary had taken weeks to like his new surroundings well enough to sing. Smiling, she rushed into the living room.

"You've a beautiful voice. I see why they named you Sing Sing but, we do have to change that name. What about Larry The Canary, Harry's little brother?"

He looked at her, then pecked at his millet spray.

"Happy Harry?"

He kept on pecking.

"Come on. A house bird has very little responsibilities."

He turned away from her and she went back into the kitchen, turned the water on again. Hearing a series of beautiful warbles she quickly returned to his cage.

"Okay. You like running water. How about someone who lives over the ocean? Pavarotti maybe?"

When he shook his feathers, she took it that he didn't care for Italians.

"Julio Iglesias? He's a marvelous singer and a very good looking guy."

When the cage jiggled, and he sat on his perch preening himself, she decided they had an agreement.

"Julio it is."

By three, she'd eaten lunch, cleaned up her kitchen, paid two bills, practiced what to say to Ginger before the meeting and was unhappy with all of it. She'd worked herself into a horrible underarm odor, noticeable as she went out into the lounge and looked out the front window.

Ginger's flashy, silver sports car was not parked at the curb. She went back to her apartment a few minutes later there was the familiar tap, tap, rat-a-tat-tat on her door. Libby practically flew to let Ginger in.

"I didn't see your car."

"I'm around back by the kid's center in case I need to make a quick get away."

Libby threw her arms around Ginger then flushed with relief when she was hugged back.

"I'm sorry I was so pissy the other day. I had no business saying. . ."

"Nothing to be sorry about, Lib. Only a good friend would dare mention my drinking."

"There that's enough of the huggy stuff."

As Ginger pulled back a hint of alcohol brushed Libby's nose.

"Yes, I've been drinking too much lately. I'm cutting back as soon as this Anna Mae issue is done and gone."

Libby just nodded. Disappointed with Ginger's solution of cutting back, this wasn't the time to start another argument.

Ginger turned saw the birdcage and welcomed the diversion. "Somebody left a bird in your living room."

"I need someone to talk to. My refrigerator makes such useless comments."

"Okaaay." Ginger looked around the living room. "Where's this journal Anna Mae gave you? You must've read it by now so just tell me about it."

"Right. We don't have the time for you to go through it anyway." Libby stared at the battered blue book on the coffee table. In worse condition since she'd gotten her hands on it.

"If reading that thing made you cry I don't want anything to do with it."

The edge in Ginger's voice, a rare sign of nervousness from Ms. Hide It All, surprised Libby. She'd expected Ginger's dislike of Anna Mae to make her leap at the journal.

Libby picked it up and sat down on the sofa.

"Eventually you'll want to read this. So." She turned the first page to Ginger.

"The first thing you'll see is Anna Mae's tiny, precise handwriting as she writes about the marriage of a Marian and David Thurgood."

"Who are they?"

Libby shut the notebook. "They are Anna Mae and Benny and they had two kids."

"No. You've got that wrong. They could never have been a parents."

"Trust me they were. Anna Mae was sixteen and P.G. when she married Benny who was twenty-one. Their first child was a boy. Benny was mean to their son right from the get go. Probably thought the boy wasn't his. He beat the little boy, shamed him. Hit him with his belt. It's all in there."

She pointed to the notebook on the coffee table. "Five years later, they had a girl and Benny loved their daughter. Doted on her. Then one morning Anna Mae found blood in her four year old daughter's panties."

"No!" Ginger jumped up.

"Yes. The little girl said daddy hurt her. Finding the blood, finally woke up Anna Mae and she did something awful."

Ginger pressed her hands over her ears. "Don't tell me. I hate killings. She killed him didn't she?"

Ginger took her hands away from her ears. "That was stupid of me. You said he was Benny and Benny just died." She sighed. "Tell me what she did."

"Anna Mae sent her kids to her sister and brother-in-law."

"That's good." Seeing the distress on Libby's face, Ginger added. "Isn't it?"

"Anna Mae put her four year old daughter and nine year son on a bus in Phoenix and sent them all the way to Flagstaff. Alone. all by themselves, up to Flagstaff."

Ginger stood up. "No. This is far too crazy to actually be Anna Mae."

Ginger clapped her hands. "I know. Anna Mae has written an outline for a novel and for some stupid reason wants you to check it out."

"No, it is Anna Mae, and that's not all."

Ginger slumped to the sofa. "I can't stand this."

"We're almost done. Remember Marian and David Thurgood at the beginning?"

Ginger nodded. "Well after this Marian sent her kids away, this David guy moved them to Tucson and changed their names to Benny and Anna Mae Brown."

Ginger shook her head. "Let me see that."

Ginger grabbed the book from Libby, sped through each entry, then flung it to the floor.

"She just sends them off? Never calls Social Services or the police? She just let them go?"

Libby nodded.

"Is there anything else in here that I need to know?"

Libby picked up the journal, turned to the last page. "I quote. Now I remember that I killed Benny. It's signed Anna Mae Brown and dated the day she shot his grave to shreds.

Silence filled the room until Julio moved in his cage.

"I don't understand any of this. Anna Mae just now remembers she killed the bastard? That's nuts."

"I think so too Ginger but we have to go. Cece's Anna Mae meeting is about to start and all I want to do is run out of here."

"No, Lib. The woman is saying she just now remembers she killed the bastard. Then she puts it in writing. We must stay. Tell Cece to throw the crazy bitch out. If Anna Mae moves back in here, Lib, you are to come stay with George and me."

Libby looked at Ginger. "You don't think Anna Mae is just crazy enough to believe that by giving us this journal we'll help her find her kids?"

"Tucson will freeze over in July before that'll happen."

Chapter 16

A tap, tap, tap on Libby's door made them both jump.

"That's Birdie's knock." Libby opened her door to a smiling Birdie looking past her to Ginger just emerging from the sofa.

"Ah, you're both here. I told Lissa that sleek car out back was your, Ginger. Chop-chop gals. We're closing in on six-thirty."

A second look at them reminded Birdie of her day old salad wilting in her fridge. This was not the time to make light of it, she turned and beckoned them toward the back stairs.

Still reeling from Anna Mae's journal, Ginger grabbed Libby's arm. "Give me one minute alone then I'll be there."

At Libby's skeptical look, she added. "I promise."

Like a gosling following its mother, Libby followed Birdie down the stairs, out the back door, across the play yard, past the carriage house and into the daycare center. Once inside the door, Libby, seeing child size chairs set up like a horseshoe, groaned.

Four tenants were already seated so low their knees poked up to their chins.

"We're supposed to sit in kiddie chairs?"

"Looks that way."

A chorus of hello 'Birdie, Libby, Where's Ginger? Greeted them as they marched in.

"On her way." Birdie looked around. "Where are the big people chairs?"

"We've checked everywhere and these were all we could find. Lissa says she likes it if visitors if come down to her kids level."

Birdie diddled a green chair with her foot. "I'm mostly Irish, so I'll sit on a green one." She then crumpled herself into her chair in one smooth motion.

"Libby, you should take a blue one to match your slacks."

Too tired to argue, Libby lowered herself onto a blue chair.

Just then, Ginger walked in.

"Ginger, you take the red one. It'll spiff up your outfit."

She bristled. "What's wrong with my outfit?"

She'd worn her tamest outfit so she wouldn't outshine the Bordello Bunch.

"It's too quiet. We always count on you to cheer up us dullards."

Ginger, never one to be ordered around, slid a purple chair next to Libby's blue one then lowered her protesting body on to it. Her gardening and months in Yoga classes just saved the day again.

Leaning forward she put her elbows on knees and felt like Rodin's 'The Thinker.' Straightening her arms, her hands rubbed the floor like an ape. Behind her head, she looked like she was being arrested.

Trying Birdie pose of turning her knees to one side, while keeping her head forward, made her neck crack. Libby hugging her knees to her chest looked like a wrap-around scarf.

She stretched her long legs out, sat back, and prayed her chair wouldn't snap against her weight.

The woman walking in now, somewhere over two hundred pounds would break a kid chair. Instead of sitting she walked to a portable blackboard, moved it, opened up a closet door, pulled out a tall cardboard sign, then lifted out a full sized chair. Dragging it over, she sat down and towered above the rest of them.

"Alice helps out with the kids." Birdie hissed out of the side of her mouth.

Useless thoughts rattled around in Ginger's head. Was Alice the leader of the pack today? From the little she knew of Alice, she was sure Alice wouldn't like that. Her next thought was how clever it was of someone to put the chairs in a horseshoe facing what looked like the teachers desk and that it was nasty to have only child size chairs. Smells of crayons, paper, chalk, old food, warm bodies, reminded her that school had once been her escape.

More tenants marched in, filling all seventeen chairs. The creaking and stirring that ensued, warmed Ginger's heart. At least everyone was equally uncomfortable. Cece set up kid chairs so the meeting couldn't last long. Once again, Cece was a step ahead of most people.

Finally Cece came in, sat on a corner of the desk. She tapped a ruler on the desk and the room quieted.

"Thank you all for coming."

Thank them? Libby frowned. Armed guards couldn't have kept them out. She welcomed the diversion. Anything to stop worrying about Ginger's drinking, about being invisible, about how to get past her anger with Benny and Anna Mae.

"Please accept my apology for ignoring our approval process and moving Anna Mae in here without first talking to all of you."

Libby tilted her head. The Bordello had an admission process? They voted on her before she moved in? At least someone had approved of her lately. The difficulty of sitting on a chair ten inches above the floor pulled on her hips.

"As I said, this mess is my fault."

Heads bobbed in agreement, especially Trish's tightly coiled, dyed black hair. Libby nodded to herself. This was going to be a very interesting meeting.

"Don't be so hard on yourself, Cece." It was Grace. "If you'd asked us, we'd have said Anna Mae could move in. She was quiet and friendly enough at the beginning. The day you moved her in here she looked like she'd been run over by a giant truck."

Libby was sure Grace's parents knew her before she was born. They gave her the perfect name. Grace always tried to quiet things down. She'd probably never let out more than a whimper while giving birth to her five children.

"Speak for yourself, Grace." It was Trish. "I for one do not accept your apology, Cece. You should have known Anna Mae was a wreck. When are they going to let her out?"

Let her out? Like Anna Mae was in jail? Libby sat up straighter, got closer to the action. Of course Trish would say 'let her out.' She sighed; told herself not to get upset over verbiage. It was the least of her worries.

"I've no information about when she'll be discharged from the hospital." Cece emphasized discharged.

"Because I don't know when, I thought it urgent we meet tonight." Cece edge more to the center of the desk.

"We need to hear from everyone A frank and open discussion will help me, we, to decide if Anna Mae can move back in here or be tossed out. Everyone, please, speak your mind."

Toss her out. Ginger groaned. With the kind of comment, chairs or no chairs, they could be here until midnight and she was in dire need of the cool liquid sitting at the ready in her fridge.

"Anna Mae is too fragile to be left all alone, Trish." It was Grace again. "That's why Cece brought her here in the first place."

Grace looked at the whole group. "Do any of you know if Anna Mae can afford to pay for some kind of supervised living quarters? If she should need it."

"Of course she needs to be supervised." Trish cranked her long neck, looked past two tenants, to glare at Grace. "She's not our problem to fix. She tried to shoot five of us."

Hands shot up all over the room. "First, I'd like to hear what really happened."

"Yes, I heard her gun wasn't loaded."

"Then why'd she wave it around like it was?"

"Because she thought her TV was being stolen."

"Come on, it was Carlos who had it. That shows how bad off she was, she didn't even recognize him."

"That's really bad."

"I've heard from several people it was Trish's squeals that provoked her."

"I did not squeal!"

"I heard that Libby and Ginger tackled Anna Mae."

"No. That's not true." They spoke in unison.

"Then what is? Trish tells us she could have gotten killed. You others say Anna Mae was just having a bad day."

There were shouts of tell us the truth, we need to know. Did the paramedics say what's wrong with her? Who's her doctor?

Birdie clapped her hands to get their attention. "I was there when the cops said Anna Mae's gun wasn't loaded. And, when she dropped her box, her glasses fell to the floor. She couldn't see it was Carlos with her TV."

"Wait one damn minute!" Spittle shot out of a red-faced Trish.

"See him or not, that idiot woman knows men aren't allowed up on the second floor. It had to be Carlos. There! That proves how unstable the woman is. Waving a gun, unloaded or not, at someone she should know by now."

A couple of mumbled yeses came from the room.

Birdie looked at Ginger and Libby then hissed. "One of you, say something. We need to settle this. I can't sit ten inches from the floor much longer."

She looked over at Cece. "And thank-you, Cece."

"For what?"

"For getting off the desk. Your crotch was practically staring me in the face."

Laughter lightened things up until Trish stood up. "Stop it! None of this is funny. We must decide what to do right now. The woman could be let out tomorrow."

Grace waved to Libby to get her attention. "Do you think she's Dangerous? You too, Ginger. You both were right there in the thick of it."

"Just because we were there doesn't make us experts." Libby ran her tongue over her teeth. She was a coward sitting on a fence. Did she want her back or not? Anna Mae giving her kids away had nothing to do with this. Her anger with Anna Mae was getting muddied with sympathy.

"But you are the expert, Libby. You were married to a policeman, you must have heard about tough situations like this."

Glancing at Ginger for help, her head jerked back. Anna Mae's journal was under Ginger's chair. Dangerous. There'd be a lynching if this group of mothers found out Anna Mae had given away her two children..

"I say we get the doctor's diagnosis before we make a decision."

Who'd said that? Someone on her left? No, it had come out of her mouth, without her permission.

"Medical files are privileged information." It was Eleanor, the widow of a lawyer.

"If you let her back in I'll move out." Trish looked sick as she stood up. "Anna Mae could, will, very likely do something like this all over again. I say we vote now to see where we stand."

Cece shook her freshly dyed auburn head, no. "It's too early to vote, Trish."

She then looked directly at Libby and Ginger.

"Please, tell us something. Anything. Help us understand what was going on in her head."

Ginger was suddenly up and walking to the right of Cece still sitting on the desk.

Glancing at Ginger, Libby clenched the edge of her chair. Ginger had the journal in her right hand!

"After listening to all of you jabber on, I've decided you are worrying over nothing."

"Nothing? That's crazy, Ginger. If Anna Mae's gun had been loaded, she could be in jail right now for mass murder." Trish walked to the other side of Cece.

Ginger nodded to Trish. "If you can make assumptions I have one of my own. Since the gun wasn't loaded, Anna Mae must have known it wasn't loaded."

"Then why wave it around?" Trish jutted her chin out, glared at Ginger.

"It's what you do if you think you are being robbed." Libby spoke as she struggled to stay calmly in her chair.

"That's true." A chair tipping to its side, made a loud clatter.

"I heard that Anna Mae was at the cemetery earlier and shot Benny's grave to shreds."

"She did?" Birdie slapped her knees. "Anna Mae should get a medal for pumping that bum full of lead."

Ginger held up her hands. "Stop! Listening to all of you makes me believe my other assumption is right. I'm pretty sure Anna Mae won't want to come back here and face all of you."

Now she had the complete silence she was looking for.

"Oh my, such shocked looks on your faces. Anna Mae might not want to live here? Be honest girls. We women aren't the easiest beings to live with. Have you heard yourselves? Facing a whole Bordello full of you opinionated women is more than a little intimidating. I suggest you don't crush her by saying she can't move back in. Wait to hear what she decides."

"Wait to hear?" Trish was now purple. "Anna Mae could waltz in here in the middle of the night."

She cast a dark eye at Cece now standing next to Ginger. "When are you going to change the entry locks?"

"It's not necessary, Trish. I have Anna Mae's keys."

Trish faced the room. "No one buzzes Anna Mae in!"

To a chorus of 'yeses' she turned to Ginger. "I've always had the impression you don't like Anna Mae."

"I don't have to like her to defend her against a lynching." Making her point, Ginger had waved her hand around and almost let the journal fly. "Anna Mae is still a person. She caved into Libby and me as soon as we got you to shut up and go behind the piano."

"What's that in your hand?" Trish took a step toward Ginger. "Does it have anything to do with Anna Mae? Does it?"

Libby, still in her chair, considered faking a faint. It wasn't too far to the floor and it would stop the meeting. She tensed her thighs. Put a hand to the side of her head to protect it if she should take a hard whack.

"You and Libby are obligated to tell us anything you know so we can mull it over."

With Trish closing in on Ginger, Libby decided faking a faint was too iffy and forced herself up and out of her chair.

"There you go, Trish Williams, wanting a trial without the defendant being here. I think that's still illegal in the U.S. At least it used to be. Ask Eleanor and Ginger's right. If I were Anna Mae, I wouldn't want to come back here to live."

The fervor in Libby's voice silenced the room but, her voice wasn't shaking because she was defending Anna Mae, it shook because she was worried about the journal. That and she was talking too fast.

Cece stepped between Ginger and Trish. "Libby and Ginger make a whole lot of sense to me. Give me time to find out what Anna Mae wants to do. Then, if necessary, we'll meet again to decide what we want to do. Thanks everyone for your candor. It's cleared up a few questions I had."

Then it was over. Chairs scraped. Women groaned as they rose up from the depth of a small person's seat. Giving limp smiles to each other, they tucked away their feelings and went their own way.

Libby and Ginger ended up alone standing next to Ginger's car.

"I was afraid you were going to tell everyone what's in that thing."

"No, no. I have to sit down and read it all the way through. I might even ask George's opinion, since men have a different slant on things."

"A man's view. Absolutely. Good idea!" Libby leaned over to give Ginger a 'things will be fine' final squeeze but, of course, the escape artist was already inside her car and out of reach.

Chapter 17

Thrilled to see George's car in the garage, Ginger parked next to it, then rushed inside, to what they called the 'dust of the day' room. Taking off her shoes, she went into the kitchen then stopped dead.

She counted twelve bottles of gin, some never opened, others near empty, standing in a perfect line on their center island. George, next to them, looked miserable. She opened her mouth to ask if his cancer was back when both his hands shot up, stopping her.

"I talk first, Ginger. On my way home from work, I stopped in at the club to thank Jeremy for helping us out the other night. He wasn't there. Ralph was."

Her heart stopped.

"Ralph gave me a worried look, like he knew about it."

She was in trouble. Big, big trouble.

"So, I asked him if he'd ever put you in a cab. He said he'd done it twice. Both times while I was in the hospital. I asked him if there might be other times. He said there could be, but the staff know enough to keep their mouths shut about what goes on at the club."

George tilted his greying head at her. "Were there other times?"

"It was a really bad day, George. I truly thought Anna Mae was going to shoot us."

"Don't dodge the question, Kiddo. A cab. Have you had to take other cabs home?"

Her George looked so worried. Worry was completely opposite of what his cancer doctors said he should do. She had to smooth things out.

"Ralph's gotten me mixed up with someone else." She started to move toward him. This time he pushed both his hands out.

"Don't come close to me and try to smooch your way out of this, Ginger. Nobody gets you confused with anyone else. Especially Ralph and Jeremy. Now. How many times and why?"

First Libby, now it was George, getting after her about her drinking. She'd never thought she'd be in this situation with him. Except for his cancer she'd been able to control her drinking.

"Two times." She hoped he'd buy that.

When he just stared at her, she said again. "It was two times. Plus the other night when you brought me home."

The concern, or was it anger in his eyes, intensified.

"I didn't tell you because your doctors said I was to keep stress at a minimum. You were fighting your cancer. I was scared."

"I might have bought that until I found all this." He pointed to the bottles. "These look like you are planning on doing a lot of drinking."

"No. No! There was a sale, George. We entertain."

"Sale? That's crap, Ginger. Pure crap." His voice tightened. "Earlier today some clown at work spilt coffee on my shirt. I came home, threw it in the laundry basket then I decided to help you out and do the wash."

She was dead. Dead. No lies, or crying, could get her out of this. "I got knocked on my ass when I pulled out two unopened bottles of gin tucked neatly into the bottom of the basket."

Her face must have shown her distress because the air seemed to go out of him.

"I get it that you were worried about my cancer. I get it that seeing your mother's bloody body tore you apart, but I don't get all this is planning for tomorrow and the next day."

With her whole body shaking, Ginger grabbed onto the back of a chair. "Who told you about my mother? Libby? She had no right."

"You told me."

That sent her against the sink. "No! I never did!"

Looking as if he was about to cry, George stepped away from the center island.

"You did the night I brought you home, and if you can't remember, then you are having blackouts, Ginger. You didn't remember your car was still at the club."

Blackouts? No. Blackouts were a bad sign and she wasn't having them. "I was drunk. How was I supposed to remember getting home?"

"What do you remember of that night?"

She stared at him, couldn't think "I can't remember now because you're mad at me. You've got my brain all muddled up."

"Don't put this on me, Ginger. What happened after we got home?"

She thought for a minute. "You put me to bed."

For effect, she slammed her purse and Anna Mae's journal down on the table. "Enough! This is too much aggravation for either of us. I've just come from a mess at the Bordello. I don't need this too."

He took a step closer to her.

"I've been battling cancer and I don't need my wife hiding her drinking. Remember telling me about when you were twelve and your mother gave you sixty dollars to buy clothes? About your mother sneaking the two of you into the swimming pool without paying?"

Her knees let go and she fell into a chair. She had told him all that? She'd shut out those memories years ago. No one knew about them. She shuddered, tried to change the subject.

"That was one very bad day, Sweetie. You have to see that."

He turned around, stared out their kitchen window to the flowers beyond.

"What about all those bottles, Ginger?" His voice was barely above a whisper.

She was getting more than scared. He wouldn't let go of this and he kept calling her Ginger, not Babe.

With his back to her, he let his tears flow. "I'm so sorry I didn't pay attention to all the strange things going on with you recently. I thought it was just us getting back to a normal life. Not you drinking a lot. Me, who ignored years of my sister's drinking until she drove drunk and wiped out that guy's life. She's still got years in prison to go."

He turned, grabbed her. His wild eyes scared her and she slapped her gentle husband of ten years. Slapped him hard.

"Oh, dear God. George! I'm sorry, so sorry, I didn't mean that."

She touched the red mark she'd made on his face. Her slap, so wrong, seemed to calm him.

"I won't let you get like her, Babe."

Things were better now. He'd called her Babe, not Ginger.

"I'll stop all my drinking. George. Sweetie, I promise."

As he let go of her, she staggered back, watched him reach into his pocket, pull out a small piece of paper. As he put it on the counter she recognized one of the numbers and felt like throwing up.

"While I waited for you to come home, I made some calls. Here are the telephone numbers of three rehab centers around here. One is just for women. I stopped looking when I heard you drive in."

He wiped the tears from his face, picked up a bottle of gin, opened it, poured it down the sink, then another, and another.

She wanted to yell stop. Why pour out money? Unopened bottles could be taken back. As he reached for the last bottle, she grabbed his hand.

"That's a lot of money you're throwing away, George. We do entertain, you know."

He took her hand off his, emptied another bottle. "I'm throwing them away Babe, because I will not throw us away."

Seeing his tears, she stared at him in stunned disbelief. He'd said throw us away, Babe. She couldn't throw George away. No. Not her George. No one before him had ever cared when she'd gotten drunk. Well, no one except her kids and Libby. They'd pushed her into her first and second stint for treatment. The top telephone number on his list was from where she'd been both those times and a short third stint.

As he took her by the shoulders, looked deep into her eyes, she thought, this was good. She relaxed a little. He'd beg her to stop. She'd promise him she would, and she would.

"I believed you, Babe when you said we were soul mates. Best buddies, joined at the hip. For ten years we've been like that, then came my cancer. All my tests say it's gone. I need you now more than ever. I won't let you turn into a drunk. If I've caused any of this I'll change."

He paused, waited. When she didn't speak, he added. "We've always had each other's back. Lay it out in front of me, Ginger and we'll get through this together."

Too dazed to say again she'd stop drinking, she watched him reach into a drawer, take out a large trash bag, go to the doorway then stop.

"My sister hid booze all over the house. Where's yours? You need to show me or I could destroy our house looking for it."

Numb, she watched him leave. Staring at all the empty bottles in the sink, she tipped up two, let the liquid drip onto her tongue.

Why had she done that?

Frightened, she ran after George hoping she could remember all her hiding places.

Chapter 18

Libby crawled out of bed, her thighs a searing pain, making her pay for her reckless stint on the bicycle yesterday. She cringed as she went into the bathroom and to her medicine chest. Opening the door, she stared at the arsenal she'd accumulated over the years. Aspirin. Tylenol. Aleve. Motrin. Excedrin. Ibuprofen. Then there was her Bengay, her Icy/Hot. Her heat wraps. They all irritated her. One could tell a person's age by what was in their medicine cabinet. Hers made her look at least eighty.

She certainly didn't have any birth control pills, acne drugs. No menopause drugs or lubricant items. She did own about all the 'miracle worker' meds they advertised on TV. That was a hoot. None of those people looked a day over forty. Not even when they had fake gray hair. Did those pills also make you look young?

She should be glad she could still take two of her favorite pills, gulp down water and get on the bicycle again today if she wanted to. She went to her living room window and looked out.

What was it they said about real estate? Ahh, it was location, location, location. She'd gotten a prime location at Cece's. She was second floor, back left corner. Away from the street noise she could open her windows and let fresh air in whenever she wanted.

As she did most mornings, she looked down at the Daycare kids racing up, down and around the huge play yard. Even with the window closed against the morning breeze their shouts and laughter reached her. She envied their attitude that life was fun.

If she were at her bedroom window it would be a whole other story. The side yard looked like an archeological dig that had lost funding.

Cece wanted it to be a fruit and vegetable garden in the shape of a huge wagon wheel. The wheel spokes were to be walks dividing the different kinds of fruits and vegetables. The hub would be circular seating.

Trying to be magnanimous, Cece had made the mistake of asking the tenants to decide what should be grown and where. A room filled with feathers and a fan couldn't have caused more chaos than the Bordello's amateur gardeners.

Dancers of the Third Age

Now she had made an even worse mistake by letting them all have a say over Anna Mae moving back in. Hopefully, Trish's tirade taught Cece that she had to make the decision on her own. A vote on it could turn the Bordello women against each other.

A shout from the play yard below interrupted her reverie. One girl, whose name she thought was Jenna, picked up a ball that had just catapulted off another kid's head. Marching over to the boy who'd thrown it, she pointed to the hit kid, then popped the culprit on the head with the same ball. Libby almost applauded.

Lissa, the Daycare Guru came rushing over, knelt down to their level, looked from one child to the other, then back to the culprit. The three kids were pointing at each other, shaking their heads. Eventually it looked like Lissa was explaining life to them, because the kids nodded, then they all reluctantly shook hands.

Libby grimaced. She wished forgiving Anna Mae were that simple. She'd hightail it over to the hospital and give the woman a good tongue-lashing. First about the gun then tell her that to stand by while Benny abused their children was more than wrong. Then, hopefully, Anna Mae would say something to make this evil urge inside her to hang the woman up by the thumbs, naked in the street, go away. They'd shake hands, but not hug. She would refuse to hug the woman.

She looked down at the yard again. Lissa was gone. She counted the kids. Yup, still twelve of them. One kid was missing today, home sick, she imagined. A boy looked up, waved at her. She smiled and waved back.

She'd begun to think Ginger was right that she'd become invisible, but the boy had seen her. She wasn't invisible. She was the watcher at the window. Watching. Never taking part. Watching was as worse as being invisible.

Her life had turned into one of no place to be and all day to get there. What kind of life was that? Ashamed she was again throwing herself a pity party she turned away from the scene below, went over to Phil's chair, lifted upshocked that the time had gotten the sagging seat cushion, pulled out his worn flannel shirt and rubbed it against her cheek.

She covered her face, inhaled, drew in his smells and barely got his scent. Tears stung her eyes. No matter what she did, how she protected his shirt, her Phil was fading. Only his after-shave remained and how long would it take for that part of him to be gone too?

No, her Phil would never be gone. Smiling, she put the soft shirt on, curled up in his chair and waited. Soon she felt his strong arms claim her and she remembered how their foster kids would laugh when he said hold the pickle, hold the lettuce, hold the tomato, I just found a dollar. We're going out to eat.

"I'm tired, Phil. Tired of trying to get me a life without you. Last week

97

I got all dolled up in my navy blue pants suit. No make-up. You know me. I marched out of here with my head held high and visited the charities with the stars on my list. I did all the right things. Smiled. Shook hands. Downed really bad coffee, smiled some more, said I'd love to volunteer two or three times a week.

They all offered me something menial or redundant. One wanted me to unload boxes of things, answer the phone. They said I had a good phone voice. Mostly I would be their 'gopher' person. I'm not a 'go for' type person, Phil. You know that. I've always been a 'go to' person. I can't turn errand girl now, so I told all of them no. It's put me in such a foul mood I'm pretty sure that if Oprah Winfrey or Bill Gates had approached me last week, I'd have turned them down too."

She paused, shifted in Phil's chair.

"Are you ready for what else I turned down?" She sat up straight.

"Of course you are. Lissa asked me to be a fill-in at the Daycare center. She says working with the kids is what gets her up every day, makes her feel useful. My, oh so brilliant, answer was that it might work for you Lissa, but I've had enough of teaching kids to cut, color and play nice. I meant my comment to be cute but it cut her in half. I don't know way Lissa is still being nice to me."

She nuzzled the collar of his shirt, picked up his picture, rubbed his lopsided grin.

"I know. I know. I'm not the Queen anymore. I'm only mad at Fate, not you."

She shook her grey head. "I feel better now and one of these days I'll get me figured out. I just needed to dump my misery somewhere and Julio isn't up to it yet."

She smiled. "Who's Julio? He's the canary you told me to buy. He's so busy hopping around his cage and getting used to being here, that he doesn't have time to listen to my sad stories."

Taking his shirt off, she tucked it under his chair cushion and went into her bedroom. The top of her dresser was filled with photos of her life. One in front was of them signing their first adoption papers. Six year old, Robert, their fifth foster child, was in the middle holding up a pen. He'd told the judge, since he was being adopted, mom and dad had to be adopted too and he had to sign that it was okay with him.

Another picture she loved was of Phil and their daughter Carrie dancing at her wedding. She had hundreds pictures of all their kids. Some stayed a while, others only a short time. They'd adopted three. Putting it back she bumped a picture of her children and her parents standing in front of an ice cream truck named Anna's Icees.

Suddenly her heart clutched and she felt ashamed. Anna Mae didn't have memories of family. None. She'd given all that up when she sent her children away.

Out in her kitchen, pouring a glass of grape juice, thinking about how Phil always softened her blows, she poured the deep purple juice up and over the rim of the glass.

Grabbing some paper towels, with what she called 'goodie two shoes' sayings on them, she mopped up her mess. She'd bought the towels for inspiration but mostly found them irritating. She crumbled up one that said smiles are for sharing; carry a spare. Another said seconds are golden; minutes beyond price. That was a rotten one to show to a widow who was closing in on seventy. The one that said the afternoon knows what the morning never suspected sounded nice, but she didn't have a clue what it meant. Today the whole roll felt like a pat on the head.

The one with 'Make a difference' on it did give her a poke in the nose. There was her trouble. She'd made a difference, a huge one for years and years. Now she was knocking one the useless door. She tore off several sheets.

Layering them she mumbled, "I made a marriage last fifty years." She ripped the pile in half.

"We took in sixteen Foster kids, adopted three." She ripped the halves in half.

"I arm twisted hundreds of companies and got tens of thousands of dollars for Phil's home reconstruction charity." She ripped again.

"Now I'm sixty-five and no one needs me."

She stacked them up again, pulled hard but nothing happened. Her pile of inspiration had grown too thick for her arthritic hands. Balling up the whole mess, she threw it in the trash. Washing her sticky hands, she pulled out a tea towel, read what she'd needle-pointed on it years ago.

Never give up. Never give in. Fall down nine times; get up ten.

"Damn!" Why had she looked? One always got to her.

The shrill ring of her phone had her jumping backwards and whacking her hand on the edge of the counter. Cutting off a screech, she grabbed the phone, got out a weak, "Hello."

"I slapped George!" It was Ginger. "Slapped him hard, right in the face!"

George was Ginger's perfect husband. "Should I come over?"

"No. I just had to tell you before we went out to dinner."

Ginger had slapped George and they were going out to dinner? Then it couldn't be too bad.

Ginger let out a long breath. It was foolish to lie to Libby.

"Forget what I just said about going to dinner. George is taking me to that drunk tank you and my daughters sent me to all those years ago. They want to talk to me, then George, then us together. If we all think we can work together, they'll draw some blood; look for drugs. Since I'm dead

99

sober today I'll probably come back home and wait for my blood tests results. We all. No. I have to decide if I'm bad enough off to go in for a while or, I can I stay sober using their drunk day care program."

"Drunk Day Care?"

"It's their out-patient rehab. I can probably use that as long as I don't drink. If I end up staying in rehab you tell anyone that asks about me that we've run up to Tucson. Bye."

Libby stared at her dead phone.

At last, Ginger's drinking was out in the open. She was facing her demons.

It was time for her to do something useful like locate Anna Mae's kids. A name like Timothy Thurgood shouldn't be too hard to find. It wasn't like trying to find the right Timothy Smith or Jones.

When the Phoenix telephone directory didn't have even one Thurgood she contemplated using the Internet. No. She'd go straight to the well.

Down in her car, she turned on her air conditioning against the building heat and drove off praying that Joe Pasternak was at the station house and not out on vacation or assignment.

Twice Phil had saved Joe's life. That made him the easiest mark at the station. But, if need be, she could arm-twist someone else. By the time she was almost there, Rosa Rita's air-conditioning was sputtering on and off like it had on her way back from the mountains. The last time she'd had it fixed her, mechanic of ten years, had said it would be unfixable the next time it died.

"It may be time to put you to rest my dear, dear, Rosa Rita." She patted the passenger seat as if a good friend sat there.

Pulling into the visitor parking lot, she felt alive for the first time in months. Looking at herself in Rosa Rita's small rearview mirror she smiled. "Mirror, mirror on the visor, should I go in all harried? Hectic? Full of dire straits?"

She fluffed her hair out like she'd been in a windstorm then patted it back down.

"Sad? Depressed? No, It's best I'm honest. I'll just say the mother is about to be deported."

Getting out, she closed Rosa Rita's squeaky car door, then jumped ten feet when a hand gripped her shoulder. Turning around, she saw Joe Pasternak grinning at her and punched him in the shoulder.

"You want to kill an old lady?"

"Sorry, Ms. Price. I thought you saw me waving at you." He gave her a sheepish grin. "I see you still got your beater car. Some of us could help you find a better one."

The growl in Joe's voice let her know he'd not quit smoking, like he'd promised her. If she wanted his help, she'd better not bring that one up.

"I don't think I'm ready for a new car just yet. Rosa Rita and I go way back. Way back. Got her after the last of our foster kids left."

"My point exactly." He looked down at her. "You here for pleasure or business?"

"Business. I need a huge favor from you." She hooked her arm through his, the way Ginger did to George when she wanted something. Phil would have said she was being 'frilly'.

"This old lady is in dire need of your assistance. I have to find two people right away and I don't know how to do it."

"Okay."

She quickened her steps to keep pace with him. Inside the station house, she waved at the intake officer, smiled at others she knew as she followed Joe into the Inner Sanctum.

"One of your foster kids go bad?"

"Nope. Can thank our lucky stars on that one. Thirty plus years ago, a long time friend of ours sent her two young kids away because their father was abusing them. Now that he's dead, she's desperate to find them before she dies."

It wasn't a lie. Anna Mae would eventually die. Playing the old lady card to the hilt, she plopped wearily down into a chair.

"When it comes to the computer, I'm almost as useless as two tails on a donkey and my friend is worse. If you tell me how to look up a missing person, I could go to the library and use one of their computers."

Joe tilted his head at her as if he knew she had a computer. She'd said *library* because that made it seem harder for her. She had her fingers and toes crossed in hopes he'd do the searching.

Digging around in her purse, then digging some more she pulled out tissues, a small calendar, two pens, laid them on his desk, then latched onto a quarter folded piece of paper she'd avoided from the outset. Opening it, she handed it to Joe.

"This has the names, birth dates and birth place of the brother and sister I need to find."

She took in a breath. "Is that enough info for someone smart like you to pinpoint what computer thingies I need to use when I go to the library and try to look them up?"

Nervous, she puffed it all out a few breaths. "Right now their poor mother is in the hospital and finding them would be such a big help to her in her fight to live."

It was amazing how a person could tell the truth yet, at the same time exploit the situation. It was as if she'd been in politics, or was a financial adviser.

"Let me see what I can do."

Joe took her slip of paper, nodded her over to a chair several feet from his desk. "Can't have you peeking over my shoulder. Actually, go over and visit with some of the guys."

An hour later she had an address and was humming as she left the station house. Next week she'd come back with a huge pot of her Texas chili she'd promised them. It always amazed her, what a smile and some home cooking could do. With men at least.

Chapter 19

Ginger drummed her red fingernails on George's desk. She hadn't had a drink in two and a half days and it was making her edgy.

Her blood tests had come out pretty well. No liver damage, no bleeding, but this time she was more anxious than she'd been the other times she'd stopped drinking. Probably because she knew now she had to stop drinking completely. Forever. No teensy nip at weddings, holidays, funerals, or because the day was sunny.

Their day program was full to the brim. They'd offered to get her into another facility immediately but she'd refused saying they had her records, she'd wait until they had room for her.

In her heart she felt she didn't need immediate help. She preferred them because they were a good drive away from her side of Tucson. She'd smiled nicely, thanked them, when they handed her a list of AA programs near their home. Even though AA programs were anonymous, she'd never gone, didn't plan on going now. Someone she knew might be there. She hadn't filled the prescription they'd given her to get through the next few days either. Her body might not react badly to being dry.

At loose ends she went into her bathroom, looked in the mirror, poked at her jaw line. "At least I'm not so puffy today."

Remembering her red azalea bushes still needed more trimming she put on a hat and headed for the garage. Instead of picking up her gloves and clippers, she got stopped by the metal trashcan she and George had filled with empty liquor bottles. Stepping to the side, the other side, something held her in the garage.

Earlier this morning she'd told George not to put out the bottles out with the recycle. Said it was important that she get rid of them. They both knew the noise of bottles being dumped into the recycle truck bothered her. People would wonder why so many. Especially Sally Long Nose.

But what to do with them? She could put some into the regular trash each week. No, the smell of gin she couldn't have, would eventually send her to the nearest liquor store. To test herself, she braved it and lifted the metal lid up and off.

Judith Granahan

The smell floating up clenched her jaws, knocked her backwards. Her throat tightened in anticipation of a bump. The urge was so strong, she put her hands to her head, paced in circles. Thank God she hadn't opened the garage door for someone to see her.

Would booze ever become a repulsive smell? Like rotting food? Or dog shit? Probably not.

Best she go back into the house, get away from the smells. Fast. George would take the bottles elsewhere when he got home. That was hours away. This was now and her first test. To fight the urge to lift a bottle or two and let the contents drip onto her waiting tongue, she jammed her fists into her pockets

Desire made her whole body shake. Desire, the name she'd given her urges on her last rehab stint, was trying to sway her. Like in the past, she pictured Desire as a huge black figure swirling around like smoke. Waiting until it's huge head, arms, body closed in on her, she grabbed at the air and threw Desire to the floor then crushed it with her foot.

Even though it was fantasy, it made her feel in control. Before Desire hit again she had to do something real. Grabbing a large can of turpentine from a high shelf, she sped back to the trash can, opened it then sat it on the floor. Pinching her nose, she took the lid off the trashcan, laid it down, then poured turpentine back and forth over the bin of empty gin bottles.

She took the fire extinguisher they kept in the garage, stood it on the floor next to the trashcan, lit a match and tossed it in.

The sudden whoosh of flames, sent her sideways, knocked over the extinguisher and sent it rolling toward her car.

"God damn it!"

Running, she gabbed the extinguisher just before it slid under her car. In a flash she was back at the trashcan and spraying the flames licking the wall. When they were out she aimed at the flames spilling from the can. As she had imagined, black smoke swirled up around her head. She coughed. Her eyes burned. But she never let go of the trigger. She sprayed until only a fizz came from the extinguisher.

She'd killed her tormentor. Well, it wasn't dead, but she'd hurt it.

Blinking her burning eyes, she tried to see into the can. Smoke was still sputtering up but the flames seemed gone. Slapping the metal lid onto the can she peered around the garage for more fire or smoke damage. It seemed there was nothing on fire except her lungs. And her eyes. She couldn't rub them with hands as black as shoe polish.

Shaking, she punched the garage door opener button with her elbow, sat down on the cement steps into the house. She could have burned the place down! It was one thing to defy her addiction, she shouldn't be stupid about it.

"At least I now can picture booze trying to kill me one way or another."

She coughed, started to rub her burning eyes then remembered her smoked covered fists. "You'll not beat me. Not ever again."

When she started to cry she couldn't stop. No matter how George, her daughters, or Libby, stood by her, supported her, she was alone in this. As alone as in giving birth or in dying.

"Stop it Ginger Logan! You are not a victim!" Anger stood her up. Her tears had flushed some of the pain from her eyes. She touched the wall behind the can. Not hot. She had to wash off the smoke damage before George got home. A few cracking glass sounds from the garbage can had her taking the lid off to check for flames.

She sniffed. "Now there! That stinks!"

Back in the kitchen, she washed her hands, face, splashed water in her eyes, swallowed water. Coughed, coughed deeper. It hadn't gone exactly right. It could have been worse if the can had been plastic. She hadn't considered that before lighting the fire. Sunshine in a dark time.

The phone rang, peeking at it she saw Libby's name and turned away, then turned back.

What had Churchill said? 'There's nothing to fear but fear itself.' Or was it FDR. Or was it 'nothing is as bad as you think it's going to be'. Oh hell, who cared who said what.

She picked up the receiver. "Hello "

"You and I need to meet with Cece right away. Now."

Libby never announced who she was.

"What on earth for?" Ginger held the phone slightly away from her ear to keep it from the soot in her hair.

"Because Cece just called me all in a dither. She thinks Anna Mae could be discharged late tomorrow and she can't decide what to do. Cece needs to read Anna Mae's journal today."

"No!" Ginger almost shouted. "You promised Anna Mae you'd keep it a secret."

"I've already shown it to you and I assume you've shown it to George. Cece has to know who and what she's dealing with. Trish is screaming lawsuit if Anna Mae comes back. Cece's lawyer says kicking Anna Mae out could land her on a lawsuit claiming age or disability discrimination."

Ginger shifted the phone to her other hand.

"Cece wants our advice. She'll be at your house in an hour."

"My house? Who invited her here?"

"She invited herself. Don't worry about lunch, she's bringing it."

"Cece's buying lunch? She still has the first nickel the tooth fairy gave her. Hey, wait a minute. We haven't spoken since I told you I was checking out rehab. What made her, or you, think I'm here?"

"It's Wednesday, your never fail garden day."

Remembering the smell in her garage, Ginger groaned. "Call her back, say we'll meet her at the Bordello. In two hours. I need a shower."

"I tried that. She says she can't go there. She's laying low until the Anna Mae thing is settled. That's why she's coming to your house."

"And her house? What the hell's wrong with her house?"

"It's being painted or something. I could drive by to see for myself. Ever since Benny died, Cece's been acting as strange as a three-legged bird."

"Right, and if you show her the diary it'll send her to the moon."

"We have to. Should I call Anna Mae at the hospital and ask her permission?"

"Yes, then stall Cece, Lib. I need time to clean up. Tell her our landscaper is here showing George where to lay pipes for the pump you gave us."

"Is he?"

"Of course not, he's at work." She finally caved in, gave up fighting Whirlwind Cece.

"Okay, here in an hour but, we eat first. See how things are riding in Ceceland. We are not to give Cece advice. If it flops, she'll blame us."

"Got it."

Ginger, picturing Libby nodding yes to herself, hung up. Racing to the bathroom she shampooed her hair three times until her hands came away free of the smoke smell. Dressed and checking out her face, the doorbell rang. Zipping over to her long living room window, she was relieved to see Libby's Rosa Rita parked at the top of her driveway. No Cece yet.

Ginger pulled her shoulders back, lifted her, not 'so puffy today', chin up and put a smile on. Opening her front door she gave Libby a quick squeeze. More than that and she'd be blubbering all over her.

"Move back, Ginger so I can shut the door. My radio says it's already a hundred."

"Your radio still works? That's a surprise."

"Why is everyone picking on Rosa Rita? She's pretty sharp for an old girl. Sorry I haven't been in touch. I needed time to recoup from Anna Mae. How are you doing?"

"I haven't had a drink since the Anna Mae meeting. Even the pitcher that had my gin-aide mix in my fridge went in the trash. I'm okay." I hope, I hope, I hope, slipped around on Ginger's tongue.

Libby squeezed Ginger's arm. "Anything I can do, I will."

A car door slammed, then her front door burst open almost hitting them. Cece barged in with two large white deli bags.

"How about we eat in your kitchen? It's not so sunny out there."

Ginger nodded. She'd found it best to let Cece run the small things, even when she was in someone else's house.

Libby, taken with the smells escaping Cece's bags, missed Ginger's irritated look as they followed Cece's swishing hips through the living room, and into Ginger's huge kitchen.

Setting her bags on the counter, Cece hung her Coco Channel purse on the back of a chair, turned a smiling face to Ginger and Libby then, frowned. "I smell smoke."

Ginger stepped in front of the door to her garage. "George left our garage door open when he went to work. The worst burning smell ever blew in from our neighbor's yard. I've no idea what it was. They're a bit off base these days."

"Really?" Cece's look said she didn't believe her. "It was so bad you had to take a shower? Your hair's still wet."

"I slept in this morning." She and Cece had fought over more than one real estate deal. It looked like it was going to be more of the same for lunch.

"Well, anyway. Gals, gals, gals." Cece clapped her hands. "This is my first chance to personally thank you for taking that gun away from that foolish old woman. I can never, ever, thank you enough for that. Both of you were so brave. Braver than I'd be. You saved my people from getting shot. And thank you for your support at the meeting the other night."

Ginger shook her head. "Enough, Cece. The gun wasn't loaded."

"You didn't know that. You two are real superwomen. My lawyer says I'm in a bind about that gun."

Cece opened a bag, sniffed. Opened the other bag.

Feeling it was as obvious as a stone in her shoe that Cece was about to ask them for a huge favor, Libby glanced at Ginger.

"Girls, a gun, loaded or unloaded, pointed at my renters by another renter, can get me sued if anyone proves I knew Anna Mae was a little nuts when I, me." Cece dramatically pointed to herself. "Moved her into my apartment building. Trish has already said I could have seen the incident coming. Could have seen it coming? Meek, mousey Anna Mae? A woman who's probably never farted in public? My lawyer says I'm lucky no one had a heart attack or a stroke."

"So are we who didn't." Libby gave a thin smile.

"What? I don't get you're meaning." Cece pulled out a carton.

"Never mind." Libby studied the carton. "This smells Chinese. If it is, I hope you said no MSG. It gives me a headache."

Cece lifted out another carton, waved it at Libby. "This one's Greek. No MSG in either. I've got to handle Anna Mae right or I'll lose everything I've worked so hard to get. How do I tell Anna Mae she can't move back into my grand old apartment building and not get sued?"

Ginger, focusing on the cartons thought Chinese and Greek? For Cece to buy lunch, and go to two different places to get it, meant she either wanted the combination to her safe or George for a sleep over. She'd learned a long time ago with Cece it was all me, me, me. I, I, I. She hoped Libby was right when she'd said her face didn't show surprise or irritation.

"October will be my forty-fifth year in real estate. They're planning a big celebration dinner and a plaque for me. Unless, of course, Anna Mae gets me in the headlines."

Ginger smiled at Cece. "Hmm. Then I guess it's time you stopped telling people you are fifty-five."

"I'm counting all the years as a little girl in my father's office."

Ginger would have raised an eyebrow, if she could. "Quit the drama queen act, Cece. You've had worse tenants than Anna Mae."

As Cece nodded, her crimson hair bounced up and down. "I can't afford a scandal right now."

Wanting to get to the point of the meeting Libby dropped her bombshell. "Before Anna Mae was carted away, she gave Ginger and me her diary."

The swift kick from Ginger made Libby squeak out, "It'll explain a lot of things."

"About what?" Cece closed the distance between her and Libby.

"About her and Benny's life before they came to Phoenix."

"Their life before? Oh good. Let me at it."

When no one moved, Cece added, "I'm her landlady."

Ginger slid in front of the drawer holding the notebook. "Anna Mae asked us not to show it to anyone. It's her secret life. Libby thinks you're entitled to read it because you are her landlady. I say we need to ask Anna Mae first."

"I called her and she said yes."

Ginger frowned at Libby as best she could.

"Good. Let me at it."

When the worry on Cece's face didn't seem like acting, Ginger reached into the drawer, pulled out the battered notebook and handed it to Libby.

"This was your idea. You can explain it to her while I set out lunch." She yanked the notebook back, looked hard a Cece.

"Wait. The only way I'll let you at this Cece is your promise not blab about what's in here. Not to anyone. If you do, I'll go straight to Libby's police friends and say you broke in and stole it."

"You will?" Libby looked up from the carton of Chinese.

"You bet, and I'll take you with me as proof you told Cece about the diary."

Cece nodded. "Don't worry. I'll read and not tell."

"You can't get out of that promise by saying it's for the safety of your renters."

Waiting for Cece's answer, Ginger tucked the diary under her arm, opened the Greek deli box, took in a deep breath then gave an exaggerated reaction.

"Ohhhh my. Greek pasta. Olives. Fete cheese. Heaven." She looked at Cece. "Well?"

"I nodded yes."

"Nods can be misinterpreted. If you are promising to keep this to yourself say yes."

"Yes. Y. E. S."

Happy to see she'd irritated Cece, Ginger gave the blue notebook back to Libby. "This is your deal, you explain the confusing parts. My stomach's reminding me it's time for lunch. I'm going to eat."

Ginger turned away from them, bent over the cardboard boxes to soak up their pungent odors. Meals and drinking had too often gone hand in hand. From now on, smells and food would have to do and maybe some chocolate later. "Did you bring desert?"

"Yes." Cece was eyeing the small notebook. "What confusion?"

Libby pulled out a chair. "Sit down, Cece. It's complicated."

Chapter 20

Eager to fill Cece in, Libby tapped the first paragraph in Anna Mae's notebook. "The mystery starts right here Cece."

Cece glanced at the page then got out a pair of glasses. "Anna Mae's handwriting is too tiny to read without these." She glanced at Ginger.

"I've never seen you wear glasses. I suppose you had the Lasic surgery everyone's getting."

"Yup." Ginger picked up the second white box. "Why did you get both Chinese and Greek?"

"Because I didn't know what you gals like. I thought one of these would do the trick." Cece put her glasses on, leaned over the notebook.

Libby pointed to the first paragraph. "See where it's written Marian Wilcox is marrying David Thurgood?"

Cece peered at the notebook. "That's Anna Mae's weird tiny writing. They must be sisters. She's never mentioned having a family."

Libby shifted in her seat. She could drag this out, make Cece suffer like she had but it was best she not get on Cece's bad side again.

"Most of it is about how David Thurgood abused their two children."

As Ginger put plates and silverware in front of them, Libby showed Cece a couple of vivid descriptions.

"This is awful but why are we reading it?"

"Here's why." Libby turned to where Marian and David Thurgood became Anna Mae and Benny Brown.

Cece jumped up. "Benny and Anna Mae can't be Marian and David. They never had children. Thank God for that. They'd have been horrible parents. Maybe they robbed a bank and then changed their names."

Libby and Ginger shook their heads.

"I can't believe it. There's something wrong here."

"Nope."

Libby held the notebook up so Cece could read the page where Anna Mae wrote about stepping in between Benny's swinging belt and their son.

Cece looked, flipped a page, read and shoved it away as Ginger put Greek on one side of her plate, Chinese on the other.

"Should I get us second plates."

"I'm fine."

"So am I."

Thinking she'd never seen such a strange combination that she wasn't going to miss one bite of, the urge for a quick gin-aide hit so hard she nearly dumped the rolls from the bag out onto the floor. Grabbing the last one, she saw the bag as something to attack. Crumbling it, she threw it in the trash compactor, stepped on the crush pedal several times and felt a little better until she saw Libby and Cece staring at her.

Her blood tests, and the center's assessment of her, had her in what they called, 'the mild' zone. Relieved when they recommend she enter the day treatment center, she about lost it when they said their staff was currently stretched to the maximum. As soon as she said she'd go elsewhere they promised to fit her in, in two weeks. Then said if things got bad, she could show up on their doorstep at any time.

Hating her grumpiness she stared at her plate. Her best chance of ignoring the cravings was to keep her mind and stomach happy, very happy. If she gained weight she'd have it suctioned off later.

Cece, back to reading, looked up with tear-filled eyes. "That son a bitch, David broke his son's arm! He sure does sound like Benny and she just stands by like mealy-mouthed Anna Mae would."

She read again, stopped again. "Anna Mae was dumb enough to have a second kid? A daughter? This is far worse than robbing a bank."

Cece laid the book on its stomach, looked at her plate, shoveled in several forkfuls of pasta, ate a roll.

"Okay. Now I can get back to this thing." She flattened the notebook, read, slapped the table with the journal, which bounced up her plate. She read more, slapped harder and in between gobbled up all of her Chinese. She looked up. "Tell me if he killed them. I can't bear to read this if he did."

"No one dies, but it gets even harder to read." Ginger put her fork down, divided up the last of the pasta.

"None for me, Ginger." Cece tapped the journal. "This thing has ruined my appetite and to think I went all the way across town for that deli. I surely can't eat a bite."

"Look at your plate. You've wiped it clean."

Cece stared at her empty plate. "I couldn't have."

"You did."

"Then just a tiny bit more for me. I didn't have breakfast."

"None for me. I had breakfast." Libby took the smallest of the whole grain sour dough rolls. They were the ones she drooled over, but rarely bought since Phil was gone.

Cece turned a page. Read. Looked at Ginger, then Libby. Went back to the journal, ran her finger over the spot, read it again. She slammed the journal shut and pounded it with her fists.

"Why didn't you tell me that sick bastard molested his daughter?"

Ginger toyed with her tall glass of iced tea. "Telling you would have taken the sting out of it. We want you as upset as we are."

"I can't read more until I know why the Browns never mentioned kids."

"Okay." Libby tilted her head up, ran her tongue over her top teeth to try and speak without crying.

"When Anna Mae saw those bloody little underpants she became so afraid he'd eventually molest their daughter, that she put their kids on a bus and sent them, by themselves, all the way **to** her sister. Later on, she writes she never saw them again."

Out of breath from speaking so fast, Libby stared at the wall.

"On a bus? By themselves? They were only four and nine."

Libby nodded.

"I hate them. He beats and berates their son for years. Tries diddling with his daughter. And that coward, Anna Mae, punishes the kids by giving them away! I wish I'd killed her when I killed him."

Ginger's glass froze halfway to her mouth. "What did you just say?"

Libby sat as still as her mountain.

Cece swallowed. "I meant to say I wish she'd died when he died."

"I may be getting old but," Libby tilted her gray head. "I distinctly heard you say you killed him."

"Me too." Ginger put her glass down.

Cece looked from one to the other then stared at the widow over the sink.

"Okay. I'm eighty percent sure I killed the bastard. I'm only sorry he had a quick death and I'll deny it all if you tell anyone, even Anna Mae."

Cece a murderer? Ginger turned her sweating glass around on the table. Cece may have a fire-ball temper but, she was no murderer.

"If eighty percent of you says you killed him then twenty percent says you didn't. You can get bitchy but, a murderess No."

Libby moved her plate aside, took the notebook, found the page she wanted.

"Read this. It's dated the day Anna Mae waved the gun around at us." She slid the journal back to Cece, tapped the spot.

Cece, pushed her glasses closer to her eyes, read, looked up. "She probably killed him? That can't be. Anna Mae was over by the door to the house when he fell."

She handed her glass to Ginger. "I need something a whole lot stronger than iced tea."

"We don't have anything stronger."

She gave Ginger a 'you must be kidding' look.

Ginger, feeling a twang of malicious joy from cutting someone else off the booze, swallowed hard.

"George and I are now teetotalers " She'd flung her news out with a little pride, and a lot of fear. The room went quiet, the hum of the refrigerator the only distraction.

Cece looked at Libby, then Ginger. "Since when?"

"If you can confess killing someone, I can confess I have a drinking problem. After taking the gun away from Anna Mae I got roaring drunk. That did me in. "

"Oh! Oh my dear," Cece took Ginger's hand. "I'm so sorry, Ginger. Are you getting treatment?"

Are you getting treatment? Envy made Libby lock her jaw. Would she have gotten the same concern she saw on Cece's face if she'd popped up out of her chair and said, I've become an invisible, unseen, useless old lady and I've no idea what to do about it.

Nope. No way. No concern would come her way. Cece might give her a strange look, but there'd be no suggestion of help because there was no AA for people who'd run out of ideas.

Libby sat up straight as if stuck by a pin. What was wrong with her coveting Ginger's drinking problem? To clear the junk thinking out of it her head, she tapped the line where Anna Mae had written she'd killed Benny.

"She says she killed him. The police say it was an accident. Exactly how did you kill him?"

Cece forked in the last of her pasta, cleared her throat, let out a breath, but didn't answer.

"Don't stall, Fontaine." Ginger gave her a stern look.

"Okay. Okay. Remember when Benny broke Anna Mae's ankle and she refused to report him?"

They nodded.

"I started dropping in unannounced at their workshop after that. I though maybe I could catch him abusing her."

Ginger and Libby nodded again. "We know all that. It was over a year ago and you asked all of us to watch him during bridge."

"Yes and it didn't help. Benny knew how to behave in public. On the day he died, I showed up with an old picture frame I wanted refinished. As I opened the door, I heard Anna Mae screaming, cussing him out just something awful. It got me so excited I almost wet my pants. Now I could catch the S.O.B hurting her. So I slid the picture frame to the floor, set my cell phone to take a video and got Anna Mae on film screaming he'd killed her cat. That made me zoom down to a dead cat on the floor next to her feet. Then I heard Benny, high up on his big ladder, laughing and goading her."

Cece stopped, smiled. "I got him on film."

Picturing Cece doing all that, Ginger topped off Cece's glass of iced

113

tea and hoped Cece would take a sip but she kept right on going. Like the Eveready Bunny

"Have either of you ever been in their workshop?"

Libby shook her head no. "Not me. I never wanted a long conversation with him. Because of the way he spoke to Anna Mae at bridge, I wasn't about to contribute to his financial success."

"Ditto here." Ginger took their empty plates, rinsed them off, put them in the dishwasher, nodded for Cece to continue.

"That monster garage of theirs is over two stories high and he was ordering her to throw his tools up to him, saying her fucking cat's hair had plugged up his ventilation system. Loud and clear he said it deserved to die. They were going at it so furiously they didn't see me."

Cece's hand shook as she lifted her glass. "Benny ordered her to throw him another tool. She picked one up, flung it right to him. It was amazing. Two stories plus and she lands it right in his hand as if he was three feet away. Benny threw it back, barked she knew better than to throw him that tool. By that time my hand was so sweaty I had to switch to my left hand and pray the shots would come out clear."

Cece gulped down half her tea.

"Anna Mae threw him a couple more tools he didn't want. It was easy to see she was baiting him and I loved it. It was a sideshow like I've never seen before. My fun ended when he threw a tool back so hard it stuck into the plasterboard just inches from her head. She didn't even see it coming. I took that picture. I was sure he was trying to kill her. I yelled for them to stop. They paid no attention to me, so, dumb me, instead of calling 911, I ran over, grabbed the ladder with both my hands and shook it to get their attention.

They still didn't notice me. Anna Mae threw him another tool. This time, when Benny reached out for it, I must have shaken the ladder at the same time because it wobbled. It actually twisted out of my hands. In the middle of the night I can still hear him scream as he fell. Hear the horrible thump his head made when it hit the edge of a metal workbench. I still see him all crumpled up on the cement floor, blood oozing from under his head."

Ginger tilted her platinum head at Cece. "Are you saying you shook Benny off his ladder?"

With tears running down her face, ruining her mascara, Cece nodded. "Yes."

"No way. You don't weigh over a hundred ten pounds with your purse full. Benny was six feet plus, with a good size belly. You couldn't have turned that ladder with him on it. You've never even set foot inside an exercise club."

"I have too been in a gym."

"To exercise or to pick-up Jack?"

Cece gave Ginger a dirty look. "What's your point?"

"You couldn't have twisted a two story high ladder hard enough to throw him off."

"Absolutely not." Libby was sitting on the edge of her chair.

"I see this whole thing like a triple play in baseball. First, Anna Mae throws wide, maybe she meant to, maybe not. Your film can't prove that one way or the other. Second, Benny, being the fool, stretches out to get the tool, just as you wiggle the ladder to try and make them stop fighting. Third, Benny's weight turns the ladder, not you and he falls and gets called out."

Libby grinned to herself. Phil would have loved that she'd come up with a baseball metaphor.

Ginger nodded her platinum head. "That fits. I agree. Benny killed himself by going after his tool and falling."

They both stared at Ginger.

"Well? Does anyone really care how he died? I know I don't."

"Me, neither." Feeling relieved, Cece fanned herself, looked at Libby. "You're a cop's wife. You must care."

"The triple play was my idea, wasn't it? Benny caused his own death by leaning out and making the ladder twist. The police declared it an accident. Why second guess them?"

Cece, rapidly patting her chest, looked at Ginger. "Are you sure you don't have anything to stronger to drink?"

"Our liquor is gone. All gone. Burned up in the garage. That's what you smelt. I've water, tea and coffee."

Ginger almost smiled. No booze, meant Cece wouldn't be hanging around for hours. Silver linings often showed up at the oddest of times.

Cece tapped Anna Mae's last entry. "But, look. Right here. You two. Read where Anna Mae says she probably killed Benny. That scares the hell out of me. When she gets out of the hospital she'll probably be pretty stable. What if she goes to the police and confesses?"

"She'd be confessing to killing him. Not accusing you."

"They'll open up the case and find my fingerprints on the ladder."

Ginger and Libby spoke almost in unison. "Stop this!"

"I can't."

"You have to calm down, Cece. If Anna Mae really feels she did it and confesses, then the police will close the case. You'll be off the hook. Just like you are now."

Cece glared at Libby. "I just told you, my fingerprints are on the ladder."

"A smart lawyer can prove you were trying to stop the wobble."

Cece slumped and studied their faces. "You really think the cops'll buy that I was just trying to help?"

Ginger sat forward. "Well, weren't you?"

"Yes!"

"Then drop it, let the police do their job."

Seeing Cece squirm sent a warm pleasant feeling, through Ginger. It was payback for the time she'd stolen that huge real estate offering out from under her.

"When is Anna Mae getting out?"

"Getting out, Libby? Now you sound like crabby old Trish."

"Discharged. I meant to say discharged." Libby pushed away the last of her pasta. "I don't sound like Trish. Do I?"

"No, you don't. I was just trying for a little humor. Wanted to break the tension. This is the first time I've ever discussed if a person we actually know was murdered or, if it was an accident."

"You're tense?" Cece jumped up. "Think of me, Ginger. I didn't want him to die. I was only trying to help. We're always being told to help. Damned if I'll ever do it again. My fingerprints are on that damn ladder. Why did it have to break and kill him? To top it off, I move her into to my apartment building and she holds her gun on my tenants! Whooee."

Cece sat down again. "Plus now, if I decide to let her back in I'll get sued for endangering my tenants. If I lock her out the ACLU or the ADA will knock on my door! She keeps me up most of the night."

Cece drained half her tea, sat down in her chair. "Okay. Panic is out of my system. She thinks they'll discharge her tomorrow afternoon, unless they decide to fix her 'plumbing down there', as Anna Mae put it."

Cece, smiled a weak smile, put her hands together as if praying. "Please, please, fix her plumbing. I need more time to figure out what to do with her."

Libby touched Cece's arm. "It'll all work out. Let it go."

"I can't. What if she remembers I helped her bury her cat? I made her put the tools back. I also hid the hole in the wall with a calendar. We were both very vague with the cops."

Ginger tilted her head. "Oh stop it. You're being your usual drama queen."

Cece looked insulted, she added, "I've seen you do it over and over at real estate dealings."

"Ginger's right. You aren't making sense. You think Anna Mae will come after you? The same Anna Mae who gave her kids away rather than provoke her husband? What would make her tell the cops you held onto the ladder?"

"So she can get off, damn it." Cece's voice trailed off into the atmosphere.

"She's already "off". The last thing she'll do is ask them to re-open the case."

"So you say, Libby."

Ginger picked up the plates, leaned against her dishwasher.

"I've an idea." Ginger said then waited for Cece to look at her. "If you can locate Anna Mae's kids, she'll focus on them. You may even be able to send her back to them."

"Send her back?" Now Cece was up. "She's not a dress that doesn't fit."

"If it makes you get your head on straight, think 'find her children, and reunite them."

Libby looked at Cece, put her paper with the information about Anna Mae's son back in her pocket. Ginger was right. Cece should get busy looking for the information.

"I like that idea." Cece looked at them. "Anna Mae getting back with her kids should keep her distracted enough so she wont think about Benny or the police. But, how do I find them?"

Ginger turned the dishwasher on. "You get the guy you hire for digging up real estate info to track them down."

"He's for my real estate business, not personal business."

"So what? He's very good at snooping."

Cece gave Ginger a dark look. "What excuse do I use?"

"You could start with the truth, Cece. Tell him your nutty tenant held people at gunpoint then, you lie. You say you promised her you'd find her long lost children, if she'd put the gun down. If you have to, get down on your knees and beg for his help. I've seen you do it."

"I really don't like him messing in my personal business." Cece thought for a minute. "Anna Mae gave you two the notebook. Shouldn't you be looking for her kids?"

"As you said, Cece. You shook the ladder. Not us."

Ginger's smile reminded Libby of the evil Cheshire cat in Alice in Wonderland.

Chapter 21

Libby stood in the doorway with Ginger, while Cece got in her car, waved at them, then headed down the driveway. As soon as she was out of sight, Libby held up her crushed paper in front of Ginger's nose.

"I've found Anna Mae's son."

Ginger pulled her head back. "What?"

"I've found Anna Mae's son."

Libby jiggled the note above Ginger's head, twirled it away to keep it from her out stretched hand, then with a bow that would satisfy a queen, she handed Ginger the paper.

Ginger, grabbed it, undid the folds, read it and looked at Libby.

"Anna Mae's son, Timothy Mathew Thurgood, lives up in Sedona? Good God! That's only a few hours from here. If I'd been him, I'd have gotten far away from his father. Like, Chicago, New York, London, even Toronto. But certainly not Sedona."

The surprise rolling across Ginger's usually immobile face made Libby bounce up and down on her toes. "Keep reading."

"Four years in the Army." Ginger nodded. "Smart. Then he went to the University of Arizona right here in Tucson? My God! He was just a bus ride away from his parents."

"When Anna Mae reads that, she'll want to go out and shoot Benny's grave all over again and I'll drive her there."

"I'll go with you."

They both laughed, stopped, stared at each other. "No, how terrible. They could have passed each other on the street."

"I hate this." Ginger leaned against the door.

"I do too."

With Libby leaning against the glass, Ginger read on. "Now he's a high school science teacher in Sedona and has a wife and three grown children."

She smiled at Libby. "You couldn't have dug up all this on your own. You went to your cop friends."

"Fast as I could. I went right to the Station and smiled at Joe

118

Pasternak. The way you do to George when you want something. He's the Detective that Phil. . ."

Ginger finished for her. "Pushed out of the way of gun shots."

"Yes." Libby smiled. Their years of shared memories helped her keep sane since Phil's death.

"By the way, Joe agrees with you. He says I need a new car."

"Everyone says you need a new car." Ginger studied Libby's paper, turned it over. "There's nothing here about Anna Mae's daughter."

"No. Joe said females are a little harder to locate but he'll keep on digging. All we got was that she graduated from high school. We women get married, maybe even more than once. At least he didn't find any death or criminal records on either of them. Joe said Anna Mae's son should know where his sister is. I'm to let him know if I need more help."

"Why didn't you show this to Cece?" Ginger cocked her head, smiled a little in anticipation.

"I was going to, until you gave me the idea she should look it up herself.

Libby looked down Ginger's drive. "Don't turn. Your neighbor Sally Long Nose is watching us."

Ginger turned, waved. "I always let her know I see her."

"Maybe that's why you don't get along with her."

"Ya think?" Ginger smiled.

Libby sighed. "You know that before Cece walked into your house with our lunch I was furious with Anna Mae for dumping her kids. Somehow the way Cece reacted, made me think of Anna Mae without her children all these years."

"Same with me, Lib. It was so easy for us before, when we played cards with her and Benny and didn't know all this stuff about them. Everyone just ignored his meanness and her wimpy ways and went home."

"I guess now we can't ignore her." Libby stared out at Ginger's rolling front yard, then sighed. "Such a innocent little thing, me sitting down to talk to Anna Mae, led to us taking her gun away and now we're involved in her life."

"Life's always been full of little things wandering around the world waiting to punch us in the belly. That's the way it is, Lib."

"Yes but so often? I'd better go."

Ginger grabbed Libby. "Stop right there, Kiddo. Good things do happen. If we hadn't been there, Anna Mae could've gotten into worse trouble. Me, seeing my mother's body, sent me on a drinking spree so bad I slapped George and now I have to quit drinking."

She paused then, added, "Totally."

Libby hugged her. "I'm so glad for that. Now, I really do have to go."

Opening her car door, Libby stopped, crumpled onto the seat.

Ginger ran to her. "What's wrong?"

"I just got punched in the stomach with a most horrible thought."

"What?"

Libby patted her chest. "Let me think about what I just saw." She took in deep breaths.

"When I opened my car door, it was like I was at my apartment door and with Phil standing out in the hall looking in."

She sat back, smiled at Ginger kneeling in front of her. The worry on her face was defying the skill of her plastic surgeon.

"I think Phil was telling me that when Anna Mae meets with her son, she'll be an outsider. Only looking in on them."

Libby nodded. "Yes, that's what my Phil was trying to tell me."

"At first, yes. Let's think positive. They'll have a great reunion."

Libby listened as a car went by, heard birds singing, finally turned to Ginger. "Maybe not."

"You can be such a downer these days."

"Okay. Think about it. When your second husband died, you and he loved each other very much. Right?"

Ginger nodded.

"So now, what if Bill somehow was alive and knocked on your door? He'd want to know who George was. He'd want to know why you went on without him and had a fourth husband."

"You're right Lib. My life has gone on without Bill."

"That's what Phil was saying. What if there is no a place for Anna Mae in theirs? Here's another thing. Anna Mae's so mousey I can picture her going to a lawyer and just sending them money."

They fanned themselves in heat.

"She might do that. Actually, my dear friend, what Anna Mae does, after you hand her your note is none of our business."

"True. Life's a bundle isn't it?"

"You've got that right."

*****

Early the next afternoon, Libby stepped into the tiny office of Charlie's Auto Repair Shop. The smells of grease, oil, metal, hung thick in the air, as did the whine of a machine grinding something beyond the door marked, 'No Amateurs Allowed'.

"I hate to bother you, Charlie, but could you please stop a second and look for my bill. You didn't have it ready when I picked up my car, last week. I've called twice, and now I'm here in person."

He frowned at her, shuffled through mounds of papers on his long desk. Picking out one, he leaned on the cluttered counter between them and waved a bill smudged with dirty fingerprints.

"I hate to lose a good customer like you, but please, buy a new car. Or, if you want to keep coming here, I can help you find a good used car."

She shook her head as she took her bill.

"That beater you have is on its last mile. It's going to drop dead any day now and that could happen up on the Freeway. I almost didn't fix it this time. In fact." He paused, looked hard at her. "I'm serious. Get a better car."

Her phone sang out that Cece was calling.

"I have to get this."

"I've found her son! Found her son!!!" Cece's shouting over the phone made Charlie lean back.

"I told you, you would."

"You won't believe what he found. I've already called Ginger. She'll be here in about a half hour, you too."

She handed Charlie her credit card. "I gotta go."

Twenty minuets later she was climbing into the front seat of Ginger's car parked around a few blocks from Cece's house.

Ginger pressed a button and shut off her calming CD. "Did Cece scream at you when she called?"

"Nearly threw my phone out of my hand."

"She's going nuts over this thing."

"By thing, you mean Anna Mae." Libby started to reach for her seat belt then remembered they were parked and going nowhere.

She turned to face Ginger. "I've been talking to Julio about her."

"Julio? Oh good. You're dating now."

"No, Julio is my replacement bird for Harry the Canary."

"I hope he's smarter than Harry the Canary."

"Smarter?"

"Harry told you we should go to that MADD protest didn't he?"

"He also told me I should like Ginger no matter what she said."

"Okay. What did Julio have to say?"

"Well, since he's new to the consulting business, he didn't chirp much. He had to make his point by turning his back on me when I said Anna Mae was none of my business."

"And that said?" Ginger looked at her watch.

"Look at me. Perched here all alone, looking at a wall. Then I imagined Anna Mae sitting in a dark room, holding two small toys against her chest. I decided she stole them from a box of toys Benny left in the hall for the neighbor kids."

Libby turned to look out the side window, tried to take in a deep breath, but it hurt. "I'm so ashamed of me. All I've been thinking about is how she let Benny hurt them. I didn't give any thought to reality and that he was impossible to stop. She lost everything a mother wants by sending them away."

Ginger squeezed Libby's shoulder. "Don't feel bad. I was angry with her until George mentioned how painful their passing birthdays must have been."

"I know. She's had a terrible life." Libby wiped a tear dripping from her chin.

"Yes, and it seems she was all alone after she lost touch with her sister."

A truck rumbled by.

"So, Ginger. I say we jump in. See if we can become her friends."

"If she wants us."

"I think she will. Now I'd better get out so we can get over to Cece's."

"Wait. Lib, we forgot all about Cece. I'm sure she's up to something. You remember yesterday Cece went out of her way to bring us lunch at my house. That's very suspicious. Now she's insisting we rush over here because she's located Anna Mae's children, or son. She rushes people when she wants something from them."

"So, what do we do? Your real estate scuffles with Cece must have taught you something we can use."

"Yes. We have to slow her down. Take a potty break. Change the topic. Do something to get her off track so we can think." Ginger reached back, took her phone our of her purse, tapped in a few things then put it back.

"There, that will ring in thirty minutes and George will need me at home."

"Perfect."

Five minutes later, Libby parked in front of Cece's just as Ginger was getting out of her car. Walking together up to the cozy two-story house, Cece's door flew open before they could ring the doorbell.

"It's a scorcher today Come in out of the heat."

Inside, Ginger twirled, sniffed, stepped into Cece's living room, spun around to study the walls, one at a time.

"What are you looking for?" Cece's eyes narrowed.

"Signs of painting. Yesterday you told Libby that lunch had to be at my house because your house was being painted. I don't smell paint. I don't see anything that says painting was, or is, about to begin."

Cece gave Libby a dark look as if the lie were Libby's doing. "We canceled that because of the price. I've such exciting news. Anna Mae's son lives up in Sedona. Isn't that wild? He's only a three hour drive away."

"It's a four hour drive, Cece."

"Well, that's closer than L.A. or New York or Cairo. He could be anywhere in the world, Ginger."

Libby looked around her landlady's living room. If it weren't for the grand piano sitting in a far corner, it could be called the quiet room. Two sofa's, three whicker chairs, all done in pastel greens, blue, rose, against a back ground of soft white walls made her want to whisper. The only bright color in the room was the red fluid in a pitcher sitting on the coffee table separating the two sofas and Ginger's turquoise blouse. She corrected herself to add Cece's red hair.

"I've made us a pitcher of my very berry, smoothies. No alcohol."

Ginger, remembered sweet comments like Cece's from years ago, when she was drying out. "Ginger, I'm so happy you suggested I use my guy. He found Anna Mae's son in five short hours."

A pang of pity hit Libby and "Five hours?" popped out of her mouth.

Pasternak had her information in less than an hour. She brightened. Maybe Cece had found Anna Mae's daughter.

Cece nodded and sat down on one of the sofas. "Yes, Libby. I did think locating a person by the name of Timothy Mathew Thurgood would go quicker." She held out a folder for them.

Libby and Ginger sat opposite her, leaned forward, to take the light blue folder with CeCe Fontaine Properties embossed across the top.

"The names and birth dates on this match the information in her diary." Cece tapped the paper. "Until they graduated from high school, they lived up in Jerome with their aunt and uncle. Then her son went in the army for, I think, four years."

Already knowing that, Libby for show, peered at the paper facing them. "Yes. I see it here. Four years."

"There's a space of time unaccounted for, but eventually he went to the University right here in Tucson." She looked at them. "Can you imagine that? Their son walking right by them on the sidewalk? I feel so sorry for her. My daughter ran away for a week. I was in a panic."

Cece brightened, sat back. "Now he's a high school teacher in Sedona and married with three grown children. There's no mention of his sister after graduation."

"We women get married. Change our names. Sometimes several times."

Cece had so much less in her report that Libby decided she should bring the guys at station house cornbread to go with the chili. Should she tell Cece her guy ripped her off? No. Then Cece could figure out she'd held back her information.

Ginger took a piece of chocolate sitting on a dish next to the pitcher of the very berry stuff. Biting in, something awful insulted her mouth. Chewing fast, she swallowed the horrible piece before it could kill her taste buds.

"What is this stuff?"

"Isn't it marvelous? It's synthetic chocolate, fake sugar, some tofu, lots of antioxidants all rolled up together with oats inside. Oh yes, there's some cinnamon and ginger mixed in too."

"I didn't know they could do that."

Ginger put the rest of the dreadful thing on her napkin as Cece poured three glasses of pureed red stuff and ice.

"She's so lucky her son lives in Sedona. It got me so excited, I called him to say I know his mother."

"What?"

"No! You didn't."

Libby and Ginger nearly knocked over the glasses.

"I did. When no one answered, I didn't think it would be right to leave him a message."

Ginger swallowed a string of cuss words before she could finally find her voice. "That was a hell of a thing to do!"

"Oh, I know." Pride radiated from Cece. "It was gutsy of me. But, that's just the way I am. I take the bull by the horns."

"That's not what I meant, Cece. What I meant was that you are either an imbecile or inhuman."

"Right!" Libby hit the sofa with her fist. "You can't contact him and open a door Anna Mae shut all those years ago."

Cece just stared at them.

"Lib's right. Anna Mae has to contact her children. Not you."

"And why isn't she here? You said she was to be discharged this morning."

"I was only trying to help." Tears finally filled Cece's pale blue eyes. "It got moved to late tomorrow, or the next day. A bladder test; or something like that. I wanted him to know his mother is alive. That's all."

Ginger tilted her head at Cece. "Why would you do that? You know better than to stick your nose in her business."

The quick flash of guilt on Cece's face wasn't missed by either of them.

"I was so excited I didn't think." Cece slowly stirred the blood-red mixture in the pitcher. "What do we do now that we know where he is?"

Ginger took a small sip of her blood red mixture, put it down. "For starters, you give her your information."

"Me? Why not one of you? She trusts you two. She gave you her gun. She gave you her life's secrets for cripes sake."

Cece took one of the chocolate things, bit in, chewed, shook a little, then swallowed it.

"And I wouldn't be in this conversation if you hadn't given me the journal to read. You need to talk to her."

When they didn't say anything she gave them a small smile. "Look, let's just put all that behind us. I'm glad I told you about me holding the ladder. At least I can talk to you."

She held up her hands to stop them from talking. "I need her out of Tucson fast." She sat back. "I guess that's why I tried to call her son. Maybe, if I tell her about her son, you two could convince her to fly up to Sedona."

"Fly to Sedona?" Libby looked at Ginger. "You ever hear of anything so impossible?"

Ginger shook her platinum head. "Nope. You know Anna Mae is far too timid to fly. Just get to what you want from us, it's getting late."

Cece gave off a coarse laugh. "It's just my panic speaking. What are our options? A bus ride would bring back such painful memories for Anna Mae. That leaves driving. She does have a perfectly good car and it's an easy drive, except for going around Phoenix."

"You want her to drive when she never drove further than the nearest shopping center? Benny was always saying that."

"Well no. I was thinking she could hire a driver."

"A stranger." Libby shook her head. "How about you drive her?"

Ginger stood up. It was too early for her phone to ring and Libby was getting too involved.

"I can't. My daughter is due to deliver her baby next week. I know. You two take her up there. My expense."

Ginger edged her way around the coffee table. Libby followed her.

Cece was close behind them. "Wait. Stop. My brain really is not working today."

Ginger turned around. "That's true. Just give Anna Mae your information. It's up to her to decide what to do next."

"What? No! Anna Mae will just get a lawyer and send money."

Cece wedged herself between them and the door. "If we don't do something, she'll never, ever see her children. And they'll never know what she gave up to save them from his cruelty."

"Then you take her after your daughter has her baby."

Cece pressed her back against the door and held tight to the doorknob. "The longer Anna Mae stays in Tucson the more likely she'll remember I held onto his ladder and go to the police."

"Stop with the paranoid stuff. You've beaten it to death, Cece."

"My problem is real. Once police start looking at me they'll dig up my police record and decide I did it."

Police record echoed around the room and, in their heads.

"You probably won't believe me, but please hear me out."

Cece pressed her lips together to stop them from quivering. "My first husband routinely punched me around. The day I finally understood it would never end, I got out his baseball bat to teach him a lesson and went to where he was fixing the car in the driveway and hit him on the back of his legs. When he fell, I hit his hands. I did it all outside so our neighbors would see and protect me.

Instead, I was arrested on battery charges and got a year in jail with three years probation. By the time I got out our divorce was final and he'd found himself another fool. He's the reason why I kept an eye on Anna Mae. He's why I can't get involved in a police investigation even though it was a long time ago. That's why I don't dare count on Anna Mae to stay away from the police."

She let go of the door. "I can show you the papers. Jack knows all this, but our kids don't."

"No, we don't need to see the papers. It's all over your face."

Ten minutes later they were walking out the door with an agreement. Cece would go to the hospital and give Anna Mae her the information about her son. Then mention Ginger and Libby had offered to drive her up to Sedona to see her son. Cece would also pay all trip expenses. Libby would have a month's free rent and Ginger a hundred dollar donation for Emerge, Tucson's Center Against Domestic Abuse. Cece could not contact any of Anna Mae's family or all agreements were off.

"Cece's jail time was a shocker." Libby muttered out of the side of her mouth as they walked away. "I watched her face crumble when she told us. Her perfection façade is beginning to crack and I'm beginning to like Cece."

"You go right ahead. It'll take my time to let go of all our real estate head butting." Ginger's phone rang saying George was calling.

"Well, I didn't time that right."

Reaching her car, Ginger faced Libby. "I agreed to this monumental undertaking because I need a diversion until I can get into treatment."

"Taking Anna Mae to see her son will certainly be a diversion for both of us. I agreed to it because I haven't been to Sedona in years."

Seeing Ginger press her thumb to the door, then it opened, Libby got her car keys out of her purse.

"It looks like we all got what we wanted, except we completely ignored what Anna Mae might want."

Ginger leaned on her open door. "We did, didn't we? We just assumed we'd talk Anna Mae into going, even if she doesn't want to go."

"Yup. We planned it all as if she didn't even exist."

Chapter 22

Anna Mae stared at the door Cece had just shut behind her as she left, then hugged herself in disbelief. Cece had said she wanted to stay and visit longer, but she'd thanked her over and over then, politely asked her to go. Cece had found her son. Her Timothy. Her little boy who was all grown up now. She knew that much from the pictures in Benny's cabinet.

"My son is alive and he lives in Sedona." Anna Mae said out loud, turned and said it to the TV in her small, very white, hospital room then said it to the chair. Her heart filled with light, as it had done on the day he was born. Picking up the piece of paper from her bed table, she put her finger on his address. Her Timothy lived right there. It said so on the paper.

The man who'd found her son had told Cece that Sarah was probably married. That would change her name, and that was why he couldn't find her Sarah. Tim had kept his name. She'd always worried he'd change it like Benny made them do. so he could never be found.

Her heart was racing so fast it made it hard to breathe. Timothy would know where his sister was. He would know where her Sarah was.

She crawled up onto the bed, pulled her knees to her chest. She'd waited for this moment from the time her children's bus drove out of sight.

Joy, happiness, swirled inside her so intensely, it just had to be true. Not a dream. She pressed Cece's paper to her chest. Pressed his address to her heart. Her son had a home, a wife, three children. There was even a telephone number. Proof that he was alive. She could pick up the phone and call him right now. Imagine that, she could call him. Again she said, thank you Cece for bothering to find my son.

She was so happy she needed something to shake. Getting off the bed, she took a pillow, shook it, then hugged it in joy.

"My son lives up in Sedona." She went to the window, looked at the courtyard below. Many people were walking around. A man and woman with their arms around each other. A man carrying a small child on his shoulders. A woman alone on a bench, and a few feet away a man sat eating something. None of them were aware of the each other's worries or joy. None of them knew her son had been found. If she could only open the window and shout it to them she knew they'd smile, then continue with their own business, just as she was doing.

Loneliness flooded her, making her step back. Unsettled feelings swirled around her so thick she could pluck them from the air. Yes, her son had been found but would he want to see her? She wiped away the tears rolling down her face as she paced her small room always looking at the telephone. Staring at it. Willing it to ring and say, *Hi Mom, it's me Timothy.* But it sat silent. She could pick it up right now and call him. It was near suppertime, her son might be home. She didn't have to say a word. Just listen to his voice or, if someone else answered, she'd know that person belonged to her son.

No, she couldn't call him from here. The hospital staff was always walking into her room. Breakfast, dinner, pills, make her bed, tests, time to wash up, talk to the psychiatrist again. They said she couldn't go home until they decided she was mentally stable.

Her therapists understood her anger when she'd found the pictures Benny had of her children with her sister Ruth and Charlie. One therapist thought her shooting Benny's grave was funny. None of them liked that she'd pointed her gun at all those women, but she could tell they were beginning to believe she would never do it again. And it wouldn't.

Cece's paper would prove to them that her children were real, not made up. Cece had said her son was a science teacher at Sedona High School. Teachers were kind. They were smart. They thought other people were important. And he had three children. She was a grandmother. She went to her tiny closet, picked up a white plastic bag holding her clothing and hid the paper in the toe of her shoe. She couldn't have the doctors calling her son. Her children were her business.

Would her son now look like his father? She wouldn't like that. Would Sarah look like Benny's mother? That wouldn't be good either.

She smiled. Timothy must have done well in school. He was a teacher. And Sarah looked so sure of herself in her graduation gown. She must have done well too.

"Did my children play sports? Join the band?" She had so many questions to ask, but the paper had no answer.

She started to curl up on the bed, feel sorry for herself but stopped. Benny was dead. She was free to go to her children, find out if they wanted her. Maybe Ruth and Charlie were near. She still had many years ahead to share with them, watch them, love them. She had grandchildren.

She went to her bathroom, washed her face. Looked in the mirror. What was she thinking? Go see them? They would not want her. She was the mother who's stood by while their father hurt them. Timothy would remember she tried to stop it all. But Sarah? Sarah would hate her. She'd torn Sarah from her beloved Daddy. A little girl of four, so full of laughter, wouldn't know that the man who made her laugh, helped her with her puzzles, played hide and seek, built her a swing, read to her at night, had made the blood stain her panties. All Sarah knew was that her Mother sent her away from her beloved Daddy.

And now Cece had said, Ginger and Libby were busy making plans for a big reunion.

Benny had controlled her all her life, she wasn't going to let them, or others, do the same.

*****

Mid morning, two days later, Libby and Ginger were walking up to Anna Mae's front door. A door neither had ever entered.

"I don't think we should start with offering to take her to meet her son up in Sedona. Do You?" Libby looked at Ginger.

"No. Let's see how it flows. It would be better if we could get her to ask us to take her."

"In other words, manipulate her. That's no better than Benny making all her decisions."

"Let's call it giving Anna Mae her options and letting her decide."

"Ah, now we are sounding like politicians."

"And sales people, Libby. It's the way I got people to buy their dream home."

They knocked several times and were about to leave when the door flew open and they jumped back. Libby let out a feeble hello.

"I startled you. I'm sorry. After Benny died one person after another came here trying to sell me things. I had to listen at the door until I heard your voices. Cece told me you'd be here but not when."

Anna Mae motioned them in and shut the door against the late morning heat.

"I tried calling you both from the hospital, but neither of you are ever in. I have to apologize for what I did to you and everyone. I'm so sorry I pointed Benny's gun at everyone. I didn't mean to. I really thought that man was stealing my TV."

Libby nodded. Relieved to be invited in, Libby was surprised when Anna Mae wouldn't meet her eyes.

"It took me a day or two to remember that I gave you my little book. I don't know why I did. I've never been one to tell people my secrets, but ever since Benny's death, I've been so mixed up in my head."

The words had rushed out of Anna Mae.

"We felt honored when you gave us your book, Anna Mae." Libby hoped Anna Mae had forgotten she'd said *for your eyes only*. We should have asked if we could share it with Cece."

I'm so glad you did, because now Cece's found my son."

"Your gun was unnerving." Ginger said as she looked around the darkened room. When she didn't know someone very well she usually was able to comment on how nice their home was. Her realtor's eagle eye always assessed a home as if it were for sale. This place would be hard to sell.

The smells assaulting her nose were of dusty, old furniture. And something else? Ginger took in a breath. Yes, sawdust, turpentine, other chemicals that must have seeped in from Benny's furniture repair business. The house had been built before the air conditioning was put in. The living room had the typical small, high, widows meant to keep as much of the Arizona heat out. It was quite obvious no one cared what seeped in from the garage.

There was very little natural light. Two dim floor lamps cast a yellow glow onto the fifties styled stuffed furniture. None of it looked good enough to have ever been on someone's 'to buy' list. What could one say about it? Cozy? Quaint? Charming? Even Anna Mae would see through that. Now she was being a snob. This house had been their home.

"Anna Mae!" Libby's near shout, startled Ginger. "You've got the very same lamp Phil's mother gave us on our tenth anniversary."

"I do? Where?" Some of the tension drained from Anna Mae's face and she almost smiled.

"Over there." Libby pointed to a square lampshade sitting on top of a dull gray, round, ceramic base.

Anna Mae smiled. "That's at least thirty-five years old. They made things to last back then. We got it in a second hand store. Benny put in new wiring."

Libby, giving thanks to her years of raising money, was able to jabber on about small things like a lamp, when she so wanted to spit out, why didn't you just leave him? Her feelings pulled her in every direction. She felt compassion for Anna Mae then, even without Anna Mae speaking she switched to not liking her one bit. These were the times envied those who could take one side and stubbornly stick to it. Her mind always seemed to be arguing with her heart and confusing her.

Ginger studied the lamp and decided Libby was lying. She'd never seen anything that ugly in Lib's house. The stifling heat in Anna Mae's house, arguing with Cece yesterday, her not drinking, had given her a nagging, back of the head, headache. Not drinking. Damn! Why did she always go back to thinking about not drinking? She was foolish to think she could she do it on her own for at least ten more days. Ginger sat down on the rumpled brown chair and fanned herself.

It was early in the day and she already felt out of steam. Another ugly sign that age was creeping up on her. She thought about that. No, her age wasn't creeping up on her, the threat that it could was nibbling at her. She had to shut those thoughts out. Thinking old would get her old fast. She still ran three miles a day, three times a week. Her shoulders were fine; she could swim laps and played a damn decent game of golf or tennis. Dance most of the evening away. And now she was going to start a business with her husband.

"I'm sorry I can't offer you gals a cold drink. I've just gotten back here and I've no ice."

Anna Mae's voice brought her back to the present.

"How are all the other people I frightened?"

"They're calming down. You gave them something to talk about for awhile."

Libby laughed at Ginger's comment, then wondered why the first thing out of Anna Mae's mouth hadn't been to ask about her children. Sitting down in a chair next to Ginger's, she watched Anna Mae twist her hands, look around the room as if she didn't know where to sit.

"Since Benny died, his ghost sits in that chair all the time." She nodded toward an old recliner chair halfway across the long room.

"He's why I moved into Cece's apartment building. Benny never liked Cece so his ghost didn't go over there with me. Now that I'm back here, so is he."

Ginger looked at the chair. Benny as a ghost. That was an unexpected surprise. Unexpected surprise? Weren't all surprises unexpected? Well, she had one. Today, with almost every breath she took, she wanted a drink. Not so yesterday. Today she turned almost anything into a drinking issue. She couldn't remember it happening before when she quit drinking. Yes, it had, but she'd been in rehab with lots of distractions.

Before, she'd always thought she could get well enough to go back to moderate drinking. This time her not drinking was forever. She looked at her hands. Good they didn't even feel like shaking today. Maybe she was gaining control. There, that was an unexpected nice surprise.

"Sometimes I see Phil." Libby nodded toward Benny's chair. "But I loved him, so I like him around."

Libby saw Phil's ghost? She'd never mentioned it. Ginger tried to raise an eyebrow, but it didn't move. Lib wasn't paying any attention to her anyway.

Anna Mae was standing behind a chair near them, looking as if it protected her from Benny's ghost.

"I never loved mine, not even in the beginning. After I shot his casket to pieces I was sure he'd go away but, he was here just before you knocked on the door."

Trying to banish the somber atmosphere, Ginger smiled at Anna Mae.

"I still have a great picture in my head of you shooting up his grave. I say hurrah for you."

"Really? You aren't just saying that? You don't think I was crazy?"

"Benny deserved every bullet for all that he did to you and your children."

"Well, he didn't dare visit me in the hospital, but he is over there right now, watching and listening to us."

Libby stared at the empty, dark brown, recliner, near a newer TV, the only newer thing in the room. "I believe he is."

"Thank you, Libby. He either sits in his chair or bounces on his bed in the other room. He kept me up all last night. He's why I lost so much weight living here alone. Benny wasn't at Cece's, but I can't go back there after what I did."

Ginger looked at her. "Get rid of the bed and chair."

"He'll sit somewhere else."

"True." Libby nodded. "I think we can make Benny's ghost disappear just like that." She snapped her fingers.

Going to his chair, she sat down hard, got up, sat down harder. Repeated it several times then beckoned Ginger to her. "Want to have a go at him?"

"Be glad to." Ginger flounced over to the chair, turned around, lifted her skirt, gave off a little gas, waved it at the chair.

"Shoo. Go away. This isn't your house anymore. Scoot."

She looked at Anna Mae.

"Is he still here?"

"Yes."

"Then it's your turn to do something about him."

They beckoned Anna Mae to them.

"Put your foot on the chair. Now stand on the seat. Libby and I'll hold you. We won't let you fall."

Her whole body shaking, Anna Mae put her good foot on the seat then hopped up like a child.

"Now stomp him out." Ginger and Libby steadied Anna Mae as she lifted one foot, then the other. Marching as if she were in a band.

"Stomp 'till you can't breathe."

Anna Mae sped up to almost fast. Quickly out of breath, she stopped. "He's gone. I felt him go."

As they helped her down, Libby patted her on the back. "Well done. Now, lets finish him off. You had a cat. Do you still have its litter box?"

"I've three in the laundry room. I couldn't bear to throw them away."

"Three! That's perfect! We'll put them to good use."

Libby went to the laundry room, picked up a clean litter box and marched over to Benny's chair. She considered dumping the contents onto the chair, but instead, she sat it firmly on the seat.

"My turn." Ginger shook a second box. "Where's Benny's room?"

"Follow me." Anna Mae turned, went past the dining room table, down a short dark hall and into Benny's room. "In here."

Ginger, looking at his narrow bed with its ugly plaid bedspread, sat her litter box where his pillow would be. "His ghost'll get a good whiff of that, and won't come back. Now you, Anna Mae."

Anna Mae held a third box over the area where Benny's private parts would have been. Tilting it sideways they watched its contents spill onto the bed.

Libby smiled. "I think the dust floating into the air is Benny."

Tears streamed down Anna Mae's face as she nodded. "I should have thought of that. Benny hated my cats."

Going back to the living room, Ginger sat down again on the worn brown chair. Three chairs in the room, but no sofa. Anna Mae must have taken it with her. She'd enjoyed the litter boxes but this was taking too long. They still had to discuss Sedona.

"You haven't said anything about seeing your children."

Anna Mae fell into her chair, having friends wasn't so bad. Maybe they could help her to decide what to do about her children.

"No, I haven't. I was so sure they were gone from me forever. I could hardly breathe after Cece told me she'd found my son. I hope it's not a mistake."

Libby was surprised when her hand reached out and patted Anna Mae's shoulder.

"It's not a mistake. I also had someone look for your son." Libby handed Anna Mae the information Pasternak had gotten.

"A man with the same name, birth place and date that's in your journal, is alive and living in Sedona. Neither Cece's detective or mine could locate your daughter, but I've found out she is alive because I called your son's house."

"What?" Ginger gave her a hard look. They'd agreed not to forewarn him that his mother was alive.

"Yup. Last evening I called his home. When a woman answered I asked her if she was Sarah Thurgood. She said no; she was her sister-in-law. So I said I needed Sarah's telephone number because she'd won ten thousand dollars and all she had to do was to send me and the the woman hung up before I said what she was to send. Which was good because I didn't know what she should send and to whom."

Ginger's laugh filled the room. "You are one sneaky woman."

It took several minutes for Anna Mae to stop rocking back and forth muttering Sarah too, Sarah too.

"I had to send my children away. Benny was hurting them. You do understand that, don't you?"

133

The anguish on Anna Mae's face, the way she couldn't look at them, melted Ginger's anger with her. It had been so easy to rain down scorn on Anna Mae after reading her journal, but not now.

"It must have been an excruciating decision."

Anna Mae brushed Ginger's comment aside as if she didn't deserve consideration, and turned to Libby. "Do you think I'm a horrible mother?"

The nicer answer would be, *no you aren't,* but Libby just couldn't say that when Anna Mae seemed to be asking for the truth, as they believed it.

"Because I hate abusers, I've gone up and down over this. Your journal made me so angry with you and Benny. I thought it was simple. You should have either reported him or run away with your children. A few nights ago changed that when a news flash said an abuser had just killed his wife and two kids. You did the only thing possible to keep your kids safe, Anna Mae by sending them to what you were sure was a loving home. You sacrificed your happiness for theirs, and put yourself in danger."

Anna Mae stood up, went down the hall, looked at the litter on Benny's bed, turned around and came back to Libby and Ginger.

"Cece wants me to go to Sedona to see my children. She said you two have agreed to drive me up there."

"Please sit down so we can talk. We thought it would be easier on you if we offered to take you, but just talk to us. Tell us how we can help."

Ginger leaned forward in her chair. "First, how did you and Benny change your names? I know you can go to court and do it, but I'm thinking he didn't."

Her years of selling real estate had taught her to talk far from the problem at hand; it often helped her gain her client's trust.

Anna Mae smiled at her.

"Benny found out that when a person died it never got connected to their birth record. So we went to a few cemeteries in Phoenix, and took names from the graves of very young children of our sex, born in our year of birth. Benny thought that most young children who died had lived near where they were born. We sent in a request to the Phoenix government for their birth certificate as if we were them. Once we had their birth certificates we got social security numbers then we got married under our new names."

"It was that easy?"

"Not exactly. The first birth certificate Benny asked for came back saying birth unknown. He figured the child wasn't born in Phoenix so asked for a different certificate."

"So why did he change your names?"

"He didn't want anyone to find us. He felt really bad for hurting our daughter, and he promised me he'd never hurt another child ever again if I stayed with him."

Anna Mae looked down at her hands. "My son's a school teacher."

She looked up, smiling. "That means he had to go to college doesn't it?"

They both nodded.

"I don't know if I can face my children. I could get a lawyer to say I died with Benny then divide my estate between Timothy and Sarah with the suggestion they give my sister Ruth and her husband some of the money for all they must have done for them."

"What?" Libby glanced at the chair with the kitty litter pan and ignored the tears rolling down Anna Mae's wrinkled face.

"Send money to your children and they will know you knew where they lived and never bothered to contact them. You'd devastate your children!"

Leaning forward, Ginger felt more like marching out than talking. "Yes. Better you give your damn money to charity."

"Not only that." Libby waved at Anna Mae to get her to look her in the face. "Most young kids, like Sarah and Tim, blame themselves for trouble in their family. They take the blame for everything that goes wrong with their parents."

Libby leaned forward like Ginger. "See them and you have a chance to undo that."

Anna Mae let out a low moan and started talking to herself.

Libby hissed to Ginger. "What do we do now?"

"I'm alright. But I'm old and my children will think I'm there because I want them to take care of me."

"Limp excuse, Anna Mae. At sixty-five, or whatever you are, you are not old."

"You know where they are. You need to see your children."

Ginger sat back, she was ready to leave if this kept going this way.

Anna Mae sucked in a breath then, in a shaking voice, mumbled "I'm scared of my daughter, really scared of what she'll say to me."

"So what? We all get scared of things. No excuses. We will go up to Sedona, drive around the town where your son and maybe your daughter lives. Drive by the school where he teaches. Park near his house, watch people come and go. We don't have to go up to his door. Maybe Sarah will show up. If she doesn't, we'll try something like Libby did. Try and trick them into giving out her address then see where it goes from there."

Anna Mae sat up straight. "Really? I can just look at his house? I don't have to actually talk to him?"

Then she got up, limped to Benny's chair and hit it over and over. "You can just get out of here!"

Going back to her chair, she sat down, and pressed her fists to her face. "I am so confused about what to do. My children could love me or hate me. I see a reunion where they hate me then I picture us running into each other's arms. I don't know if I'm strong enough to do this."

She sat back, sighed. "It might help if I could see their faces, even from a distance. Then, with you two beside me, maybe I can talk to my children and tell them what really went on and why I did what I did. You are right; they need to know the truth."

Surprised by Anna Mae's sudden surrender, Ginger cleared her tight throat, to make her words come out firm and clear.

"Then tomorrow morning we'll drive up to Sedona."

Ginger didn't know she was fully committed to the trip until she'd actually said it.

Libby joined in. "Yes. If we leave early in the morning, we'll get to Sedona in time for lunch and some sight seeing."

"Perfect." Ginger swished a thick strand of platinum hair off her forehead. "You must see Sedona, Anna Mae. Surrounded by magnificent red rocks, it's gorgeous. Some even call it a magical place. Good things will happen to us up there, I just know it and tomorrow's Friday. Your son will be working. We can drive by his house as many times as you want. You might even see him outside."

Anna Mae smiled. "Is it really that easy? After all these years?"

"Yes." Ginger pushed on the chair arm to get up from the sagging chair. "There are lots of great places up there. I'll book us into a peaceful hotel so we can relax a little. We'll be here by nine tomorrow morning and get on our way."

The plan had rolled off her tongue without her thinking at all. It was as if she were back to her old self.

Anna Mae looked at them from her chair. "You have to promise me you won't pressure me to meet my son."

"We promise." The lie had rolled easily off Ginger's tongue.

Libby nodded her agreement.

"Then I'll be ready. I could never do this on my own. I can't thank you enough for doing this for me."

They were half way out the door when Anna Mae shouted, "No! Wait!"

Ginger shut her eyes. Libby ground her teeth and turned around.

"The most miserable drive of my life was leaving Phoenix and my kids to come down here. I've never had the courage to go near that highway since. And I know I can't bear to see Phoenix. Can we leave here when it's still dark? Say about four?"

"Four in the morning? I'd only get up at that time if my house was on fire." Ginger shook her head.

"Come on, Ginger. You could do it just this once. I bet you've never even seen a sunrise."

"Please." Anna Mae had come over to them.

"Leaving at four means I'd have to get up at three. We'll leave at five." Ginger couldn't believe she'd said that.

"And I have seen pictures of a sunrise. They look just like a sunset."

Chapter 23

Anna Mae watched Ginger and Libby drive away, then let her curtain drop. They just didn't understand her life. They hadn't lived with a monster day in and day out, dodging his rages over nothing. Being careful with her every word. Never disagreeing with him, but never agreeing too readily. That was when he called her an ass kisser, or he'd kick her ass.

She'd dreamt up trick after trick to stop him from hitting their children. Promised him the moon, if only he'd calm down. Many times she jumped between her husband and their son to take the beatings. She'd even held Benny's arms. Pulled him back whenever he'd let her. Benny had shredded Timothy with words so often that he'd quit baseball; the only thing her son loved.

Rushing into her bedroom, she grabbed the large envelope from the hospital bag with her belongings. Tearing it open, she looked at the photos of her children Benny had somehow taken at Sarah's high school graduation. She kissed them, held them close to her heart. In the hospital she'd tried and tried to figure out where the pictures were taken, how Benny found out where they were living. She shouldn't care about that anymore. She had the pictures. He was dead. Now she could go see their grown children. Find out how they'd done without her. She smiled. Benny couldn't do anything about that.

Collapsing onto her chair she stared at the picture of Timothy. He had a lanky body and he was wearing a military uniform. She'd decided he'd been in the Army. Sarah was tall and beautiful in her graduation gown.

"My Timothy. My Sarah." Saying their names out loud in this house felt so strange. She'd never done that while Benny was alive. Not even when he was gone off somewhere, because he always came back.

To stop her tears, she pressed her hands to her cheeks. If she saw her children, what would she say to them? Would they believe her? She sighed. Timothy and Sarah looked so happy. It was best she leave them that way.

Through all the years, she'd kept her small children frozen in time, but the photos reminded her they'd grown up and she'd missed it all. She was a little hurt that they were happy without her. What kind of mother was she to feel that way? She quickly packed the pictures away, went into the bathroom and splashed water on her face, combed her hair.

Tomorrow would be here soon. Time to go to the store to buy a nice traveling outfit. She didn't want them to think of her as shabby. And at least shopping, would get her away from his ghost for a little while. Ginger had said she should get a swimsuit, but a swimsuit was out of the question. There'd be no time for fun.

*****

Libby turned to look at Ginger now that they were out in the sun. She looked weary. Her color, always perfect, was a little pale today. Not drinking seemed to be taking its toll on her friend. Dealing with Anna Mae's family problems could make Ginger want to drink.

"We're going to do our darnedest to get her to face her children. Right?"

"Absolutely, Lib. Do you have a swimsuit? I've a feeling we'll be needing some pool time."

"I've an ancient one. The Bordello doesn't have a pool. I just hope A M, as you call her, doesn't worry-whine all the way up to Sedona like she did at her door as we were leaving. My fingers just itched to reach over and pinch her mouth shut."

"She wasn't whining, Lib." Ginger made a left turn, then headed toward home.

"She wasn't?" Libby tilted her head. "Let me quote her. I don't have the right clothes. I've no nice over-night bag. I need a haircut. I need to shave my legs. All that when she doesn't plan on seeing them. She went on and on and 'ad infinitum.'" Libby paused, smiled.

"How'd you like that? At least my brain cells haven't lost all my Latin lessons."

"Lotta good Latin'll do you these days. And AM wasn't whining, Lib. She was making a list. It's what most women do. Not you so much, but the rest of us have oodles of things to do before going on a trip."

"Okay, call it a list. I just got irritated, that's all. Woman's wimpy personality drives me nuts. I think of all she's lost, and I start to feel unbearably sorry for her but I'm planning on putting her in your trunk if she whines past the outskirts of Tucson."

Libby adjusted her seat belt, pulled it away from her neck. "I guess it's me who's whining."

"Seems so. Split in half. I know what you mean. When George looks at another woman, I get so jealous. When he doesn't, I get scared he's lost his sex drive."

Ginger pulled up behind a small red convertible with its top down and remembered the days when her top was always down. Now, in her older age, the heat and the wind were too much for her thinning skin and hair. Moods had a lot to do with it too. Today her mood was definitely not a top down mood.

It was a gin-aide mood and that mood was simply out of the question. Stop! Stop! Damn! I've gotta stop thinking about drinking! Her head felt like it was about to explode. Their trip to Sedona could turn out to be one very long drive not just a distraction.

"Oh Lordy!" Libby almost shouted in her ear.

"What?" Ginger stomped on the brakes, looked left and right. "What?"

"We said five o'clock. That's gives AM plenty of time to skedaddle."

"Damn it, Libby! Skedaddle? You made me think I was about to hit something."

"Ooops. Sorry. We should go now, before she has second thoughts and runs out on us."

"Now? No way. It would be light out all the way to Phoenix and dark when we try to find Sedona. We will go at the stupid hour of five. If she wants to skedaddle, as you put it, she could be backing her car out of the garage right now."

Ginger smiled as she pulled into her driveway. Home at last. "Wait! Where's your lovely Rose Rita?"

"What?" Libby looked around. "Oh, for Pete's sake. It's at the Bordello! You picked me up, remember?"

Ten minutes later, Ginger dropped her off at her car. Libby waved goodbye then looked in at Rosa Rita's peeling dashboard. "

Okay Rosa Rita, you'll have to wait here while I go down to my storage bin and see if I've an overnight bag that doesn't look like a doctor's kit from the nineteen thirties. Ginger'll get us a nice room, a really nice room, probably in a swank hotel. So I will need to buy me a swimsuit. And some new slacks. Might as well get a new blouse too. Oh my, I've turned into one of those listy women Ginger was talking about."

An hour later, Libby stood up, arched her back in the dusty smelling cellar. She'd been rummaging through stacks of belongings from her and Phil's house and all she had to show for it was a sore back. Nothing even faintly resembling a decent overnight bag had surfaced. She'd found several boxes filled with desert artifacts. She'd have to look at them when she got back from Sedona.

"I could just give them to Birdie. The Daycare kids would love them."

"Give what to Birdie?"

Libby spun around and nearly dropped her box. "Dang it, Birdie! Cough. Or something. Warn me you are sneaking up on me!"

"Sorry. Warn you that I was sneaking up on you? You must have been terrible at hide and seek when you were a kid. When you said 'give them to Birdie' I figured you knew I was here." Birdie smiled.

Embarrassed, Libby balanced the wide box on her hip. "You're right, I was talking out loud. I've been doing that lately."

"I like talking to myself. I don't have to answer back if I don't want to." Birdie pointed to the box in Libby's arms. "Is that what you're thinking of giving me?"

Libby's irritation quickly settled down. Not smart to tick Birdie off, if she was going to dump this stuff on her.

"I've boxes and boxes of desert lore. Dried lizards, snakes, scorpions, cacti spines, red rocks. You name it. I've got it. I've artifacts from all over the Arizona desert. Phil used to call me the Collection Queen."

She shifted the box from her left hip to her right.

"Our foster kids loved the stories I conjured up about this stuff. Most kids start out scared to death of crawly things. Phil and I taught them to love the heat and sand of Arizona. Plus, everything crawling, walking around in it. We all got comfortable with our desert friends. In fact, most of our foster kids still live in Arizona."

"That says a lot about how good a mother you were to them."

Embarrassed, Libby shoved her box at Birdie. "Here."

"What am I supposed to do with it?"

"Pick through the stuff, show it to the Daycare kids. They'll love you for it."

Birdie, refusing the box, stepped back, hands up.

"No way. I'm not touching dried or dead bugs. Or any other of that kind of stuff. I'm a city person. You're the perfect person to conjure up stories for our kids. You know the desert."

"Really? If you're a city person, how'd you get Birdie for a nickname?" Libby sat her box on a chair, arched her back again.

"I used to be Bernice Birdsel. In the middle of fifth grade my friends and I decided we needed nicknames. They said I should be Bernie but I refused, saying we had a scary neighbor guy called Bernie. So my friends called me Birdie. My enemies called me BB eyes."

She peeked in the box, pulled her head back, waved her hand in front of her nose.

"Whew, that's a smell and a half. Libby, but it's a match made in heaven. Cece's free Daycare doesn't have an extra dollar and you've got free desert stuff. I can set up whatever time you want to teach the kids. You can change it every week, if that works better for you. The kids will be so excited to learn about the desert."

"I can't do it."

"Of course you can. You taught your foster kids. Do it for us."

"I don't have the time. Besides, we had sixteen foster kids, plus all their friends, I want to be with adults."

The scowl on Birdie's face, along with her beak-like nose, had Libby thinking 'she's going to peck me to death,'

"You don't have the time?" Birdie gave her the teacher's tilted head, eye squint, kind of look. The kind that sent lying children automatically to the chair in the corner.

"I swear just last week, you Libby Price, said to me that all the good volunteer positions have been sucked up by the sixty-year olds. That all they offered you was coffee making and filing. I'm offering you a gem and you can't be bothered?"

Birdie, waiting for her to say something, stared at the box, then looked at Libby.

"Okay, let's see what you've got in there. Maybe I can find someone to explain these things to the kids so you can play dead while you're still walking around."

Insulted by Birdie's comments, but not enough to do the teaching herself, Libby opened the lid and carefully lifted out one of her jewels; a dried rattlesnake skin.

"I'm amazed this is still in one piece. I was so excited when I found it."

She held it up to the light so Birdie could see through the skin but she hadn't counted on Birdie squirming a little. That wasn't good since she planned to ask Birdie to take care of Julio while she and Ginger were gone.

"It's almost impossible for the casual hunter to find a complete snake skin and I found three of them. Kids, especially girls, scream when they first see it then they want to know how it came off the snake and why. If you do it right, some kids will even get to like snakes."

"See? That's what I'm saying, Libby. Come on. Try it a time or two. We so badly need you and you'll love our kids. Teach them about the land they live in."

Libby shook her head no. "I've answered the same questions too many times."

"Not for my kids you haven't." Birdie's scowl made her uncomfortable.

"The invite stands. If you change your mind, just show up any day. We've some pretty bright five-year-olds, but this isn't why I tracked you down. I've great news. One of the women scheduled for our Alaskan cruise has had to back out. I asked for, and got, first dibs on replacing her. She's going to lose her deposit, so that will come off the price for whoever takes her place. I put your name down as being very interested. My travel club meets in three nights. You've got until then to snap it up. How's that sound to you?"

Dancers of the Third Age

The dim light of the cellar, the shadows falling across Birdie's face, didn't hide her concern for her. A flush of sadness rolled over Libby.

"Birdie, I just can't make myself go. Phil and I were going to go to Alaska and now he's gone. "

She gave a weak smile to Birdie. "I'd feel like a traitor."

"That's nuts. You'd be honoring him if you went."

Libby stepped away. "I can't go. I've more boxes just like this, full of more desert artifacts. You can share them all with the Daycare kids."

Birdie shook her head. "I think you're being a bit selfish. That's what I think, Liberty Price. I offer you a terrific opportunity to teach some very nice kids at your convenience. Offer you a fabulous trip with money off, and you refuse both. Might as well add that our ESL classes need you too. They are booming."

Birdie turned away, turned back again to glare at her. "None of these offerings comes with a guarantee you'll be happy, but, it's easy to see you aren't happy now. Some people, some, not you of course, but some people are so tied up by what they were, that they can't see who they can be. In fact, I just heard one groan that 70 is the beginning of the end. I've got news; the beginning of the end starts on the day we're born. Opportunity has knocked. It's up to you to open the door."

Then Birdie was gone. A slight rising of dust was all that was left to say she'd been there, and a twist in Libby's stomach and a realization she'd have to find someone else to watch Julio.

Muttering, "It's not as easy to change as you think." She sat down on a wooden chair, her box on her lap.

What was wrong with her? She really didn't have any excuse not to help out in the ESL classes. She spoke Mexican as well as anyone. Trouble was, she didn't like Lissa's bossy ways all that much and Lissa was the ESL leader. She did like Birdie so why not show the kids her desert artifacts? Staring at her box her heart twisted. The truth was it would hurt too much if she got attached to more kids who'd leave her life. She had grandkids from her three adopted children. She'd give them this stuff.

She hadn't thought it would be this hard getting old. She and Phil had planned for it; they hadn't planned for his death. They'd expected to continue their work of turning shacks into homes until they wanted to quit. Back then her days had been full. People needed her. Now, they needed her for coffee and pencil sharpening. Now, she was left in this limbo terror. She sighed. She was in good physical shape; no old age surgery, no memory loss.

She looked down at her clothes. Plain grey slacks, lemon yellow shirt. Boring. She'd once worn a tee shirt of a woman leaping in joy from one side of a canyon to the other. Where had that woman gone? Instead of leaping, she now stared into the abyss and saw the other side as unreachable. Simon and Garfunkel sang it right; her life was *slip sliding away*. She would not cry. She was tired of crying. She carefully put her box of artifacts away with her other memories.

"There you are."

She spun around to see Margot, the quiet widow of a doctor of something, coming down the stairs.

"Did Birdie send you to talk to me?"

"Birdie? No. I've not seen her. I've been looking for you for two days. I knocked on your door several times but you always seem to be out doing something. I didn't leave you a message on your machine because I wanted to thank you personally."

"For what?"

Margot actually walked up and hugged her. "For taking the gun away from Anna Mae before calling in the police."

Then she let go of Libby.

"The police could have misunderstood things. They do, you know. If they'd seen Anna Mae with her gun we could have had a shooting tragedy. I hope they've set her up with the right people at the hospital. She's so shy. I think Cece was wrong to tell us to stay away from her. I'll vote to let Anna Mae back in and I'll ignore Trish when Anna Mae returns. That said, I'm so glad I finally tracked you down. I do need your help."

Oh yes indeedie, Birdie had sent Margot after her.

"You and your husband renovated homes for the poor. Am I correct?"

"Yes." Libby squirmed a little. Another volunteer opportunity coming up.

"I've just come from my Yoga class where they have the most marvelous poster on the wall. It's a dance line of older women of all different sizes and colors. Tall, short, skinny, chunky, middle size, dark, light. One gal, with her ponytail flying high, reminds me so much of you. There's such joy on their faces as they lift their legs like the Rockets in New York City do. Mind you, they aren't in sync, but they look happy. Every time I see it I get the urge to turn these ugly storage rooms into a dance studio. That's where you come in, Libby."

"Me? I've never been a dancer."

Margot's laugh echoed around the large dark room. "Me either. I'm a clunker. Here's the thing that caught my attention. The poster is titled Dancers of The Third Age. Those women, look like all of us here at the Bordello. We are in our Third Age and most of us are doing it well. We're very busy, productive. Some, like Anna Mae, are stumbling a bit."

Libby was relieved not to hear her name on the stumbling list.

"Libby, experts are now saying that exercise keeps senility away a bit longer. I'd love that, wouldn't you?"

Not waiting for an answer, Margot continued. "Living here has made me feel so much younger. I've made friends who socialize, argue politics. I eat better. I've lost some weight. I'm so fired up I believe that together we can make the Bordello an even better place to spend our Third Ages."

Together We Can, echoed in Libby's head as she watched Margot turn on all the lights.

"Look around. I've measured these rooms. Instead of using it as a storage bin of our past lives we can turn this into a hundred square yards of dance space.

Last week I came down here, opened up my boxes and threw out almost all my history. It's lifted my spirit." Margot took in a breath.

"It could help us live years past our expiration dates. So, I need you to tell me if these two walls can be taken down and the door too?"

Margot spun around. "If we could take them out it would double the room size. After all the houses you and your hubby did, you must have an eye for something like this. If you don't, do you know someone who'd tell us how to open up this room? I know I can talk Cece into opening her purse strings and turn this into a perfect dance studio. We'll put up a wall of mirrors, smooth out the floor, add more lighting. It's cool down here no matter how hot it gets outside."

Libby looked around. If her opinion was all Margot wanted of her, she'd help out. It could even be fun. Thumping the wall, she knocked a pitcher frame crooked.

"This whole wall can go."

"Wonderful!" Margot, straightened the frame, looked at Libby. "Have you ever read this through? Really taken in the words? It keeps knocking me sideways. Before moving here I spent most of my time worrying about my health, my brain. How long I'd live. When will life stop being fun? Making sense to me? Let me read this to you."

Libby groaned inside. Everyone seemed to be trying to make her over. She read as Margot spoke.

Life is not a journey to the grave with the intention of arriving safely in a pretty and well-preserved body.

But rather to skid in broadside, totally worn out proclaiming, Wow! What a ride!

"It still takes my breath away. Literally." Margot ran her hand over the words and smiled. "I've always been the prefect one. The child who gave no one trouble. The wife smothered by her husband's success and his mistresses. The mother who made her daughters in her image. I've written down the saying and given them all copies. You know what, Libby, I keep one in my wallet and one on my bathroom mirror. I've never run further than a block, now I'm in training for a five K run. At seventy-two I won't miss my uterus if it falls out. I'm trying to do at least one WOW thing a day. This "third age" is my last chance to make something of me."

Margot glowed, as if she'd just had good love making.

Libby chewed on her bottom lip. First it was her do-good paper towels. Then Birdie jumping on her to teach the kids. Now Margot was wowing everything and it somehow included her.

"Okay." Libby looked around the room, sat down next to her cardboard boxes. "Give me a minute."

A half hour later, Margot with Libby's design for on a box cover, headed out to find Cece to talk her into the project.

Libby smiled, now she had a bird sitter.

Chapter 24

Ginger leaned against George as they stood outside staring at the water pump Libby had given them. She liked it that they were both tall, stood eye to eye. "The water's still coming out a little cloudy, George."

"It'll run that way for a day or two more, Babe. You sure you're okay to drive Anna Mae up to Sedona tomorrow?"

"I am, George. She's got to face her kids and Libby and I are the only way she'll get there."

Deciding she might as well face the elephant in the room, she added. "I won't drink, George. That's done. I'm not scared about your cancer any more, and I'm signed up to start treatment when we get back."

She couldn't tell him she needed this distraction to keep her sober until then. She smiled and kissed him.

"Just worry about what you're going to eat while I'm gone and stop worrying about me." The smell of his aftershave tightened her heart. "Remember when we met? Neither of us was supposed to be at that dinner where you spilled your red wine on your white pants."

Laughing, George hugged her. "I did it to get you to notice me."

"So you've said but, you engineer types can be real klutzes sometimes. We're ten years into our marriage, and it's the happiest time of my life. I wanted you to know that, Goerge."

She put her fingers on his lips to stop him from speaking. "I do think there's a cosmic reason that Libby and I are taking Anna Mae up there when Cece should be doing it. Just like us meeting."

"Cosmic reason?. You and Libby, together, in Sedona, the Spiritual Seat of the Universe. Yes, Sedona could be in trouble." He grinned at her.

"I'm serious, George. This Sedona trip could be another moment like us finding each other."

"You think Libby or Anna Mae will find a husband?" He chuckled.

She raised one eyebrow at him. "No, George. Strange things have already happened. Stingy Cece popped up with a bunch of money for the woman's shelter so Libby and I would go." She looked at him.

"I think our biggest problem is that Lib and I might clap hands, say hurrah, if Anna Mae's children ream her out."

He shook his head. "You won't be happy and they won't ream her out. With the cosmic forces at play, you'll have no control over it either way so don't worry about it."

"The reason I owned my own business was so I could be the ruler of own my Universe."

"Just let things flow. If it gets too tough call me, Babe and I'll fly up on a moment's notice. I mean it."

He turned her to him. "Speaking of controlling things, I've decided to retire."

Her heart thumped in her chest as she pulled sharply away. Retire? If he didn't trust her to stop drinking, if he didn't have faith in her, how could she do it?

"Say it isn't to watch over me."

"Me watch over you?" He gave her a deep look. "First, that's impossible. Second, I'll help you all I can but, it's up to you to fight your addiction. And, this place you're going for treatment must be the best in the West, to have a waiting list. They'll help you put it all behind you. We saw that with my sister."

Ginger looked at their rock filled back yard, and how perfect Libby's pump fit in. When George saw a problem he took it as a challenge, not as a weight dragging him down. His cancer fight proved it. What would he think if he knew this was her fourth try at quitting, only her dear friend Libby knew that. Those other times she'd fooled herself into thinking she could drink socially and not let it get out of hand. This time life had to be different. From now to her grave, she couldn't take another drink. No more refuge in the refrigerator. And, the thought scared her to death.

"Hey, where'd you go?"

She shook the thought out of her head. "I was thinking about you retiring."

Taking her hands he walked her over to the mounds of rock he called his work in progress.

"I'm bored with my job. I've been there for a long time. I'm retiring because the cancer scared the shit out of me, made me realize I wasn't doing much with my life. I envied you your retirement. At first, when you couldn't sit still, I thought nope, retirement bad idea. Then I watched you turn our boring, as you called it, sand and rock front. Then the side yards into an oasis for birds and humans. You loved every hard minute of it and I want that excitement for me."

He hugged her, nuzzled her neck.

"Babe. Remember the way we envied how Phil and Libby worked together to rehab those houses and did it for no money?"

She quickly pulled away. "Oh, no, no. We aren't fixing up houses. I've had enough buying and selling real estate to last two lifetimes. Three, maybe."

"Not real estate." His lopsided grin exaggerated the scar on his chin she loved to touch.

"I keep thinking about what you've done, Babe. Taken penny cheap plantings, made them thrive in our dry, hot weather. You've won six big garden awards. I plan on developing reasonably priced solar water pumps. Making it a self-sustaining watering system. Together we'll teach people to bring the desert alive without lining the pockets of the power or water companies. While our friends spend their lives working, playing golf, traveling, eating too much, we'll be here making a difference."

She looked at his flushed face, his eager eyes. "Isn't that a little lofty?"

"Aim high, fall short, still good."

"No golf? No travel? None? "

"Well, sure some."

"Then it's a deal." She leaned against him, thanked whatever kind spirit had sent him her way and hoped that kind spirit would follow her to Sedona.

Chapter 25

At quarter to five the next morning, Libby pushed open the heavy oak door leading out of Cece's Bordello. The weather guy had gotten it right last night. It was already warm and going to be another scorcher day in Tucson. A perfect day to be in a car going north to the cooler climbs of Sedona, if they actually went.

Staring at the empty street, lit up by the bevy of lights on the front of the Bordello, she proudly set her brand spanking new overnight bag down next to her Birkenstock clad feet. Yesterday she'd found the bag tucked in among a haphazard pile of fancy flowered suitcases in the luggage department of a discount store. Its brilliant red color had instantly snapped her out of thinking about her upsetting encounters with Birdie and Margot.

When she'd discovered she could wear the bag slung over her shoulders like a backpack, or carry it like a humungous purse, or fill it to the brim to make it into a suitcase the way she had it now. It had made her feel like she'd stumbled onto her new best friend. The swimsuit inside it was probably a mistake.

Swimsuits these days were all about saving material. Crotches headed north to within an inch of the waistline. The vacated space between a woman's breats opened up a whole new set of problems, especially sagging ones.

And her legs in daylight? Not a pretty picture. Her muscles were as firm as someone twenty years her junior. It was her skin that was the problem. Crepe paper was smooth compared to her skin. The thing that might save her from total embarrassment was the sun block imbedded, in the beach wrap-a-round, that a size two clerk had sold her. Shopping for their trip had been a sobering event. The price of her new swimsuit and cover-up alone, would have fed her and two friends for a week.

A deep, mellow, car horn made her look up so fast she almost stumbled over her bag. It was Ginger and she was on time. It could be a foreshadowing that a very strange day was about to unfold. They were going to Sedona, the center of the Spirit world. At least it had been, before all the tourists started showing up.

Dancers of the Third Age

Libby mumbled shut up with all the negatives. She picked up her bag and as if her lover were waiting in George's sleek silver car at the curb, and practically flew down the steps.

The car trunk popped open without Ginger ever leaving the driver's seat. Now, that was handy. Maybe she should replace Rosa Rita. These new toys these days were fun. While she was shopping yesterday an idea had snuck into her head of some work she could do to keep herself busy and happy. It would require a car with a lot more space and amenities than dear Rose Rita had ever dreamed of. If she could get the ladies of the Bordello to cooperate on a side garden they'd have to haul a lot of dirt and plants.

Life was changing fast. Car trunks that opened weren't new, but ones that closed themselves were. Cars in the ads on TV parked themselves. She'd have to see that one to believe it. She had sun block in her clothes. Tinted car windows for ordinary people, not just for criminals.

Cruise control had been something a girl worried about in the back seat of a car. It seemed to her the ink was barely dry on the instruction booklet, when the new and improved version popped up for sale. Tossing her purse and overnight bag into the trunk, she counted four bags already in there. Four? It was supposed to be a three or four day trip. Ginger was just being Ginger.

"Your ride awaits, Ms. Price." Ginger called to her from the driver's seat.

"And the top of the morning to you, Ms. Logan." Libby yelled back as she waited for the trunk to shut itself. Going around to the passenger door she got in, looked Ginger up and down.

"You look fabulous, Ms. Logan."

Even the puffiness under your eyes is going away Ms. Logan was her added thought. Addictions were bad things. What was her addiction? Being needed was a big one for her. Ginger was right; she could never be Ms. Assistant.

"Why are we taking George's car?"

"He offered it to us because the back seat has so much more leg room than mine."

Sitting down in the passenger seat, she watched as the seat belt automatically snaked down over her right shoulder, slithered across her chest, to disappear beyond her hip then snap itself into place without so much as a thought from her.

"I'm locked in. How does it do that? "

"I've no idea. George, being the engineer type, had it added because a couple of his golfing buddies refused to wear their seat belts. They said a belt made them feel old. George said they are old and gave them no choice. Are we ready to go?"

"Yes. You drive while I tell you about my awful nightmare of Anna

151

Mae meeting her kids. They were telling her off big time, and there I was, wedged in between them grinning like a pissing camel."

"Grinning like a pissing camel?" Ginger looked her. "That's a new one."

"Well, camels do smile. My grin in the dream reminded me of a visit to the zoo several years ago. I was standing with a couple of our foster kids in front of the camel exhibit and telling them how camel humps store water. One camel suddenly leaned forward and grinned at us. I swear it, Ginger. That camel had a grin from ear to ear. Our oldest son said the camel was peeing I heard running water and looked down. The camel really was pissing. Its grin disappeared when it stopped going. That's how I got that one."

Ginger shook her platinum head. "You've had the strangest experiences. I gather this means you were happy about Anna Mae's kids reaming her out?"

"Yes and no. I had another one and we were all having fun at a picnic."

Ginger sped up to get through a yellow light. A few blocks later, pulling up to a stoplight, Ginger pointed to a sign in front of a church.

"That sign says, Potluck Supper Sunday 5 pm. Prayer and medications to follow. I had to read it twice to get it."

"Get what?"

"It should say meditation, not medications."

"I might need both of them so I can stop thinking that I'll be letting down our adopted Foster kids if I forgive Anna Mae."

"Yeah. Right. I keep mixing her up with my mother killing herself and Anna Mae. A horn honked behind them. Ginger, having slowed to a crawl, stepped on the gas and caught up with the red sports car ahead of them.

"This is turning us both into a mess and it isn't even our problem. Promise me one thing, Ginger. We will walk away from Anna Mae's house if she won't go up to Sedona. We won't beg her and, we won't come back to try again."

"Absolutely. I did call her last night to tell her that our hotel rooms are reserved and can't be canceled. The rooms have to be paid for, no matter what."

"What'd she say?"

"She said thanks and hung up."

"Okay." Libby fished for a lighter topic. "I counted four bags in your trunk. You need four suitcases?"

"Usually I do, but I managed to stuff my things into the matched pair. The one that looks like a flying saucer is my make-up case. The fourth bag is in case A. M. tries to get out of going because she doesn't have the right bag."

"Excellent. Did you notice my bag? The clerk said it's a cross between a backpack and a duffle bag. Sitting out there in the sun though, it sure looked a brighter red than it did in the store."

"It's the perfect bag for you, Lib. I'll bet it's why you came bouncing down those stairs like a fifty-year old."

"That's what I mean. A red bag when I haven't seen fifty in ten years?"

"Red is your color and backpacks are all the rage right now." Ginger gave Libby a wicked grin. "Today, Ms. Price, with your juicy red bag, smart pants outfit, pony tail, you are part of the in-crowd. You didn't know that, did you?"

"Phil would turn over in his grave if he knew."

"He's smiling at you, Lib. Happy you're finally moving on. Some."

Unbidden tears welled up in Libby's eyes. "I'm having a hard time wanting to move on, Ginger. Birdie says I'm sinking into oblivion." Libby swallowed hard. "Lets find a better topic of conversation."

"I've one!" Ginger passed a car going below the speed limit.

"Yesterday my horoscope said things have been hard, but now the planets are lined up in my favor. It says things will turn around. I'm thinking I should buy my very first lottery ticket. Yours said you either need a pet or a husband."

"Well, there you go. I just got a replacement for Harry the Canary. We've agreed his name is Julio Iglesias, and I'm Ms. Iglesias. There, I've got a pet for a husband."

"Don't we all." Ginger, slowing to a crawl, watched a kid standing at the corner a half block ahead.

"See that boy with the paper delivery bag? Kid's why I don't go out before nine in the morning. They're like fleas. Darting all over the place, jumping, skate boarding their way to school. There's no way I can tell if he'll dart out in front of me and I'll kill him or, if he's going to stay put. I won't know until I'm right on top of him, when it's too late."

She peered over the hood of her car, sat back. "Good. He's staying put."

Ginger kept driving. "He's on his newspaper route. And he's not a boy, he's a man."

"I've some news. I don't know if it's good or bad, but George is taking early retirement. He wants to develop a solar water pumping system that doesn't cost a fortune."

Suddenly they were at Anna Mae's door. "We're five minutes early."

Ginger popped out of George's car, went to the trunk, grabbed her extra overnight bag. "I'll tell her this was a gift from a client and I can't use it. You ready?"

"As I'll ever be."

Judith Granahan

Side by side, they walked up to the door, glad that Anna Mae had left the light on. Libby rang the bell, rang it again. When the door didn't open, she rang again, then again.

"Enough dinging, Libby. She's either run off or she's hiding in there."

Libby looked at Ginger. "Well, should we go."

The door opened a slit, then all the way as Anna Mae peered out. "You're early, but I'm mostly ready. I didn't recognize the car so I waited to hear your voices." Anna Mae, looking nervous, beckoned them in.

"I hope you remember your promise that you won't force me to see my son."

"Absolutely." Ginger nodded. She was counting on the draw of motherhood to make that promise fall by the wayside. Besides, once she got Anna Mae in the car, she'd be at their mercy. She held out her blue bag.

"Could you use something like this? A client gave it to me and I've others of my own."

Anna Mae quickly nodded. "It's lovely and, yes I would. Mine's as ugly as a cardboard box. I'll be right back. Please, please come in."

Anna Mae took the bag, started off, stopped, turned around. "Thank you so much."

Once Anna Mae was out of sight, Libby rushed over to the desk and grabbed Anna Mae's journal, hissing to Ginger, "She needs to bring this."

Ginger whispered back. "Great idea. I've never ever seen anyone as stone-faced as A.M.is. I can't tell if she's happy, or miserable, about this trip."

"There are other stone faced people" Libby looked Ginger up and down. "The four Presidents in the Black Hills. Joan Rivers, Carol Burnett, Dolly Parton and you."

"Ouch!" Ginger, laughing, felt something good release inside. She looked at Libby. "When I called to tell her about the hotel arrangements I told her there's a pool and she should bring a swimsuit. Do you think she will?"

Libby raised an eyebrow. "Anna Mae's more likely to bring a coat than a swimsuit. I bet she's never even worn shorts."

"Shorts? Yes, I have them."

If Libby had false teeth she'd be bending over to pick them up off the floor.

"Benny especially didn't like shorts on men or women. I forgot to ask you. Will the hotel take money? I don't have a credit card in only my name and I won't touch anything with his name on it."

Anna Mae set her suitcase down.

"Yes, they still do."

"I heard you laughing. What was so funny?"

"Libby thinks I look like Joan Rivers or Carol Burnett."

Anna Mae, not understanding the connection, stared at them as if she were deaf.

Ginger changed the subject. "Your outfit is perfect."

And it was, she wasn't just being kind about it.

"Thank you. A dear clerk helped me pick it out last evening. You did promise me that I don't have to meet my children. Right? It will be okay if all I can do is sit and stare at Timothy's house. Yes?"

Ginger, feeling a little uncomfortable, having been asked it so many times, crossed her mauve painted fingernails behind her back. "Yes, and you can stop asking now."

Anna Mae's need to ask permission again and again made Libby realize how very far apart they were. She couldn't remember the last time she'd asked for permission. Not even from Phil.

No, that wasn't true. Ever since he'd died, she'd been asking, begging, for someone to give her a useful job. Give her! That sickened her now. It was time she stepped up and made her own way again.

Brushing the thought away, she held out Anna Mae's journal.

"We've put you in such a rush, I don't want you to forget this, so I picked it up. If you do decide to meet your children, they'll want to read this."

"Thank you! I would have forgotten it."

When Anna Mae reached out and actually took the journal, the tightness in Libby's stomach gave way to relief.

Chapter 26

Two hours later, into the drive, Anna Mae's light snoring from the back seat stopped and she sat up.

"It's light out. Where are we?"

"You couldn't have timed it better." Libby turned around to look at her. "The last exit for Phoenix's northern suburbs is just a couple of miles away."

"Phoenix? Really? Ginger's driven us all the way through Phoenix while I slept?"

"She did and we've decided to stop at the next exit for a pit stop. Get some coffee, a little food. The gas stations are scarce from here to Sedona."

"Thank you. You don't know how much I was dreading living that drive again. I know things have changed, but the memories are still there. How long before we get to Sedona?"

Ginger glanced back at Anna Mae. "About an hour and a half after our stop at the gas station. Sedona isn't big on advertising. Unless things have changed since my last trip up here, there's only one highway sign for Sedona and it's close to the turn-off. My theory is they think we should know where to turn."

Anna Mae, peered out the side window and mumbled, "I'm over half way to my son's home."

She was quiet for a moment then she just had to explain it to them. How it had all gone wrong. How it wasn't supposed to be.

"I was so sure my sister and I had set up their escape so perfectly. It started when our neighbor heard Benny yelling at Timothy. When she saw his bruises she told me to call the police but I got her to secretly pass letters back and forth between my sister Ruth and me instead. Ruth's husband Charlie was an engineer who was looking to re-locate. They knew what Benny was doing to us so it was the perfect time to run away from him. We all grown up with mean families and Ruth and Charlie weren't telling anyone where they were going. The plan was to get on the bus, meet them in Flagstaff and go off with Ruth and Charlie. But at the last minute I got scared Benny would figure it out, so I just sent the children with a note to

Ruth telling her to write my neighbor where she was going and to send some money. I had to keep my children safe from their father. The lesser of the two evils was to punish me and not let my children get hit.

But Benny was smarter than all of us. Three nights later he tied me to a chair, packed our belongings in a truck he'd bought then he left the children's things in the hall for the neighbors to pick over.

When we got to Tucson he made sure we didn't have a phone and our mail was delivered to a locked box. Benny had the key. The first day he was out looking for work, I went to the drugstore and called my neighbor. She didn't have an address for Ruth yet but I promised I'd call her again soon.

The next day Benny came home and said we had a job together delivering produce. I was never out of his sight for a whole month. By the time I called my neighbor, her phone was disconnected. She was old. She must have died or moved into a nursing home.

If I'd run away with the children, even as far away as Montana or Wyoming, I knew Benny would find us, no matter what. I even thought about killing him by running him over with our car."

Anna Mae sighed. "I didn't do it because I knew I'd get caught and sent to jail. Then who'd take care of my children?"

Libby turned all the way around in her seat saw tears running down Anna Mae's face.

"The important thing here Anna Mae. is to remember you did what you set out to do. You got your children to safety. You don't know what would have happened if you'd run away or kept them there."

"I know." Anna Mae turned to look out the window. "But do my children? Maybe they think I gave them away because I didn't like being a mother. Even though my sister Ruth and Charlie had two children of their own, I know they would have taken good care of my children."

Having children of her own, tingles of unease ran through Libby's body and made her reach around and squeeze Anna Mae's shoulder.

She'd gotten that from her grandmother who always said it was better to give a person a hand up, than a shove down. Her mother believed people were responsible for what they did.

"I thought Benny might kill me when he found out our children were gone, but he seemed relieved. Death would have easier than living all these years."

With her neck cramping, Libby returned to looking out the front of the car.

That caught Ginger's ear. "You'd have let him kill you?"

"Not right away. After I lost contact with my sister I knew it would be a long time before I'd be free of Benny He was very healthy. He'd still be alive if he hadn't fallen off his ladder."

Ginger, thinking about her mother feeling trapped, stepped on the gas

157

and swerved onto the shoulder. Quickly gaining control, she bounced the car back onto the road.

"Whoops. Sorry."

"What happened?"

"I started to nod off. Gotta get to that gas station and coffee." Lying was easier than saying she needed a drink to get thoughts of her mother's death out of her head.

Trying to get away from the depressing talk she added. "We don't need gas yet, but cross your fingers they have coffee and something to eat. Just something small gals. We'll get brunch at a great restaurant I know up in Sedona."

"I could use some food and a fresh bottle of water. Maybe a chocolate covered donut."

A few miles later they were inside a giant rest stop that looked ready to sell them anything they could possibly need for the day. Ginger went to the DVD rack to find a movie to slide into the player in the back seat, to keep Anna Mae occupied for awhile. All she'd found so far was Motorcycle Madness, a couple of Vampire movies and several children's cartoon DVD's.

Cartoons in Arizona? In the land of grey heads and golf clubs? The world had truly gone nuts.

Where were 'Thelma and Louise' when she needed them? She looked down at Anna Mae's hand. "What's that?"

"A notebook. I think I should write down all the things I need to say to my children; even if I don't have the courage to actually talk to them."

Surprised and pleased, Libby turned away from the donut display. "Good idea. I used to write things down whenever I needed to have a serious conversation with one of our kids. I rarely got to say much of what I'd written, but it helped settle things in my head."

"Really? Did you use key words or full sentences?" Anna Mae had a pen ready to write down Libby's wisdom.

Anna Mae's hopeful face tore at Libby. Anna Mae had lived in a very small world and they were about to throw her into the jaws of family life. See if she would sink or swim without any lessons.

"Both. I wrote whatever came into my head. The good things and bad things about the situation from my point of view, then what I might do if none of it worked out my way. That always seemed to settle me."

Ginger turned from the coffee machine. "When I was trying to make a real estate sale I made a list of all the important things I needed to tell my clients. I went over it and over it until I knew it by heart. But, I learned something important from it. My clients often had different things on their minds and I had to be ready to listen to them. Your kids will remember things differently than you. They could even have some good memories of their father."

"I'm sure they do. He wasn't always mean and sometimes I was crabby."

Libby, trying to decide between a donut, and a banana, interrupted the conversation. "The important thing is to tell them over and over how much you loved them. We should have suggested you to bring any pictures you have of your children. To help them remember their time with you."

"I've only a few baby pictures, plus the graduation ones Benny had. The rest of our pictures I put in the children's suitcases when I sent them on the bus."

All these years only a few baby pictures? Mothers needed pictures. She was beginning to actually respect Anna Mae.

"We'd better get on the road again." Ginger nodded toward the coffee machine. "Coffee anyone?"

"You get the coffee. I'm getting us all a banana and a donut." She turned back to Anna Mae. "Write down whatever you think. I know it'll help."

As the miles rolled by, Anna Mae sat in the front seat, writing page after page. Finally Ginger, thinking about her dream, reached over and stilled Anna Mae's hand.

"Let's say the worst thing that happens is your children are about to slam the door in your face."

She caught the stern glance Libby gave her in the rear-view mirror. "They could scare you so much you wouldn't know what to say. So write this down now. I love you and I'm sorry. Write it over and over, think it over and so that's the first thing that pops in your head and out of your mouth."

Anna Mae looked at Ginger. "You promised me though I wouldn't have to see them if I couldn't do it."

"You don't. I just threw that in in case you decide you must see them."

Ginger sighed to herself. *Here we go again. Same question over and over.*

Anna Mae shook her head. "They'll think I'm there because I'm old, alone, and in need of their help. That's the main reason I don't want to knock on their door. Plus, they may hate me."

"You can't control what they think, or do. Only what you say and do." Ginger couldn't believe she was actually trying to help Anna Mae.

"We can't run away from our pasts. We are who we are because of it. Your son's life with your sister and brother-in-law must have been good since he teaches high school science. Benny can't stop you from having a second chance with your children he's dead."

Her experience said Anna Mae should see her children. When her father, years later, finally knocked on her door, she'd slammed it in his face and turned the lock. Later, when it was too late, she'd tried to find him and couldn't. She gripped the steering wheel and focused on driving. What she'd done was done. It was easier to tell someone what to do than to do it yourself. Still, she couldn't let it go.

"We all have troubles, Anna Mae. That's what life is about. Libby is spending her time mourning her husband's death instead of putting together a life without him. Me, I'm going into treatment for alcoholism because my mother's suicide, over forty years ago, made me afraid that people I love will leave me. If you don't move beyond your past, or learn from it, you will ruin the years you have left."

She'd done it again. Spouted something she couldn't yet do herself.

Anna Mae tapped Libby's shoulder as if she'd heard none of Ginger. "Did you ever see your foster children reunite with their parents?"

"No, not really. It wasn't allowed."

She knew Anna Mae wanted her to say that all their kids had run joyfully to their parents. That blood was blood, after all. Some had seemed like they would, but every child was different. The three they'd adopted had begged to stay with them. Still, she sometimes felt less by not being their birth mom. But that was her issue.

"I forget that you two know all about abused kids."

Anna Mae's comment felt more like a dig, than a compliment. It actually cheered Libby. If Anna Mae had meant it as a dig, she must be growing a backbone. Time for her to stop preaching and sounding smug.

Libby put her head back and closed her eyes. Ginger concentrated on the traffic. Anna Mae went back to looking at the scenery going by and writing until she pointed to the sign for Sedona.

"There it is!"

"Sedona coming up. Wake up Libby. You don't want to miss the drive down into Oak Creek Canyon. It's a must stop place for everyone. Time to feast our eyes on some startling landscape after the long, boring scenery up from Phoenix. Drink in the beauty of the gorgeous red rocks."

Drink, drink, drink. That word came up when she least expected it. And, yes, she wanted a drink, a real one. Needed one.

Chapter 27

Anna Mae stepped out of Ginger's car. Looking up. Looked left, right, shaking her head. "Yes, This is real. I am awake."

Excited now, she moved away from the row of parked cars over to a small grassy area to marvel at the wall of red. To see such beauty, it about stopped her heart. How could rocks be so beautiful? So towering. So majestic and intense in color.

"How did we get here? We were just up there on that boring highway only a few minutes ago. I didn't see any red rocks or even red dirt. And now all this. It's fantastic."

Expecting someone to talk to her, she turned around and saw only empty space behind her. Ginger and Libby were still back at the car, looking like they were having some kind of dispute. Either with each other or the man walking away from them.

Turning back to them she could almost feel the steam coming from Libby and Ginger as they glared at each other.

"Do *not* fix me up with him."

"He's a really nice guy, Lib. I worked with he and his wife."

"I don't care, Ginger. I've told you a dozen times, I'm not in the market."

"Yes, and I've told you a dozen times I won't do any more protest marches or picket lines. Yet, you keep bringing them to my doorstep."

Worried about the time she had left to sit in the car with them would be unpleasant, Anna Mae stepped in between them.

"Look around."

She pointed up, all around them. "Magnificent, red rocks, are everywhere. They're so bright against the clear blue sky and go on for as far as I can see, like they're protecting us from the world."

She turned around, turned again. Then, with amazement in her heart, she scolded them. "How can you two argue in this place? We're looking at the most fantastic, towering red rocks I've ever seen. What's their color? Some place they are red, orange, crimson?"

Libby and Ginger stared at Anna Mae, at the majestic spires of crimson red, rocks, at each other, then wrapped their arms around Anna Mae who's knees went weak with relief. She'd just scolded someone and hadn't been punished.

They let go of each other as if they'd bumped into a hot stove.

Ginger cleared her throat. She should have known this would happen. Sedona did things like this to her. The last time she was here, she told George she'd go on that Montana fishing trip with him. They'd gone, and now she had her favorite picture of George and her, grinning with their catch of fish with the snow-capped mountains behind them. As if called, a warm wind blew dust at her making her clear her throat again.

"Right. No fighting. Not here. No matter how many times I've seen these red rock beauties, they still take my breath away."

Libby, shaken from arguing with Ginger, agreed. "They are beautiful. They are so fantastic. Amazing, really. And yes, Anna Mae, naming their color is a problem. It changes all day long depending on the sun's angle. I usually say their color is all variations of Arizona orange. From barely there, to as intense as the center of a campfire."

Anna Mae sighed. "I've seen pictures of them and I was so sure the color was enhanced. You know, as an advertising gimmick? The pictures didn't show their huge size, or that some are rugged and right next to smooth ones that look like they've been sanded."

"Sanded by time." Libby held up her cell phone, snapped a picture of Ginger and Anna Mae with the rocks as a background.

"Show me how to take a picture of the two of you."

Libby quickly showed Anna Mae what to press, then put her arm around Ginger. "Sorry about yelling at you."

"Me too."

Anna Mae pointed the cell phone at them, walked backwards, looked then pressed the button. "You two are so tiny against the rocks." She handed Libby her phone. "This world is amazing. A few minutes ago we were on an ordinary Arizona highway, now we're in fantasy land."

Suddenly she slumped to the ground.

Libby and Ginger were beside her in an instant.

"What happened?"

"Are you having a heart attack?"

"Do you have pain?"

"No." Slowly the tears flowed down Anna Mae's face. "I just realized again, how kind you two are to me. Bringing me up here where my children live. We've known each other a long time and we've never been friends. I feel so blessed."

Libby and Ginger, stunned into silence, stood her up, waved a man and woman away, crossed the parking lot to sit down on low rocks. People walked past, car doors shut, the was a long silence, before anyone could speak.

"I didn't mean to blurt out my feelings like that."

Ginger, thinking they'd covered up their disapproval of Anna Mae fairly well, brushed the dirt from her knees, then helped Anna Mae up.

Looking at Libby, then Anna Mae, she said. "I thought we all got along pretty well for being cooped up in the car for hours."

"We did."

Ginger nodded. "Ahh cards. We didn't communicate very well. Benny irritated me when he chewed you out in front of all of us. It was humiliating, and embarrassing, we didn't know what to do or say. After that I just wanted to play cards and not get involved. I had my own life to figure out. When Cece said he broke your ankle and you refused to report him, in my eyes made you look weak. I really don't like weak women."

Even though it was a horrible conversation to have when surrounded by such beautiful mountains, Libby just couldn't let it lie there.

"That's true of me too. I felt the same way without really knowing you. Now that I know more about the circumstances, I'm ashamed that Phil and I acted so detached about the way Benny treated you."

She pressed her lips together. "When you gave us your journal I was eager to read it. Then, because I was a foster parent to abused kids, I got angry that you let Benny get away with hurting your children."

"Yes." Ginger nodded. "When I found out you and Benny weren't who you said you were. That you'd lied to us for years, saying you never had children, this really upset me. I screamed when I read the part where you sent your children away. I felt for your children because My mother killed herself which left me in the care of relatives, like your kids."

With the toe of her shoe, Ginger brushed a smooth arc in the path. "When I read it all a second time I realized how frightening Benny must have been for you."

Libby tilted her gray head. "I do have one question but you don't have to answer it. Why didn't you leave him after your children were grown up?"

"I did. I saved the change from the grocery money he gave me until I had a thousand dollars. Then I took a bus to a town in western Arizona and found out how hard it is to get work without references. Finally, with my money almost gone, I got a job as a waitress. I lasted until the lunch crowd came in. I got so flustered they fired me.

So I took a bus to back up to Phoenix, went to family assistance. They made me fill out this paper, that paper. Said I had to wait for the state to decide what they could do for me. It could take weeks, maybe months.

People told me, I could sleep in the shelters when they had room and I should get a job. Doing what? All I'd ever done was help Benny repair things. So I came back to Phoenix and Benny. I was sure he'd beat me; instead he laughed. Said now I knew that people weren't nice out there. I stayed with him until I killed him."

Libby looking around saw no one was listening. "You didn't kill him, Anna Mae. He killed himself by going after that tool."

"But I sent the tool wide, purposely."

"Well, he didn't have to reach out for it, did he? And you know, Cece said the ladder twisted in her hands. The police called it an accident because Benny didn't have it securely connected."

"I know, but I still threw it wide."

"Why the hell did you decide to do this after all these years?"

Anna Mae looked at Ginger. "Because he'd killed my cat. Because he'd thrown a tool at my head and missed me by inches. Isn't that enough reason?"

"Wow. Then Benny also chose to reach for that tool." Overwhelmed with her own feelings, Ginger headed for her car. "Girl's, I need lunch. We'll save these rocks for another time."

Libby hooked her arm through Anna Mae's and they all headed for the car.

Chapter 28

Twenty minutes later Ginger was driving into a nearly full parking lot when Anna Mae grabbed the steering wheel and yelled. "Watch out!"

Ginger slammed on the brakes. "What?"

"See that family? I was sure they were about to step in front of your car."

"Where?"

"There. Them." Anna Mae pointed past Ginger's nose, to a man and woman with two kids.

"They aren't even close to us. Anna Mae. Don't you ever grab the wheel again."

"I'm sorry. It won't happen again. Now I can see that they really weren't close to us. I'm just so nervous about today. Please, both of you look at him. See how he holds those little girls by their upper arms?"

Ginger, the pounding in her head quieting, drove past the foursome. "I'm driving. I can't look."

Anna Mae turned to Libby. "You can look. See how tight he holds them?"

"Yes. I'm sure he's making sure they don't run out in front of a car."

As they drove past the group, Anna Mae turned to looked at them. "We're the only car around, Libby and he's really pulling them very close to him."

Ginger swung into an end spot. "I've found the perfect parking spot. Only one side of George's gorgeous new car can get hit by an open door." She giggled.

"Anna Mae, you can't tell how hard anyone's holding someone else."

Anna Mae opened her door. "Maybe not. But why is he holding their upper arms, not their hands? You can hurt a child up there and leave no easily seen marks."

Libby, now out of the car looked at the man and nodded. "Anna Mae's right, Ginger. It does seem odd, but some parents are just overly cautious." Her nerves frayed from driving, arguing, listening to Anna Mae's story, Ginger wasn't about to get into it about strangers. Instead, she got out of the car, walked over to a large barrel cactus. "I've been thinking some of these would be perfect for my front yard."

Tugging at Libby's sleeve, Anna Mae turned her toward the restaurant.

"Look at him now!" She nodded ahead. "He's actually pulling the girls across the lot and the woman is looking away, as if it's not happening. Like you said I did when Benny acted mean to me."

As a concession to Anna Mae's obsessing, Libby checked them out again.

"I still don't see that there's anything wrong, Anna Mae. The mother could be looking out for other cars. The girls are just pups. He's keeping them in hand so they won't get lost or hit."

"I hope you're right, but I don't think so."

Anna Mae walked quickly ahead hoping to hear what the man was saying. She'd nearly caught up with the foursome, going up the steps to the restaurant door, when five laughing women came out and covered up the man's voice.

Libby stopped one of the women. "How was your lunch?"

Ginger smiled. Libby always asked that of anyone who looked liked they'd eaten.

The woman in a sequined baseball hat and wearing the reddest of lipstick Libby had ever seen, even on Ginger.

"We had breakfast and it was simply delicious. Healthy. Well prepared. They always use only the freshest of organic ingredients."

As soon as the group left, Ginger hissed to Libby.

"You can't take her word for it. She's either the mother, or the wife of the owner."

"You don't know that."

Anna Mae pushed herself between the arguing Libby and Ginger and hissed. "They're going in the door and he's still got a tight hold on the older girl."

"There's no way to tell if it's a hard hold or, just hard enough, Anna Mae."

Ginger didn't care to pay attention to the family. She had to check out the results of the renovations that were being done the last time she was here and she was starving. Looking over the entryway as if she were pricing the restaurant for a sale, she noted how well the expensive soft lighting brought out the high quality artificial cacti clustered near the gift shop. She really liked the intricate wrought iron wall divider. The person that had done that was very skilled in mingling cacti and birds of the southwest into the structure.

"This was an expensive renovation. I hope they aren't planning to sell out to a chain."

Anna Mae, busy watching the troublesome family, paid no attention to

Ginger. Now they were following the hostess to the left side of the half-filled dining room. Then hostess came back, picked up menus, was starting to lead them to the right when Anna Mae touched her arm. "Could we sit back there?"

She nodded to a table being cleared and two just tables away from the couple she'd been watching.

"Of course."

Sitting down, Ginger and Libby took their menus, listened to the hostess enthusiastically spew out the breakfast specials.

"I know it's early, but we'd like lunch."

"Not a problem."

They ordered ice tea, waited for Anna Mae to order but she seemed to be off in la-la land. Ginger tapped the table. "Anna Mae?"

"Yes?" Anna Mae kept watching the other table.

"Do you want iced tea, coffee, water, wine? What?"

"Yes."

"Give her the same as us." Ginger, very tired from the long drive, had snapped it out.

The minute the waitress left, Anna Mae put her menu in front of her face. With Libby sitting across from her, she could pretend to talk with Libby while watching the man two tables behind them. Ginger was on her left. Ginger should be able to see the man out of the corner of her eye.

"Act like we're friends just having lunch. That family we followed in is just two tables behind you, Libby."

"I know, and I don't think you should stare at them." Libby glanced at Ginger then looked down at her own menu.

"But he'll think I'm looking at you. But you can't turn around Libby. He'll notice that right away. Ginger, when you to talk to Libby, you can glance at them but don't be obvious about it."

"What?" Ginger looked past Libby. "That's the same guy you said yanked his kids arms. How did we get seated near them?"

Anna Mae put her menu to her face. "Keep your voice down. He might hear you. I asked the hostess for this table."

Without thinking, Libby copied Anna Mae, and put her menu to her mouth then took it back. "Anna Mae, don't put your menu up. We'll look like we're conspiring to blow the place up."

Whispering back, "Oh my, you're right, but I bet you this man is abusive." Anna Mae moved the salt and pepper, shakers an inch or two, dusted the tablecloth, while keeping a close eye on him.

"I studied him the whole time you two were ogling this place. I tell you, the man kept a white-knuckled grip on both girls right up until they sat down at their table."

Ginger flattened her menu. "White knuckles is one big leap. You can't see white knuckles any more than a hard grip."

Anna Mae hissed back. "The woman walked with her head down, like she's afraid of him."

"Even if you are right, it's all circumstantial and not any of our business."

Now Libby wished she had paid attention; she knew a victim's walk when she saw one. That head-down walk was another reason she had decided she would probably never like Anna Mae right from the get go.

Ginger, trying to get off the subject, ran her finger down the salad listings and said nothing.

"At the entrance," Anna Mae hissed. "I heard him tell the girls to keep their mouths shut or he'd lock them in the car without lunch."

"Were those his exact words? Or was it, be polite, mind your manners or back in the car you go? Like I use to tell my girls." Ginger, seeing margaritas at the next table, shuddered.

Anna Mae's lips were now a tight line.

"I suggest you watch the children, Ginger. They haven't once lifted their heads to look around. What kids do that? I tell you, they're scared of him. The woman must be the mother, because she and the girls have so many similar features."

The waitress was now at the man's table. "The woman is looking down away from the waitress. Typical powerless behavior. I should know."

Libby, turning to get her phone out of her purse, gave the family the once over. "They are the gloomiest bunch I've seen in a long time. It looks like he's ordering for all of them."

Ginger closed her menu, sighed.

"Come on, girls. A lot of men do the ordering. They think it's sexy. I don't see anything wrong with them. Even if he is abusive, he's behaving in here so we can't even report him. There's nothing we can do. I'm ordering the chicken oriental salad."

"Order one for me." Anna Mae was suddenly up and heading toward the man's table.

Libby didn't dare turn around. "Oh, Lord. What's she doing?"

Ginger had a clear view. "She's exaggerating her limp. Now she's past his table and heading toward the restrooms. If A.M. has to pee that suddenly, she should see a doctor."

Ginger paused. "That's weird."

"What is?"

"The woman is gone and both girls are barefoot."

Libby stood up. "Order me the chicken salad too."

Suddenly Ginger was alone at the table and looking up at their smiling waitress. "We'll have three chicken salads."

Anna Mae pulled open the door and walked into the fanciest restroom she'd ever seen. Huge gilded mirrors, marble sinks, marble counter tops, sage colored floor tiles, fake flowering cactus orchids in pots, but there was no sign of the woman. She was sure she hadn't made a wrong turn. A noise behind her spun her around.

Libby whispered. "Aren't you going in?"

"It seems empty."

Libby checked out the long hall they'd just walked through and whispered. "She's got to be in there. The men's restroom is the only other door. Hurry up. If he is an abuser, he'll give her only a brief time away from him."

Going to the first stall, Anna Mae peeked under the door, moved to the second stall, at the third one she spied the scuffed tennis shoes the woman had been wearing. She pointed to the door. Libby nodded.

Anna Mae knocked, muttered, "I'm a friend. I saw how he treated your children coming in."

Silence. Anna Mae cleared her throat, ordered herself to speak firmly.

"I've been abused all my life. That's how I recognized your husband's hold on the tender spots of your daughter's arm."

"He's not my husband." The woman's voice shook.

"Are they his daughters?"

"No. They're mine." The toilet flushed and a woman, about thirty years old opened the door. She had dark circles under her darting eyes and looked exhausted. Anna Mae felt an instant kinship with her.

When Libby approached, the woman stepped backwards into the stall.

"It's okay. She's with me. Has he hurt you?"

The woman nodded.

"Then why are you still with him?"

Wrong question, flashed in Anna Mae's brain, followed by, be kind, but firm, when confronting. She'd read that advice somewhere before giving up on Benny.

"He's an old high school friend. His wife and two sons left him a few months ago. I didn't have the heart to turn him down when he asked us to go for a ride. Everything was fine until my youngest daughter said she wanted to go home. He turned onto the freeway and locked the car doors. That was three days ago. The doors can't be opened even from the inside except with his remote."

"We'll call the police for you."

"You can't do that. He has a gun and he'll shoot my girls if I try anything. He's very clever. He always keeps one of my daughters next to him. I have to get back to our table. He's expecting me." As the woman stepped all the way out of the stall, went to the sink, Anna Mae followed her.

Libby, looking for any signs of abuse saw none. It was a scam to get money. But then how would the woman know Anna Mae would follow her or, be worried about her?

Anna Mae leaned close to the woman. "The restaurant is getting full. Right now, we can walk calmly back to your table. I'll fall on him while you two grab your children and run to our other friend's car. She can take you to the police."

It had popped out of Anna Mae's mouth before she could think clearly. She'd never told someone what to do. Her second thought was Ginger wouldn't know to run with them and that thought tightened her stomach.

"No! He'll shoot at anyone if we try to get away. He's always flashing me his gun. He'll shoot us. He'll shoot us all."

"In front of a bunch of witnesses? That's a little far-fetched." Libby's doubts were knocking on the door. They were either facing a huge problem or a great actress.

She could hear it all now. Please, he has a drug problem. He'll let us go if you just give him a hundred dollars. Blah, blah, blah. Stories like that were on the news all the time. How clever women especially, were getting good at pan handling. To find out if it was trick to get money out of them, Libby pulled out her cell phone. "I'll call the police for you from in here."

The woman grabbed at Libby's phone.

"No! I told you he'll shoot us if he sees any signs of the police."

She'd heard enough, Libby turned to go.

"Wait, Libby! Didn't you hear her? He kidnapped them! We have to help her."

As Anna Mae, stepped in front of Libby to block her exit she bumped into the woman, who let out a loud moan.

Anna Mae reached out, lifted the woman's shirt then smothered a cry. Raw, red, swollen slashes, some still with dried blood on them, wrapped around the right edge of the woman's back. Scattered amongst them were many, fist size, bruises. She quickly lowered the woman's blouse.

"He used a belt with a heavy buckle, didn't he?"

"Yes, when I begged him to let my daughters go and keep me. Then he locked us in the car and bought me some antiseptic cream. He really thought I'd be pleased. That's how crazy he is."

Anna Mae turned her back to the woman, lifted her own blouse and exposed her own crescent moon scars, now silver-white. "I too, was beaten with a belt."

The woman, now shaking, faced them. "Please, just go. I don't want you to help. He's says he'll let us go as soon as we get to the Grand Canyon. That's where and his wife got married. I thinking he's planning to jump off and kill himself."

Libby looked carefully at the woman's face. Their foster kids had taught her how to spot a liar.

"I still don't get it. He goes into a store to buy things, takes you out to eat, and yet you can't get away? You say you've been gone three days, so he must sleep. Still, you haven't run."

"I'm not lying. When he goes anywhere, he locks us in the car with his remote. Usually he takes one of my girls with him, then points his finger at me then mouths bang, bang. This is what he does to me so he can sleep."

The woman held out her hands as if she were being arrested, exposing wrists that resembled raw meat. "He uses rough farm ropes to tie my wrists to a bed or to table legs. Then he gives my girls a sleeping pill."

"Dear God." Anna Mae steadied herself against the counter. The man was far worse than Benny. She couldn't bear to ask if he touched the girls in the night. "There must be a way to get you away from him!"

"No! He'll shoot us. I've gotta get back. He times how long I'm gone."

As the woman turned to go, Libby moved faster and blocked her exit. "Will he come back here to pee before you leave here?"

"Yes." The woman's chin quivered as she fought back tears. "Yes. He has to follow his routine. He'll take us out and lock us all in his car. Then he'll come back in and use the restroom."

Libby tilted her head. There was the lie. "Why not scream for help then?"

"Would you believe me if you heard me? No. You might call the police. They wouldn't get here in time but he'd see you and shoot. Forget you ever saw me."

Libby held tight to the door. "Can you find an excuse to come back in here?"

"When we're done eating he'll let me bring my girls in here, one at a time."

"Good. One of us will meet you in here with a plan."

"There's no way." The woman pushed open the restroom door.

"We'll have a plan ready!" Libby hissed at her retreating back.

Anna Mae waited until the door shut then fell against the counter. "A plan, Libby? How? Ginger won't believe a word of this."

"We've got about a half hour to convince her and to set something up. They say old age and treachery beats youth and beauty every time. So get your thinking cap on."

Libby pushed open the door, hissed to Anna Mae. "Here, take my arm. Limp hard. Act like you're in a lot of pain."

Lurching past the woman's table, Libby patted Anna Mae's hand. "I'm so sorry I bumped into your leg. I had to pee so badly. Do you need to go see a doctor?"

"Let's wait until after lunch. It's just my bad leg. It could get better."

Easing Anna Mae into her chair, Libby sat down, grabbed her silverware and squeezed it hard to stop shaking.

Chapter 29

Ginger stared at them. "You two look sick. And what were you doing in the bathroom so long?"

Libby picked up her napkin, fluffed it lightly in the air. "Ginger, do NOT react to what we tell you; no matter how upset you get with us. Pat Anna Mae's hand. Pretend to worry over her. I hope that'll help you remain calm."

Ginger, sensing this wasn't a joke, nodded. "Do you give me any choice here?"

"No. We've uncovered a very dangerous situation. Anna Mae was right. He's kidnapped them. He's beaten her. They are his prisoners."

"Oh come on. That can't be true. He wouldn't dare bring them in here to eat. They could yell for help at any time."

Ginger's low growl made Libby hand her a roll. "He has a gun and promises to shoot the kids if she does anything wrong. Anything. You should see her back. It's covered in horrible slashes and some very ugly bruises from a belt."

Ginger picked up her glass, smiled at them. "She says he has a gun, shows you some bruises? That's a con game if I ever heard one."

Libby patted Ginger's arm and did a poor imitation of a laugh. "No one would take that much of a beating just to con us. Her injuries are real. Her wrists are cut raw from the rough ropes he ties them up with at night."

Ginger waved her fork at Libby. "Anna Mae's got to be overly sensitive about this, but you? I can't believe you fell for it. Where's the Libby who checks for bogus twenty dollar bills?"

Anna Mae took a roll. "It's all true, Ginger. Her injuries are horrible."

"It's a con job. One or both of them are druggies." Ginger dipped a roll in garlic-laced olive oil. "They want money."

"She didn't mention money or come to us, Ginger. Anna Mae approached her. Anna Mae got her to believe she could talk to us."

"I did. She couldn't fake how bad she looked. She was shaking from head to toe and her breath really stinks."

"That's what drugs do, Anna Mae. They make you shake."

Anna Mae looked at Libby. "I told you she wouldn't believe us. Right now, you call the police. I'll run over there, land on him, knock him off his chair."

"Wait a minute. That's too chancy Besides you can't hold him down. He'll bounce up and shoot someone. Here comes our waitress with our food. More later."

Libby pretended to be interested in picking out the best roll. Precious time flew by as the waitress smiled, placed their salads, asked them if they needed more rolls or iced tea.

Seeing that the other table was already eating, Libby was wound up so tight, told the waitress to go away. The second she left, Libby dug into her salad and whispered, "Ginger you don't have to believe any of this."

Ginger nodded. "Good, because I don't."

"I've a way that'll give you time to check this whole thing out for yourself. After lunch the woman will take her girls, one at a time, to the restroom."

She prayed it would happen.

"Then you go in and talk to her, Ginger. Check out her injuries for yourself. If you decide it's all a scam, then come back here and say so and we'll leave. But, if you think it's real, then you can tell her my plan."

"You've a plan? Already?" Anna Mae's face filled with amazement.

She did, but it was a crazy to think three sixty-five year old women could pull it off against a young guy with a gun. Well, Anna Mae was only sixty, but she had a bad leg.

On the other hand, Anna Mae had given up her kids, and dealt with Benny. She'd shot his grave to shreds. Ginger had four marriages under her belt, built a multi-million dollar real estate company, had great kids, was edgy because she wasn't drinking. She and Phil had taken in sixteen kids in from the street. She looked over at the guy and almost felt sorry for him, knowing what they hoped to do to him.

"Both of you eat while I talk."

Anna Mae eagerly nodded. Ginger groaned.

"Ginger, when you meet her in the restroom, if you believe her, you'll have to spell out our plan to her very fast. I know we can get them away from him."

"IF all of it is true." Ginger felt the hair on her arms rise up. "There's no way we can snatch and run from a guy with a gun. I don't want any part of trying this thing. I've been sober four days. George's cancer is gone. Life is good. I want to keep it that way."

"You're right." Libby nodded at Ginger. "We can't grab the girls in here and run for it because he will shoot someone. So, we'll have to wait until he locks them in his car and comes back in here to pee. Then we break them out and take off in your car."

Ginger clamped her hand so tight on Libby's arm pain shot up to her shoulder.

"Break them out of a car? You've really gone around the bend this time, Liberty Price. She can get her own damn self out of the car!"

"Nope. He remotely locks the car, Ginger. You must know about remote locks. Now, please laugh a little, eat something and listen to my best idea ever."

Libby felt a rush of excitement for the first time in months. She was back in life.

Ginger took a small bite of salad. "You're being Ms. Castro again, trying to con me into an insane idea. Why didn't they run away at the restaurant entrance?"

"He has a gun, Ginger." Anna Mae chimed in. "A gun. And a tight hold on the girls. Remember? I told you he did."

Ginger, giving Anna Mae a dirty look, picked up her iced tea, put it down. Peach tea was not a substitute for a gimlet. Their lovely lunch had turned into a situation just because Anna Mae, and now Libby, couldn't mind their own business.

"This is all too much."

Anna Mae burst out with a nervous laugh.

Ginger pushed her fork through her salad, speared a piece of chicken, ate, then laid her hands on the table.

"See these blue veins. The ugly brown liver spots? Arthritic knuckles? They belong to a woman old enough to be his grandmother. You can rush him, I'm staying put."

"Just listen to my plan, Ginger." Libby reached into her purse, slid a six-inch silver tube onto the table, showed them a button on its side.

"This is what I call my poke stick. If I push the button, which I won't do right here, and out pops a thin, incredibly sharp, stiletto knife making the tube into a handle. Phil confiscated it from some hoodlum and gave it to me for protection."

"Oh my God! You're gonna to kill him?" Anna Mae put her hands to her face.

With her heart pounding in her chest, Ginger shook her head no. "There's not a chance of that. Libby can't kill even a lizard."

"Right." Libby faked another laugh. "When he comes back in here to go to the bathroom, I'll use this to puncture two of his tires. That way he can't follow us after we rescue them."

Anna Mae stared at the pen. "Are you sure that thin little thing will cut his tires?"

"I sliced one of Phil's tires when I was furious with him." She didn't have to tell them the tire was old, did she?

Anna Mae gulped. "I wish I'd been that brave, even once."

"You are now." Libby gave her a wink. She was beginning to think they were smart enough to get this done.

"First, I'll slash one tire. You Ginger, when you hear the hiss of air, you'll smash in the back passenger window with a rock while I ruin the second tire."

She prayed her face didn't show that she was making it up on the spot.

"I'm to break his window? Which window? With what?" Ginger stared at Libby. If it weren't so utterly insane it almost sounded like fun. A hoot, even. She'd already begun to calm down.

Libby gave her a small smile. "Driver side back window with a rock. Then we'll all get them out of the car and you'll drive us away."

"And where will the bad guy be while we do all this?"

"As I said, in the restroom."

"And, how will we know that?"

Ginger was staring at her as if she knew the answer.

"I can take care of that."

They both looked at Anna Mae. "You haven't given me anything to do so, I'll stay in here, just inside the restaurant front door. When he comes back in to go to the bathroom, I'll run out to tell you."

"Yes!" Libby grinned at Anna Mae. "The gift shop. You can hide in the gift shop."

There was so much excitement on Anna Mae's face Libby worried if she could really pay attention to the details.

"This is not going to work." Ginger gave them a fake smile. "Men pee fast and never wash their hands. Four or five minutes, tops. That's not enough time to break them out and get away."

"You have to add the time it will take him to walk back in, then come out. That could be another four or five minutes."

Ginger shook her head. "Why am I arguing with you? This is all a ruse. A scam, a trick. I still think it has to do with them somehow getting money out of us! And if it isn't, and if he has a gun, he'll come out, see us at his car, and shoot the nose off my face. Or call the cops on us. Count me out."

"As I said earlier Ginger, you go into the restroom when she takes one of her kids in there. Check out her injuries. Hear her story. Tell her our plan is to ruin his car, then take her and her kids straight to the police. If she balks, you walk out. One way or the other, you get to decide this. Can you do that?"

"I'm going to lay it on thick about wrecking the car and going to the police."

"Absolutely."

"And if I say it's a con, you will let it drop?"

When Libby and Anna Mae both nodded yes, Ginger let out a

minuscule breath. "Then, since it's all up to me, I can at least put some more details to the plan."

At the tail end of the sentence Ginger's voice had risen sharply. Her face was as white as her hair.

"Good God. He just scratched his leg and I saw a gun strapped to his ankle. Libby, call the cops right now. Tell them they have to break the family out of the car."

"Why would they do that on my say so?"

"Because you asked? I don't know. Because your husband was a famous cop."

"Not up here, he wasn't. We have to do this ourselves."

"The car probably has an alarm." Anna Mae, oblivious to their conversation, was cutting her salad to shreds. "What if it goes off when Ginger breaks the window? Won't he come running out? Won't people try to stop us?"

"I'm sure it does have an alarm. We'll just ignore it and anyone who comes by."

"That'll take three minutes off the time we have to get them out. And, there'll be broken glass on the seat. How do they get over it?"

"I don't know."

"There are too many I don't knows." Ginger now felt like the hair on the top of her head was saluting the flag. "I'm going in there and tell the mother that when he marches them through the restaurant, they are all to run in different directions."

To let that one sink in, Ginger took a bite of something. When no one said anything she added. "He won't know which way to go. All of us screaming won't hurt either."

Libby shook her head, her gray ponytail bouncing from shoulder to shoulder. "You don't watch enough TV. They'll run. He'll catch the littlest girl, make it look like a game, then drive off with her, never to be seen again. Then how would we feel?"

Anna Mae nodded. "Or, he just starts shooting."

"Floor mats!"

"What, Libby?"

"Ginger wanted to know how they get over the broken glass. It's floor mats. You tell her to put them on the seat after you break the glass."

Libby couldn't believe how well her mind was working today. It was as if she'd done this all her life.

Ginger sighed. "Okay, okay. I've got a window hammer out in the car. George got us both one after we were almost caught in a flash flood. It's supposed to break a window with one stroke."

"How do you know it will?"

"Because, Anna Mae." She so wanted to call her A.M. "They are made to actually break car windows. I can't believe I'm actually saying I might do this."

Libby smiled at Ginger. "Atta girl. And, I've just come up with another bright idea."

She pulled a small calculator out of her purse, handed it to Ginger. "Tuck this into your bra. Tell her our plan, then tap your chest, say you've recorded the whole conversation. Say the tape will go to the police if this turns out to be a scam."

"Great idea!" Anna Mae looked as if she were going to high five them. "Make sure she knows we're taking her straight to the police station where she is to charge him with beating her and kidnapping them."

"You can take it to the bank."

When Anna Mae just stared at her, Ginger added, "Count on it."

She shoved her plate aside. "Tell me why it's us that's doing this."

"Because we're the only ones who've noticed." Anna Mae just had to glance at the man.

"Ginger you'd better head to the restroom. The guy's putting the youngest girl's shoes on. Mom will probably take her to pee any second."

Libby laughed at nothing. Anna Mae joined in. They clasped hands with Ginger under the table as if they might not see each other again.

Ginger put her purse on the table. "Money in there. Pay the check, but wait here for me to come back and say yes or no."

She slid her chair out and headed for the restroom.

Chapter 30

"How does your leg feel now?" Libby spoke to Anna Mae as if she were deaf so the man's attention would be on them and not on Ginger heading for the restrooms.

"Not too good. I know I can't go shopping."

Shopping? That was good. Anna Mae was catching on. Libby waved at the waitress for their check.

"I'll take you to my healer. She'll shoo away your aches and pains."

"I doubt that," Anna Mae whined.

With their voices fading away behind her, Ginger swished her hips as she passed the table. The man was putting a second shoe on a worried looking little girl. An urge to reach over and punch him hit Ginger so hard her hand came up without thinking. Fortunately, restraint kicked in and she brushed her hair back, then got an underarm whiff and found out that even very expensive deodorant quit when she was scared stiff.

Inside the restroom, she took a long look at herself in the mirror. Libby was right. Happy, angry, or scared stiff, her face didn't show it, except now her face was flushed. The woman's cuts had damn well better be fresh and they'd better be dreadful.

That was awful thinking, wishing the woman had really been beaten. She could tell the truth by looking at the woman's face. Her years of searching faces for scammers trying to buy real estate with no money, or credit, was going to pay off today. Libby had been as shrewd as ever, sending her in here to make the decision alone. That way she had only herself to blame if this was a scam and she fell for it.

To test her nerves she stuck her hands out as if reading a paper. "Three elderly women have been arrested in a parking lot after wrecking a car."

She shook her imaginary paper, changed the headline. "Three women risked their lives today to snatch a young family from an armed kidnapper in crowded Sedona parking lot." She hated how her voice had risen up. "

"Calm down. Pretend this is just another multi million dollar sale." Ginger put her hand across her mouth. She'd lost her senses. Giving a quick glance around, she let out a sigh. Thank God the place was empty.

Dancers of the Third Age

She'd never broken a law worse than a speeding ticket. If she okayed this deal, in a few minutes they'd be smashing in a car window and stealing children. Could she even trust Libby to slash the tires? Of course she could. Libby might be a softie but not when she was on a crusade. Lib had been arrested in several protest marches. Ginger shook her head. Focus! You're in here to check the woman out. And I'll kill Libby if I have to spend the next ten years in jail.

Ginger turned the water on, wet a towel and was dabbing her forehead when the door opened. The woman and youngest child walked in. She refused to think of them as mother and child until she knew for certain that they were.

"I have to poop, Mom."

Well, there it was.

"That's fine, Emily. Take your time."

Ginger gave the woman a quick once over. Pretty. Early thirties. Edgy. Short hair cut, tan face. Seemed the out-doorsie type. She looked intelligent, but that *contrasted* the fact that she was mixed up in this mess. She touched the woman's elbow, kept her voice low so the daughter wouldn't hear her. "I'm with the two women you talked to earlier."

"Yes, I saw you at their table." Tall like Ginger, the woman had leaned forward to whisper to her.

Ginger stepped behind her. "Lift your shirt so I can see your injuries for myself."

The cuts and bruises sucked in Ginger's breath and she turned away as if hit. "My God! That's far worse than they said! He must have gone at you more than once."

"Shh. My children don't know about the beatings. It happens after they're asleep."

The woman turned around, showed her scarred breasts. Ginger wanted to hit something. Instead, feeling sick, she grabbed the counter.

"You can't help us. His gun is always in his belt. He has another one strapped to his leg and he keeps one of my daughters with him at all times. Did the other tell you that? I'm showing you what he did to me to make you all stay away."

Ginger shored up her strength with anger. This was unacceptable! The woman was badly beaten. Worse, it was all over her face that she was petrified.

With her doubts leaving faster than a flushed toilet, Ginger pulled the woman into a corner.

"Tell me about him going to the bathroom."

Libby and Anna Mae could have gotten that one wrong. "How long does he take?"

"He's hung up on his habits so I'm sure he'll do the same thing today.

He'll lock us in his car then leave to go to the bathroom. It'll only take him less than six or seven minutes and that's why you can't help us."

"There's absolutely no way for you to get out of his car?"

"Believe me, I've tried. I've kicked the windows but nothing happens. His remote is the only way out."

"Okay. Here's our plan. Two of us will be out in my car watching for you to come out and get locked in the car. Our third person will stay inside to signal us to be sure he heads back to the restroom. After Libby slashes one of his tires, I'll smash in the driver side back window."

She probably shouldn't have said Libby's name.

"It won't work. As soon as you break the window his alarm will go off. He's says it rings on his remote. He'll come running out."

"We were sure of that. The restroom is so far back here he'll probably be in the middle of pissing and he'll have to zip up then run out. The second you see him go into the restaurant, get everyone to the back seat on the passenger side. Hold up the floor mats to protect you when I smash the driver side window. Oh God! Does he have floor mats?"

The woman nodded.

Relief flooded Ginger. "Cover the broken glass with the floor mats and hand the kids to us. We'll get you all out, run to my car and take off. My doors will be open."

The woman was shaking from head to toe. "No. You could all get killed."

"We can beat him if you almost throw your kids at us."

"You could call the police when he locks us in."

"Don't go rational on us now. We need hysteria to pull this off."

The woman still looked petrified. Ginger, cupping the woman's face in her hands, tried to pour her own strength into her.

"Take a breath. You're strong. Take another breath. Let it all out. You're brave."

Son of a Gun. It was working. The woman was calming down.

"You're young and strong. We're old and sly. Between us we'll beat the bastard. Being a bit afraid is good. Your girls must not scream. That would make it look like we're the bad guys."

Something smacked Ginger hard in the thigh.

"Let go of my mother!"

She glanced down. The child's fists were up. There was fire in her eyes.

"No, no, Em. The lady was just helping me feel better."

"Yes. Your mom has a headache. I did some pressure points on her." Ginger tried to pat the small girl warrior on the head, but she'd already backed away.

"Are we set?" She smiled at the woman and hoped her face showed she cared.

"Yes."

Marching out of the rest room, Ginger felt Libby's calculator slip and inch or two down the crevice between her breasts. She'd forgotten to threaten the woman. Well, it hadn't been necessary. It was real. It wasn't a scam. She was sure of that.

*****

Waiting for Ginger to return had been excruciating for Libby and Anna Mae. They'd paid the check, said they didn't need their lunches boxed up. Even so, the waitress returned with three boxes and their change. Cleaning their plates into the white boxes, they groaned when the man signed his credit slip.

Libby hissed, "He can't be too smart if he's signing credit slips. I know Ginger told us to wait here for her, but it'd save time Anna Mae, if you went out and found your hiding spot now. If Ginger comes back and says it's a scam, we'll find you and go some place where we can actually eat lunch."

"Okay. Yes. Okay." Anna Mae stood up, adjusted her hips to walk as wobbly as possible on her bad leg.

Libby looked at the large white bag with three boxed lunches sitting on the table. There was no place for the bag in their plan, but she couldn't just leave it sit here. Some diligent person would run after them waving the thing. She sneaked the bags under the table.

Clenching her fists to her side, Anna Mae headed out exaggerating her limp the whole way. It was finally paying off that Benny had broken her ankle, plus it was her daily reminder that men like him existed. Muttering, *It's going to work. It's going to work. We will free them. I believe it. I believe it.* She made her way to the entrance gift shop.

Several chattering people blocked her way. In a panic she turned and bumped into the cluster of fake Saguaro cacti. Set deep into the corner, and a foot taller than she, they made a much better hiding place than mulling around in the gift shop. Standing behind the cacti, she could see everyone passing by. She couldn't see into the parking lot, but that wasn't her job. Her job was to let Ginger and Libby know if the guy came back in and actually headed for the bathroom.

She stared at the loitering people, wished them a table and was shocked when the hostess immediately showed up to take them away. A cleared entryway and the perfect hiding spot, both very good omens. As she slid in behind the tallest of the tall cacti she kept whispering, *Benny's dead. He can't spoil our plans.*

Ginger, coming back to their table, picked up her purse, hissed at

Libby. "You were right. That man's a bastard. I told her our plans and she's ready. Where's Anna Mae?"

"I sent her on ahead to hide. If we don't see her, then she's in the right spot."

"Brilliant, Lib. Let's go."

Libby picked up two squares of butter.

"You're stealing butter at a time like this?"

"To lubricate my knife, make it slide in and out of his tires. Two tires should be enough to keep him put. Right?"

"Right. Come on, let's go." Ginger, seeing the bags under the table, reached down, grabbed them and headed out.

"My fingers are so ready to smash in his window. I do like the way, every now and then, how those hoodlums you and Phil raised have come in handy. I told the mom to make sure her kids keep quiet. Do you think Anna Mae can really help lift them out of the car? What with that bad leg of hers."

"She got her husband to fall off a ladder didn't she?"

"We'll never know." Ginger was moving as fast as her mouth. Libby grabbed her arm. "Slow down. They'll think we're running out on the bill."

Reaching the exit, Ginger gracefully turned to the hostess. "We've lots of shopping to do. Please refrigerate our lunches."

"We don't do that."

"Oh, yes you do. Your manager was very helpful last week. Just put my name Cece Fontaine on the bag."

Ginger smiled. Cece was the reason they were here. Cece deserved to have her name on the bag. She set it on the consul, pushed open the door, and got slapped in the face by the late morning heat.

"Damn! Lib, we forgot to look for Anna Mae in the gift shop. Did you see her?"

"Yes. She's behind some fake cacti near the gift shop. She stuck out her hand and waved."

"She's behind a fake cactus?"

"It's better than lurking in the gift shop."

"I suppose, but now she's already changed things. Cross your fingers, Lib. As far as we know, Anna Mae has never done a daring do."

"Sure she has. I just reminded you she helped her husband off his ladder."

"Only a rumor, Lib. A rumor spread by her."

Libby somehow managed to keep up with Ginger's long legs as they rushed to her car. Ginger looked calm and collected, but she always did. Anna Mae had seemed okay. That left herself to worry about. Did she have the strength to flatten two tires? She had to shove hard and straight and her shoulders had bothered her for months.

Ginger spoke her mumbo jumbo to her car, the doors opened and heat poured out. Getting in, Ginger turned the car around to face the restaurant, got her cell phone ready to take pictures or to call for help.

She looked at her thermometer, snapped a picture. "That says it's over a hundred in here. It's got to be that hot in his car. I've a movie thingy on my cell phone. I'll catch him locking them in his car and walking away. At the very least, we can say he locked them in a hot coffin and we had to get them out."

"Oh, I like that!" Libby wiped her brow, leaned forward. "There they are! They're just coming out the door now. Get ready!"

Libby held up her own phone, snapped a picture through the front window as the man, the two little girls and their mother walked down the stairs.

"They look like a nice family, but my camera on my phone picked up his grip high up on the older girl's arm just like Anna Mae said." Libby smiled, then added. "Please, oh please, have his car parked back here near us."

"Why?" Ginger hissed out of the corner of her mouth as if she could be heard outside the car.

"We're about to make a lot of noise. It'll take more time for a crowd to gather back here."

"Oh, right."

They nervously peered out the front window as the man walked his captives past the first row of cars, past the second, turned left, then stopped three cars down in the middle of their row.

Libby gripped Ginger's knee. "They're back here? We all should have been watching when they parked and we would have known that."

The man pointed his clicker at the car, motioning everyone in. When he also got in, Libby and Ginger groaned.

"No! Don't do that." Ginger couldn't believe the emotion flooding her. "Damn him! He's backing out! What do we do now?"

"We keep taking pictures. If he comes by here, I'll get a good shot of his license plate, and everyone inside while you drive."

"Are we're going to follow them?"

"Yup."

Libby leaned forward, clicked away as the car pulled out and went left around the end of the row. "He's going for the exit. It's a good thing we didn't call 911. They sure look like a normal family just out for a nice drive."

Ginger started to pull out to follow him then stopped, grabbed Libby's arm, shook it.

"He's not going for the exit! He's parking in the front row. There! He's getting out so he can see his car the second he comes back out. Smart of him. Not good for us. We'll be in everyone's face when we wreck his car.

An audience will be a big problem."

"We'll just punt. I got shots of him pointing his clicker at his car after he got out."

Libby took pictures of him heading back into the restaurant. "Now quick, Ginger! Park as close to him as possible."

Libby traded her cell phone for the stiletto knife Phil had given her. "I'm ready. You got your glass breaker?"

"Right under my thigh." Ginger drove out of their row and parked directly behind him.

"Because I've got a spot right here. That says It's going our way. I about cried when I thought the S.O.B. was getting away. Get ready, we'll pulverize him!"

Chapter 31

"Where is he?"

Anna Mae fought the doubts in her head. It shouldn't be taking him this long to walk to his car, get everyone in, lock them up tight then come back inside. She couldn't see much out the door, just the door. An urge to step outside and search for him was so strong her feet started to move; instead she pressed herself into the back wall. Relief soared when the door opened, then came crashing down when she saw it wasn't him.

Where is he? She stomped her bad foot, looked up to see him just inside of the door! He was handsome, in a cruel sort of way. She sucked in her breath and didn't move an inch. Now she'd find out if he were a kidnapper or a scam artist. He stopped, turned around, stared out at the parking lot and her heart fell to the floor.

It was a scam! He was waiting for someone to break into his car and free his fake captives then he'd rush out! It was a darn good thing Ginger and Libby needed her signal.

No! Now he'd turned and he was coming her way. Then he was passing the cactus. Breathing in, she gagged on his sweet, heavy cologne.

As soon as he put a foot into the dining area she headed out the door. Shielding her eyes against the bright sunlight, she was careful to wave as she went down the stairs. Not waving was the signal it was a scam. It was, wasn't it? Her memory wasn't as good as it was even a year ago.

Adjusting to the intense sunlight, she spied Ginger's car parked behind a black one in the front row. Flush with relief, Anna Mae fled down the stairs, limp and all.

Libby, seeing Anna Mae burst through the door with her arms high in the air, got out and ran to the black car. Peering inside to make sure everyone was away from the back side window she wished she hadn't. The fear and hope she saw on their little faces looking up at her was so intense she feared she couldn't slash the tires. This just had to work. They had to free them.

Dropping to the front tire, next to Ginger's feet, she slammed her silver poke stick into the tire. Ignoring the searing pain in her shoulders, she twisted it in up to the hilt, then heard the sweet sound of a soft hiss.

"It worked!" Yanking hard, she fell backwards, landing with a thump. Hissing filled the air.

Rushing to the back tire, she heard Ginger hit the window but no shattering glass.

"Harder. Ginger. Hit harder!"

Ginger swung again and it caved in but didn't shatter. Now what? She didn't have anything to shove it all the way in. Then a purse came flying as Anna Mae finished off the window.

Libby, hearing the air swoosh out of the second tire, stood up. Ginger was just handing the older girl to Anna Mae, whose face was covered in tears. Then the smallest girl popped up to the window. Libby easily slid her up and over the floor mat the mother had put over the rim of the door.

"Run to the car with your sister. Stay in the car but tell that lady to yell at us if that guy comes out."

As Anna Mae helped the crying child into the back seat of Ginger's car she whispered. "It's okay. Those women are going to get Momma out right now."

Well, they weren't if the man who'd just clamped his big hairy hand on Ginger's arm had anything to do with it. "What the hell's going on?"

Libby pushed in. "Stop that language! There are children here. We're their grandmothers and a guy has kidnapped them and he has a gun."

"Please, get me out. He'll be here any minute." Ginger put all her strength into it and pulled the mother through the window as far as her waist.

"My wife's calling 911." The man reached for the mother.

"Perfect. Now you get her the rest of the way out. We'll guide her legs."

The man pulled the woman out as Libby and Ginger carefully guided her legs up and over a few shards of glass still in the window. Then he helped her stand on the ground.

Libby hissed. "Ginger get your car started." She turned to the mother. "Run to the car. A crowd's starting to gather. Where are the 'mind your own business' people when you need them?"

Looking at the man she pleaded, "Help us."

"You gals git! I'll take care of them."

Ginger, Libby and the mother jumped in the car, slammed the doors shut. Ginger stomped on the gas, then hit the brakes bouncing everyone forward.

"Sorry. I have to take it slow. Can't get stopped for running people down."

She drove toward the exit as Libby tapped her side window.

"I think that's him coming out the door now."

"Yes and he's racing down the steps." Anna Mae, nose pressed against the back window, squealed. "Now he sees his smashed window! We should have taken the mat."

"Why?"

"So he can't use it."

"Ha! He's kicking his car." Libby spoke from her seat. "Break your foot, fella."

As the car bounced up and down, over a speed bump, if finally came to a dead stop, Ginger gripped the steering wheel as if it were her plastic surgeon trying to move far, far away.

"Oh sugar, sugar, sugar." Remembering the kids in the back seat she'd put a clamp on her desire to swear.

"There's a car stopped right in front of me waiting to get out to the street. Brace yourselves. If the guy comes running at us, I'll have to drive on the sidewalk."

Libby pressed her face against the window. "Oh hey! Wow! This is beautiful. The crowd seems to be pointing in every direction like they're trying to confuse him. Great! Now I see a cop car pulling in!"

"Two of them." Anna Mae shouted from the back seat.

"The cops changed the light to red. That's why we're blocked at this exit." Ginger drummed her nails on the steering wheel as Libby sat down on her seat.

"I didn't hear any sirens." Anna Mae's mouth was so close to Libby's ear that she jumped.

"No." Libby shook her grey head. "The police often run silent when there's something in progress. They don't want to scare off the culprits."

"And, they don't want Sedonan's knowing that something bad is going on in their town. The lane's clear. We're out of here!"

Ginger shook the steering wheel in sweet relief as she pulled out into the street, driving away from the turmoil they'd started.

"Wowser! We did it! I've always wanted to drive the get-a-way car."

Libby grinned. "I've always wanted to ride shot-gun. Be the look-out."

Anna Mae shook the back of their seats. "I've always wanted to do something."

"Us too." Three voices chimed in.

Chapter 32

Ginger slapped hands with Libby. "We were amazing!"

"We ARE amazing! My arms are still throbbing from shoving Phil's poke stick into those tires. But I didn't lose it! It's in my pocket."

"And, I've got Ginger's hammer. She dropped it." Anna Mae waved it at them, put it under the seat.

"That was the most exciting thing anyone could do! Yahoo, we were all brave, very brave."

Anna Mae hugged the littlest girl. "You, your sister, your mom, us. We are all very brave women today."

Turning, Libby caught sight of Ginger's wild platinum hair. Grinning, she felt a laugh tickle up inside her then escape in blessed relief.

"Ginger, your hair's sticking out like you've been in a wind tunnel."

Seeing Libby point at it Anna Mae let out a chortle.

Ginger looked at her hair in the rear view mirror and joined in. The two girls and their mom also started laughing, making it hard for Ginger to concentrate on weaving through the heavy traffic.

"One minute we're ordering lunch." Ginger took a breath to stop laughing.

"Next thing I know, you two come back saying we have to plan a kidnapping. Then boom, we pull it off and now we've escaped."

"Stop crying, Mom, please stop."

Libby turned to see the oldest girl patting her sobbing mother.

"These are happy tears, Lizbeth." She hugged her daughters to her.

"These ladies saved us. We're safe now. You know that. Right Em? Right, Lizbeth?"

"Right, Mom."

"Are we still the three Misketeers?" The oldest girl, who looked to be about nine, stared up at her mother.

"Misketeers?" Libby asked.

"Misketeers 'cause Em, Mom and me are all girls, not boys like the Musketeers."

"Today Lizbeth, we are the six Misketeers."

"That lady broke Kevin's car really bad, Mom."

The younger girl who Libby thought she was about four was pointing at Libby. "Kevin will be very, very mad. He might come back and hurt them."

Libby thought, so Kevin is his name. She'd always liked the name Kevin but now she took it off her list. She put her hands together at her mouth, tapped her fingers, then gave Em her most serious look. A pose she often used to get a kid's attention,

"You are right, Em. Kevin will be mad. I flattened his tires so he can't drive his car and I saw the police talking to him."

Libby waved her phone at them. "I'm going to call them right now to tell them they should arrest Kevin and that we are coming to the police station. Your mom and both you girls will have to tell the police all the things Kevin did to you."

"Yes." Anna Mae smiled down at the chestnut haired child. "Tell them the truth and Kevin will have to stay with the police."

She hoped she was right. The news always told about the ones who got away or who were let out on bail to do whatever they wanted. They had no real way of knowing if the police had arrested Kevin or if he'd run off. Maybe mom and her girls should come live with her. They'd be safe far away back down in Tucson.

Ginger slowed down, turned into the back lot of an art gallery. "I've got to get out and walk around for just a minute."

Getting out, her knees wobbled. She grabbed the door, stood straight, stiffened them, willed her strength back as the others peeled out of dear George's car. Dear George. She had to call him. Tell him what a day she had! Tell him they'd just stepped in and done something huge and she wasn't drinking. He'd be so proud of her. And he'd want to come right up here to be with her. That's the way her husband was. She was lucky to have him

Heading for the back of the building and some privacy, relief that it was over made her chant, *I don't need a drink. I don't need a drink. I just need George and some air.*

He would flood her with questions. Questions he would say she should have thought of earlier. Like, what was the mother thinking, getting into a car with a maniac? Where was the children's father? Why hadn't there been an alert sent out about them missing? Questions to throw some sense into her; the kind that made people turn away. He'd say she should have called the police and waited. And she'd say Ha! Did he do that the day he took the knife away from the pissed off guy at work? No!

She slumped against the building. They'd been so lucky the guy hadn't caught up with them. Or hadn't shot wildly downing them with bullets. Her eyes filled with tears and she hated tears. They always gave her a headache and ruined even her most expensive make-up. Bending down, picking up some stray papers blowing around, the anger that they were there took away her tears. Why didn't people clean up after themselves?

Then she thought about the little girls. They didn't deserve any of this. Standing up, she caught a glimpse of her hair in the reflection on the window and patted it back down.

"Libby was wrong. My hair looks like I stuck my finger in an electric socket."

"But it's cute."

Arms flew around her, squeezed her hard. Everyone was hugging and she was hugging back, hanging on for dear life. Their nervous laughter mixed with tears of relief as they all seemed to be shaking like jello.

Thank-yous rang out from all of them like church bells.

Libby whispered in her ear. "You're the best friend a person could ever have."

*****

It was nearly three by the time they poured out of the police station.

"Oh this heat feels good. So, good. " Libby rubbed her arms. "My teeth were chattering in there."

"Is Kevin in there?" The smallest girl, holding her mother's hand, looked up at them.

Her mother knelt down beside her.

"No, Em. He isn't. The FBI is taking him to a jail in another town. Kevin will be in jail for a long time."

Em scowled at her mother. "Kevin can still get out of jail, Mom. Lizbeth and me saw it on TV."

Both the girls looked so small and frightened that Libby had to kneel down beside them.

"My husband was a policeman for a very, very, VERY long time. Which makes me an expert on all police things. So, if you will sit down with me on this nice warm curb, I'll tell you all about the police."

"Can we, Mom?"

"Yes, Em."

Putting an arm around each child, Libby with snuggled them in as if she could shield them from more bad things. Patting the tops of their heads, made her feel like the Universe had returned all the parts of her it had taken away on the day her Phil had died.

"Listen to me girls. And really listen. Can you do that?" She smiled when the two small heads nodded a big yes.

"First, did you girls tell the police how mean Kevin was to you and to your mom?"

She knew the answer was yes. She'd seen them talking away. She wanted them to admit it.

Both heads nodded.

"Fantastic. Your mom did too." She'd gotten that information out of the detective she'd cornered.

"We three ladies told the detective how we saw Kevin lock you in his hot car and leave you there. That we saw him squeeze Lizbeth's arm really hard."

"I showed the police lady the marks on my arm." The older daughter looked over at her mother talking with Ginger and Anna Mae.

"Mom, did you tell the police how Kevin hurt you with his belt?"

Their mother sucked in her breath. Her daughter knew?

"I didn't know you knew about that, Lizbeth. Yes, I told them every bad thing Kevin did to us. I signed papers saying so."

"And the police told me,"

The girls looked back to Libby.

"That Kevin guy has done bad things to other people. Even the FBI wants to talk to him. So, there it is my Miskateer friends, we all did it perfect! Kevin will stay in jail until you both are all grown up like your mom."

"Really?" Em's eyes got big. "That's a long, long time."

She held them close to her, felt them meld into her. This was where she belonged. Ever since Phil's death, she'd spent her time looking back at where she'd been and tried to get there again. Her life was different now and she had to face that. All her adult years, nothing had warmed her heart like a child's hand in hers. Maybe she could learn to fall in love with small children again then, let them go and not die a small death. She especially loved four and five year olds who saw the world as beautiful.

"I'm glad you saved us." Tears spilled from Em's eyes.

"And you know what?" Libby pulled back so she could look at both girls at the same time.

"I'm gladder than you, because now I have you as new friends. Maybe someday you can help someone too. Helping feels very good."

"Our mom tried to help Kevin and he hurt her really bad." Lizbeth looked angry. "He was supposed to be her friend."

Libby nodded. To talk about this would be stepping on parent territory. Even so, she didn't want to lose this moment.

"What Kevin did to all of you is very hard to understand, and it could make you not want to help other people. Right?"

The girls nodded.

"And that's too bad because it's important we help other people."

"Like you did us."

"Yes! Like we did you. Remember us and not Kevin. See, here's what

191

I'm thinking. Someday you will see someone, who needs your help. Like maybe a friend in school who wears glasses and the other kids pick on him or her."

Em put her hands to her mouth. "How did you know about that?"

"Because, my dear Miskateers, my grandson was just about your age when he had to start wearing glasses. He got picked on because he was different. And do you know what his friend did for him?"

"No." In unison.

"His friend got his mother to tell the teacher about it. So their teacher got some play glasses and made the children wear them."

"Did that make it stop?"

"Good question, Lizbeth. No, it didn't. So then the teacher smeared Vaseline on the glasses and told all the kids to read with them. That's when they stopped teasing him."

"Why?"

"Because they understood why he was different."

Lizbeth she looked at Libby. "Is that the truth?"

"Yes." Libby dug through her purse. "Here's a picture of my grandson. Someday someone will need your help. Don't let Kevin spoil that for you. You can check it out with your mom."

A shadow at Libby's feet announced Ginger's arrival just seconds before she knelt down in front of them and looked at the girls.

"Libby's right. Helping people, well, it's like getting the best ever present. You should always talk it over with your mom. I had a fun idea while we were all sitting in the police station. Something very important."

"What?" Libby and the girls asked.

"I bet those are the same dresses you girls had on when you got in Kevin's car way back in Denver."

Em pulled her skirt over her knees. "My mom tried to wash them but she couldn't get all the dirt off."

"I happen know a very nice shopping center that's not far from here. We'll drive over there right now and get you some new clothes and some things for the next a few days. While all of you are shopping, I'm going over to our hotel and get you a room near us. They've a really nice swimming pool, so you must buy swimsuits."

The girls squealed, jumped up and ran to their mother.

Libby stiffened. Ginger leaving them when she could easily call the hotel could mean trouble was looming. She'd been dry just long enough for the flush of success to be wearing off and it had been one whopper of a day. She forced herself to count to five, let out a breath. She had to trust that Ginger would make the right choice and Ginger did hate shopping in ordinary stores.

Now Anna Mae was clapping her hands. "Shopping with you will be so much fun. Children, have I ever been to any of your birthday parties?"

"No."

"Then, as my birthday present to you, I will buy you new clothes. It will be my treat." Anna Mae patted her purse. "It's been a long time since I've bought things for children."

"Can we, Mom?"

She looked at Anna Mae. "We do need new clothes. Just after we passed Colorado Springs Kevin threw my purse in a river. I'll pay you back when my parents get here tomorrow."

"Grandpa and Grandma are coming?" The smallest girl jumped up and down.

"Yes. I called them when we were inside the police station. They are going to fly her and we'll fly back home with them."

"We're going on an airplane? Really?"

"Yes."

"Lizbeth, we're going on an airplane. Did you talk to daddy?"

"No, Grandpa is still trying to get ahold of him. You know that China is a long ways away."

Their mother turned to Ginger, Libby and Anna Mae.

"My husband is in China for a conference on robotics. That's the reason no one knew we were missing. I'll pay you back as soon as my parents get here."

"No, you didn't hear me." Anna Mae shook her gray head. "This is my treat. I've not had anyone to buy for in years and years. Please, let me have the pleasure of doing so now."

She put her arms around Anna Mae and hugged her hard. "Thank you again for believing me in the restroom. We are alive because of you."

For a moment, Anna Mae felt like she could be hugging her own daughter then, not used to touch, she stiffly patted the mother's shoulder.

"How can we thank you? I haven't even had time to tell my children your names."

Anna Mae looked down at the girls. "I'm Anna Mae."

Well, that wasn't true, but she wasn't going to explain that to them.

"The lady with the big blond hair is Ginger. Libby is the woman who was sitting with you on the curb."

Libby looked at the youngest girl. "I heard your mom call you Em. Is that short for Emily?"

"Yes. My sister is Lizbeth. That's not short for nothing. Our mom's name is Nikki Pearson."

Anna Mae looked at the mother, then at both girls. "And I'm Anna Mae."

"You told us that already."

"So I did. Sometime old people forget things."

Judith Granahan

"Older." Ginger and Libby spoke together and smiled.

Seeing their puzzled looks, Ginger added. "We are older, not old. I believe there's a difference."

As everyone piled into back Ginger's car, Anna Mae thought some people would say they'd been foolish today. She was glad they'd been foolish.

Settling into the front seat, Libby started humming *I Am Woman*.

Ginger and Anna Mae joined in with the words until both girls started to giggle.

"You don't sing good like our Mom does."

"But we're having fun." Anna Mae said, freeing Em from her seat belt the second Ginger pulled into the parking lot of the large shopping center.

"Vamoose all of you. Go shopping. I'll meet you back here in an hour and we'll eat."

Relieved to finally be alone, Ginger drove down the street, pulled into the first parking lot she saw, put her head on the steering wheel and started shaking. The guy could have shot them. Easily shot them all. She gripped the steering wheel. She'd been so dumb to say yes and so grateful she had. Headache be damned, she let her tears flow.

Chapter 33

Drained, Ginger forced herself to stop crying. Sitting for a moment, she got her make-up kit out of the trunk and re-did her face. Her body was still shaking but it wasn't giving off signals she needed a drink. She was sure the shaking was a reaction from almost getting killed. Things might be turning around for her if she could get through this day without a drink. She should call George.

Before she could sort out what she wanted to say to him, her cell phone started meowing like a cat. She grabbed it.

"George! Thank God it's you! You won't believe. . . "

He cut her off. "I've had a game changing day, Babe. It's why I'm calling. It all started with."

Ten minutes later she was saying she loved him madly, that she was with him all the way, and they'd talk tomorrow. She clicked off her phone without mentioning their rescue. George had put in his resignation, effective in three weeks. Then he'd taken the rest of the day off to visit several companies interested in his solar pumping system. Just over a half hour ago he'd signed a second contract. The numbers were a little frightening, but they were now small business owners. She'd not gotten in one word about rescuing Nikki and her girls.

Sitting there trying to figure what would be asked of her in their new joint venture, her phone rang again. 'Caller unknown.'

Thinking it could be the police, she reluctantly answered. "Hello."

"Ginger! It's Birdie. I've a huge favor to ask of you. You know about my travel club's trip to Alaska?"

"Libby told me you asked her to go."

"I did. But you know her these days. She kept hemming and hawing until it was filled up, as she knew it would, but,"

Birdie paused. Ginger drummed her nails on the car dashboard and waited.

"A woman backed out of the trip last week. I told Libby about that. Of course she hasn't gotten back to me. Someone here thinks she's with you."

"She is."

Ginger smiled. Five minutes later she'd signed Libby up. She deserved it as payback for all the picket lines and protest marches she'd talked her into. She'd given Birdie her credit card numbers, signed Libby up for the trip had even promised she'd badger Libby into teaching at least one class on desert lore to the Daycare kids. With far too much to think about, she spoke the address of the hotel to her GPS system, then drove out of the parking lot.

Pleased to see their hotel was set far enough away from the road that it would be quiet during the night, she parked George's car in the only spot of shade. Getting out she looked around. A gurgling waterfall, hibiscus trees even taller than hers, reminded her of her home and calmed her a bit.

Even her feet happily marched along the stone path leading to the office door. She was good. Very good! With just a few clicks on her computer she'd found this beautiful hotel, and made reservations at home in her nightgown. She was almost keeping up with the times except for the newest, do everything but cook dinner, cell phones. They seemed a bit over the top for their life style but she'd need to learn about them now for their new business.

In the lobby, intending to instruct the owner not to give out any information about them, she stopped dead. Booze. She smelled booze! Her back bristled. She'd specifically booked a no bar hotel! Looking around, seeing no signs indicting there was a bar, her nose traced the source to a man huffing and puffing past her carrying two large suitcases out of the lobby. His companion gave the tall woman behind the counter a ferociously dirty look then walked a small yipping dog past Ginger and out the door.

The woman behind the hotel desk smiled at Ginger. "Sorry about that, they were sure my 'no pets allowed' sign was for other guests, not them."

The clerk waved her hand slowly back and forth over a clay pot, filling the air with the sweet smell of jasmine. Ginger smiled. Now, that was service.

Within minutes she knew the woman was fifty-eight, had moved from Oregon almost thirty years ago, owned the hotel on her own, and loved Sedona. She was very sorry she didn't have a fourth room available.

A few flattering comments from Ginger about the hotel had the woman searching through the reservations and changing their three single room reservation to one single and two rooms with queen size beds. She and Libby would have to share a room, snoring or no snoring. Nikki and her daughters would have the other, with a cot added. Anna Mae still had her single room, but all their rooms were near each other and facing the quiet beauty of green grass, brush, leading the viewer's eye to a range of low, Sedona's red rocks. It was as if they were being rewarded for their hard day.

Ginger explained about the bust-out at the restaurant. Asking for secrecy, she watched the woman sign Anderson, Johnson and Brewer on the forms in front of her.

"Thank you. Why do I smell wonderful food? Is there a restaurant near here? I didn't see any signs."

"Just go out our side entrance, through the arches, into the courtyard. That will put you next to the best restaurant this side of town. I've accused them of having a direct conduit into our air ducts."

With her stomach growling, Ginger followed her nose to the outside seating. It was almost full. Inside the restaurant was a bit less crowded. Making reservations for four thirty, she eyed the long bar at the back of the restaurant. Behind it were three lit up shelves, showing off their evil temptations. Today, with all that had gone on here and at home, she felt strangely whole. The bottles didn't beckon her, but she knew they could at any time.

It had been a memorable day. She didn't feel the need for a drink, but her legs acting as if they had a mind of their own, strolled her past the bar and into to the restroom. Using the facilities, she came back out and very quickly passed the bar. Turning around, she headed toward the restroom as if she'd forgotten something, then found herself sitting down on a barstool.

The bartender wiped the pristine wood in front of her, laid a napkin down, smiled, showed his remarkably white teeth and asked, "What can I get you, pretty lady?"

He was handsome enough to make her want to fool herself with a Virgin Mary. That could lead to one drink and then another. The smiling bartender, bottles all in a row, with their familiar smells hit her so hard, her purse fell to the floor. *'Have a drink. Just one. You deserve it.'* Flashed in front of her eyes.

What the hell was wrong with her? She didn't want to drink ever again. She'd felt so sure of it when she promised George her drinking days were over. When she walked into the restaurant she'd felt on top of things, now she wanted to drain the bar. Get the old comforting feelings back. Who was she kidding? How could it be good when she hadn't even remembered how she got home that day?

George pouring out her gin, the bottles on fire, flashed in her head. She bent down, picked up her purse, returned the bartender's smile and fled. One day, one minute at a time.

Not this time, not ever, sang in her head all the way out the door and into the late afternoon sunshine.

Looking across the street she saw a cafe with lots of outside seating. From here she could read the 'all organic' sign. She'd be much safer over there for dinner and it was a perfect place for children. She quickly cancelled her reservation and made one there.

Back in the safety of her car, and half way to picking everyone up, her cell phone honked like geese. That meant it was Lib. She'd given her that sound because Liberty Price never announced who she was, no matter how bad the reception might be. Ginger pressed the talk button.

"We're done, but we're not where you left us."

"Where are you?"

"Outside Walmart."

"Walmart? I dropped you off blocks from there."

Ginger pressed the volume button as if more of it would make sense of what Libby was saying.

"Nikki wouldn't let you shop where I dropped you off? Too expensive? She's nuts. It's not her money."

She listened a minute.

"Okay, I'm too late to the party. If Nikki thinks those stores were too expensive, wait 'till she sees where we're staying tonight. Oh boy."

Ginger was behind several cars waiting for a line of tourists to cross in the middle of the street. A horn blared.

"Did someone just honk at you? Are you driving and on the phone?"

Libby, thinking Ginger sounded good, not jittery, spoke so loud, Ginger was sure she was just outside her car.

"You called me, remember? I answered. I'm stuck in traffic. That's not driving. Some guy in an exotic sports car wants a sexy blond to notice him. I'll be there in ten if these tourists ever get moving. Some are pretty slow and old."

Ginger giggled. Snapped her phone shut, tossed it on the passenger seat as if Libby would catch it for her.

Studying the line of people she became irritated with herself. Again. She'd seen gray heads and thought old. That was a rotten thing to think. They were moving slow because it was just too crowded to move fast. Something must have just let out.

Her nerves were screwing with her head and, she still had to tell Libby about signing her up for the Alaska trip. That could get touchy. Best she wait until after dinner, maybe even after Anna Mae met her kids, if she actually would.

Maybe telling Libby about her cruise could wait until they are almost home. One thing at a time. One thing. One day. One person.

She spotted them as soon as she swung into the Walmart parking lot. Nikki's girls were standing next to dozens of white plastic bags whipping in the wind and waving for her to stop. There was no way she could miss them.

Ginger stepped out of her car. "Trunk's open, girls. Go to it."

Anna Mae grinning a grin Ginger had never seen on her, helped the girls stuff their bags into the trunk next to the suitcases she should have left at the hotel.

"We had so much fun shopping."

"You'll have loads of fun with your grandchildren too."

Dancers of the Third Age

The light on Anna Mae's face vanished. "Assuming I have some."

Ginger wanted to step in front of a car and die. She'd crushed Anna Mae's moment of happiness. Taken it from her. It was inexcusable. Yes, not drinking had her off kilter. She didn't need a drink Yes, her body craved the relief gin gave her, but there was no excuse for hurting others.

She had felt good smashing that car window then driving away like they'd robbed a bank. Great even. It satisfied her urge to strike out at something but not these people. She valued them so she had to be careful, control her urges.

Suddenly Nikki pulled them all together for another big circle hug. Right there. On the sidewalk. In front of strangers. What would they think? She didn't care. These dear people made her feel better. She gave Anna Mae an apology squeeze, then mumbled. "I was a bitch and I'm sorry."

Before Anna Mae could reply, Nikki was thanking them again.

"Thank you. Thank you all for saving us. We almost d. . . " Her chin quivered. "What you did for us is still so unbelievable."

"What we did for you?" Libby turned Nikki to her. "Getting you free of him, woke me up. Taught me that there's still a lot of fire left in this here woman. I'm so proud of us I could just yell!"

"Me too." There were tears in Anna Mae's eyes.

"Ms. Ginger!" Lizbeth touched Ginger's sleeve. "Ms. Anna Mae got us all swimsuits with flowers. You too, 'cause we are the six Misketeers."

She'd just crushed Anna Mae, who'd thought enough to buy her a swimsuit. Ginger looked down at Lizbeth.

"Anna Mae got me a new swimsuit?"

"Yup, 'cause she said it wasn't fair if we didn't get you one too."

Ginger looked at Libby. "I have a suit?"

Libby smiled. "Wearing Walmart will be good for you."

She touched Anna Mae's hand. "Thank you."

"Mine's blue, like my eyes." Em lifted a blue suit with multicolored fish all over it out of a bag, then another.

"This one is yours. Isn't it pretty? It's yellow like your hair and lots of flowers. Ms. Libby says you love flowers."

Libby grinned. "The girls had great fun picking them out. Didn't you girls?"

Two little heads nodded in unison. "We all have matching yellow, happy-smile, tee shirts."

"Of course we do."

Thank God they were staying at a small hotel way up in Sedona, far away from any of her boring Tucson friends.

Chapter 34

Nearly exhausted, but dressed for an early dinner, both Libby and Ginger looked out the hotel room window, down to the swimming pool. Nikki and her girls were testing the water for a swim in the morning.

Mother and daughters were laughing at something. Libby put her arm around Ginger's thin waist. "We did good today, didn't we?"

"Yes. We were incredible. A bit insane too. It turns my stomach to think what would have happened to them if we'd just taken a few minutes longer enjoying the red rocks or, picked out another restaurant. Or."

Ginger couldn't help giggling,

"If mousey Anna Mae hadn't stood up and roared like a lion. They'd still be in that frightening guy's hands if Anna Mae hadn't started the whole thing. I'm beginning to think Anna Mae will actually meet with her children."

The littlest girl, looked up at them, waved, Libby waved back at Em. It seemed a long time ago that she'd stood looking out her window at the Bordello watching the day care kids play. She'd thought of herself as the Watcher at The Window. She smiled now. Not any more. She'd come alive today.

"When I sat down on that curb and hugged those two sweet, little girls."

When Libby didn't continue, Ginger finally asked, "Yes?"

"When those little bodies pressed against me, all the parts of me that went missing after Phil's death came roaring back. I became me again. Liberty Price is back in action."

"Does this means you'll start helping with the Daycare kids?"

Libby nodded. "Yup."

Ginger smiled. One hurdle gone and she didn't have to bring it up. Maybe if she rubbed ice on Lib, she'd be hit by an urge to get away from the Arizona heat and sand. See some icebergs. Feel cold, sea air against her face. From the deck of a cruise ship.

*****

Dinner had been full of laughter and stories. Nikki's parents had called, full of thank you's and saying they were leaving in a half hour Denver and would arrive in Flagstaff late this evening. They would then drive to Sedona tomorrow. Hopefully they could all leave Monday morning.

By nine-thirty Libby and Ginger were dressed for bed, when a quiet knock had Libby jumping up from her bed, going to the door to face a distraught Nikki.

"I was just trying to help a friend and I've hurt my children so badly, it's not fixable."

"Where's this coming from?" Libby took Nikki's hand and, steered her into the room.

"It just hit me that my children will never forget this. And now I'm lying to myself and my daughters. I've been telling them over and over, that we will be all right. I don't believe we will be all right. They'll never be right again."

"No, that's not true." Libby sat her down.

"I have three adopted children who were abused by someone in their families. They are grown up now and are happy, well adjusted adults. You have to worry about yourself. You have to worry how to heal yourself."

Ginger looked at Nikki. "Are your daughters sleeping?"

"Yes. I cuddled them until they fell asleep. When I tried to sleep, my mind went crazy thinking back to today. I can't thank you enough for all you've done for us. But while I was hearing my children softly breathing, I felt like I was hit with a brick. I'm scared I can't handle the repercussions that are coming. I've got a splitting headache." Nikki took a long breath. "I do think I'm over reacting some. When I talked to my parents and they told me my husband Bill, blames himself because he asked me to befriend Kevin. Bill has always worried about Kevin."

"No, don't got there." Ginger said.

"Everything's gone so fast today. Try to take some breaths, calm down. Let it all settle down. Tomorrow your parents will be here. Soon you husband will be home. You have love all around you. Just love yourself and your children. That will get you through until tomorrow."

"Ginger's right." Libby sat on the bottom of the bed. "Why don't I go check on Em and Lizbeth? Do you have your room key with you?"

"It's here somewhere." Nikki patted her pockets then handed Libby the key.

Taking their room key too, Libby left, Entering Nikki's room she stumbled in relief seeing the girls curled up together on the bed. Their chests rising and falling; their color was a bit flushed. They looked so normal. She'd been nuts to think Nikki would ever hurt them?

This day had been too much. The children were asleep and they looked just as if nothing had harmed them. Touching them, their arms were a little cool and she pulled a blanket up to their shoulders then tip toed out of the room.

"Your daughters are are sound asleep all snuggled together. They're breathing easy."

The last part was for Ginger, looking worried sitting on the bed with an arm around Nikki.

"I wish I could sleep. Just before I came in here I got an update from my husband. He'll arrive in Denver a few hours after we do. We all thought Kevin's divorce was his wife's fault. She was so emotional and he was so quiet. Now we know he's a quiet nut case."

Ginger pulled the bed covers back, took Nikki's shoes off.

"Libby, could you sleep with the girls? I'll stay here with Nikki."

"I'd love to."

Ginger crawled in the bed and laid down with her. "I'll lay here with you. If you can't asleep in a half hour I'll get you something."

It wasn't long before they were all sound asleep, except for Anna Mae. She was dressed and sitting on her bed, with an open phone book on her lap and her finger pressed on the listing for her son. His name spelled out in official print finally made her believe her son was alive. Now she had to decide what to do, which was proving as difficult as when she'd sent her children away.

Libby and Ginger had said she deserved a medal for saving Nikki and her girls from Kevin. Maybe she did, but she needed now to make herself actually talk with her own children.

Life seemed easy for them. They handled things so well. They would never understand why life scared her so. The only time it hadn't was when she sent them away. She'd been strong that day. She'd even risked her own life for her children by staying with Benny. Risked it over and over. She'd done the right thing then.

Tears rolled down her face, dropped onto the telephone book. From across the bed, her reflection in the mirror startled her. Her face drooped in sadness, when it should be happy. She tried to smile, but it looked fake.

No, that was what Benny would say. She sat up straight, looked again and saw a kind person. She was a woman who thought before speaking. Who loved her children enough to send them to safety. Benny was dead. He couldn't stop her from seeing their children. But Libby was right. If she didn't meet with her children, now adults with children of their own, Benny would win from his grave. Then she'd have to go back and shoot the son of a bitch again.

"And, if I don't talk to my children, Ginger will never let me back in her car."

Her voice startled her, but lightened her spirits a little. Her children

202

had better lives because of what she'd done. They looked very happy in Sarah's graduation pictures. Her sister Ruth and Charlie looked proud, and happy too.

She wrote down Timothy's address, turned to the yellow pages, picked up the phone and ordered a taxi. Minutes later she snuck out of her room, sauntered through the hotel lobby, smiled at the clerk as if her life were in order, then limping as fast as possible to the street a half block away from their hotel. The taxi was there, waiting for her.

Fifteen nervous minutes later, she sat staring at her son's home from the back seat of the cab. The lights on in front of the house made it clear her Timothy had a nice home, in a nice neighborhood.

She felt herself relax a little. Impulsively, she leaned forward, tapped the driver on the shoulder then wondered if she should have touched him. She'd never ridden in a taxi before. When he turned and smiled at her she could see he was clean-shaven with no rings in his ears, nose, or lips. She'd been afraid he might be one of those modern men wearing all kinds of jewelry and covered in tattoos. His face was years younger than the wrinkles around his eyes. That puzzled her until she saw racing car tags hanging from his rear view mirror.

Benny used to say the brutal Arizona sun rotted rubber and faces. She shook her head to get Benny out of it.

"Do you race cars?"

"No. I'm in charge of the pit stop."

"I'd like to sit here for a few minutes. Can I do that?"

"Yes, ma'am." The cabbie turned back around.

She looked out the window again. Timothy's one story house was sprawled across a wide lawn. No bikes or toys littered the front yard. Well, her grandchildren, if she had any, were probably older than that by now. Her heart raced when a light went on in one of the front rooms. With the curtains drawn, it was impossible to see if it was her son. No dogs barked and no cars drove by.

All of her years of wondering would be over in just minutes if she could just make herself get out of the cab, walk up to his door and ring his bell. She moved toward the door handle, but her hand stayed at her side. The cabbie sat very still, staring out his front window. The quiet became so unnerving she cleared her throat.

"My son lives in there. I haven't seen him for thirty-seven years, nine months and six days." She hated that her voice shook. "I've no idea where my daughter lives."

"I'm very sorry to hear that ma'am." He turned around. "I have children of my own and I know how hard it can be sometimes. I'd be glad to walk you to his door, ma'am."

"That's very nice of you, but if it's alright with you, I'll just sit here a bit longer."

Chapter 35

Early the next morning, Nikki returned to her room rested and in much better spirits. Her parents would be here soon, they'd spend some of the morning talking with the FBI.

If there were no police delays, Nikki and her family would see some of Sedona then leave for Flagstaff and home.

After an enjoyable breakfast together, there were more group hugs in the hall and waves of thank you, thank you and trading of addresses.

"We'll keep in touch."

"You bet we will." Libby smiled at them. "We want to see pictures of our new family and where you live. How our Miskateers are doing. And all big events coming up in your lives. Us too. We'll send pictures. Maybe someday we can all come back here and have a nice time?"

Nikki nodded. "Yes. That would be wise too."

"You could fly into Phoenix, we could drive up from Tucson we pick you up and off we'll go."

"No, Lib. We'll need a van. We'll rent a van so we can all sing together. Especially, *I Am Woman*."

"Maybe we can even visit with my family who lives up here." Anna Mae lips trembled as she spoke.

Libby put her arm around her. "That we could do, Anna Mae. That we could do."

Minutes later they were nudging Anna Mae toward the stairs.

"I can't go looking like this. I'm in a dress. You are both in slacks. I'll go to my room and change out of this dress. I'll be just a few minutes."

Not trusting her, they followed her back to their rooms where Ginger gave her, her marching orders. "Ten minutes, no more. You come get us."

Twenty minutes later, Libby, looking at Ginger and couldn't resist. "Now you know how much fun it is waiting for someone."

"You sound just like George. I never pay attention to him, but this is ridiculous. I'm not waiting."

A sharp knock, knock sent Ginger heading for the door. Opening it, she was relieved to see Anna Mae in slacks and a blouse.

"Sorry I took so long. I stopped in to tell Nikki we're leaving now. I've been thinking."

Fearing another delay, Ginger stepped them into the hallway.

"Before we leave shouldn't we call my son's home to check if someone's there?"

Libby had followed them into the hall. "I thought you said you wanted to see his very first reaction to you."

Anna Mae looked a little puzzled, then brightened. "I do. I'd hang up if someone answered."

"Then why call. It's best we just go over there." Libby hooked her arm through Anna Mae's right arm. Ginger took her left arm.

"You're thinking I'll try to escape, aren't you?"

"No, we're just being cozy." Libby moved them forward.

"Don't lie, Lib." Ginger smiled. "Yes, we think you might try to escape."

Anna Mae squeezed their hands against her sides. "Don't let me out of your sight."

Once they settled into the car, Ginger spoke Timothy's address into her GPS, listened for instructions, then headed left out of the parking lot.

"I still don't know how a car can give you the correct driving directions." Anna Mae tugged on the seat belt to loosen it from her neck.

Trying for levity, Libby leaned forward from the back seat. "Ginger's other car has George Clooney and Brad Pitt impersonators telling her which way to go. When she fails to follow instructions, Andy Rooney comes on and says, 'get a grip'."

"And famous people do that? Amazing." Anna Mae's admiration was genuine.

Ginger slowed for a car turning in front of her. "I call them modern miracles. I can even download other voices to talk to me, Anna Mae."

Any kind of chatter would do to help eat up the time going to Timothy's house.

Unfortunately, no one had more chatter so they spent the next few miles in silence. Finally, Anna Mae cleared her throat.

"Do you think you should start calling me Marian? My children don't know me as Anna Mae. And I will be so happy to get rid of that name. I've always thought of myself as Marian. Now I can be again."

"Will do, Marian." Libby emphasized Marian to make the name stick in her head. Over-joyed that Anna Mae, no she meant Marian, was making plans to actually talk to her children, she pointed out more of the stunning red rocks.

A few miles later, Ginger turned up a winding hill, and suddenly they were on Timothy's street. Her GPS was counting off house numbers when Anna Mae AKA Marian tapped her arm.

"There it is!" She pointed left, across the steering wheel and down several houses from the car.

"How do you know that's his house? You can't possibly see the numbers from here."

Marian didn't answer that, instead she said, "Please, park back here, on the this side of the street. I want to be far enough away that he can't see me looking at his house. I may not be able to get out."

Ginger parked, then turned to her. "You didn't answer me, Marian. How did you know that's his house?"

Marian looked straight ahead so she wouldn't have to face them. "I took a taxi out here last night."

"You did what? That's fabulous!"

"Good for you!" Libby reached forward, patted Anna Mae's shoulder. "Why didn't you tell us? Did you go see him?"

"I sat out here for over an hour watching his house, hoping to catch a glimpse of him but the curtains were closed. The taxi driver was very nice about it."

She continued when Libby and Ginger just looked at her.

"I just wanted to experience my feelings all by myself when I first saw my son's home. That's why I asked a stranger to take me here. All Timothy's driveway lights were lit last evening, so I saw the shape of his house, but not much more. Seeing the grass now, and his shrubs, tells me my son must be very neat. He has a very nice home. Don't you think so?"

She liked that both Libby and Ginger smiled and nodded.

"I tried so hard to get out of the taxi. I wanted to ring his doorbell. I really did. I told the taxi driver that I hadn't seen my son in a very long time and he offered to walk with me to his door. I just couldn't do it."

"Maybe you need your friends at your side."

Libby and Ginger always seemed to know what she needed. They looked pleased with her, even though she'd failed to go to see Timothy. They didn't think she was a fool, or a coward.

Benny would have called her worse than that. He always got mad when he found out she did things for herself.

Marian kept staring at her son's front door.

"I wasn't very brave. Anyone can sit in a taxi wondering what to do next, then do nothing The hotel was so close to my son I just knew wouldn't sleep until I saw his home. Last night was only my fourth big decision of my life."

Ginger mentally shook her head at Marian. *Only her fourth big decision?* That was followed by, *give her a break, Ginger, four is better than two.*

"What were the others?" Libby quietly undid her seat belt.

"The first one was when I decided to marry their father. He'd made me pregnant. My parents said I either had to marry him or run away. The second decision was almost impossible. Send my children to their aunt and uncle or what? Three was easy. I had no trouble deciding to throw his tool wide. I knew Benny would reach out for it. I hoped he'd fall off the ladder, and break his neck. I didn't think he'd die. I wanted him in a wheelchair and to be at my mercy for the rest of his life. But he died."

Libby squirmed in her seat. "You have to stop talking like you killed him, Anna Mae. I'm sorry, I meant Marian. Stop saying you killed Benny. You'll crush your children if you so much as hint that you had a hand in his death. Even if they are happy about their father's death they won't want their mother to be the one who caused it."

"Libby's right Marian. Come on." Ginger chimed in. "Give the police some credit. After testing all the evidence they declared it an accident. Your kids don't need to know any more than that."

Marian sat back. "This is too complicated. Take me back to Tucson. I'll make out a will that says Timothy and Sarah will get all my money when I die."

That may be sooner than you think, was on the tip of Ginger's tongue but, she wasn't a three year old, or a hundred and three, so she corralled her anger.

"And just when are you going to die? Ten, twenty, thirty, maybe even forty years from now? They could be dead by then. You march up to that door right now and be with your kids. That'll get rid of Benny's ghost damn fast."

"You mean David."

"Who cares what we call him. David, Schmabid. Mean Benny is my name for him. My point is, don't do his bidding any longer."

Ginger got out of the car, went around to the passenger side to find Libby already there and holding her hand out to Marian. Libby snapped her fingers.

"Come on. Get out. I was terrified, really terrified yesterday when we were rescuing Nikki and her girls, Marian. It taught me a little bit of what you and your children went through every day living with him. You gave up your life to get them away from him. Now, get out of the car, hold your head up high, and go get it back. We'll knock on your son's door with you."

When Anna Mae didn't budge, Libby growled. "Look at me."

Waiting until she did, Libby added. "Good. Now listen. This is the last piece of advice I'll ever give you."

My facelifts will be free before that happens, ran through Ginger's head.

Libby took Marian's hand. "The first step is the hardest. They even write songs about it. Now, come on, woman, your friends are right here beside you. We'll walk you to the door."

Dancers of the Third Age

For thirty-seven years she'd yearned for this day and feared it. Wondering what would her children say when they met. With shaking legs, she took hold of her friends hands, leaned forward.

"Both of you must go in with me. If, they ask me to come in."

"Rabid dogs can't keep us out. Let's go."

Tears ran down Marian's face as Ginger took her elbow, Libby her hand, and together they stood her up.

"One step. Now another. See? We're walking."

Surprised that her legs actually were moving, she let Ginger and Libby nudge her forward. Holding at a steady pace, they crossed the street then walked down the sidewalk. Soon she was there at her son's cobblestone walk. Her feet stopped as if they were frozen in cement. She tried walking but they were stuck. Nothing moved, until her knees buckled. Only Ginger and Libby's strong hands held her up.

"If one of you kicks my left foot, maybe it will move."

Libby's nudge made her foot move. Made her move so they were all walking on up to her son's front door.

Marian straightened, then reached out over the chasm of time and rang her son's doorbell.

Chapter 36

The door opened so quickly it startled Marian and she jumped back, knocking both Ginger and Libby sideways. Quickly re-gaining their balance, the three of them stared at a woman who could be Marian's daughter-in-law.

Disappointed it wasn't her son who answered the door, Marian looked past the woman, to an entryway. Every part of her wanted to push the woman aside, run in, call for Timothy to come to her. But, that was not her way of doing things. So she stretched her neck as far as she could and looked further into the house.

"I'm sorry." The woman smiled at them. "I should have known my answering the door so fast would have startled you ladies. I saw you coming up our walk, arm-in-arm, and the three of you looked so eager, I just headed for the door."

Still straining to see her son, the woman's words passed by Marian unnoticed. She stared at the brightly colored entryway tile floor. It was cheerful. The colors lit up her heart and carried her gaze into a wide, bright opening, to what looked like it was the dining room.

Yes, there was a large dinner table. And a master chair was facing their way. Past it, was an upright piano, a cello, and guitar. An unusual sight for a dining room. Music must come from her daughter-in-law's side of the family. None of her relatives had any musical ability at all. Her sister Ruth had once said the only way any of them could carry a tune was in a shopping bag.

"How can I help you?"

The question jolted Marian into the present. She stared at the tall, very pretty woman in front of her. She had a kind face, looked to be the right age to be Timothy's wife and, she had a puzzled look.

Of course! It was because Timothy's wife would know her sister Ruth. In their younger years, everyone said she and Ruth could be twins. Maybe they still looked alike. If they did, it would be easier for them to believe she was who she was.

"And who are you?" Marian's question jumped out without warning.

Clamping her hands over her mouth, she just quickly removed them thinking they made her look a bit crazy.

"That was rude of me! It doesn't matter who you are." She shook her head at her foolishness.

"I didn't mean that either. Of course you matter. I'm so anxious to find out if Timothy Thurgood lives here that everything comes out of my mouth wrong. Is this his house?"

She held her breath. Not for one minute, had she ever thought, she'd get to ask that question.

"Yes, it is." The woman smiled while looking a bit wary.

Marian's legs gave way. She grabbed onto Ginger and Libby for support, looked at them.

"Did you hear her? Timothy lives here."

She'd not seen him since he was nine years old and now they were moments apart.

"I'm his wife, Allison. How can I help you?"

This woman was her son's wife! She was her very own daughter-in-law. It was all unbelievably wonderful. She wanted to clap her hands, jump up and down, like a child.

"Yes! Oh yes! I'm Timothy's mother!"

Her daughter-in-law stiffened as if struck. She shouldn't have said it so fast or so loud. She'd planned to ease into who she was, not shout it out like that. Things were going badly and only she was to blame. Shaking Benny's opinion of her away she stood up straight. There was no easy, or right way to do this.

"I am Marian Thurgood, Timothy's mother."

"I heard you, but you can't be. My husband's mother died a long time ago. If this is some kind of scam it's not funny."

"No, I'm alive. I've always been alive." Now she sounded insane.

"No you aren't." The woman looked very angry.

"Why am I talking to you? You can't be her. We hired several top-notch investigators to find Tim's mother. None of them located even a trace of his parents, beyond their apartment in Phoenix."

Marian grabbed Libby's arm.

"Did you hear her? My Timothy has looked for me! He tried to find me. He doesn't hate me."

"Exactly what we told you." Libby smiled, steadied Marian.

A pale Allison now held onto the doorframe. "Please don't do this. You can't be his mother. Every detective said that given his father's violence, he most likely killed her then disappeared."

Marian looked at Libby, Ginger, then at Allison. "It makes sense they'd say that, but it isn't true."

"No, too many experts have told us she's dead for me to believe you

211

now." Allison shook her head, at the woman in front of her.

"And who are these ladies with you? You all look like a bunch of Evangelists."

"We're her friends. We're here to give her support."

"Well, she can't be Tim's mother so I'm shutting the door now."

Ginger pushed on the door. "Well, experts said we couldn't walk on the moon either."

They stared at Ginger who shrugged. "Just a thought."

"You have to prove to me first that you are Marian Thurgood. My husband can not survive another let down."

She couldn't prove she was Marian Thurgood. Benny had changed their names, destroyed all their old identity.

Excited, Marian almost shouted, "I put my son and daughter on a bus and sent them to Ruth and Charlie to protect them from their father."

She held onto Ginger's arm so hard, pains shot to Ginger's shoulder all the way up to her ear.

Allison shook her head again. "Everyone knows how my husband and his sister got here. They know about Ruth and Charlie. You aren't even close to proving who you are."

"Look at me, closely. Everyone always got Ruth and me mixed up."

Marian tilted her head up, and to one side. She was at Timmy's door. She'd not gotten this close to give up. Not now. She'd sit outside all night if she had to.

"My son'll know me."

The suspicion on her son's wife's face didn't change a bit. "Let me see your driver's license. A charge card, maybe."

She couldn't do that. They'd all say she was Anna Mae Brown not Marian Thurgood. A tug on her purse made her look down. Libby was digging through the side pocket of her purse.

"Show Allison the journal."

"I'm so mixed up. I should have thought of that." Marian squeezed Libby's hand. "Thank you, thank you."

She held out the journal to Allison. "In here it tells when we got married." She flipped some pages and stopped.

"Right here I tell about the beatings and how Timothy hid in his room."

Impatient to see her son, she didn't give Allison time to read before flipping to the most important page. "Here, here. Read this."

Marian pointed to the day she gave her children away. "I put them on the bus, then hid behind a pillar until they were gone."

Allison's eyes narrowed. "This only proves you have his mother's journal."

"I am his mother!" She was near tears as she finally came to the page she needed to show Allison.

"See here? Timothy's father changed our names from David and Marian Thurgood to Benny and Anna Mae Brown. I can prove that I am Anna Mae Brown."

Fishing in her purse for her wallet Anna Mae nearly dropped the journal. "I can prove it. I can. It's here."

"Slow down, Anna Mae, I mean Marian." Libby pressed the pictures into Allison's hand. "She found these just a few weeks ago."

As she looked at them, Allison's face filled with fury. "You got pictures of Sarah's graduation but you never contacted your children? That's enough! Get out! Get the hell away from here."

Ginger held tight to the door Allison was trying to shut. "I know this is crazy but wait, give her a minute to explain."

"Their father took the pictures. I didn't know about them until they fell out of his cabinet just a week ago. Somehow, he found out where the children were. He never told me."

Allison looked past them to the street. "If he's out there, I'm calling the police."

"He's dead." Marian turned to Libby. "I've forgotten her name."

"Allison." Libby whispered into her ear.

"I still need proof that you are his mother."

"Timothy has several half-moon scars on his back from his father's belt. I have the same scars."

She turned and lifted her blouse. "See? They match his."

"Hers are from the bastard's belt too."

This time they all looked at Libby.

"Well, there's no other name for him. We saw her scars when she took her shirt off at the pool."

Allison sucked in a breath. "As horrible as they are, people have seen my husband's scars. I give you it's impressive. There's only one thing myself, Tim and his sister know. If you are his mother you will know it too. Not even Ruth knows it. What did his father call his son?"

"Timothy. That's his name."

"What about a knick name?"

The color drained from Anna Mae's face. "Timid-thy."

Tears ran in torrents down her daughter-in-law's face as she pulled Marian in for a huge hug.

"He'd given up. We'd all given up."

Despite all the hugs from Nikki and her girls, hugs still felt strange, and uncomfortable. Group hugs weren't so bad, but from one person? A person she didn't know was hugging her. She pulled slightly back.

"I'm so sorry. I just had to be sure you're his mother. He's worried about you ever since you put them on that bus."

This time, when Allison pulled her to her chest, Marian stayed there, felt her daughter-in-law's trembling body. She gave way to a rush of love and hugged back. Releasing each other they parted.

"Come in, all of you. I'll go get him. First though, I must tell you, your son hates the name Timothy. It reminds him of his father. He had used his middle name ever since I've known him."

"You call him Mathew?"

"We've shortened it to Matt. I'll go get him." Marian grabbed the sleeve of her daughter-in-laws blouse.

"Wait! Please don't tell him I'm here. Please don't. I abandoned my children. I need to see their first reaction to me. Before they can put on a proper face. That's why we didn't call to say we were coming. First, I need to know. Is my daughter alive? Is Sarah here?"

Allison held onto Marian's shaking hands. "Sarah lives just a few miles away."

"Oh, thank God."

Tears streaming down her cheeks, Allison smiled. "Matt is out back in his workshop. I'll take you to him."

"Workshop?"

Marian's heart nearly stopped. Benny loved his workshop. Had her son turned out like his father after all she'd sacrificed? If her son were a bad man, she didn't know what she'd do. No. She wouldn't jump to conclusions. Good men had workshops. She tried to smile as her wobbly body followed Allison through the living room, into a kitchen smelling of homemade bread.

At the back door she became afraid again. Libby and Ginger had to gently nudge her through it and into son's back yard. A big and beautiful back yard.

There was a pleasant round building, she thought people called it a gazebo, to her left. It had red, yellow, orange flowers, clusters of succulents, all across the front. It reminded her of an artist's rendition of the days of old. On the other side of the yard there was a low brick wall. Green low bushes, a mix of flowers, succulents, three low benches were near it. Everything looked so inviting. The only things out of place in this natural beauty of a yard were the cement walkways crisscrossing in the green grass. Why cement when the grass looked so healthy?

Allison pointed to the round building. "The gazebo is his workshop. Matt has it so crowded in there we won't all fit in."

Reaching up, she pulled a cord and a soft bell rang out. Seconds later a honk sounded from the gazebo.

"That means he's coming. Two honks means I have to wait, three says he's not available right now. I'd like to put a phone out there, but your son doesn't want to be disturbed when he's working."

Marian stiffened. One ring, two rings. What did her son do if someone broke his rules? Benny rained down terror. The gazebo door inched open and a man in a wheelchair backed out.

Marian opened her mouth to speak then clamped it shut. Her son was in a wheelchair!

"No, no, no." Her barely audible wail tore at Libby. "My son is crippled. I waited too long to send them away. "

She dare not ask if it had been from a fight.

Allison looked at her. "Don't call him crippled. Your son is the most able man I've ever known. "

"Why didn't you warn me?"

"I had to see your first reaction to his wheelchair just like you want to see his. Only my husband's mother could possibly have that much pain on her face. That told me you really are his mother. You just passed with flying colors."

She should have stayed in Tucson and imagined he was fine. Muttering, "I shouldn't have come here."

Marian squeezed her fists, to force her bad thinking out. There were many, many reasons, for a person to be in a wheelchair. And many happy people were in wheelchairs.

"Why is my son in a wheelchair?" Saying 'my son' and wheelchair in the same sentence, cut like nothing ever had.

"It's best you hear it from him. Just focus on your son, not on his chair."

Ginger loved what she was hearing. Don't say crippled? Most able man you'll ever meet? Focus on your son, not his chair? This Allison was a gem, a pure gem. Marian's whining wouldn't get far here.

Chapter 37

Instinct told her to run away and her feet twitched to go, but she held fast. Watching her son spin around as easily as if he'd turned on his feet, she whispered, "My son is alive, at least he's alive."

That he needed a wheelchair was another reason for him to be angry with her. She'd made him a cripple. No, not cripple. She wasn't to say cripple. And she wasn't to say Timothy. He was Matt now and she was Marian. She needed to touch his face, hear his voice. Make sure this wasn't a nightmare.

Allison gently pushed her toward her son. "Go to him. Hurry, go to him."

Her son was real.

As she stepped forward, the picture of her son in his Army uniform came to her. That was it! The Army had done this to him. Not her. The thought stopped her heart from flopping around in her chest and she took a few tentative steps toward him.

"Aunt Ruth?"

Patting his denim shirt pocket for his glasses, he remembered they were on his workbench back in the gazebo. The woman coming toward him was listing to one side with each step. It wasn't Aunt Ruth's walk; he could see that now.

She could be a custodial grandmother from school. No, he knew every one of them, and none of them limped. Older women often meant trouble for him. Most wanted a piece of his work for next to nothing.

"They usually said, Mr. Thurgood your carvings are so wonderful. But the price! Can't you come down just a teensy bit?"

They'd dicker with him, but they never came into his back yard.

Staring at her, he realized the familiarity came from her head being down and a little to the side, not quite looking at him. His mother sometimes held her head that way, when dealing with his father. He dismissed the thought. He'd been disappointed too many times and his mother had, had no limp.

But, still his heart raced. His hope had never really died.

Limping badly, Anna Mae closed the distance between them and saw the puzzlement on his face vanish. There was shock, but thankfully he didn't frown. Then a burst of sunshine filled her son's rugged face.

"Mom?" His voice broke. "Mom?"

"Yes, son it's me, Momma. Oh my dear, dear, Timothy." Her trembling hands reached out and touched his face. The darkness in her gave way to light, as it had on the day he was born.

Her frightened little boy had become a man. But his hazel eyes, his beautiful smile had stayed the same. The love on his face was the love she'd always seen in him. He was crying! Her boy was crying as he pressed her hands to his lips, kissed her palms.

Voices behind her said, "Sit."

Libby and Ginger pressed her into a chair then left before she could introduce them to her son.

Bursting into tears she disappeared into his shoulder. Her son felt warm, smelled of freshly cut wood. His arms were strong, muscled as they held her.

"Yes cry, Momma. It's okay to cry. Look at me I'm crying too. Everything's going to be alright. I love you so much." His deep voice whispered in her ear.

"I love you, son. I've missed you so much. You are so grown. I love you, love you."

There they really saying this to each other? Or was she remembering it from when he was a little boy trying to quiet her? She leaned into him, wept silently in his arms, the way he had wept in hers all those years ago.

Then she was spitting on her fingers, and gently rubbing sawdust from his chin as if he were five and coming in from the playground with dirt on his face. Laughing and crying, they held each other tight as if to keep the other from escaping.

"I didn't know how to save you from him, I just didn't."

Her son stiffened, looked beyond her. "Is he here?"

"No. No, he died a few months ago."

The flush of relief on her son's face tore her up. He was a grown man and still afraid of his father. Gathering a breath, she explained how he'd died. Never saying Benny had killed her cat, never saying she'd gotten him to fall off the ladder.

"You, Sarah and I, had nowhere to go. When we ran to my parents they called your father and sent us back to him."

"I remember that."

"You do?" She marveled that he did. "You were only six then. The only thing I could do after that was to send you to Ruth and Charlie. I had to. Did they treat you right? Were you happy with them?"

"Yes, Momma. Yes. Ruth and Charlie treated us just like we were their kids. They told us good stories about you."

His words loosened the band around her heart. "I'm sorry I couldn't fight him."

"It's okay, Mom. No one could. You stood between him and me so many times. Taking his hits for me. Hiding me from him."

His voice, so strong, so full of love, it eased her pain. As his warm hand gently caressed her back and quieted her, she sobbed out her life.

"Mom, I saw you limp. Did he do that to you?"

"No need to talk about him. He's dead."

She didn't deserve her son feeling sorry for her. She just wanted some forgiveness. She'd tell Libby and Ginger not to talk about Benny either.

"Your wife said you hired detectives to find us."

"Three different ones and they all came up with nothing. We wanted to find you, Mom. Not him. We wanted to get you away from him."

"I think he knew that. That's why he moved us to Tucson and changed our names."

"Tucson? I went to the University there. We could have passed each other in the street."

Her hand bumped the wheel of his chair making her suck in a quick breath. How could she have forgotten his wheelchair so quickly? She'd spent their time talking about her. Benny had been right to call her selfish.

She managed to whisper. "How did this happen? Was it because I sent you away?"

He gave her a kind smile, shook his head. "No. You are not to blame, I am. I was taking some stuff to a teacher friend and thinking about other things. I didn't see a car skid into the playground until it was too late. The accident broke my back."

Maybe he just sometimes needed the chair. "Can you walk at all?"

"No. But being in this chair has opened up a whole new world for me, and my family. You ever hear the saying that when one door closes, another opens?"

"I have, but I've found it very hard to believe."

Watching them from the patio, Ginger, Libby and Allison heard the murmurs, felt the joy radiating their way.

"The way Matt is hugging her tells me she is his mother." Allison, pressed her lips together, tilted her head, to hold back her tears.

"He hired people who promised they could find her. When even the third one couldn't find any trace of her and said she'd most likely died, Matt finally gave up thinking he'd ever see her again."

"Evidently miracles can happen." Ginger's sad look cut Libby to shreds. She leaned in, whispered, "I think your mother's here, with you right now."

Startled, Ginger stared at the yellow pitcher of lemonade sitting on the patio table. "It would be nice."

Libby switched her worry from mother and son scene to Ginger. She'd seen the anxiety creeping up on Ginger. Last evening, enjoying Nikki and her kids at the pool, Ginger had tap, tapped, her foot so much Libby changed chairs.

This morning, waiting for Anna Mae, she'd paced around their room like a racehorse. Now she was brushing imaginary dust off the table, off her shirt.

It could be a signal Ginger wanted a drink, it could be all that had gone on had her upset. It did her. There was still a lot that had to happen and Ginger hated sitting around. Had said she'd only come up here because Ginger needed distractions to get through the time before going into rehab. Well, they'd had enough distractions and she was sure there were still more to come.

She looked at Allison. "I know it's rude to ask, but why is your husband in a wheelchair?"

"It's not the least bit rude, Libby. That's your name, right?"

Both Libby and Ginger nodded.

"I'm glad you aren't ignoring his wheelchair. That would be rude. Fifteen years ago, Matt was a Sedona Fireman. As part of the Technical Rescue Team, he volunteered to talk to school kids about water and rock climbing safety. He was going through the elementary school parking lot to do that when a car bounced up and over the curb and skidded toward some children. Matt got there in time to shove three kids away but the edge of the car's bumper hit him and broke his back."

"Dear God!" Ginger looked at Marian's son. "Was the driver trying to hit kids?"

"No. Several bees had gotten into her car and were stinging her face and she lost control."

"That's horrible." Ginger wanted to cry. "Were any of the children hurt?"

"One got a few scrapes and cuts. Two were scared, but not hurt."

"Then he's a hero." Libby nodded yes to her own statement.

"Please. Don't call him a hero. Since his accident we've learned that labels are good on food, but not on people. Sometimes we even think his accident was a good thing. We had gotten into such a rut that we'd started to ignore each other. Focusing on our children, his job, my job, left no time for us as a couple.

"It took us all almost a year to accept that Matt was in a chair for the rest of his life. Because of the accident, we've been receiving a paycheck that will last for life. That gave him time to focus on getting stronger. One day, he just looked at me and said he couldn't sit around for the rest of his life, not doing anything constructive. So we rented out our house here, took the kids out of school, moved to Tucson where Matt got his teaching degree. We're so proud of what he did and now he's a high school science teacher who wheels around the school halls so often the kids call him Mr. Wheeler. What he likes best is when a kid comes to him with their problems. He helps them look for the good in a bad deal."

Libby, watching Anna Mae's, no Marian's son talking with his mother, rubbing her back. She leaned over to Allison.

"I think all of you are heroes, but I won't say it." She smiled. "I smell fresh cut wood. Is it from his workshop?"

"Yup. When he's not teaching, Matt's a Master Woodcarver. You'll love his work. Everyone does."

Ginger tapped the table. "Libby's not the only one with a rude question. I have one. How will Sarah react to her mother?"

Allison stood up. "That's hard to say. Sarah doesn't talk about her parents. I've got to get more ice and glasses. I'll be right back."

As she left, Libby nodded toward Marian and her son. "They seem to be getting along well."

"They do. And I'm happy about it," Ginger touched her dear friend's hand. "I didn't know it until now, but their reunion had me tied up in knots."

"Me too." Libby nodded

"Sometimes on our drive up here, her whining had me wanting to sew her mouth shut. Did you know I threw up at the police station? I didn't tell you that, did I?"

Ginger laughed. "Rescuing Nikki and her girls had me more scared than I've been in a long, long time. We were so close to getting shot. Now we understand what Marion and her kids went through with Benny. I still shake."

She held out her hands to Libby. "See?"

"I don't see any shaking, but you do look a little green."

"Thanks." Ginger nodded toward mother and son. "I hope she's not apologizing too much for sending them away."

"I'm afraid, if he asks about his father she'll jump in and take all the blame and go with her spiel '*I'm a terrible mother*'."

"You don't have to worry."

They looked up. Allison was standing there with ice and three new glasses. "His father terrified him, you know. Matt'll never let her take any blame for any of it."

"Oh, dear, we've been caught being nasty."

Allison put the tray on the table then sat down.

"You're not alone. I flipped out when Matt told me about his mother sending them on that bus. His loyalty to her drove me nuts. It's also what I love most about him. Then, seeing how our kids adored us at his age, made me accept his feelings."

Allison laughed. "Of course our kids changed their minds about us when they became teenagers. You asked about Sarah. Sarah gets touchy about life in general. Ruth says that after arriving at their place, Sarah cried herself to sleep for over a year. Then one day she just stopped, and got on with her life.

Sarah's had two very short marriages. Now she's married to a great guy. They've been together fifteen years and have a son and a daughter. Shouldn't tell you this, but you both seem so close to her.

Eight years ago when Sarah's daughter turned four, the same age Sarah was when they were sent away. Sarah started having nightmares about those days. We think that's also when she started drinking. Eventually it got so bad Sarah had to be hospitalized. She and her husband don't talk about that time. Not even with us."

Pouring them lemonade, Allison continued. "We've often seen Sarah get thrown off by surprises. That's why I called her when I was in the house. It's a good thing I did, because she was already on her way over here."

"Oh boy. Two reunions in one day."

Allison put the pitcher down. "It could go well."

"You don't sound very convinced." Libby tightened her hold on her lemonade, then nearly spilled it when Marian plopped down in a chair right next to her elbow.

"These are my very good friends that I told you about. Libby and Ginger drove me up here. This is my son, Matt."

Libby reached out and shook his hand. The happiness on the two faces that looked so much alike, tugged at her heart.

"I have a hard time believing this is happening." Anna Mae hugged herself, took in a deep breath.

"My son teaches science at the high school. He and Allison have three grown children and two grandchildren I'm a grandmother and a great grandmother. And they all live here."

She loved saying my son. She didn't want to sound puffed up, but it was a long time that she had something to brag about. She touched her son's wheelchair.

"A run-away car broke my son's back. That's why he's in a wheelchair."

Libby smiled at Matt. Evidently he hadn't told his mother he'd saved three kids. She liked him and his wife too.

"Helloooo."

They all turned to see a tall, smiling, dark haired woman walking toward them.

Matt whispered to his wife. "Tell me you called her."

"Yes. She was on her way here with a frame she wants you to match."

Libby crossed her fingers, and thought; oh boy, here we go.

Chapter 38

Matt leaned into his mother; spoke quietly, "Mom, Sarah's here."

Marian followed his look.

Patting her hand, gently. "Sarah gets excitable, Mom. Let me tell her who you are."

The woman coming toward them was her daughter? Just like that, her Sarah was here. She held onto her son's hand. Smothered a cry, she pressed her feet hard into the ground to stop from jumping up and running to Sarah.

Forcing herself to sit very still, she studied her daughter. This woman was not her four year-old Sari skipping across the lawn in her pretty, new, blue dress. This woman was her grown up Sarah with the confident walk of a strong woman. Matt knew his sister best. It was best she take his advice.

Sarah was pretty with Benny's height, his black hair. It was so hard not to jump up and hug her. Looking surprised, Sarah stopped a few feet from them. "Allison, why didn't you tell me you had company when we talked?"

"You wouldn't have come over, if I had,"

"That's true." Sarah laughed.

The light, spicy perfume, smells whirling through the air were from her daughter. Marian smiled. Sarah's perfume was what she would have bought, if Benny had allowed artificial smells in the house. She tucked her hands under her legs to keep from reaching out, and touching the edge of her daughter's sleeve.

Sarah smiled so nicely at Allison. Nodded to them, the strangers. Bent down to hug her brother. Sarah was not shy like she always was. And not superior like Benny thought he was. Ruth had done a good job with her. Better than she would have done.

Time stopped as she and her daughter locked eyes, studied each other.

"You look a lot like my Aunt Ruth. Are you a cousin she's never mentioned?"

Joy tickled Marian. Her daughter's voice was as light and cheerful. The way she'd dreamed it would be.

"No, Ruth and I are not cousins."

"Would your turn your head, please."

Doing her daughter's bidding, she turned toward her son for what to do next, but he was intent on watching his sister.

"Now, please look at me." Sarah peered at her, squinted, backed up, looked briefly at her brother, then back to Marian.

"You could almost be Aunt Ruth's twin."

Matt pulled out a chair. "Sit down Sarah, and we'll explain."

Sarah continued staring at her mother as if she hadn't heard him. "Ruth's never mentioned a twin. Although, my family's so crazy, she could have had one in hiding."

The roaring in Marian's ears cut off whatever it was Sarah said next. Her heart was pounding so hard in her throat, she could hardly swallow and she couldn't wait any longer.

"Sari, I'm your mother!"

Sarah looked at her. "You're my mother?"

Anger filled Sarah's face. "Don't say that! Do not say that! She's dead."

Marian started to get up, but her son's hand clamped hard on hers kept her seated. "I am your mother."

"No! She's dead. Dead. She's dead."

Unable to bear the pain on her daughter's face, Marian closed her eyes.

"What's going on? All of your detectives said our parents are dead. Tell this liar to get out of here."

Marian opened her eyes to see Sarah glaring at her.

"Sarah, we were told our parents were probably dead because no one could find even a trace of them after they left Phoenix. This is our mother."

"Damn it, Matt! She's lying. It's your wishful thinking again. She's an imposter. Someone who knows our story, knows Aunt Ruth, must have looked at this woman and seen the resemblance. Then they figured you'd fall for it that she's our mother. I bet she told you a bunch of stories that everyone knows. Like, how she dumped us out at the bus station. She's here to get money out of you because you are now famous. Your carvings are selling for big bucks now."

Marian tried to speak, but couldn't even shake her head.

"The only thing I'll give this liar is to say she does look a bit like Ruth."

Matt rolled his chair over to Sarah. As he started to put his arm around his sister's waist, she shoved him away, glared at him.

"It would be better if you didn't touch me right now."

"Okay, let's do this." He turned to his mother. "Do you remember what Sarah stole just before her fourth birthday?"

Marian thought back to her last birthday party for Sarah. "Sarah didn't steal the kitten. She brought it home because she thought the neighbors were hurting it."

Sarah jumped away from them as if they were on fire. "No. No. No. Something's very wrong here."

"Even Ruth and Charlie don't know about that cat, Sarah." Matt looked at his mother again. "What color was the kitten?"

"Grey striped with a black tip on its tail. Your sister wanted to call her Tip Top."

Sarah turned, walked away. Stopped, came back, raised her hand as if to strike her mother, then let it fall limply to her side.

"You can't come back now! Not after all these years."

The pain on Sarah's face ripped through Marian like the claws of a bear. Sarah couldn't possibly love her. It was hopeless. Still, she had to defend herself before she left.

"Your father was hurting you both. I had to send you away." Marian's voice barely rose above a whisper.

"That's not true! Daddy loved me. You hated me."

Sarah was five foot nine inches of anger. "You alone put us on a bus, by ourselves. A four year old, supervised by a nine year old. My feet didn't even touch the damn floor. I kept sliding off my seat. The bus driver was huge. All you said to us was that you'd forgotten something and left. When the bus started to go and you weren't back I was such a stupid kid I jumped off my seat and ran up to the bus driver. I told him to wait because you were coming right back. He told me to sit down because the bus was moving."

Red faced, Sarah pounded the table next to Libby's glass of lemonade, nearly tipping it over.

"I stomped my foot and said no. Wait for my Momma. She's coming right back. He stopped the bus, reached into the pocket of his shirt and showed me a piece of paper. I knew it was from you because it was your handwriting. The driver said, in a big growly voice that you told him Matt and I were to stay on the bus until some people came to get us."

"Get us? The bus driver said some Aunt Ruth and Uncle Charlie that I didn't know would get us. I sat on that bus terrified some stranger was going to take us away before you could get back. All the way to Flagstaff I watched people in case they were the ones who wanted to take us. How's that for a bus ride?"

Sarah threw her purse across the table, nearly missing two glasses.

Tears rolled down Marian's face. "I couldn't talk to you about it. If I'd looked into your eyes, touched you, I wouldn't have been able to let you go. I thought it would only be a little while until I could be with you."

"Liar! I knew you'd sent us away for good when Aunt Ruth opened my suitcase and there were my dolls. I ripped every their heads off, stepped on them then threw them in the garbage."

Marian wanted to rip her own head off, Benny's tirades had never cut her deeper.

Libby, listening to Sarah, had been watching Ginger and couldn't believe what she saw. Whenever Sarah flicked her hands to make a point, Ginger flicked hers, only in smaller swirgs.

Ginger leaned forward when Sarah did. Mouthed something when Sarah yelled. Waved her finger back and forth, as if she were scolding someone. Ginger looked angrier than she'd ever seen her. Something very strange was going on. Ginger never gave into emotions in front of strangers. Never. Ginger never made fun of people either, but today she was mimicking Sarah's every move.

It could be the DTs. Some people did see imaginary people, did weird things when they went off liquor. No, that wasn't it.

"Calm down, Sarah."

When Allison slid Sarah's purse back to her she took Libby's attention away from Ginger.

Sarah collapsed into a chair, bumped the table.

Matt wheeled over to her again. "This about knocked me off my feet too."

"Quit it Matt! I can't take your weird humor now."

"I was just trying to get you to take a breather for a second." He put his arm around her.

"I remember more of them than you do, Sarah. She is our mother."

Seeing her children hold each other comforted Marian a bit. It was clear they loved each other. That was enough for her to know. If Sarah told her to leave, she would. She'd be content with this small look into their world.

Sarah lifted her head, leaned forward, glared at her mother.

"Let's say you are her." She pressed her lips together. "Why now, after all these years? Are you broke? Maybe you're sick. I sincerely hope so. Now you'll find out what it's like to have your family dump you." With that, Sarah stood up, started to leave, came back. "What did you say?"

"I'm a horrible mother."

"A horrible mother?" Sarah bent down close to Marian, and growled. "Horrible would have been so easy to live with."

She stood, stiff as a board. "You have no idea how hard it is to forget a mother. The whole world conspires against that. Teachers say have your mother sign this or that. They asked to talk to *my mother.*

Kids asked why I lived with my aunt and uncle, so I finally made up the story."

"No, Sarah. Stop it."

Shaking her head at Matt, Sarah continued. "I said my father and mother were fishing in a stream. My mother went too far and got pulled by the current towards a waterfall. When daddy tried to save her he drowned too."

The weight of her daughter's pain fell on Marian like a death would.

"It doesn't go away when one gets older. As I grew up, I needed a driver's license, college entrance papers, papers to get married, a passport, checking account, credit cards. They either asked for my birth certificate or my mother's maiden name. Ruth had to show them my birth certificate, I couldn't look at it. When they ask for my mother's maiden name I say Ruth. That fits because Ruth is my mother. You only happened to give me birth."

Marian could hardly breathe. "I'm so very sorry."

Sarah tilted her head up to stop the tears from spilling down her face. "Sorry is not even close."

A plane flew overhead and Marian she wished it would crash down and kill her. Just her. When it didn't, she cleared her throat.

"Once again. I'm sorry, so sorry. I love you and Matt with all my heart." Her voice shook, but she was determined to get this one thing out. "I had to send you away to protect you from your father. If I'd gone with you, he would have chased us down."

"Bullshit, Mother!" Sarah had spit out the word mother as if it was a crawling bug. "You didn't want us. We were baggage. Admit it."

"No, Sarah. Your father had a violent temper. He did. He cried in relief when I sent you away, then said he was always afraid someday he'd kill you or your brother."

"Lies, these are all lies!"

"You don't know much about them, do you?" It popped out of Libby's mouth, surprising her as much as it did everyone else.

"And who the hell are you? Are you another dead relative?"

Libby, looking straight into Sarah's dark eyes, so much like Benny's, pointed to herself and Ginger. "Your father was a very difficult man. We knew, , ,"

Sarah spun around. "Is he here?"

Marian shook her head. "No, Sari. He's dead. That's why I could come here now."

"Dead?" Sarah turned to her brother. "And you knew this?"

"Yes, Mom said he fell off a high ladder in his workshop."

"Ah. See? I was right. She's here because she's broke and alone. She wants our help."

Sarah brushed away her tears from her face and turned to her brother. "If you let her stay here, it's the end of you and me, Matt."

"No, no. That can't happen. I'll leave." Marian stood up.

Limping across to the other side of the wide yard, Sarah voice trailed behind her. "Waddling like a duck won't get you any sympathy from me."

Libby had had enough. "Stop! Your father kicked a wooden bucket from under your mother. When it broke her ankle he took her to a quack he knew wouldn't report him for what he'd done. The guy didn't even have a

226

clue on how to set a bone."

"So say she." Sarah glared at Libby, then moved away.

"No, your mother said nothing. It was a friend of ours that went to your parent's workshop the day it happened. She saw your father drive off in fury. She went into their workshop and found your mother. He'd not only kicked her off bucket, he punched her a few times."

"No way. She would have reported him."

"Then what?" Libby kept her voice as level as she could.

"Well, Ms. Know-It-All, they would have arrested him."

"And?"

"What do you mean? And."

"They arrest him. Does he stay in jail for life or get out and come at her harder? That was why she stayed with the brute for thirty seven years."

"She's right, Sarah. It's time you give Mom a break. She always protected us and threatened Mom."

Allison touched Sarah's arm. "This is a huge shock. Try to give it time. Let it settle in."

Sarah yanked her arm away. "You all are big time suckers." I'm out of here."

Marian, too far away to hear what was being said, collapsed onto the low wall near her son's workshop. Looking behind her for a way to escape, she saw more flowers, large rocks, some brush, fir trees that almost hid a six foot high wooden fence. Even if she could get over the fence, she couldn't go there. There were children laughing on the other side, as if they were in a swimming pool. Her only way out was to try and run past everyone on the patio.

Trying to decide what to do, she adjusted her hips on the hard stone, saw Sarah grab her purse, turn, and head for the side of the house. Suddenly Ginger, with her platinum hair fluttering like the wings of a bird, was right behind Sarah.

Something even more horrible must have just happened.

Chapter 39

Ginger, got up, turned to Libby, Allison and Matt. "Keep her here. Tie her to a chair, if you have to."

With her sandals flip-flopping, she took off after Sarah. Rounding the corner of the house, thick shrubs grabbed at her bare legs, setting her well behind Sarah who seemed to be headed for the sleek, red, convertible parked in Matt's driveway. Sprinting at a pace she hadn't attempted in months, a few agonizing sharp breaths later she realized she'd never catch up with a young gazelle like Sarah.

Ginger stopped, yelled. "Somebody help. Help me."

Surprised when Sarah stopped and turned around, Ginger bent over and started fanning herself. "Need some help."

Even more surprised when Sarah came running back, Ginger put her hand to her chest and tried to stutter. "C-can't get breath. S-s-s-it on c-curb."

"You're really red in the face! I'm calling 911."

"Wait!" Ginger held up a hand. "Old lady. Hot run. Be fine soon."

The uncertainty on Sarah's face had Ginger fanning harder and holding out her arm as if she expected Sarah to take it. "Help me sit on curb."

"Are you sure?"

"Yes."

Sarah took Ginger by the arm and helped her up. Then she led her to the curb, and sat down with her.

"You're still so red. I really think I should call 911."

"I get easily flushed. Let's wait. See how it goes." Ginger sucked in a long breath.

"That's better. I'm just not in shape for a hot run. Pain's gone. My friends had pain with their heart attacks."

Relieved to see Sarah put her phone away, Ginger added. "Thanks for coming back for me. It must've been hard for you to stop to help one of your mother's friends."

Sarah's face hardened. She looked Ginger up and down, leaned away, stared at her. Ginger couldn't tell if Sarah was going to hit her or laugh.

"You faked all that! You scared the living shit out of me."

Sarah started to get up and leave, but Ginger clamped her hand hard on Sarah's knee. "Stay a minute. Talk with me."

"No way. You'll just tell me I'm an ungrateful brat."

"I wouldn't do that." Ginger hugged her own knees. "I'm the older version of you. Your mother sent you away on a bus. My mother blew her head off."

Pain briefly brushed across Sarah's face. "I'm sorry that happened to you, but I'm in no shape to listen to your sad story. I just can't do that."

Suddenly Ginger was having second thoughts. What was she doing here? She had no training on how to deal with something like this. Well life had taught her a lot.

"Allison told us you're in your third marriage. I'm in my fourth and am about to screw that one up too. I wouldn't want you catch up with me. It's too painful."

Chuckling, she only got a cold stare from Sarah. "Besides that I'm an alcoholic."

"I should care? Life is tough lady. Get used to it." Sarah started to get up again.

"Wait! Wait, please! Sit with this old lady for a couple minutes. What I have to say is very important to you. Crucial really. Please."

Sarah settled back down, looked at her. "You'd better make it quick. I've got to get out of here."

"Okay, back there while you were yelling at your mother, it let lose something inside me and because our lives are a lot alike, it's important you know about it. That's why I ran after you."

A boy riding by on his bike stopped, backed up. "Hey. Are you okay? Should I get somebody? My mom's just up the street."

"We're fine. Thank you for asking."

They watched him ride away. Giving them one more look, he disappeared around the corner.

"Sarah, your anger somehow reached down into a part of me I didn't know existed. Seeing your rage set my emotions free and I started mimicking you. I was yelling at my mother. I was copying your gestures in my head. Then, suddenly I found myself I flinging my hands around when you did. I shook my fist right along with you. I don't suppose you noticed?"

"I was a bit preoccupied. Do you have a point to all this shit?"

"Yes. What I'm saying I denied my anger, made excuses for her. Wished she'd show up so we could go have lunch."

Ginger squelched the tears boiling up inside her, took a deep breath, patted her fly away hair down to somewhere near reasonable.

"When I finally let my anger go I began to feel at peace with her. Well, the long story is there are many sides to a tragedy. I stuffed my anger. I drank. I made several marriage mistakes. You on the other hand, seem to be very good at anger but still you drink and have had marriage mistakes."

"This is why I quit therapy." Sarah got up.

"Wait." Ginger grateful her gardening kept her limber, was up almost as fast.

"What I'm saying is, you got me really mad at my mother and it's changed me. I feel."

She paused. "I don't know how to put it in words but I feet better. That's why I ran after you. You have no trouble with getting mad at your mother. Now you need to learn the truth about her. Pause your anger and see what she was trying to do."

"No way. Your mother died a zillion years ago. I have to deal with one who's just risen from the dead. Now that's crazy."

Seeing Sarah with her car remote in her hand, Ginger waited for a car to pass, then pointed across the street. "Do you know that guy over there? The one that's heading right at us?"

When Sarah looked, Ginger snatched the remote from her, dropped it inside her blouse, shivered as a cold key touched her sweating breasts.

"Hey! Give me that back!" Sarah clapped her hands. "Give it to me!"

Standing nose-to-nose, Ginger shook her head. "You give me five minutes of your time, then you get it back."

"Keep the damn thing." Sarah took out her cell phone. "My husband'll bring me his."

"Can he get here in less than five minutes?"

Sarah sighed, grabbed at Ginger's arm. "No. Give me my remote."

"Not until we talk."

"No."

With Sarah's hand tight on the sleeve of her new Gaultier blouse, Ginger smiled. "My lawyers will be real happy if you shove this old lady around."

"You're playing the old lady card?" Sarah let go of her just as the woman across the street looked up from her gardening.

"Whenever I have to." Ginger tilted her head. "Now, cane we all calm down here and listen to me. You got your yelling out back there, now do yourself a favor and find out about her."

"Lady, that was only the tip of my anger. She abandoned us!"

"She didn't really abandon you. She sent you to safety and you miss her."

"Really? I was very happy until she showed up."

"Really?" Ginger stepped back a little. "It's not yet noon, and you've already had at least one drink."

Sarah looked at her. "I have not!"

Ginger gave Sarah the saddest look her face could muster. "We drinkers can pick up the smells from ten feet away. Next week will be my fourth time in rehab."

"It's not booze! My perfume's stale."

Ginger tilted her head at Sarah. Waited.

"Okay, so I've had a drink. One drink doesn't make me an alcoholic. I've just had a few bad days."

Sarah's quick denial was so familiar to Ginger.

"There's the trifecta. *I've had a bad day. It was only one drink. I'm not an alcoholic.* Do you see what I'm saying? Look me in the eye and tell me you aren't planning on rushing home to pour down a drink or ten."

A child yelled from somewhere, finally, Sarah glanced at her, then quickly away. "I want to punch you for brining my mother here."

"Well, I might punch back. You stirred up painful feelings I didn't know I had." Ginger raised her fists, laughing.

"We'll look like idiots. Hopefully that woman across the street can rush over here and stop us before it gets too bloody."

"I'm not falling for that one either."

"No, she's really gawking at us. Is that red convertible over there, yours?"

"Yes."

"We've looked at those, so I know what you paid for it."

"It's leased."

"Then you get a new car every other year or so. Nice, designer car. Great designer clothes. What college did you attend? I'll bet it wasn't a public one."

When Sarah didn't say anything, Ginger added. "From what I can see, your mother took you from a dangerous life and sent you to a good, safe, life. By the way, Libby and I and a bunch of friends knew your parents as Benny and Anna Mae Brown. Your father changed their names so you couldn't find them."

*****

Marian, still sitting on the low wall in her son's back yard, stared at the corner of his house wondering what was keeping Sarah and Ginger. Why hadn't they come back?

I should be the one out there, not Ginger. I should have followed her Sarah and at least tried to speak with her. Ginger is out there probably being the mother I should be.

Yesterday, I helped save three strangers from an armed kidnapper. Today I'm right back to my old frightened self, running from her own daughter. I even ran across my son's back yard to get away from Sarah's anger.

Running from fear is what I do best. She pounded her legs that ran away from things. Wiping perspiration from her forehead she wondered if it was the sun in a clear blue sky, or fear, making her sweat.

She thought about Ginger and Sarah. They were strangers. No, they both had bad mothers and bad marriages. They had children. She relaxed a little.

Her Sarah and Ginger were not strangers. Ginger could be good for Sarah, maybe even fix some of Sarah's hurts. There I go again, making excuses.

What is wrong with me? I ran from my daughter. I'm even willing to leave here and never see my children again if Sarah says I must go.

She sighed, slumped a little.

Yesterday I risked getting shot to save three strangers. Strangers! I goaded a husband who petrified me into falling off a ladder because he killed my cat. A cat! I even fired his gun into his grave, and got arrested, yet I'd walk away now. She looked over to the patio to her son, his wife. Libby.

Mathew is living his life as it was handed to him. He's a husband, a father, teacher, wood carver, and he's doing it all from a wheelchair!"

Marian slid off the wall, stepped onto the stone path meant for her son's wheelchair, not his feet, let out a slow breath and headed back to them.

Chapter 40

Arriving at the patio, Marian stopped next to Libby. "Does anyone you know where I put my purse?"

"I do." Bending under the table, Libby retrieved a worn, black leather purse, came back up and handed it to Marian. Then she gently squeezed her hand.

Marian gave her a son a thin smile. "I'm going to find your sister and talk with her. But, please, none of you follow me."

When they all nodded, she took her small blue notebook out of her purse and headed for the corner of her son's house where she'd seen Sarah and Ginger disappear.

Avoiding the sharp barbs of a shrub covered with red flowers, she peeked around the corner and saw Sarah and Ginger sitting on the curb like little children. Their heads were moving as if in a quiet conversation and Sarah wasn't angrily waving her hands about. Relief washed over Marian as tears filled her eyes.

Ginger, with her arms wrapped around her knees, appeared to be relaxed. It seemed peaceful between them. There was no way she would sit on a curb like that. Matt's neighbors could see them. Checking the front yard, she saw a red convertible, with its top down, parked in her son's driveway. That had to be Sarah's car since it wasn't there when they'd arrived. It certainly would be more comfortable than a cement curb and the only place she saw for a little privacy.

As she walked across the lawn, the soft murmur of their voices calmed her a bit. To not startle them, she stopped several feet behind them and cleared her voice.

Both quickly turned to her.

"Ginger, please leave. I need to talk with my daughter."

"That'll never happen." Sarah was up and off the curb so fast Marian jumped back.

Then Ginger was up, pressing something into Marian's hand. "Tuck

Sarah's car remote in your bra."

"What?" Sarah stepped between them. "Give me that."

Sarah swiped at Ginger's hand but not before Marian had the remote wedged safely between her breasts.

"I will not talk to you." Sarah turned and stormed her way up the front yard to her car.

Ginger smiled at Marian. "I was wondering when you'd get here. No matter how badly your daughter acts, stand your ground, don't back down from the truth."

Don't back down from the truth hung in the air as she watched Ginger head for the safety of Matt's back yard leaving her alone with Sarah. Touching the remote in her bra, a power surge similar to the one she'd gotten when she'd thrown the tool wide to Benny sent her after her daughter.

Sarah was pacing back and forth beside the red convertible, not looking at her. Marian walked up, opened the passenger door, got in and sat down.

"I've your keys and I plan to keep them until you get in here and talk with me."

"Keep them. I'll walk home and get my other set."

"Then I'll lock the car in your brother's garage until we talk."

"You can't do that." Sarah stopped pacing and came back to the car to glare at her mother.

"I need my car."

"All I ask is a few minutes Sarah. Then I'll leave." Marian twisted her hands in her lap.

"No. You've risen from the dead after thirty-seven years and you expect me to sit down so we can have a nice chat? Go to, , ,"

Sarah stopped, folded her arms across her chest.

Marian took heart that her daughter couldn't tell her to go to hell.

"I expected you to be feisty. You certainly were when you were a little girl. One morning I popped you on the seat of your pants for something you'd done then I turned and went into the kitchen. The second I stopped walking you whacked me, with all your little might, on the butt. Then you grabbed my leg and cried."

"Sweet stories won't make up for what you did. I'll rent a car for a few days until you get tired of this and climb back into obscurity."

Sarah turned to leave.

She had to stop her. "Your father told me to abort you."

The retort nearly knocked Sarah to the ground. "Abort me?"

Clenching her fists, Sarah forced herself to go back to the car where she pounded on the hood. "What sweet loving parents I had. One sent me off on a bus and the other wanted me dead."

She gripped the front window of the car. "If you came here to destroy me, you just did."

Sarah headed down the driveway.

Marian was instantly out of the car and chasing after her. "No. No. Don't take it like that."

Sarah turned. "Really? Is there another way to take your planned death?"

"Yes. You are alive because I didn't do what he asked. I loved you even in the womb. Your father fell in love with you the instant you were born. He doted on you. Jumped to your every need. All three of us loved you so much."

Sarah started to leave then turned around so fast she nearly bumped into her mother. "If you loved me so much why did you give me away? Answer that one!"

Marian reached out a shaking hand and touched her daughter's sleeve. Sarah yanked her arm away.

"I had to let you both go. I was afraid of what your father would do to you and your brother if you stayed with us any longer. We'd already hurt you so much. Please, sit with me in the car, Sarah. Please. You need to hear about your life when you were a little child. I won't take long. Then you can decide to hate us, or forgive us for what we did. Either way, you win."

Suddenly the ground seemed to be moving and Marian felt woozy. Sarah grabbed her. "Are you about to pass out?"

"Yes, I think so."

Sarah steadied her mother. "Only because you didn't abort me I'll help you back to the car, sit you down. No other reason. Then I'm leaving."

The pain on her daughter's face had Marian's heart pounding in her throat.

"Please, Sarah just listen to me for a few minutes. Your father couldn't control his temper with your brother. He said having a second child would make things worse. We both had violent families."

"Ah, here she comes with the excuses."

"Excuses yes but, they are reasons too. Your father's family settled everything in cuss words, yelling, throwing things, hurting people. Your father, his bother, they were routinely beaten by their father. My family was that way, only I learned to keep my mouth shut."

"You sure must have kept it shut when he brutalized Matt. I've seen the scars on his back." Sarah stared coldly at her.

"I'll never forgive myself for my part in all of this, Sarah. I owe your brother a bigger apology than I do you. At least for you, I stepped in the moment I realized the danger."

"Realized the danger? I wasn't in any danger from daddy. He loved me. He called me Daddy's Girl."

Sarah's belligerent shake of the head scared her.

"Yes. He couldn't do enough for you. Marriage was our way out of our miserable families. We thought if we got away from them we would be normal. And it worked for a while. Your father took care of me and I gave him a sense of peace. When Matt was born your father slowly changed and became like his father. He'd punish Mathew, hard. He kept saying he'd change Sarah, but he never did. So the abortion wasn't about you. It was about him."

"Get to why you sent Matt and I alone on a damn bus." Sarah had her hand on the door handle.

"I am. Things got better after you were born. He was a wonderful loving, caring, attentive father to you. Like you said, you were Daddy's Girl. And he wasn't so hard on Matt because it made you cry."

Marian took in a ragged breath, pressed her hands together.

"When you were about three and a half, his sister, your aunt, came to me and said their father had molested her. It wasn't long after that that I noticed your father kissing you on the lips. I told him not to, but he ignored me. When he started jiggling you on his lap, then rushing to the bathroom I became terrified."

"Ahhhhhhhhhh." Sarah buried her face in her hands. Her shoulders shook.

Marian reached out, put her arm on her daughter's shoulder.

"That's why I sent you children to Ruth and Charlie. I stayed behind because I thought I could keep him from you. When your father found out you were both gone for good, he went into our bedroom. I could hear him crying in there all night. Two days later he said if I hadn't sent you away he would have someday ruined you and your brother's lives more than he already had. Then we gave everything we owned to the neighbors and moved from Phoenix to Tucson. That's when he changed our names so you'd never find us."

"It's the truth, Sarah. The brutal truth."

The curtain in the living room closed and the four heads turned to each other.

"My God, my sister's hugging our mother."

Chapter 41

Shock, disbelief then a smile spread across Matt's face as he looked at his wife. "I know I saw it, but I still can't believe it. Sarah's hugging mother? What made that happen?"

"Ask questions later, Sweetie. Just get out there and join them." With tears running down her face, Allison rushed ahead of him to open the front door.

"Aunt Ruth! Charlie! Call them."

"Yes. I'll invite them for dinner."

With her words trailing behind him, Matt was out the door and heading for Sarah's car.

Ginger quickly handed Allison a business card. "Here's where we're staying tonight. Can I tell them someone will pick up your mother in-law's things by ten tomorrow morning?"

Allison frowned at them. "You're leaving, now? In the middle of all this joy you helped bring us?"

Libby nodded. "We are. This is the time for your family, not us."

Fifteen minutes later, they were walking into the lobby of their hotel and the owner was waving them to her.

"Come over here girls. You have to see something on my computer."

Libby and Ginger stepped behind the desk with her. "It'll take me just a minute to find it."

"Is it the helicopter tour of Sedona we asked you to set up for us?"

"Nope. You have to stand right next to me and bend in close. Really close for the best view."

The owner clicked on start and a video began. "Here we go."

She pointed to a figure low on the screen. "Keep your eyes on the kneeling woman. Watch how her ponytail swishes as she shoves something into the car's tire."

Libby stepped in for a closer look.

"And here." She pointed again. "Right here, a woman with hair suspiciously like Ginger's, slams the car window with a hammer."

Now Ginger moved closer to the screen.

"Next we see your friend Marian swing her purse at the window and shoving it in."

"What? No, that's not us. It can't be."

"Ah, but it is." The owner replied. "This video has been on YouTube all day. The third time I saw it, I just knew it was you gals."

"I know it looks bad." Libby, her nose practically on the screen, watched as Marian limped to Ginger's car with little Emily.

"We didn't do anything wrong. We stopped a guy from kidnapping Nikki and her children."

The owner, now smiling, nodded. "I know that. Now I know why you didn't want me using your real names on the register. The news people in Arizona can't stop raving about you three. I can even quote them.

'Saturday, in a daring rescue, three elderly women risked their lives to snatch a mother and her two daughters from the hands of their kidnapper.'

"Elderly?" Ginger straightened.

Libby hugged her friend. "Your hair did come out sort of white, Ginger and Anna Mae, I mean Marian, does have a bad limp."

Ginger hugged her back. She looked at the owner. "I suppose you also know how we got on the video?"

"Yup. A nine year-old girl used her mother's cell phone. By ten this morning it had ten thousand hits on YouTube."

"Ten thousand hits?"

Libby looked at the computer again. "Wow! That camera phone even got a clear shot of your license plate, Ginger."

"Dear God! George! I forgot to tell him about it."

Their laughter filled the room.

~~~~~

Some Thoughts

The road of life is always under construction.

The friends we meet on the highway of life make the trip worthwhile.

If you want a place in the sun you have to put up with a few blisters.

Some people succeed because they are destined to; most people succeed because they are determined to.

A vacuum cleaner works best if you first empty the dirt out of the bag---your opinions work better the same way.

We make a living by what we get. We make a life by what we give.

It doesn't do any good to sit up and take notice if you keep sitting.

A good way to forget your troubles is to help others out of theirs.

The joy you give to others is the joy that comes back to you.

The nicest thing about flattery---- you don't have to believe it to enjoy it.

Life is a continuous process of getting used to things we hadn't expected.

Sometimes we have to replace the "what ifs" with "so whats".

An apology is the superglue of life. It can repair almost anything.

Minds are like televisions sets. When they go blank it's best to turn off the sound.

Who you are, is not always significant: what you are matters the most.

Smile, you don't own all the problems of the world.